Another Kind of Concrete

Koushik Banerjea

JACARANDA

This edition first published in Great Britain 2020
Jacaranda Books Art Music Ltd
27 Old Gloucester Street,
London WC1N 3AX
www.jacarandabooksartmusic.co.uk

A CIP catalogue record for this book is available from the
British Library

ISBN: 9781913090081
eISBN: 9781913090074

Cover Design: Aase Hopstock
Typeset by: Kamillah Brandes

Printed and bound by CPI Group (UK) Ltd, Croydon, CR0 4YY

To Ma,
For the spelling tests. But mostly for carrying it with grace under
pressure, and really, in the end, for making the whole thing possible.

'It takes nerve to walk down the street when you fall between the cracks.'

-- Nan Goldin

'Anyone who has felt the drive to self-destruction welling up inside him knows with what weary negligence he might one day happen to kill the organisers of his boredom. One day. If he was in the mood.'

-- Raoul Vaneigem

Prologue

London 1977

Peace of mind had been in short supply back then too. The National Front in Lewisham yet even so K. was still pre-occupied with buses, and with the uncertain protocol around ducking the fare on a highly unusual day. Actually, even though he'd snuck on without any intention of paying, it was still hard for him not to think of the 'Routemaster' without acknowledging that in some ineffable way the conductor was indeed the master of ceremonies. The ultimate arbiter of whether an incident would need to be referred on to the proper authorities or nipped in the bud.

And in between times the bell and the banter, which on good days could even involve the mysterious voice from the driver's cab. Which is how K. knew on that particular day the conductor's name was 'Vic'.

#

On quiet days, when everyone seemed wrapped up in the details of their own existence, the bus would make its functional way from one part of town to another, largely without comment or distraction. But the overriding feeling was one of impatience, passengers and conductor united in their desire for as short a journey as possible, the sense that everyone had other, more pressing destinations to reach.

Yet at other times the journey itself could feel more unpredictable, as if the disparate energies of its human cargo had somehow altered the entire dynamic. On these occasions the bus would become a timetabling casualty, jerky and uneven as it jockeyed for position amongst the other road traffic. Its frequent spasms adding some engineering clout to the low level hum of enforced conviviality.

#

K. found himself on a bus in another part of the Borough the day that the Front, which basically meant the cops and a few North Kent diehards, had tried to march through the area.

The taste of the exhaust mingling with his own excitement as the bus became concertina'd in diverted traffic. Then the happy realization that no one was going to be asking him for his fare today, nor chiding him for ducking it. Oddly followed by what he'd now recognise as a kind of melancholy. Though it was only when the driver cut the engine that the real bus, its commons, sprang into life again. Some speculation about Millwall and the overspill of local disputes from the Pepys Estate. Vague talk of reprisals, and in at least one case mention of someone called George Davis.

He'd been struck even then by how nervous some of the passengers were, and the contrast with the conductor whose face, though alert, seemed preternaturally calm, as if every other journey he'd previously made had really just been a dress rehearsal for this. The man was more in charge of his vehicle than ever, which was odd given that it was now stationary and effectively off the timetabling grid—the hallowed framework which gave him his authority in the first place.

#

Taking a moment to study his face, K. could tell that the conductor was Indian, and a particular kind. It wasn't so much the almond eyes or the brown skin. More the snapshot of his own uncle in those eyes—distant, forever looking at a slight remove. If he'd even had the fare, he'd have bet the lot on this being little more than a minor skirmish in the wider scheme of things for the man from London Transport.

The only skirmishing in K.'s world was that single minded dedication to the present he'd witnessed time and again at school. Kids mobbing up to avenge some perceived slight or another. The speed, the lack of respite between one act of foolishness and the next. The necessary showboating, the predictable outcome which even as a young boy he felt to be limited. The boys taunting the girls, then other boys, then the teachers. Little stabs at classroom immortality—the theft of pencil cases, the sniffing of marker pens—gradually escalating into pinching and punching.

Yawns were deemed funny—he quickly cottoned on,

stored the detail for future reference. Even if they weren't, he soon learned it was best not to let on else the same fate awaited as befell the 'sensitive' boy who played in the doll's house. Or the neighbouring school which got sacked like some medieval town. Or the lanky teacher who was pushed through the plate glass window adjoining the lunch hall for telling one of K.'s classmates to queue up properly. Or himself on those occasions when the fox fancied something a little more exotic than chicken.

#

The difference between this man and the lanky teacher could hardly have been any greater though. Even as the first crack sounded outside the window, the conductor barely reacted. When it was followed shortly after by several more, he quickly established from the yellowish gunk trailing the windows that these were eggs, the shattered shell casing little more than local mischief. To K.'s mind though, the bus was coming under sustained attack and he took refuge under one of the seats.

The other passengers had already fled the scene, deciding that they were sitting ducks on the Routemaster. The conductor seemed amused, though not especially impressed, by their cowardice.

'What are you doing down there?' he asked K.

No answer.

'Why are you hiding? I can see you,' he added, trying not to laugh.

K. emerged from under the seat, saw that he was the

only person left on the bus other than the conductor. Even the driver had gone, and clearly in a hurry as he'd left the door to the driver's cab invitingly open behind him. It was just the two of them, and the faint smell of eggs. The conductor seemed pleased, if not exactly for the peace and quiet, as there was a lot of activity on the street, then at least for the timetable respite.

He sat down on the bottom step nearest the conductor's pole by the exit. To K., who was still toying with the idea of running but felt with each passing moment that scarpering was somehow inappropriate, this appeared to be a strategic move. The conductor could easily apprehend him from his vantage point if he made a bolt for freedom. Equally, he had his back covered. No other egg throwers or mischief makers could creep up on him, and he wasn't visible to anyone at street level through any of the windows.

Something in the man's eyes suggested boredom. K. found this strange, especially in tandem with the man's alertness, and with everything else that was going on outside. But really, the bit that mattered was the growing sense that today at least collecting the fare was not a priority.

#

He'd never met an Indian called 'Vic' before. Actually the whole idea that an older Indian man could have a name was odd. All his uncles and aunties were 'kakas' or 'kakimas', and he had no idea what their first names were.

Didn't ask either, not so much for fear of seeming rude, although it was that too, but as he just wasn't very interested. He barely even knew his cousins' actual names as opposed to the *daknaams* they all had, and they were the same age as him.

'Are you ok?'

He nodded.

'Don't mind me saying, but you don't really look ok.'

'No, I'm fine.'

Vic was relieved that the boy could at least talk. He'd been sat there like a statue for some time, almost as though he was waiting to be moved. But his English was good, not like the half-cut foolishness he'd sometimes hear from the Black boys on his bus; soft English boys who acted all day long as though they were from somewhere else, before hopping off without paying on Lewisham Way. Though it was hard to take them too seriously, Vic still made a point of feigning outrage whenever they absconded. It was no less than any of the other passengers would have expected, and he'd rarely disappoint.

What made him laugh though was how those boys never bothered to *listen*, else they would have long since heard the traces of 'yard' on the coolie man's voice.

This kid was a little different though. The look was still all wrong—up top a little apprentice skinhead, but then some huge collars and a pair of corduroys—yet perhaps that was what caught Vic's attention. The Black boys wouldn't be seen dead wearing crap like that, but he thought he'd spotted defiance in this kid's eyes, something a little staunch under the collars. He hadn't really seen that before in this part of town, not on an Asian kid. Most of the Indians round here carried that slump in the shoulders, then the face, that he hated. He'd seen it practically every day on the bus, the way they'd give up so easily in the after school scramble for seats and influence.

'Ah, so it speaks,' said Vic to the boy.

'What?'

Again, the slight tilt of the chin, something unfamiliar, yet wholly familiar, in the eyes.

'I thought you were just going to sit there like one of them shop dummies, but it turns out this mannequin can speak.'

'Why are you chatting to me like that?' asked the boy.

Vic smiled. He'd been right about the kid. No flies on his soup.

'So you have a problem with how I speak, then?'

K. mulled over the question. It wasn't what he'd meant. Not how the man spoke, but how he spoke to him. Why would he say anything about how the man spoke when the accent wasn't anything like as strong as on Dad? He hadn't been taking the mickey. Not like some.

'No, that's not what, I mean I didn't say that,' he blurted out. If the man was convinced, he wasn't letting on. The eyes betrayed no real emotion. Reminded K. once again of his own uncle who was currently staying with them. Had been there a month already and barely said a dozen words to anyone. Always seemed to either be heading out or sleeping. Didn't like being disturbed. Had a way of letting you know without saying much.

Actually this man's eyes seemed a little softer. When

K. looked again, there was no hint of cruelty behind the mask.

'It doesn't matter anyway,' said Vic with a bit of a smirk, 'we're under fire!' And made as if to duck. Without hesitating, K. threw himself back onto the floor of the bus, and was surprised when the only sound he could make out was the roar of Vic's laughter. They sat in silence for a while, the only sounds coming from outside. From time to time an egg would break against one of the windows, and at one point two young men ran onto the bus but froze when they saw the conductor and the boy just sat there. 'What do you want?' Vic asked, but they hadn't stayed long enough to answer. Shortly afterwards two police looked in, beyond the boy and the conductor, before deciding their quarry lay elsewhere. Every so often a face would peer in, be momentarily surprised at the two figures just sat on the three-seaters and leave it at that.

To Vic this was nothing new, whereas he could tell this was the first time the boy had encountered such etiquette. Beneath the cropped hair was a head full of wonder; the eyes darting around after the details, yet without any of that knowingness he'd seen on the after-school crowd. The many shades of English carrying on as though they'd seen it all before, when really they'd seen nothing; knew nothing.

'Why are you still on the bus?' K. asked.

It was a good question; took Vic by surprise. Why was he on the bus? He couldn't really say beyond some vague notion of duty, so he mentioned London Transport and then wondered why he was having to justify himself to some kid.

The odd thing was the kid didn't seem in any great rush to leave either. Vic thought about asking him the same question, then thought better of it. He must have had his reasons. Sitting there, collars still buttoned, acting all nonchalant like this kind of thing happened every day. After a while he became aware of the strangest thing too. He sensed that the kid was studying him, like he was some sort of coaching manual. Searching for clues as to the present situation. How best to deal with it, but more than that, how best to *come across*.

Somehow this pleased him, imbued the moment with meaning and style and, yes, even some leadership. Made him feel heard although he wasn't speaking.

'Look, I should try to get this bus back to the depot.'

As the engine roared back into life, the bus suddenly started filling up. K. had no idea where all these people had come from, but they'd clearly been watching from somewhere close. Vic's confident sing-song informed the new arrivals that the bus was just heading back to the garage, and not up west. There were no complaints, just a low level murmur.

When he looked again, K. could see that many of the passengers were in fact dripping something onto the seats and he was briefly outraged on Vic's behalf, though not so much for London Transport. The anger soon subsided once he realized that it was fresh claret staining the seats, and the murmur was in fact a collective moaning.

Vic must have already processed these details as without warning the bus pulled up outside the hospital. People spilled off and dispersed into the Victorian buildings housing Accident and Emergency, wearily grateful they hadn't had to run the gauntlet of all those meatwagons parked up off the High Street to get there.

Orderlies, doctors and nurses were already in the car park, helping to ferry the more seriously injured inside, and the walking wounded seemed to be milling around everywhere.

The bus lurched on, Vic having taken the executive decision that it would be commandeered for the wrong purposes if they stuck around outside the hospital any longer.

Uniforms had started to materialize with greater frequency, nursing their own battle scars, and it was only a question of time before they cast a covetous eye at the bus.

All the way up to the Cat, there were little groups of stragglers, the odd burnt out car. Bricks, masonry, bottles lying around, their work done. And wherever there was a broken window, there was also an angry voice, usually an older one, admonishing the stragglers, somehow seeing it as their handiwork.

But all seemed delighted by the lurching beast. K. loved the way that people smiled, gave the thumbs up, waved as though the bus itself had led the charge. Some people seemed to recognize Vic at the wheel and the shouts of 'Yes, star!' followed them all the way to the depot.

Actually the Cat marked the last open vestiges of where trouble had occurred. Some windows had been put through and a few bottles lay strewn in the road, though on another day this could just as easily have been a re-gulation liquor scrap. Seeing the Cat swiping at air through one of the side windows, K. suddenly had the strongest feeling that this was the last thing worth defending round here. Just a little further along past the cinema and the road opened up, a sure sign of cars and crazy paving. Perhaps something a little less hostile to the Front too. Another kind of concrete.

#

Part One

Barely Even Loaded

1.

London, 1976/77

The knoll was its own lookout post, affording unparalleled views of the playground and the school buildings. On a clear day, the crisp air held court to a thousand obscenities too.

What sounded at first like, 'You can't!' soon clarified itself as 'You Cunt!' But it was in good company. 'You old bike!' 'Wanker!' 'Paki lover!' 'Iron!' just some of the better ones floating over from the estate, his ears pricking up like bored antennae.

Most days, though, he'd just sit there, biding his time, running down the clock until the teachers deemed it safe to let the little cunts back in after lunch.

Thinking about it, they mostly were little cunts. Danny Heller and Lee Sagree were two of the bigger ones, and god help you if called them Daniella and Lisa. The new teacher made that mistake just last week and ended up pushed through a plate glass window for his troubles. Silly sod didn't seem to realize lunchtime was when the animals were let out of the traps, allowed to run wild for a bit, have a little taste of the unadorned. Not the moment to be telling them to queue up properly.

Under normal circumstances, K. would have felt

sorry for him. But this was the same teacher who had mispronounced his name in class, and seemed to enjoy getting a cheap laugh from the English kids. So fuck him, lanky cunt, picking the shards out, waiting to make a statement.

Good word that, 'unadorned', something classy about it. Earlier, in the library, he liked the way it looked when he applied a magnifying glass, the letters warping, the 'r' and the 'n' first appearing to fuse, then pulling apart, their domed roof lifting up, inviting him in. And he'd dive in, swimming in alphabet soup, running down the clock, Mrs J., the kindly old librarian, occasionally glancing over at the little boy who seemed to be in his own reverie.

It was usually just the two of them in there, but one time she'd noticed a pretty Black girl sitting with K. He was playing with her braids, and she was tracing invisible patterns on his back. They clearly weren't reading and for a moment she thought about throwing them out, before something in her relented, some distant echo, and she'd gone back to her crossword.

After that they seemed to be together most days, playing more than reading, but quietly, so as not to disrupt Mrs J.'s concentration.

Her name was Michelle, and K. wondered how he hadn't noticed her before, looking at him through the braids.

She was much quieter than the English girls, didn't seem to have eyes for a furry pencil case or the cocky little herberts who'd regularly take over the classroom.

That morning, Stephen, the class runt, had thrown

Sarah's pencil case out of the window, and this had led to a feeding frenzy on the grass, the other urchins picking the case clean within seconds. Everyone had laughed, Sarah cried, and the teacher, as ever, seemed unable to intervene in any way.

K. felt bad for Sarah, but was careful not to show any sympathy. Not then, in front of the others. Looking around to test the classroom temperature, only the girl with the braids stood out in a sea of snarl. So now here they were, pawing at each other in the library, all digits and drawings and little curiosities.

'A carrot?'

Actually it was a prick, but he preferred Michelle's interpretation. Anyway, arguing would just waste time, and he wanted the feeling of her fingertips tracing mysterious patterns on his back *now*.

His eyes closed, blissed out at the physical touch. Her fingers arced upwards, made a couple of loops, before curving back down again. For a moment all he could picture were a pair of huge breasts, like the ones on those seaside postcards. But some other instinct kicked in and he piped up with a hopeful, 'European Cup?'

'No, silly', she laughed.

He was stumped. It was the only other thing he could think of that looped. He'd only seen it for the first time the other night, when a lot of bubble permed Scousers had got their hands on the silverware. The commentators sounded happy enough, the whole evening a late Mersey singalong in glorious Continental sunlight. The cup itself looked huge, needed both hands on its jug ears to lift it.

Then the image of a little cartoon bird with a massively puffed out chest took over. He couldn't think of anything else with a crested dome and a downward curve. The chest was about to explode, leaving a feathery shower for the cat to contemplate. Through one lazy eye, the cat was licking its lips, knowing dinner wasn't far.

'A bird?'

'How can that be a bird? Don't you know anything?'

She was right of course. He didn't know much, and about invisible drawings even less. It was fun getting it wrong though, and her pretending to be annoyed. Mrs J. didn't seem to mind too much either.

They moved wordlessly into one of the aisles. Michelle picked out a book she had clearly seen before. It was nestled between two others on football, but was a story book. He did the same thing sometimes, if he found a book that he liked but didn't have time to look at it, he'd hide it in a completely different section. Not that there was ever anyone else in the library, but it felt like a necessary precaution.

Another good word. The 'pre' made it sound more grown up, the kind of thing a newsreader might say. And it worked. No one else ever found those books.

She showed him a page with a drawing on it. An old man wearing rags was resting by the side of a river, propping his arm up against a stick. He looked exhausted, as though this was as far as his limbs could carry him. His mouth was curved into a downward hollow, and the face was creased, deep furrows cutting into the flesh. Next to him was a small knapsack, and on closer inspection,

K. could make out a pair of eyes watching the old man through some reeds.

'I like this one,' she said.

'He looks tired,' replied K.

'So do you.'

Hearing a faint rustling sound, Mrs J. looked up once or twice, but the sounds didn't last and nine across couldn't wait any longer.

After that, most lunchtimes were spent in one or other of the aisles. But when Mrs J. got sick a few weeks later, the library was closed and they were forced back out into the jungle.

At first it was just holding hands, but soon they were getting bolder, thinking no one could see them kissing if they snuck behind the knoll. They had different smells, K. fish, rice, fear; Michelle shepherd's pie, some kind of cocoa, confidence. Running down the clock got easier, but now there weren't enough minutes in the hour. And before they knew it, lunchtime was over and the afternoon head-count was underway.

#

2.

'Wipe that stupid smile off your face!'

Stephen made the wiping gesture with his hand then ran out of the classroom, with the new English teacher in hot pursuit. It was no contest, the runt running rings around the rookie. He was small, even for his age. Perhaps that was why he was twice as cheeky?

The whole class was screaming and shouting. Except for K. and the new girl, Michelle, and Rachael Huntley, who no one would sit next to as she smelled of wee.

She seemed distressed. It was always the same story when the class erupted, the noise and the frenzy appearing to jog something else lodged deep inside. Her face made as if to scream but no sound emerged. Instead she would sit there motionless, some storm raging inside while all around her the scamps fed on nothing. Pencil cases, rumour, boredom.

Again, K. would have consoled her but she smelled of wee, and someone would be watching, so a label would form, and stick. Then she'd be his problem, and in some indeterminate way his life would become just that little bit harder. So he ignored her, trapped in a very private hell, and instead chose cocoa over wee.

Actually there *were* others who remained aloof but, as that tune went that he was forever hearing down the market, 'a little way different'.

Rosalind, Emily, Benedict, Robert, Jake. They always sat together, and the teachers listened to them when they put their hands up in a way that they didn't for anyone else. The funny thing was that even when the teachers weren't around, none of the Lees or Dannys would pay them any mind. Those accents, and the clothes, and the favourable treatment by the teachers never registered. Or if they did, then someone somewhere had decided that they weren't half as troubling as poor girls that smelled of wee, or anxious brown boys or a skin so black it was blue.

One time when they were paired up during an afternoon 'baking' class, K. tried talking to Rosalind—'Rosie'—and she gave him a look which just seemed puzzled, faintly amused even. He remembered her looking over at Emily at the next table and the two of them sharing some unspoken wisdom which left both smirking.

After that he hadn't bothered any more. The aloof girls had clearly made some early years assessment that he was a liability, so he retreated back into the books and the familiar comforts of cocoa.

Every now and then he caught himself looking over to see what the aloof crowd was up to, but they showed no interest in him so he would quickly avert his gaze. Closer to where he sat, Stephen fidgeted away, hands always moving, mischief pogo-ing away behind those eyes. The trick, K. found, was to maintain awareness through peripheral vision but never actually catch the runt's eye.

Anyway, the runt already had his muse, Sarah, whom he would torment and delight in equal measure. She of the furry pencil case, alternately giggling away or in tears. So long as he had some kind of an audience, the runt was happy, sufficiently distracted not to start with any verbals. Cropped blond hair of course, a face that looked older than it was, and under the mischief the faintest, but near permanent, frown. Something in the water perhaps? Or more likely the crisps and laissez-faire. K. had found that phrase in a book about France tucked away among the sporting digests and gardening manuals. As far as he could tell, it meant 'left to one's own devices' but in the sense of 'no government interference'. Yet he felt it could be applied equally to the runt, largely left to get on with it, rarely any parents or family in sight. Maybe that gave him a lot to think about. Perhaps that's where the line etched into his forehead came from?

Should he feel sorry for him? Just then the runt looked over, daring the eye contact which always escalated. He could feel little blue lasers boring holes into his cheek. Wisely though, he resisted the temptation to look. The game was so boring and predictable. Not yet into double figures and this little cunt had already decided this is how it would be. As far as he could tell, no one forced him. The runt chose to be this way.

Rosie and Emma were giggling away about something or another, and as usual were left to it by the Lees and the Dannys. Laissez-faire as natural as lice in this classroom.

Mrs. Allott, the English teacher, scribbled in really

large letters on the board. No one paid any attention and K. drifted off into one of his regular daydreams.

He was being pursued by dogs and they were gaining ground on him. Finally they had him cornered on a piece of waste ground and his arms were growing tired from swinging the cricket bat in a frenzied arc. One dog in particular, which seemed bolder than the others, edged forward, and he could see toothpaste foaming around the edges of its mouth. The bat slipped out of his hands. The dog waited a moment, the toothpaste now a shoelace. He heard someone calling out. Realised it was his name. When he looked up again, the dogs had gone.

Mrs. Allott. was standing next to him, glaring. The room felt quiet for once. Even the runt had piped down, and K. sensed that he was the centre of attention.

Standard issue. 'What are you doing?' No answer. 'I said, what are you doing?' 'Nothing.' 'What do you mean 'nothing'?' 'Well, there's nothing to do.' 'Get Out!' 'Fine.' Laughter (the runt, Emma, Rosie, the others). Fear (what if Mum finds out). Library. Quiet again.

#

3.

'What did you learn today?'

The question caught K. by surprise. His uncle rarely showed any interest in the outside world, still less in anything to do with school. Yet here he was, clear-eyed for once, chin propped up in a massive hand, leaning back in an office chair as if he genuinely cared about the answer.

K. wasn't really expecting him to be home. The man kept odd hours and often seemed to head out when most other people were coming home. Then again for all he knew, his uncle had been home all along. For a big man he was very quiet. Had a habit of creeping up on people unnoticed, seemed to regularly appear from nowhere. Said very little even when he did materialize.

'English.' Without really knowing why, K. instinctively knew this was the right thing to say to his uncle.

'What English?'

'Verbs.'

Quiet again.

No one else was home. Next door but one the transistor was crackling. He could tell it was cricket, just from the pauses and occasional silence. The old English lady never missed a game if she could help it. Didn't seem to mind when he was outside practicing all his shots, throwing a tennis ball against her wall, trying to mimic uneven bounce or spin by using the divots in the road. Stuck her head out the window every so often and told him to 'straighten his elbow'.

The chair groaned faintly as his uncle leaned into it, rubbing along his stubble with one hand, the other scratching his vest in a well worn habit.

'What's new?'

'Nouns.'

'Why you learn about bread?'

'No, *nouns.*'

'What's the difference?'

'Oh, nothing much, one's -' but his uncle had already lost interest, was getting out of the chair, heading out of the room.

There was no explanation, the man clearly felt no need, and K. made a note of that. *Don't excuse yourself. When it's time to go, just go.*

He tried to put some of that confidence into his batting, but the swashbuckling was cut short by a ball rearing up out of the pavement and straight into his jaw. Typically this happened during a lull in the commentary and, craning his ears past the quiet, K. was sure he could make out the sounds of an old lady's laughter.

4.

The first time it happened there was no warning, just a sharp crack, then a dull shock as the fist slammed into his cheek. It felt like being hit by a wrecking ball, not that he'd know what that was like. It was more about the image and what was happening to his cheek *now*, the delayed reaction followed by a level of pain that ought to have been less familiar than it actually was.

He felt sure some of the brickwork had come loose and checked the inside of his mouth with a frozen tongue. But there was no real damage, no stray enamel, and he realised then that this was no wrecking ball. It was barely even loaded, the man in front of him largely indifferent as he scratched his vest with a giant southpaw. No, this was just a quick warning shot, in case he was thinking of making the same mistake again. The huge man with the baleful eyes, who was also kin, sloped back into the adjacent room where he'd been trying to sleep. And K. was left holding his face but making sure not to cry, as the man, his uncle, had promised him 'two more' if there were tears.

It felt harsh. All he'd been attempting were some basic ball skills indoors, keepy-uppy, which would make it easier to face the fiends in the playground back at school. But it was one of those days when the ball kept spooling away off a foot, a thigh, once even a knee, and the tap tapping on the wall eventually roused his uncle. Stupid really, and he should have checked first to see whether the room was empty, but even so, it was a bit harsh.

No point dwelling on it though. Luckily no bruises for now, and as far as he could tell no after effects either.

#

The doughnut tasted good, sugarcoating his tongue, hipping him to the prospect of its sweet, jam centre. And though he couldn't really make out anything much beyond the hot water, it was exciting to be washing it all down with tea. This was a 'big people' drink, and there he was, sat at the counter, legs so short they still couldn't reach the floor, blowing at the steam rising from his styrofoam cup just like he'd seen the adults do.

His uncle had made a point of taking him out for a walk, and, once K. had worked out he wasn't in any more trouble, he'd enjoyed it.

For a man who spoke very little English, it was surprising how many people his uncle seemed to know, passing by doorways or generally just on the street. They mostly appeared keen to say hello and to pass on respects but not linger. One man in particular seemed very eager to get away, but with a promise to his uncle to get him 'that thing'.

When they got to the bakery, his uncle had made sure to tell everyone, in his faltering English, that this was his nephew. And he wore a rare smile as he treated K. to a doughnut and tea. At one point, bored of waiting, K. turned around to see whether the treats were ready, and caught a glimpse instead of the lady on the till fishing something out of her apron and handing it to his uncle. But he paid no mind. Today, after all, he was one of the big people.

5.

'What's new?'

'Pronouns.'

'*Pranam?*'

'No, pronouns. Instead of a noun.'

'Instead of *naan?*'

'Yes.'

K. gave up trying to reason with his uncle. They'd been sat in the kitchen performing this Punch and Judy for what felt like an eternity but was in fact a little under a minute. His mind strayed to the Banana Nesquik he'd been craving for the last couple of hours, something sweet to wash away the taste of the lunch hour gruel. They didn't have it at school, and his craving had just grown all through the afternoon Art class, and now here, feigning self discipline when everything in his gut was screaming, 'Yellow! Yellow! Yellow!' Resistance was futile.

His uncle shook his head, mystified at what passed for the boy's education. Still, his nephew had heart, he'd grant him that. Hadn't cried out or flinched that day his nap had been disturbed and he'd been forced to take steps. Hadn't told anyone either, even when his face had begun to swell up and he could just as easily have been betrayed by the pain. If he was going to be honest, he'd have to admit he'd been impressed at the time, and more than a little surprised, when his nephew remained steadfast under questioning, the lie growing in stature with each retelling.

'No, I just fell over.'

The boy's father, one of the uncle's younger brothers, soon lost interest, probably recognising some of his own stubbornness in his son's deadpanning, but also happy not to keep prying, suspecting all roads would inevitably lead to the same stonewall. Just as well too, thought the uncle. The truth rarely helped, even if it appeared to be something of an obsession over here. Every last thing in this country seemed to end in a 'public inquiry'. Take that head of the Liberal party, as far as he could tell, a sordid little man campaigning in his hat. He vaguely recalled some scandal involving another man and then a swift fall from grace. He found his mind briefly wandering to that other dandy, Nehru, who'd also campaigned in a hat. Well, a cap more like. He couldn't help feeling how differently things might have turned out if the Kashmiri pandit had spent a little more time focusing on that 'tryst with destiny' and a little less on the English mem's petticoat. The borders might have fallen elsewhere, or been avoided altogether. Perhaps he'd still be in his childhood home and that word, 'Partition', might not have leaked its poison into his life. Or maybe he wouldn't have seen people forever after as largely worthless confections of weakness and greed. Though in fairness that had hardly been a problem. In his line of work those were merely seams, profitable ones at that, to be mined over and over for personal gain.

Then again it probably wasn't fair to pin all the blame on the dandies in their hats.

What about the Lord who'd almost certainly killed his maid and then himself, or that politician who'd just disappeared without a trace? He winced at the recollection of what they'd supposedly done. The news had been full of them for a while, and then it was as though people simply lost interest. They just faded from public view, although *he'd* not forgotten who they were. Lucan and Stonehouse, the names never far from his lips, shorthand in his mind for a very local sort of disgrace. On his rounds he recalled one man complaining bitterly about the 'disgrace' of the Chancellor heading off to the IMF with his cap in hand, though this same man had nothing to say about the Lord or that other politician, the absconder. At the time he'd let it pass, largely as this was a client who did at least honour his debts in a timely fashion, but all the same the man's attitude had puzzled him. In his own way how was this man any different to the Chancellor? Had he not also gone seeking a loan from a foreigner? And why was he not equally ashamed of that?

Lucan and Stonehouse. Were they any better than the dandies? Of course not. No matter that the rest of the politician's tribe, as far as he could tell, were elected idiots one and all. These were men who couldn't so much as keep the lights on here more than three days a week, even when they weren't running away from the scene of their crimes, or shame, or whatever it was they were trying so hard to leave behind.

He had an inkling what that might be though, even if no one else let on.

In the shabbiness of this city, in its public representatives, in men like Lucan and Stonehouse, he saw the final proof of this country's decline. Her empire well and truly gone, right down to the electricity supply. Its shambling circuitry little better than in the place he'd left behind, that they used to rule, yet here they were, still acting so superior. *In spite of everything.* Of the power outages, or *load shedding* as it would have been called back home. Of the degeneracy, with the defrocked and the disappeared, and with everyone on strike. Of the fighting every night after the pub, the slurred vowels and drunken pavement ballet. The evidence mounting up and still they would carry on as though they were really the ones in charge. Men with big words, and plans. Every so often, those rare evenings he stayed in, he'd see them on his brother's television, heading up committees, councils, *enquiries.* Proposing a service for everything—social, welfare, *bachche* (children), *burolok* (old people)—but with expertise in nothing. Then again, he thought, that was also why they needed him.

Feeling under his chin, he could sense the stubble growing in confidence, thickening into something more impenetrable. This pleased him.

One time, he'd run out of razors and the first hint of beard had accompanied him on his rounds. People noticed too. A subtle change, but one he'd become aware of in a frozen glance here, or fumbling delay there, while the clientele fished around in their pockets for answers. The beard evidently unsettled them in some way too, thus handing him a competitive edge. That pleased him no less. In his line, these were the little details that counted. People were creatures of habit, liked to see the same face at the same time each week. Even the slightest variation on a theme— the appearance of stubble, or the swapping of rings from one finger to another—would ripple out into commercial transactions, his clients momentarily unsteady, blindsided by the change. And he could understand that. Routine was key, allowed for a degree of order in this chaotic world. Which was why he favoured a functional approach to where he lay his head.

#

The room was sparsely furnished. He'd kept things simple in there: a table with a desk lamp, a single bed which barely framed his bulk, and a wrought iron clothes rail, more than ample for several Van Heusen shirts, a couple of cardigans, and two overcoats. The first heavier duty, for those occasional Arctic spells, the other more of a trench coat really, multipurpose, all weather, good inside pockets, for the day to day. In the corner some drawers, rescued from the same junkyard which had yielded the clothes rail, and a toolkit. No clock, or watch, anywhere. Rather, daylight, even the watery kind filtering through the curtains, always viewed as sufficient, nature's own alarm. And out of sight, on old newspapers under the bed, a trusted suitcase, its veteran leather no stranger to sharp exits. No knowing how long he'd be here, or when he might have to leave at a moment's notice.

#

He'd try to get some much needed shut-eye, his tiredness eventually overcoming the nagging suspicion that the boy would carry on as normal with his indoor football or cricket, even after what had happened the last time. Truth be told, he didn't know if he had it in him to give his nephew another 'tap'. Although he'd toned it down, he'd still left his mark on the boy's face, and he regretted that. It was unprofessional, and demonstrated a loss of control. He'd need to be more careful in the future. But at least his kin hadn't blabbered, like seemingly every other person on this island. Crying away about their silly little lives, *he said, she said, money worries*, then overreaching, then reaching out to the wrong person, which of course was where he came in. But really, he thought, all that grief, all that worry, could just as easily have been avoided if, like him, they kept it simple. No drink, no drugs, no women, just the occasional whore for relief—something manageable to be factored in with the standard outgoings. Yet in this place where they couldn't even keep the lights on for more than half the week, they'd confuse desire with need, and before long there'd be accounts to settle. Fools.

#

The bed groaned under his weight, the mattress, like most things around here, a little soft. But compared to what he'd known before in the old country, to the floors, benches and doorways where he was rarely welcome, this was luxury.

He guessed it was around 4pm, as that was when his nephew generally returned from school. Only another half an hour of daylight to keep him at bay. Then he'd start on his rounds again.

This was his favourite time, the bit just before. Meditative, an extended moment to compose himself, limber up like a fighter, to shadow box any remaining doubt from his mind. Once in character, the feints and jabs would melt away, replaced by a stillness which always unnerved. As indeed it was meant to.

Vest, rings, inside pocket, beard. Light blue Van Heusen for the more compliant end of his register. Grey for those days when a little more sweat was needed.

He especially didn't like to be disturbed at this time. As far as he was concerned, these were sacred moments when all that heft, and some of the hurry, would congeal into one fixed mass of concrete, any lingering sentiment sloughed off into the shadows. The final moments before darkness, the curtain call, and his public stage. An important half hour or so to prepare. Method for the big man.

So when the tap tapping started up again against the bedroom wall, he felt it was more than just his sleep that was being disturbed. Something in the cosmic balance of his miniature world was being altered. And really, from where he sat, he had every right to take that personally.

Stepping out of the room he saw his nephew, still just a scrawny kid, throwing a tennis ball against the wall and attempting to bat it away with a small wooden cricket bat. When the boy looked at him, he could tell he was doing his best not to tremble. It had been the same the other day. Trying to keep eye contact and hold the face up straight. The same schoolboy error too, failing to check whether his uncle was still indoors, mistaking an absence of noise with an absence of flesh.

#

He should have been angry really but he was surprised instead by his own reaction. True, he reflected, the boy could be an annoying little bastard with his *nouns* and *pronouns* but he couldn't deny it, there was courage there under all that skinny. By rights this was the point at which he would ordinarily have handed out another salutary lesson on the consequences of a broken sleep. Yet a strange thing seemed to be happening to him, perhaps even stranger than his new-fangled sentimentality. He wasn't actually angry any more. Perhaps for the first time since he'd arrived on this godforsaken island with its runny eggs and leaky eyes, he felt genuinely encouraged. The novelty of this temporarily disarmed him, such that the look he now gave his nephew was for once devoid of rage. None of the usual fractiousness, in fact the only red anywhere was a reluctant tinge in baleful eyes robbed of their extra half hour. And if the boy was still scared, something else must also have passed between them in that instant, some shift, however minor, in the tectonic plates which meant that before long his nephew was actually loosening his grip on the bat handle.

For a while after that, things improved. At K.'s school, the librarian, Mrs J., who had been off sick, was well again, and so his lunchtimes were spent with his classmate, Michelle, sat on the floor down one aisle or another, the two of them pretending to read and stifling giggles, Mrs J. quietly indulging them because in this school children were rarely sighted near books, and almost never of their own volition. So once again the playground was left to the junkyard beasts, to the bullies and the easily cowed, while tucked away out of sight, the little brown boy and the little black girl began to explore an alphabet soup of their own curiosities.

Around a week or so later, his uncle arrived unexpectedly to pick him up from school. The big man in the gabardine trench coat was an unfamiliar face here, and one of the teachers asked him who he was. The look he gave her was entirely dismissive, but K., who'd been observing from a slightly shocked distance, inwardly rejoiced when he heard his uncle follow up with a heavily accented, 'I've come to collect nephew. He in this class.'

No explanation was provided as to why he'd come to meet his nephew, nor was it requested. K. had let go of Michelle's hand the moment he'd spotted his uncle. She'd asked him what the matter was, and all he'd said was that he had to go. But she also saw him leave with the big man in the trenchcoat, and made sure to remember to ask him who that was the next time they were in class.

#

'Who that black girl?'

They had barely cleared the school gates and already K. felt exposed. His uncle's question caught him unaware and it was all he could do to mumble, 'What?' in reply.

'What? No, *who* that girl?'

Shit, he thought. His uncle must have had X-ray vision if he'd managed to spot them together for that briefest of moments before he had let go of Michelle's hand.

'What?'

'No, *who*? I look it up. It one of your *pranams*. Interrogative.'

He looked at his uncle, walking briskly down the road. His mind was a little scrambled but, even so, he could have sworn there were the faintest traces of a smirk on the big man's face. They were nearly home. He'd have that banana drink as soon as they got in. Might even share it with his uncle.

#

6.

Bubbling. That's how things were. People, the weather, the asphalt ('*Readers' Digest*' again, Library, Aisle 3, the same day he got to kiss Michelle's neck under the braids. He liked the feeling of both—the dark buttery skin on his lips and an expanding vocabulary for something a little more exotic than 'tarmac').

That entire summer the place had bubbled. He loved the smell of the tarmac as it cooked under an unusually bright sun. One time he'd put his face right next to the freshly laid tarmac and the fumes, as beguiling as the creosote on the fence, had drawn him closer and closer until that little bit of the neighbourhood had left a dirty kiss on his boat. Of course his cheeks were freshened by another kind of slap when he got home, but nothing too serious in the wider scheme.

In class everyone caught lice, no doubt from one of the unwashed scum out of the rabbit hutches, though the teachers were at pains to point out that lice actually preferred a nice clean head on which to lay their eggs. He didn't believe that for a moment, and blamed the dirty little runts he was forced to share his day with. Had to be them, really. Every lunchtime there they were in the canteen like so many flea ridden meerkats, looking around from side to side before the furtive trip to the toilets to scrape their school dinners into the urinal. Stupid too, to think they wouldn't be spotted, day after day, plates barely concealed under T-shirts as they made the dash across the assembly hall to the kharzi. Eventually of course lookouts would be posted, and Checkpoint Charlie properly manned, forcing a change of tactics onto the runts. That was when they switched to smuggling the dregs of shepherd's pie and what passed for 'greens' back into the igloo of *aloo*. It worked for a while too, until one of the dinner ladies, who were by now the last word on nutritional values, decided, on a hunch, to perform an autopsy on the doctored plate. As the offending greens tumbled out of the igloo, the runts knew straight away that they'd have to change up again. But they were rapidly running out of options, and in the end many simply went along with the gruel, learning to cope with the watery beans, instant mash and sausages of uncertain origin with the trademark good humour of the perennially disappointed.

K. watched these developments from his table in the corner of the canteen. On good days he'd sit there with Michelle; otherwise on his own, bemused by the antics of his fellow foragers. To him, lunch was lunch, just something to get him through the day before he had some real food at home. And other than the shepherd's pie, which for whatever reason was off limits, he had no problem with the food. Though he felt a mild embarrassment on those days when 'curry' appeared on the menu, hoping that none of his classmates thought this was the kind of shit he ate at home. It even looked a bit like shit, and he was genuinely hurt when Michelle said so. Maybe that was why he made a point of eating it in front of her. He didn't say anything to her about the shepherd's pie on her plate, but had the vague sense that her diet, her tastes, were more in keeping with the rest of the class. Weirdly enough he started to enjoy the taste of 'this shit'—Knorr, Vesta, Findus—and to occasionally crave it even when he wasn't at school. But he thought better of sharing this little revelation and, as with most things, he was good at holding stuff down, keeping it in, staying *schtum*.

When it bubbled though, everything got pushed forward. 8am starts but that meant an early close of play too. And then the streets were theirs. He'd see the boys and girls pairing off and heading into the stairwells. They'd go off, then re-emerge, no smarter but somehow proud, as though the whole thing meant something. The boys especially, styling it out like little apprentice toughs. Whatever emotion they felt held in check. Expressions frozen in barely set cement.

Michelle was tugging at his arm now, and they were heading into one of the stairwells. They watched some older kids already camped out, bits of foil and a strange smell drifting across. Deciding against it, they walked round the block and tried another entrance. This time there was no one there and they found a spot a couple of flights up. He liked how her hands and her palms were different colours, also how her neck was darker than her face. Leaning in to kiss her, his eyes closed, only opening again when his tongue found her closed lips. She was looking at him anxiously.

'Are you sure?'

He nodded, then moved his hand towards her braids, the way he imagined it should be done. She closed her eyes now, letting him guide her face towards his.

A woman walked past them, muttering something under her breath. Then an older man, who stopped and turned to face them.

'You should be ashamed of yourselves,' he said. 'Did you hear me? You should be ashamed of yourselves.' K. looked up, thought about saying something, then saw the size of the man and thought better of it. Before he could respond though, the silence was pierced by the words,

'Fuck off, mister'.

It took him a moment to register that the words had come from Michelle's mouth. Those lips weren't pursed now. He could feel her trembling against him but she continued to hold the man's surprised gaze. 'Bemused disgust' was the phrase which popped up in K.'s mind as best describing the scene, but he kept his thoughts to himself. Didn't want Michelle thinking it was the words stacked away in those ancient *Readers' Digests* rather than the prospect of her buttery skin which kept him coming back to the library. The man told them they didn't know they were born, which seemed an odd sort of thing to say, and then made his way back down the stairs.

K. looked at the girl with the buttery skin who rarely said a word in class, who never mistook the carrot he would draw on her back for the prick it was meant to be, and if she did, never let on; who was never less than polite to all the teachers and the librarian. This same girl had just told a much older, and bigger man to 'fuck off'. And he had. Wonders never ceased, but he made a mental note of her actions anyway.

#

Two blazing summers on the bounce. No drought this year but his school finishing early anyway because inside all that 'award winning' design it was a furnace. Glass everywhere, with or without lanky cunts lying around in it. 'Health and Safety' the phrase he'd overheard outside the staff room. It meant nothing really, but he knew that as long as the sun burned, he'd be out of there by lunchtime.

A pity Michelle hadn't been in his class a year ago. She'd only joined this year, and he suddenly realized to his shame that he hadn't yet asked her where she'd come from. Everyone did that. Where are you from? No, where are you really from? And then when the wrong answer kept being supplied, a swift 'well why don't you fuck off back there then?' Actually he just wanted to know where her previous school was. Everyone had previous. Some of the boys in his class liked to say that and then look around to see who was listening. Furry pencil case and the smirking girls and more often than not, K., though unlike them he didn't let on. Already knew that somehow that was not the done thing. Again, to his untutored ears it was just something they said. To K. it didn't really mean anything, though he did find himself wondering from time to time if he had previous. And if so, what it was.

#

7.

K. doesn't say much. The taxi arrives to take them to the airport. It's not a good feeling, breakfast still restless, as they leave behind what's familiar, past the pink elephant dancing on top of the shopping centre, then down to the river, through some fancy looking streets heading out west. No one's saying much though looks are occasionally swapped between his parents if they think the driver is about to take a wrong turn. He's sat next to his brother, but they don't really acknowledge each other during the journey. Steeling themselves.

Things have been quiet for a while now, ever since Dad told them the tickets were booked and that was that.

Mum had got the call just a week ago. At the time he'd been in the toilet trying to regurgitate the winning mixture of banana and smarties to look like sick as an alibi for a cheeky day off. Found himself put off his stride by the sounds of sobbing coming through from the other room. When he'd gone to investigate, he put an arm around her, found out he no longer had any living grandparents, and took the day off anyway.

The rest of the summer, it's just snippets really. The good bits—fish cutlets, the occasional stray English language newspaper, and a distant 'cousin', older than him, who makes him think strange thoughts on that rarest of occasions when they're left alone on the verandah of a flat otherwise bursting with strangers in the preamble to the big day.

The bad stuff—his actual cousin, who they're staying with in Calcutta. That whole side of the family really. He can taste the hostility, though he loses his appetite for *macher-jhol, tarkari, ruti,* for the first time in his life.

They're indoors mostly. It's dull. So he invents cricket scorecards from imaginary Test series involving an Indian side that improbably doesn't wilt in the face of express West Indian pace, the rhythm of his invention spurred on by the sounds of monsoon rain, huge droplets flooding the streets below, occasionally bouncing off the open window ledge into his delighted face. He thinks of Michael Holding—'whispering death'—destroying the English just last summer on that featherbed at the Oval, imagines the raindrops like that cherry leaping into those frightened English faces. And it still makes him smile.

The Planetarium should be a treat, but it ends with him scuffling with his cousin on the forecourt, and both of them getting a slap off his old man with the full backing of the amused onlookers. A trip down to the park and a random game of football with a couple of young Sikhs goes well until his cousin, unhappy at what he sees as a heavy challenge, picks up the ball (his, unfortunately) and walks off with it. Later, when he confronts his cousin about this, they end up scuffling again, but this time he makes sure to get his blows in first before the inevitable intervention and *thapar* from the adults.

There are ants—big, fearless fuckers—and mosquitoes all over the place, but he doesn't see any monkeys until the day they leave the city and head out to his uncle's (on mum's side) in the country. He's a sweet bloke, only has one tooth, and lives simply in what looks like not much more than a glorified shack. But he shows the boy a letter he once got from Harold Wilson, and K. tries to imagine this toothless man, at another time and in another place, in a suit doing an important job, one that receives accolades from Heads of State. It's humid and there are ants and mosquitoes here too, but just outside the shack, on a dusty mound, some kind of *bandar* is sat eating a chapatti, and no one seems to mind.

The really bad stuff—boredom. Day after day lost to his scorecards but knowing there's a million lives being lived just beyond that window ledge, and he doesn't feel any of them. But if it's noisy out there, inside this place is like a morgue, nothing dreamy, only dead signals behind the eyes.

And then finally the day arrives. *Poita*. Their heads are shaved—him and his brother—and they learn the *gayatrimantra*. Three days in *dhotis* with nothing but fruit for company and typically, barely ten minutes in, another of those big, fucking ants is crawling out of the sack cloth. The ceremony itself is impressive in its chaos. Uncles and aunts, *mashis, meshos, pishis, kakas, mamas*, all having their say, telling the poor barber with the cutthroat not to louse it up. A good job the man has steady hands, and the thick black locks come off surprisingly fast. The fire burns throughout, cloying his nostrils, singeing those soft eyebrows. Fairly soon it's over, all the clamour and instructions, imploring and threats, all of it departs with the throng and it's just them, bald and skinny, left with their thoughts, the fruit and the ants.

By the time the Ambassador taxi makes the return trip to the tropical airport, a thin layer of bristle has sprouted atop their globes. He wonders if his brother is thinking the same thing. How it will be on that first day back at school, when the junkyard beasts mistake cultural ritual for the throwing down of some kind of a gauntlet.

#

8.

Bengal, 1940s

Fireflies are circling already. The storage facility has been broken into, telltale footprints zigzagging across the floor. The sawdust is lightly drizzled with blood, nocturnal *rangoli* off the books. In the corner, the nightwatchman propped up against a wall, streaks of claret dried on his face, has been bludgeoned. All that's missing are several large sacks of rice, and this, rather than the surprised look on the nightwatchman's face, is what leads the police inspector to conclude that the culprits are probably adolescents. No real conviction in the blunt-force trauma either, with the evidence pointing to an inability to lift more than a couple of sacks before fear, or a lack of strength further exposed by the famine, must have kicked in. He hates the beggary on their faces, the pleading mixed in with all the lies. When he finds the culprit, child or no child, someone will plead. And someone else will hang.

After a reward is posted it doesn't take long before names are offered up. The rice is discovered under the floorboards of a local grain merchant's house, and the urchins are flogged and locked up, while the merchant finds himself twisting in the wind. The nightwatchman eventually recovers, but his memory of that night remains vague, and he is unable to recall the faces of the young boys who had attacked him. Their fate is uncertain, but the jails, already brimming with would-be *shahids*, have no enthusiasm for these young thieves, and they are released before the genuine blunt-force trauma of Partition— the carving up of the borders, and shortly after that of the bodies. For years after the older of the boys, just too young to hang, occasionally wakes up in the night even when there are no mosquitoes. Two of his brothers, next to whom he sleeps on a park bench in a recently refugeed huddle, suspect the trauma of prison is plaguing their *dada* when they stir from their own half-sleep to find him sat up looking straight ahead into no particular horizon. But their minds are wrapped around problems of their own and there is little appetite for unnecessary questions in this huddle. So his night terrors (which only he knows are not so terrifying) remain unspoken. In his more lucid moments, always private, he recalls dealing the crucial blow to the nightwatchman's head, and not being scared when the red ink started to pour down the startled man's face. There's something else though, and this is the bit he knows he can never tell anyone. The way he remembers it, when the man's eyes went all strange and the seepage began, that was the point at which he started to laugh, for the first time in months, ever since the shortages, and the hoarding, and the thefts had started. His laughter carries him all the way to the merchant's house, and most of the way through the flogging, even when the welts begin to leak. It's only in jail that he learns to narrow his eyes, square up to men much bigger than himself, and hold the laughter down.

#

Routine sustains him in the daily fight for food and space. Though nearly every available inch of ground is used up in the cage, he learns to make his back wide or compact and perform press ups placing his hands in the uneven gaps separating the crook of a neck here, the curl of a foot there. At times there is so little space that he is forced to ball his fists and perform the exercises on his knuckles, though this has the unintended consequence of supplying him, over time, with an extra layering of skin in that strategic part of his hand. He learns to sleep standing and to feign sleep lying down. And by the time toes or hands or the dysfunctions of a gnawing hunger have set his path against one or other of his cellmates, those hands, those knuckles, all that rigour, ensure the contest is rarely that. A thief, and really still just a boy, but the mistake his adversaries make is seeing just a thief and a boy. Afterwards, when blood and teeth and collapsed ego scramble to recompose themselves in the dirt, space miraculously appears for him, so that he can step back, admire his handiwork, occasionally even indulge himself a little smile.

Picking away at the scab he feels a certain amount of regret. Space is limited here and he has taken to marking his tiny locale with whatever is to hand. More often than not this involves hair (his own), or a chipped finger nail, and on one occasion a tooth unhooked by day after day of the cage gruel. But today he has noticed a scab building up on his forearm, and the urge to scratch the itch has proven too great to resist. The skin is not yet flakey, so there is blood and pus underneath. He doesn't mind though, as it makes for a richer signature on the floor. He knows the other inmates are looking at him as he pinches the skin then releases the gunk, but they don't complain as there have been days when it is their teeth or blood which have lined the floor. His blood seems to have been corrupted in some way by the surroundings such that even the mosquitoes avoid him on their night time sorties. The moan and slap of the other wretches means they are still being plagued by malarial torments, yet his nights are oddly peaceful. He holds the gruel down and continues to build himself up with press ups on his knuckles. And he watches, and he waits. The wretches occasionally come to blows with one another, but even when this happens they are careful not to allow their dispute to spill over into the micro fiefdom he has marked out for himself. His vest fills out with this taut system rigour, vein and fibre and barely concealed violence developed in those arms; the knuckles have long since forgotten the harsh taste of floor, protected as they are by an extra layering of skin. And though he is young, there is a strong beard shielding that face now.

When it finally happens, there's little ceremony. 'You', the guard barely able to muster the enthusiasm to unlock the cage, a heavy set of keys jangling near his paunch.

Him, no name as far as the guard is concerned, just another animal languishing in the dirt. A bearded one at that, the mask of facial hair belying his tender age, the rigour in any case located elsewhere. In knuckles drawn tight, the extra layer supplying its own immunity. Bigger and older men in the cage mute witness to the system-built authority of this young man. And his eyes, quiet for now, shorn of sentiment, just waiting, waiting for the next challenge.

For now though, the metal stink, the fetid breath, that shrunken layout which has been his world for longer than the beard, is suddenly traded for something broader.

It is smoke and dust and red that fill his lungs, an inkspot near the eye where once desire might have resided. Now barely a trace, just shapes and numbers and deep crimson calculations.

Space, which he now knows to be the most precious of companions, is needed for another kind of inmate, and with a final reminder that he is a lucky *badmaash* ringing in his ears, the system spits him back out into the dust and the tumult.

No one is there to meet him, and after the initial disappointment, which is barely even that, he feels nothing. Shielding his eyes from the harsh glare of late morning, he squints at the first building which lies beyond the dirt track and at the thick plume of smoke which is rising from it.

#

'Bhaiyya,' implores the man, skeletal arms thrust outwards, that simple action so draining that no more words come.

He stops to look at the man, sees the distant saucers

of his eyes set back in hollow sockets. Instinctively reaches up to soothe the bridge of his own nose with thumb and forefinger. Is surprised when the fingers trace thick hair in the space just below his cheekbones. Strides purposefully on towards the plume without looking back.

#

As he crosses the waste ground his eyes start to pick out more stricken figures, little more than shapes really, only the occasional spasm indicating any life at all. Mostly they are just covered in rags, though one or two are sat, as though meditating, in whatever clothes they were wearing when their lives were touched by fire or tragedy or whatever it was that has left them like this.

He can't bear to look at these figures, implacable in their sadness. It's worse even than the ones who call out to him.

'*Dada. Bhaiyya. Amar ke kichu ekta ditte parben?*'

'*Dada. Amar khidda.*'

Or sometimes, just 'Dada'. *Dada*, though he's barely old enough to be considered anyone's Dada. He sees their arms, little more than flesh starved twigs, and feels something surging up within him. There's no sign of his own siblings, of any of them, though he begins to study the blank faces on display for any traces of recognition. People change, even in a short space of time. He has seen that for himself in the cage. Right in front of him, big, strong men reduced to urchins, the fight drawn out of their faces with one savage beating. The unexpectedness of it, or perhaps the shame, but either way all that swagger absorbed by the blows, repainted as something smaller and delivered in silence. These are just strangers though and even less binds him to them than to his fellow inmates. So when he looks again, this time more closely, and sees that they are in fact not meditating but sitting on recently bandaged stumps, he is as surprised as anyone that the thing surging through him, up through his gut and into his throat, then out of his head, is more primal even than anything he had experienced in the cage.

#

A vengeful fog, some loss, and then all that rigour learned in the cage, perhaps even earlier cruelties that put him there, all of it absorbed, its Spartan lessons heeded in flight. On the benches, holding together some fiction of family, of an 'Us'. In the guise of a refugee but if there's a column of misery here it's not abject.

Bloodied defiance and system rigour, the swamp-fevered red of survival. The key as ever in his ability to remain undetected, to play the role of the grateful survivor, of the responsible head of family, of the man who has learned his lesson.

And within a year it is in the guise of that invisible man that he boards the cargo vessel, undetected and even to those who do actually see him, utterly unknowable, an inkspot where other men store their weakness.

Disgorged not long after from one set of bowels into another, the engine room his delivery system, the docks just another receptacle.

#

By the time he gets to Tilbury, he is amused to find that
the docks are one of the largest facilities for the handling
of grain in this new English landscape. Something in
his bulk, or whatever it is that no longer flickers behind
his eyes, dissuades too many questions in what he
elsewhere hears described as an 'unforgiving place'.
Though personally he is mystified by such a description, able as he is to limber up, stretch out and be paid
for shifting weights here. Those countless nights and
days of boxed up system rigour serve him well in this
environment too and he thrives in its space, revelling in
the anonymity. So long as the freight gets handled, no one
comments on how his face doesn't really fit, nor on his
continued absence from the local drinking establishments.
No one even knows where he stays, though they guess it
must be nearby as he's always the first to appear for work
in the brutal early morning dark of winter while the rest
of them are still rubbing the sleep or remorse from their
eyes. He says very little, sees no reason to draw attention
to himself. It's enough that he's here, working, stretching
out, bit by bit, living. Beyond the crates, and a certain skill
with the inventory which impresses his fellow handlers,
he works equally hard to remain unknowable. The one
time he *is* challenged about an inconsistency between the
number of crates on the pier and the number noted in
the ledger, he's more annoyed at being called 'Gunga Din'

than by the accusation itself. It is a reminder of something unwelcome and the instinctiveness of his response transports him for a moment back to the cage, and the very first of the lopsided contests. Equally he makes a note of how the other men in the vicinity allow the contest to play out, how nobody attempts to stop him even when his accuser has lost the first of several teeth and his nose is broken in two places. He also makes a note not to be caught out so easily again. It is sloppy and weak and in his short life he has already seen far too much to pretend that those are virtues. So he is more careful from now on, knows he is being watched, accustomed to that too.

Some weeks later he arrives to find the docks already thronging with people. There is great excitement, a murmur rippling from one side to the other. He is surprised to see smartly dressed Black people descending from a passenger liner, their suits very much to his liking though he finds something a little suspect in the wide brim hats that many of them seem to favour. He thinks he can feel some within the crowd, where he stands, looking his way, then back at the well dressed blacks, but he can't be sure. He looks himself, sees the fineries with which these passengers are disembarking, then considers his own skittish arrival, hidden away in the engine room of a Polish cargo vessel, praying for nightfall and some kind of proximity. He is briefly angered by the memory, then reminds himself of the box he was in before, and of the new boxes only he knows about. Shortly after that he is not seen in Tilbury again, and it is only after the crowds, and the excitement, have died down, that anyone bothers to look at the inventory. And once again, grain has gone missing and brows are furrowed. But this time no one will plead, and no one will hang.

9.

London, 1976

Drought. But no famine. On television, K. is watching the tall, blond captain of the England cricket team, who seems to be a South African, repeat his promise to make the touring West Indians 'grovel'. Even to his eight year old eyes, this seems to be an unwise boast. In the *Radio Times* he has seen a picture of this summer's tourists, and they don't look the sort to grovel. He likes the maroon blazers that they are wearing—a good, strong colour. And there is a look of steely determination about this touring party. Some arms are folded, but even those at repose look as though they mean business. It reminds him of a photo he has seen recently which tumbled out of a cardboard folder containing lots of letters from 'The Electricity Board'.

'Mum, what's this?' he'd asked.

She'd been chopping some onions at the time, and seemed distracted until he showed her the photo. Then she'd wiped her forehead with the sleeve of her apron before getting back to the onions.

'Oh, that. That's your dad,' she replied, unable to fully suppress the smile.

'What's he doing?'

'What do you mean, 'what's he doing'? He's just there,'

she said, with what sounded like a touch of impatience.

It was indeed Dad, standing under some kind of a fruit tree, arms folded, looking implacably ahead. There was something familiar in his stance, the big, strong forearms, the early summer light. That is when he hears Dad, the sounds of a hammer, and nails going into wood, and he knows he should help him, at least hold the wood steady. When he goes to investigate he sees that mesh wiring has been placed over all the windows visible to the street. Extra strips of wood have been secured to the edges of each window as well. Only the most determined brick launcher is going to pierce these defences, and since the letterbox has been sealed and they are now retrieving all their correspondence from the Post Office, the hope is that the special deliveries will cease too. Of course for the time being they are holding on to the industrial quantities of Dettol which they picked up last time they were dropped off at the Cash & Carry. No knowing when it might come in useful and always better, as Dad is forever telling him, to be prepared.

'Nothing personal,' the policeman had said, though it feels quite personal when backup is called to restrain Dad after the observation that, 'your wife does wear a sari though, and maybe that makes her stand out.' K. sees Dad inviting the policeman to leave, and can make out the little snake eyes of the class runt darting around in the background scenery. The runt often appears when there are sirens. K. knows that he lives in the next block, though he doesn't yet know exactly where. He wordlessly swaps glances with the runt. Even when the policeman tells Dad, 'there's nothing we can do, not without proof,' K.

doesn't voice any of his suspicions. Besides, up to now, the policeman had barely registered his presence and keeps looking nervously behind him as if for reinforcements to his courage. For whatever reason, he clearly wasn't expecting the man who answered the door to be so big, or to be holding a hammer. He wishes he hadn't mentioned the sari now but it was just nerves really, he'd blurted it out, hadn't meant it, knew it was foolish as soon as he'd said it. Backup arrives, more doors open and curtains twitch, though the scene remains eerily quiet. Growing bolder, the runt perches on the seat of a brand new bike on the opposite side of the road. He appears more alert than at any time during class, eyes darting from the uniformed men to the big man in the doorway, then back to the scaffolding near the high rises, and the recently arrived skip.

Explaining that he has to carry out his own running repairs as there is apparently never any 'proof', Dad puts the hammer down but as he does so, makes sure to look beyond the several uniformed men now gathered on his doorstep, and into the eyes of any neighbours who happen to be around. K. stands behind him as he has the strong feeling that this will help the situation. He hears, 'I didn't know,' 'You can't blame me for thinking,' 'Like I said, we'll do all we can, but without proof,' and he takes a step forward so that he is right next to Dad. He feels a big hand come to rest upon his right shoulder, and when the lack of proof is again mentioned, enjoys the pressure of the fingers as they squeeze the top of his arm. Later, when all the uniforms have dispersed, he will take another look at the photograph, making a mental note of the stance, the way the head is slightly tilted, the arms showing more than a little flex. On closer inspection, something else stands out too. This is one of the few photos that K. has seen where Dad isn't smiling, in fact where there's not even a hint of a smile. And yet when he'd showed it to Mum a little earlier, she'd tried really hard not to smile, even though bricks kept flying through windows, and silly little men in less than dazzling uniforms would turn up spouting even sillier excuses.

It takes a while to bin all the glass, the smaller pieces routinely embedded in the carpet, the shards swept up and wrapped in paper. Yesterday's news, really, or maybe an arc stretching even further back. K. is distracted by the headlines, his mind trying to balance inflation with the task in hand. When he sees something about West Ham in Europe, he momentarily forgets that the story is wrapped around a shard, and the rivulet of blood which forms around his thumb surprises him nearly as much as the ongoing progress of the Hammers. That evening though, when he sits down with Mum to do their nightly spelling test, he correctly spells the word 'sanguine' before they both look up its meaning in the large Chambers Dictionary Mum has purposely brought to the table.

He also looks up 'runt', sees that in addition to being

the smallest in a litter of pigs, it is a large breed of domestic pigeon as well as a vague term of reproach.

#

10.

London, 1950s, 1960s

The ration books can finally be put away. In the shops there is more butter, and Black faces. He has been here some time anyway, watching, learning. It is a place of graft, and it has been long enough that the memory of the cage has begun to recede. He feels this first in his physical movements, the cramp ironed out of his arms by those long days on the docks. The ability to lie flat has returned, legs enjoying the luxury, for so long denied, of reaching for space. And once the docks are forsaken, that is just one more memory to be shed.

'Good morning,' he says to the West Indian man, tipping his hat as he walks by. Though it is early, there are already a number of people on the street heading, he presumes, to work. He has been watching for any signs of movement coming from the top floor flat in the large house across the road. So far nothing, though he has already been standing on the street for nearly an hour. It is cold and he is grateful when the little café on the corner opens its doors some minutes later. The steaming tea is just what he needs, and he has quickly developed a taste for the egg and chip option which every café seems to offer. It is an odd way to eat *aloo* but he enjoys mopping up the leaky yokes with the deep fried fingers. Looking up as the last of the chips disappears, he sees that a light has come on in the flat. For once he praises the dark smog of these wintry mornings, pays for his breakfast and strides across the road.

#

'Let me go! This instant!' shouts the woman, her hair unkempt, nightdress offering a good grip with its ample material. He pays no attention, forces her over to the window, which he unlatches using his spare hand.

She continues to scream, 'Let go of me!' He feels she is drawing unnecessary attention to both of them, so pulls her back from the window, and spinning her round with her nightdress, he backhands her smartly around the mouth. While her eyes are still registering the shock, he palms her on the other side of her face, all the while keeping his gaze focused on her. The noise immediately stops—something he has noted on other occasions—and though she continues to struggle a little, most of the fight seems to have left her with the first blow. There is no real malice in any of it. More wake up call than punishment. He releases her nightdress from his grip, lets her slump back down onto the bed. Only now does he speak.

'Where it is?'

She nods over at the dresser, ruefully nursing the blow with her tongue placed in one cheek. He looks around the room, sees little of any note other than the dresser, but makes sure to roughhouse the drawers anyway so that her few items of clothing and a couple of trinkets fall onto the floor. Predictably, the package is located to one side of the bottom drawer, under some gloves, and he feels its weight before tucking it away in an inside pocket. Turning to face her he sees that a little red trickle has already appeared at the corner of her mouth. Her eyes are leaky too. He detects a tiny flinch as he walks past her towards the door. There is no need for any further reminders in this flat, for now at least.

\#

The hairstyles, like the buildings, growing upwards now. Beehives and brutalism, the twin pillars of this new laissez-faire. Everywhere he looks he sees castles and cones in the sky, though someone should also have explained to these brash new Londoners that it was a lot further to fall when the views were cloudcapped. He's endlessly practised that line in his room, has managed to make it sound almost fluent, and though the decade, and its 'misplaced sense of priorities' (a phrase, like 'cloudcapped', that he once heard on the radio and liked), is barely under way, he has already had several occasions to apply its wisdom. He feels he has made the phrase his own; enjoys the fact that he has some kind of a signature statement. Ever since he saw 'Angel Eyes' in that strange western that was playing at the ABC, he has felt the need to develop a signature, though elsewhere in that primal soup of memory he hears another voice urging caution, the need to remain silent and largely invisible. But it's too late for that, he thinks. Apparently all the old restraints are being lifted, and from the snippets he can gather on his radio, London is the epicenter of the shift. In truth he doesn't really see it, or believe it.

On his rounds people still have the hungry look of ration books and black market butter. To be sure, there are more kettles and even one or two vacuum cleaners in evidence, but for the most part the flats he visits remain sparse, unfurnished, dingy, their inhabitants sallow and tired. On those rare occasions that he encounters surly, a quick spell in the clouds is usually sufficient to readjust their attitude, and then he's back to a mental inventory of their threadbare surroundings. He guesses that 'swinging', whatever else that might mean, doesn't refer to his domain. There are no boutiques or coffee bars around here, and the skirt length has remained stubbornly modest for years. In fact his only recollection of a miniskirt in the locality is on a young woman who was unable to honour her obligations. 'Please,' she'd said, and then again, and then she'd stopped talking, and afterwards he'd hated her more for the tears streaking her cheeks, but she'd at least had the good grace to turn away from him, had looked down at the unmade bedsheet, and so he'd left her to her fantasy of a clean slate, knowing that it wouldn't be long before someone this weak was back on his radar.

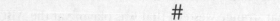

#

11.

There is change in the air though. One of his younger brothers, part of that park bench huddle, is married now and living in London. The girl, at one point also a refugee, is from a long line of books and learning, her father a renowned professor, but now as far as he can tell just an old man with failing health in reduced circumstances.

He should feel happier than he does for his own brother, but the truth is he feels hardly anything. One time when they were sleeping on the benches, he awoke to find his brother comforting a stray dog which had gravitated towards their huddle. Although none of them had eaten properly for the past few days, his brother was sharing a tiny piece of roti with the dog. He recalls the intense rage he'd felt at the time, his own hunger keened by days and even longer nights in the cage, where all he'd thought about was space, and abundance, and no more privation. Yet this brother always had a kind word for everyone, and his face bore that kindness in gentle eyes, an ever present smile. Still smiling even that day, as a young boy, when he'd fallen out of the tree near the river and landed awkwardly, smashing his forearm on the ground. Lying there preter-naturally still, blood pouring from the wound, but not crying out as it was early. Not wishing to disrupt anyone's sleep. And when he was discovered, half-conscious, even then no kind of snarl on that already handsome face. So that when people were done praising his stoicism, they went right back to praising his face. No one ever asked who found him, then carried him back to where the adults were sleeping, imploring him the whole way not to go, not now, then bore the brunt of their questions, and their anger, while wounds were cleaned and bandages wrapped. And now here he was feeding this *kutta* while half the city starved.

12.

Bengal, 1947

'What are you doing?'

He is surprised by the question, thinking he was alone. He is looking at himself in a shard of mirror which he earlier found on the dirt road snaking around the park. Gauging his reflection he tries to look haughty, then severe, by turns flaring his nostrils then dulling his eyes. He turns to see the familiar khaki uniform of the police. The man is carrying a *bhuri*, sagging over his belt, and in that one detail he sees so much of what will always divide them. As much as the uniform or the steel tipped *lathi,* it is the softness of that belly, its partiality to sweetmeats and greed, which marks out this man's tribe.

'Nothing. I was just leaving, sir,' he says to the policeman, observing the expected protocol but knowing from the deep set rituals of the cage that it means nothing.

He sees the policeman prodding a bundle of rags a little further along the path. The rags stir and a disheveled face appears, already terrorized long before the steel tip brushes its chin. He realizes he has been fortunate to even be asked a question. Standing there with a shard of glass in one hand, he could just as easily have been deemed a 'threat' by the policeman. The city is on edge, the bodies still fresh, and he is taking a risk each time he leaves the huddle. He knows he must hurry back to his brothers, still prone on the benches, to warn them about the lathi. But when he does he sees that they are already awake, sat up for the policeman's benefit like a couple of early morning *bhadralok* discussing current affairs. The lathi briefly pauses, satisfies itself that these are not miscreants, before moving on to the next set of unfortunates.

And seeing this, with the shard now wrapped in a fold of his vest, he thinks, no one ever asks the right questions.

Part Two

Half bark, half vapour

1.

London, 1976

'Hello?' Dad answers the front door, thinking he wasn't expecting anyone this evening.

'Mr. H?' replies the woman, standing there with another man and holding a clipboard.

Dad nods, still unsure as to why these people are here.

'Can we come in for a moment?' asks the woman, gesturing inside.

'Of course. But first can I ask why?' replies Dad, never breaking from the smile with which he'd answered the door.

At this point the man who has been standing there behind the woman speaks for the first time.

'Perhaps it is better if we come in, Mr. H. It is a rather delicate matter,' he says in the matter of fact way which suggests that he is in fact the senior partner of the duo. His tone betrays a growing impatience with the doorstep etiquette.

'As I said, no problem. But you still haven't told me why you're here.'

The senior partner repeats, but this time with greater urgency, that the matter is best discussed inside. Dad relents, and then all three of them are in the kitchen, where

K. is sat next to Mum, eating dinner with his brother. It is *macherjhol* and both boys are unpicking the trout with their fingers.

The man makes a mental note of who is sitting where, while the woman smiles weakly in their direction.

'They seem to be enjoying it,' says the man, pointedly not referring to the 'it' as fish.

'Of course,' replies his Dad. 'It is their dinner.'

'And your other children? Have they already eaten?'

'My other children?'

'Yes, your daughters? Did they eat earlier?'

'My daughters?'

K. shifts uncomfortably in his seat, focusing on the trout as if it is the last thing left on earth. Though he makes sure not to look up, he can feel Mum's gaze trained on him, senses this is the first time since the strange couple walked in that she has paid attention to something other than *his* dismal brown suit and *her* clipboard, which the woman seems to be holding ever more tightly.

K. makes a series of rapid calculations, realizes there isn't enough fish or rice left on the plate to use as a distraction while 'the matter' is cleared up. Even so, without any specifics, perhaps the whole thing could still be put down to some kind of misunderstanding, and that would be that. So he zeroes back in on the one remaining piece of fish clinging to the bone, and spends what feels like an eternity failing to separate the two.

'Where are your sisters now?'

The words linger over the formica top, and as they do he knows his cover is blown. Maybe he can pretend that he hasn't heard, or that the question isn't really addressed to him, but the silence all around and a quick jab by his brother under the table force him to look up. Seeing the way the adults are looking at him, and knowing he is cornered, it all comes tumbling out. *Only mucking about. How was he to know that other kid would go off and tell the teacher? He'd only said it as a joke. Why would they hide their sisters? No, that didn't mean there were any sisters. He'd made the whole thing up, remember?*

After the strangers leave, the man muttering something about the job being 'hard enough', he gets a slap off Mum, as expected, though he can tell her heart's not exactly in it, and Dad hasn't really stopped smiling throughout.

It doesn't seem right somehow, especially when the same kid he'd been fibbing to earlier on, 'tells' on anyone else in the class and the teachers never seem all that interested.

'Put it down to experience,' his brother says, and then they all get back to having a good laugh at the state of the man's suit.

#

2.

How do they know? But know they do. It's obvious from their carry-on the next day in school, little clusters made up of all the usual suspects, and he knows as soon as they grow quiet when he walks past them. Can sense that he's the topic of conversation, notices a couple of them pointing him out to their friends. When he goes into the classroom he sees the snooty girls for once making eye contact with him before quickly looking away. Then the runt, breaking off from his usual antics to stare at him with a barely concealed smirk on his boat. He takes his usual seat, tries not to meet anyone else's eyes, and wonders where the teacher is.

'You're going into care,' someone says, and then someone else adds, 'You're getting deported,' and then they're scuffling, and of course *that's* when the bloody teacher finally decides to make an entrance.

After only he is sent to the headmaster's office, K. sits outside, aggrieved, for a few minutes, before the secretary, who has been looking at him over her glasses with a mixture of pity and disgust, tells him he 'can go in now'.

It takes a moment to readjust his vision to the thick pall of smoke which just seems to hang in the air. Eventually he is able to make out a pair of feet resting on the desk, and then the homespun profile of the headmaster. He looks smaller than he does during morning assembly, certainly a lot smaller than Dad, and not much bigger than Mum.

'Now, why are you here today?' the headmaster asks.

'I dunno,' replies K. in the expected fashion.

Something in his response seems to bother the headmaster, who takes his feet off the desk and adjusts his glasses so that he can have a proper look at this boy. It comes as something of a surprise to him to see that the boy is Asian. There aren't many of them there and he's not used to seeing them in his office. Wouldn't have hurt for someone to have let him know. His secretary hadn't thought to mention it. Silly moo, probably couldn't pronounce the name, thought she wouldn't bother. Then again.

'And whose class were you in?'

'Mrs. Allott's.'

'Mrs. Allott?'

'Yes.'

'Right then. So why did she send you out of her class?'

'I dunno.'

K. is surprised at how easy it is to keep repeating that line. He knows there will be questions as soon as he gets back to class, and that for some reason it is best if he keeps saying the same thing to the questions which are being put to him now. Again it does seem strange how he is the only one expected to say nothing, especially as all of this was only happening now because of what everyone else had been saying. And as he'd already told that strange man in the terrible suit only yesterday, he'd made the whole thing up. When the man had asked him why he'd done it, he seemed surprised to hear that it was mainly out of boredom. He'd gestured to his colleague, the one with the clipboard, and she'd ticked something on the front-page. And when he'd leaned forward to ask in a voice that belonged on *Play School*, 'what else do you like to do when you're bored' and the answer had come, 'nothing much', she'd carried on ticking the boxes until Mum, watching the whole thing with arms folded and a fast furrowing brow, mentioned how he wasn't challenged by the material being taught in class and that's why he was bored. They'd both stopped what they were doing then, him with the questions and her with the clipboard, as though they couldn't quite believe that this little lady wearing the funny dress and speaking her heavily accented English was telling them about a lack of 'challenging material' in her son's class. And then about his advanced reading age, and how the books being introduced in class were the kind of thing he was devouring (and yes, she'd used that word, 'devouring') when he was four or five. Not the kind of thing at all she expected an eight year old to still be stuck on. That was the word she'd used, 'stuck', and she'd fixed both the strangers a look that made it clear that her boy was not stuck; far from it, he was bored; and when people are bored they sometimes do naughty things. But all he'd really done was tell a little story to alleviate the boredom. And yep, she'd used that word alright, seemed to really enjoy the way it pierced the low benchmark routine of the clipboard, and the early evening domestic, and the expected descent of the presumed underclass into expletive and self doubt which of course she had no intention of succumbing to. That was when the man started mumbling something about 'confusion and mix-up', and 'needing to go to his next meeting'. And within moments they were both gone, faintly trailing a muttered complaint in their wake.

K. is still marvelling at those words, all those fancy lines, when the *thapar* spoils his reverie. Even so, the focus soon switches to the man's terrible suit, which K. learns is a 'polyester nylon mix', and fairly soon they are all wheezing with laughter as Mum impersonates the look on the man's face each time she threw in something from her Chambers' Twentieth Century Dictionary.

#

'What do you mean by that? What do you mean 'you don't know'?' the headmaster practically shouts at him.

K. is surprised by the outburst as he doesn't ever remember the man getting this angry during assembly, even the special one they'd all had to attend that time one of the older boys had been run over. A tragedy alright, but then again the boy had been playing chicken at lunchtime on the dual carriageway that ran right past the school. He remembers the ambulance, and the police, and the headmaster's sombre tone that day when addressing the whole school. But not this sort of anger, which is strange, given that the boy later died from his injuries.

'I dunno.'

The funny thing is that he doesn't really care anymore. He is already used to the puzzled looks from his other teachers when they ask to see his work and find it completed and largely without error, barely masking their irritation on those occasions they catch him dawdling, or daydreaming, or looking through the blackboard into the plaster and at the very foundations the school is built on; at its glass and recently acquired grime; at the parquet floors and the special stink they give off with hundreds of little feet to baptize them each day; at the window ledge and grass verge beyond, and dreams of escape from all these shades of stifling, stinking, sugar coated silly. He has learned to slip in the occasional deliberate error, just for the way their faces light up, the renewed sense of mission always so prized by those he already recognises as the fools. For that briefest of moments they can look at him and believe, actually believe, they have something important to teach him.

He spots this the first time he genuinely makes an error, tilting the balanced vowels of 'separate' in favour of the 'e's. Mrs. Allott, who never sees anything in class, miraculously zeroing in on the error with an enthusiasm she rarely allows to get in the way of her teaching. Of course she does, they all do, look at him then like a poor little boy, starting off at a disadvantage. *They don't speak it at home you know. All that fish, it's why their hair's so oily. And they eat with their hands. I mean, that can't exactly be hygienic, can it?*

The smell in the office, so overpowering only moments earlier, is now just another detail—weak, and stale, and not much really. A little like the man standing in front of him, a study in sweat and agitation, some red in those cheeks for the first time since he's been here, but still largely unconvincing.

'This is unacceptable. I will of course be speaking to your mum and dad. Have we got their number in the office?'

K. can't believe his luck. It is an open invitation, and far too good to pass up.

'I dunno.'

#

Another week, and K. is back in the headmaster's office. His birthday is coming up and pretty soon he will be eight. But this is no treat. It is 1976.

This time he is accompanied by Mum, her nose already wrinkling at the stale smell which greets them as they walk in. She makes a note of the sign above the door—'No Smoking on School premises'—but doesn't say anything for now.

The headmaster is sat up this time, and gets out of his chair to greet them when the secretary shows them in. There are no feet planted on desks, and an outstretched hand is offered, though Mum declines when she notices the nicotine stained fingers.

'Now, Mrs. H. I understand you have some concerns about the teaching here. First of all, let me assure you ----------'

'Look, your teacher, Mrs. Allott, told my son he can't read properly. I want you to give him a test.' Mum has been rehearsing that line on the way in, and when there is no immediate answer from the headmaster, she adds,

'Now.'

'Let's not get too worried about this,' says the head-master. 'I'm sure K. is making good progress overall, and if Mrs. Allott------------'

'*Now*. I want you to give him a reading test right now then,' Mum insists, her eyes scanning the room for the very few books which are actually on shelves. She picks one out, something called '*Total Woman*', while the headmaster looks on disbelievingly.

'Any page. You choose any page and he reads. Then you can tell me if he still can't read. Any page,' and she thrusts the book under his nose.

K. is happy to read about Harriet Habit and Phoebe Phobia, and is surprised to learn that 'a slovenly wife is usually too tired to be available to him,' whatever that means, though he has an inkling.

The headmaster has barely spoken since Mum waved away his initial protests about the unscientific nature of this method, and the book not really being 'appropriate'. K. enjoys the advice to women to 'be touchable and kiss-able' and nearly laughs aloud when he gets to the line suggesting they 'remove all prickly hairs and be squeaky clean'.

'Ok, ok. I think we've heard enough,' says the head-master, signaling for the reading to stop. Something in the look Mum gives the man prompts him to add, 'I'll have a word with Mrs. Allott. There's obviously been some kind of misunderstanding, but we'll straighten it out, Mrs. H. Don't worry.'

'I always worry,' Mum replies. 'He's my son. I have to

worry about him.'

As they leave, K. spots the secretary sneaking a quick glance over her glasses at the woman in the sari emerging from the headmaster's office. He has seen that look before, though this time there's no pity commingling with the disgust.

The 'misunderstanding' is indeed straightened out, though K. is left to ponder that of late, it's been one after another of these. Anyway, he is largely free to do as he pleases during class, the assumption now being that the set work won't occupy him for more than a few minutes. He has more time to study the other children, so he notices that the snooty girls occasionally look over at the blonde boys who sit at the back, untroubled by the teacher or whatever the work might be. He sees them egging each other on to catch the eye of the boys at various times during the class. And on the rare occasions that the boys look up, he sees Rosalind and Emma immediately look away, smirking at one another and pretending to focus on their books. One time he catches Rosie (as she likes to be called) looking at him, and she seems embarrassed at being caught out. There is no smirk this time, no sharing of secrets with Emma.

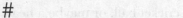

3.

When the weather warms up a little, Dad shows him how to make a bow and arrows, and he spends a whole day carving little sticks of wood into lethal points. That's the same day he overdoses on plums and spends most of the afternoon with an upset stomach while his brother pings arrows at him, safe in the knowledge that he won't be running far, unless it's to the toilet, or behind the bushes.

When the weather warms up a little, Dad shows him how to make a bow and arrows, and he spends a whole day carving little sticks of wood into lethal points. That's the same day he overdoses on plums and spends most of the afternoon with an upset stomach while his brother pings arrows at him, safe in the knowledge that he won't be running far, unless it's to the toilet, or behind the bushes.

Dad does some carving of his own, working miracles in the back yard with the tree stump they had rescued from what Dad calls the 'corporation' dump after the council had sent in the chainsaws. He works the stump with a hammer and chisel, muscles rippling in his string vest. A trilby is rakishly perched on his greying scalp, protecting him from the sun. His trousers are held up with braces, red ones, and there is no polyester or nylon anywhere in the mix. Every now and then K. pops out into the yard to sneak a look at the work in motion. Though it's early doors, something is already starting to emerge from all that rejected wood, a familiar shape which looks like a huge cricket ball, or maybe a head.

Mum briefly joins Dad outside and they share a joke about the shape before she hands him a little cloth bundle and a cup of tea.

Dad spots K. lurking in the background, tells him to come over.

'Let me show you something,' he says, removing a large knife from the bundle. He hands K. what looks like a tapered rolling pin made of stone. 'Hold this for a moment,' he tells him, and isn't surprised when his son needs both hands to avoid collapsing under the weight. 'Heavy, na?'

K. nods, relieved at not dropping the funny looking rolling pin. Dad takes it back from him, and holding the stone in one hand, he makes rapid paint brush strokes using the one knife with the other. The scraping noise quickly becomes a rhythm, mesmerising K. with its rising and falling scale of all that steel against stone.

'You want a go?'

Mum yells at Dad from the kitchen in Bengali, but by then K. is already holding the knife in both hands and running the blade across the stone sharpener, which Dad holds steady for him. He completes two brush strokes, enjoys the compliment Dad pays him and then heads back inside, where Mum is still muttering something under her breath, waiting for Dad to finish up and chop the fish.

K. is impressed by how quickly Dad swishes the blade from one side to another. He makes it look so easy, but when he'd tried just a moment before that stone *chakkudhar* had weighed a ton. It is hot and the doors and windows are all open, the aromas of *dhal*, *tarkari* and the *macherjhol* under orders, mixing with the smells of fat and red meat escaping from a neighbour's yard.

Occasionally the sound of cans being opened from next door breaks up the stone/steel rhythm, but not much is being said either side of the fence.

Dad seems to be satisfied with the sharpness of the blade, but runs it across the *chakkudhar* one last time just to be sure. Somewhere beyond the back wall whispered encouragement and then a hand up to defy the physics. A face appears with impeccable timing just as the knife prepares to make its final downward stroke. The implacable figure in the string vest looks up, eyes still partly shaded by the trilby, the knife held for the briefest of moments in mid air.

'Jesus fucking Christ!' says the face even as it tumbles back out of sight.

Only after it lands with a thump and the sound of scrambling boots trails ever fainter, 'fuck' 'fucking hells' in its wake, does a burst of laughter leapfrog the fence from the afternoon ritual beyond the creosote.

Shortly after there is a knock at the front door. When Dad goes to answer it, he sees a big man stood there, skin blushing under ink. There is a pause, string vest sizing up body art, and then a burly hand is outstretched.

'I'm J., your neighbour.'

'Pleased to meet you,' says Dad, then, spotting the cans the man is holding in his other hand, invites him in.

#

By the time J. leaves, still carrying the unopened cans, he has largely forgotten that earlier craving he'd had for steak and beer. The dhal, tarkari and rice has been washed down with several cups of tea, and much to his own surprise the afternoon heat has given way to lengthening shadows.

One tattoo in particular, of a miniature *ohm*, catches Dad's eye, and without much prompting it turns out that the trail of ink and blood leads through a stint in the merchant navy and ocean bound adventures far from J.'s native Canning Town. Bombay, and a taste for fish, have stayed with him, that little piece of skin a votive offering to the spirit of elsewhere. Which is why he could never return to those docks, that side of the drink. All those pinched faces and the freight already coming in through Tilbury. The old East End holding on to its memories but not a whole lot else, and frankly he couldn't be doing with that. A little too close to self pity, or as his old man would have described it, 'frankly undignified'. Besides, he'd had the ink put there for a reason, a reminder that there's always an elsewhere, for starters the stamps of origin for all that freight he'd seen coming in ever since he was a little boy. And in a way, little traces of elsewhere were already on his fingers from handling all that exotic cargo long before he decided to see something of the world, to put an ocean and several time zones between himself and that bit of the docks which just got stuck in one ancient hurt after another.

He wiped his mouth with the back of his hand and continued.

So he'd left it all behind, and headed off with a young

man's ambition, shedding no tears for the smallness of the departure. No one to see him off, but no one to hold him back either, and then it was just him and the vastness of all that unknown. Other places, other people, but in his experience often the same habits. Speaking of which, would you like one of these, squire? Not now. Oh, righty-oh, a cuppa it is then. Yes, two sugars please, that's perfect.

Dad doesn't say too much, can see that J. feels the need to talk, lets him supply most of the details. It is something he's noticed over the years. People generally don't like to talk much, but when they start, there's no knowing when they'll stop or where it will go.

While the tea is being poured, K. picks out another of the man's tats.

'Are those the Hammers, then?' he asks, pointing to the crossed pair of rivet hammers and the Boleyn castle crest on the man's forearm.

J. puts his cup down for a moment and turns to look at the kid, sat there in his tooth and curiosity.

'Well spotted young man,' he says. 'They are indeed. And those hammers were used to build the kind of ships that took me to India and brought your old man here.'

K. doesn't like to hear Dad referred to as an 'old man', and is also a bit confused by what the man has said. What has happened to last year's Cup winners and why is the man talking about ships?

Seeing the confusion on the kid's face, J. asks, 'So are the Hammers your team then?' and K., as much to please the man because he's shown some interest, rather than because he feels any great conviction about it, says,

'Yes'. From across the table Dad shoots him a look which strongly suggests that this is news to him.

'And have you been to see them play?' he asks K.

When K. shakes his head, the man rubs his hands together. 'Right then,' he says, 'That's settled. We'll have to do something about that, won't we?'

#

4.

A lot more words are being swapped now across the creosote. With the days lengthening and the weather warming up, Dad is out in the yard most evenings, shaping the reclaimed wood with a hammer and chisel.

'What are you making now?' comes the question from next door.

'Hopefully you'll see,' answers Dad, applying some sandpaper to what looks like a set of fingers fanning out across a forehead.

J. often turns up just as dinner is about to be served, but no one minds too much. K. thinks he's like one of those kids on the Bisto ad, unable to resist the waft of cooked rice, though he never actually tells J. this.

Mum is happy enough as he usually brings something from his garden—fresh mint, potatoes and one time even a marrow. He rarely turns up *khali haat* like most English people she has seen and among other things she puts this down to the time he has spent in India, enjoying his sailor's life among the landlocked. Swapping words and curiosities to start with—*mera naam, tera naam*– but quickly sizing up this feast of possibilities with a docker's seasoned eye. And settling on food as the best medium for any further conversation. Sizing up, and being sized up by, the locals. Eating with them too, seeing how they share, and how it's bad form to turn up at someone's home empty handed. He's also seen enough white men playing Livingstone around these parts to know that he didn't leave the docks behind for this. And he's already told Dad it was more paneer than pleasure palace, so Mum also knows. Unannounced is fine, really, but unthinking she can well do without.

#

He's a talker and the stories just keep coming once he sees how much the boys enjoy them. It's all there: the best way to grow mint, his tattoos, even the teddy boys who rose from the rubble of his East End childhood, all bomb sites and spit, snarl, polish.

In the runny egg caffs which pepper this landscape, he finds some respite from the roar of the docks. Though the strange thing is that under all that sizzle and crackle, within earshot of fat and fry, the smell of the river never lags far behind. It follows him as he slurps his tea, and stays with him as he mops up the yoke. Like a great murky tongue pressed against his ear, it whispers deep secrets to restless souls, and he knows that day is drawing closer when the tongue will finally lift him onto its endless current and take him far away from these ruins.

For him, all the area's secrets, and a lot more besides, are right there, in front of him, in front of everyone. Carving their own patterns of desire and despair, of so much lust and longing, in the mud and mayhem of the city's ancient tongue. Right there on the banks of the Thames, the forgotten remnants of untold dramas, before the strike or the scabs, or even the rumour that the original freight was words, ideas buoyed along by the eddying currents of their own fury or fun. These are the lines he traces in the mud, that swirl which goes around his head, lines forming shapes, eventually encased in steel and sweat, giving rise to the ships that would soon enough smuggle him to some other kind of alive.

#

5.

K. is with Dad, walking on the High Street. Though it's hot for the second consecutive day, some people are still out in polyester. Dad hasn't made a list, and he's already struggling to remember what they were supposed to pick up from the market. So they carry on walking, making mental notes of fruit and fish and those stallholders with a smile on their face, as well as those whose boats have only ever known a scowl.

They see M., the old lady who lives two doors up, loitering around a fruit stall, and K. goes over to see if she needs a hand.

'No, but that's very nice of you to ask,' she says, though the look on her face suggests otherwise.

Dad tells her not to worry, just tell him what she needs, and K. will bring it over later. And then they're picking up oranges and pears and a whole lot of stuff that, list or no list, neither of them can remember Mum asking them to get.

When they're done the plastic bags feel heavy, cutting into their flesh. K. still finds this funny, every time he goes shopping and sees his old woman's fingers at the end of it. But today it's just hot, and he wouldn't mind sitting down somewhere.

Dad is a couple of yards ahead of him when K. spots the sign, 'Free Public House'. A strange smell, rich and slightly rotten, wafts out of the open door and, peering in, he sees a couple of figures propped up against some kind of a bar looking out into the street. They are holding something in their hands but it's hard to say what through the pall of smoke which lingers in the air near the entrance. But that's not the detail which has caught K.'s eye. He is looking at the stools set up on the pavement outside with no label or price tag.

Testing out the first one, he lightly bounces up and down on its gently elevated seat cushion. It is comfortable, for something which looks so flimsy. Then he does the same for the other two, paying little attention to the fingers which are now pointing his way from the smoke-dimmed interior.

He is about to opt for the third stool when he spots a small tear in the fabric, so picks up the first one instead and starts to walk away.

Dad has just turned round to see what is taking his son so long when the first sound of raised voices slips out of the pub.

'What's going on here?' he asks the man with the pot belly who has just yelled, 'Oi!'

'Is this your boy?' the man asks him.

Dad nods, but isn't happy with one question being answered by another.

'Why are you asking?'

'He was about to walk off with one of these,' says the

man, gesturing at the stools with a big, fat digit.

'No, I wasn't,' says K., annoyed by the way the man had shouted at him, and more so by what he was suggesting now.

'You cheeky little -----

Dad cuts the man off with a look that suggests something else entirely, and then turns to K.

'Is this true?'

'No.'

'So why is he saying you were trying to take a stool?'

'*Aasholay or mota aar murkho, shay jonno eta bolche,*' replies K., looking not at his Dad but straight at the fat man, enjoying the man's flinch at the first sounds of Bengali. Then, pointing up at the sign, 'It says 'Free Public House,' and the briefest of pauses before the punchline, 'I thought it was free.'

A burst of laughter comes from behind them. A large man with dreadlocks who has been drawn by the sound of raised voices, and has stood by watching the whole thing with arms folded, can't contain his mirth any more.

'Stout hearted youth!' he calls out, and taps his chest a couple of times with a clenched fist.

K. instinctively does the same before he's spirited away from the scene by Dad, who looks suitably embarrassed.

Luckily it is their failure to get any of the things she'd asked for which Mum focuses on, as well as the huge amount of leeks they seem to have picked up. No one mentions the pub or the stool, and the second round of raised voices that afternoon is all about forgetfulness.

#

When K. goes round to deliver the leeks and fruit, M. has got the television on. While she insists on rummaging around in her purse for a little extra, he sees the unmistakable form of Tony Greig, the England cricket captain, suddenly flicker into life. The interview takes place against the backdrop of a county game. That much is clear from the sounds of just a few hundred people enjoying their day out in the stands. Greig's blond hair is all over the place, but it's what he's saying that makes K. sit up. 'Not really as good', 'heads above water', and then something else, which doesn't seem wise at all. Grovel. Why say that? And why bring Closey into it? M. is stood there shaking her head, but puts it down to 'the usual bravado' before slipping a couple of extra coins into K.'s hands and making him promise not to tell his Mum or Dad. K. nods. He can't think of one good reason why Mum or Dad would want to know about the loudmouth exploits of England's lanky skipper.

#

6.

It is warm again, and a lot more skin is on display . Ashen grey pins, arms like cold porridge blistering up. But undeterred, people sit out in deckchairs, just one knotted handkerchief and some misplaced optimism away from sunstroke. And though summer is barely under way, the grass is already toasting, and down the park it is one great threadbare carpet. They are all sat out in the flower garden—K., his brother, Mum, Dad, J. and J.'s stepson, S., who is rarely spotted these days, more likely to be out and about with his strange looking friends or modifying bin liners with razor blades and glue.

'Try one,' says Mum, handing S. one of the rotis she'd filled earlier with *aloo tarkari*.

He grunts, takes it all the same, not really looking up, Dad and J. both trying not to laugh.

It's a good spread, they've already finished the sarnies that J. had got up early to make, and there's still a tupperware container full of pakoras to get through.

S. doesn't seem overly keen on the small wooden stumps and tiny cricket bat that K. has brought with him. He doesn't say much to K. or his brother, and is quite a bit older than either of them. Neither of them can help it, though. They can't stop looking at his hair, which is cut short. But it's not that, it's the off centre streak running through it that they keep returning to. He looks bored, as though he's already quite used to this kind of attention.

'Did it hurt getting that done?' K.'s brother asks S., nodding towards his earring.

S. finishes his roti, looks up for the first time that afternoon.

'Why, you thinking of getting one?' he says.

Mum looks over, and though nothing is said, it's clear there will be no piercings taking place on her watch.

J. cuts in, 'Now come on son, play nice.'

S. turns to J., looks as though he's about to say something, when the word explodes around his ears. Poofter!

Two young boys, one of whom K. recognises from school, are pointing at S., laughing.

'Look at that fucking poofter!' they shout, this time a little louder.

When S. starts to get up, they retreat a few steps, wait until he's sat down again. Then, sizing up the rest of the group, the bolder of the two, who is in the year above K., sees his chance.

'Paki lover! Fucking Paki loving poofter!'

Though it's busy down the park, no one tries to stop the boys as they run off, easily outpacing J., who is left clutching at his chest, yelling after them that they don't know they're born.

Afterwards no one says too much, but they make short work of the pakoras, and a couple of other kids randomly join in their impromptu game of cricket. At one point, when the tennis ball rears up off some hidden divot and thuds into the jaw of one of the boys, K. finds himself wishing it was a real cricket ball. Other than that, S. turns out to be a good fielder, and he doesn't seem to mind the attention at all when he goes in to bat.

#

London, 1974

It still counts as a good day. And they should know as there's been some bad ones over the years, a whole lot of them packed into 1974. A bad year really.

Good natured at first, gentle ribbing about the state of Indian cricket—'Don't go to the toilet else you'll miss their second innings'—the other parents having their fun at the school gates, Mum not so thrilled but grinning and bearing it all the same.

It starts to wear thin as the Tests drag on, piling misery upon misery, each new collapse the source of fresh jokes. The scorecards, the faces, largely forgotten, but not the insult, or especially what's not being said.

We know you. We know how you crumble. We can do what we like. You won't fight back.

Though he's barely a year into school, K. senses this in the way the teachers ignore him, the benchmark already set low. He sees it in their surprise when it turns out he's one of the few who *can* read.

And he loathes the Indian tourists for making England look so good. Edges to slip, all weather collapses, no threat with the ball. Even the announcer, Peter West with his combover, wishing a bit of fight back into proceedings, wishing it were at least a contest. But night after night, he is left disappointed, with nothing else to report but dropped catches, terrorized Indian batsmen and that defeated look on Gavaskar's face. And after a while this man with a combover who is clearly a gentleman, actually starts to look bored with the predictability of it all. To his seasoned eye there's little worse than the collars up swagger of Greig and the others. Something a little vulgar about all the gum chewing and pitchside triumphalism too. He still recalls with some fondness the exploits of Wadekar's team just three years earlier. That groundbreaking win at the Oval, and how hungrily it was lapped up by a crowd largely starved of good news away from the ground. This time round there are no such heroics: boys against men, a total mismatch, but no one else seems to mind.

In class too, the tone is changing. Barely a year in, and it is just K. and a girl who smells who have found no regular table.

The only hands shooting up that summer belong to English umpires, K. sat sullenly next to the faint whiff of dried wee.

No let up in the playground either, the other boys with their collars up, sticks painted on walls and the batsman going 'bud bud ding' as he's bowled by one that keeps dead straight.

When K. bats and prospers, hitting the ball repeatedly back past the bowler, the collars up crowd lose interest. And though it is summer, sticks are soon swapped for jerseys, and once more it's rush goalies and three-and-in. The switch belies the look.

We know you. We can do what we like.

But it's laced with resentment now, an element of doubt creeping in for the first time.

We think we know you.

Peter West would have been proud, but he's covering the sorry events in St. Johns Wood. He'd have been proud that in the opposite corner of London a little outpost of resistance has been established. There is now at least a contest.

The switch is also a retreat, and everyone knows this even if no one says so. Football a sore point ever since that Polish goalie, not rush but described as a 'clown' anyway, kept England out of the World Cup with his antics at Wembley.

The next day one of the quietest he can remember at school, everyone listening to the teacher, no one mentioning the game.

And now with the World Cup approaching, and their heroes topping up their tans on the costas instead, here they all are, back to playing football in the middle of the cricket season. They don't really know him at all, and both parties know this now.

#

Those are good days, the Cruyff turn and the Dutch slicing through everyone, and then finally through themselves. And if it's sad when the Dutch fall at the last, at least *their* heroes aren't there. No Gerry Francis, no Rule Britannia, nothing for the collars up boys to latch onto.

But the bad days are never far off, and around the time of Mum's birthday are some of the worst.

When the reports start coming in of the first pub bomb they know it is bad. Just a bus-ride-away bad.

Woolwich, so close and somehow, for this as well as for every bit of collars up, tournament-non-qualification anger which has been steadily building over the year, they know they will have to pay. And though it's the Irish, and the second bombing is far away in Birmingham, it is worse. They see the news, the shock, the wreckage, and somehow they all know a fuse has been lit. The anger raw as bodies are pulled from the debris, while in the tower blocks, and under the parquet floor, those islands of resentment are conjoining into one electric charge. Collars up, and Cruyff-envy, the charge picks up the stragglers, the dregs, all those who felt mocked by 'the clown', and it reminds them, cigar in hand, that every man is expected to do his duty. But, but, they were Irish. But, bud, ding. And there are fires, and bricks, and shit, but then there are sirens, and the collars up are feeling playful again, and the chant goes up in the underpass, and on the streets, and it draws closer until it feels as though it is right outside. 'Ding dong the lights are flashing, we're going Paki bashing'. It reaches some kind of fever pitch, a vicious choreography of shouts, and hurling and shattered glass.

Then it melts away, and only after that, the uniforms.

#

There is always a blanket and a watering can near the door, but the mesh grill on the windows can only hold for so long before the defences are breached again.

They are told there's nothing anyone can do 'without evidence', and all the spitting and the snarling and the hurling is unpleasant, of course it is unpleasant, but it is not enough by itself. No you're not listening to me, Mr. H., to what I'm trying to tell you. We can't just round people up on a hunch. We don't operate like that *here*.

The gap, the pause, just long enough to let that word sink in. The fight, the sting, drawn by everything that's not being said.

And of course we'll do all we can, and we want to assure you that everything possible is being done. But Mr. H., you really must let *us* look into it. That's what we're here for.

So when they see on the news that a lot of Irish people have been rounded up, at least they can take comfort in the fact that it's not 'on a hunch'.

If eyes are blacked and faces bruised, 'of course it is unpleasant, but it is not enough'. The papers are baying for blood—'that's what we're here for'—and on the nightly updates the men on the telly with their serious faces really do give the impression that they are 'looking into it.'

But the really puzzling bit, the thing that K. struggles to understand, is this. If somewhere amongst all that blood and bruising, tucked away in the spit and the fury, are the people responsible for the bombings, then why are bricks continuing to fly through *their* windows? Why are noses even now wrinkling at the gift wrapped parcels still landing on *their* doormat?

In between times, K. learns that cupboard is spelt with a silent 'p', and enjoys the unlikely piling up of vowels in 'quay'. There is no slacking on the Chambers even if he is the only one in his class able to correctly spell and explain the word 'sectarian'.

7.

Dustbin lids become shields, dented and bruised by sustained volleys of bricks and stones. Everyone throws stones, but not at each other.

Lunchtimes are their time, pitching little missiles at the dual carriageway which runs by the school.

Every now and then the screech of tyres and the kids scattering as a furious driver pursues unknown assailants into the school compound.

'Come back here you little cunts!'

And from a safe distance, 'Fuck off, mister!'

When this happens the playground is happy again, everyone talking about the same thing, the moment somehow shared. The Granada, or Cortina, though rarely a Datsun, limping off with vague threats to 'get the law on you'.

The teachers promise to have a word, and for a day or two it's three-and-in and kiss chase all the way at breaktime.

But the larger stones are already being stockpiled, and before long there are more slammed brakes, and insults, and empty threats.

Back in class, the girl with the funny smell mostly sits

on her own in the corner, but the teachers don't seem to mind.

When the day arrives that the whole class has its picture taken, she is barely in the frame. K. is stood at the other edge of the group, and it is only after he is presented with his copy that he sees a little boy with a very serious look on his face. Some of his classmates are joking and laughing and they seem to be enjoying themselves. But his boat is looking straight at the camera, and those lips are pursed.

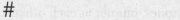

#

8.

London, 1975

At least they are out of the rabbit hutches. It happens fast, and when it does, it takes everyone by surprise.

K.'s feet are up on the wall. He thinks he has heard a sound coming from behind the wardrobe and for some reason keeping his feet off the floor seems like a good idea for now. But when he goes to investigate, the sound stops, and it briefly makes him think he'd imagined the whole thing. So now here he is lying on the bed trying to push up as close as he can to the wall. He's done this once before when he was too tired to read and enjoyed the giddy feeling as the blood rushed back into his head.

Silent waves swish past his nose and he closes his eyes. Then that feeling in the roof of the mouth, particles gently rising from his teeth, lining the cave all the way back. He knows it won't be long now, the waves crashing against his forehead, pushing down, down. All that red, inking its designs, the shapes, blurry at first, then snapping into focus, stepping out of the interfering static. Feet up, eyes shut, blood sucked back up nostrils and into the back of the throat like a waterfall in reverse. Visions.

A tap drips, but the droplets are a funny colour, and there's that smell, the smell of his classroom leaking onto the carpet, absorbed by the fibres, drying out. Ah yes, he knows what the smell is, and then he sees her, right here, resting in the carpet, no one paying her any mind, they never do, but no one saying anything either. So she lies there quietly. And after a while even she can tell that this is no ordinary spell, her body still, at rest. For once not trapped, no silent scream frozen in the mouth. No abandoned protest. No more wondering 'why me?'

The droplets are changing colour now, the yellow draining out, then colourless, clean. And they're huge, or rather he can see that *it* is huge, squeezing out of the tap with the cunning of a genie.

This time it's orange, with ears, and a little boy is holding onto his space hopper as it dances a merry jig on the hallowed turf.

Lips pursed, eyes tightly shut, K.'s forefinger works furious patterns across the middle rungs of his other palm.

The boy smiles his toothy grin, the hopper now abandoned. He makes a victory salute with the left, and a Hamlet smoke ring with his right.

Which is the point when K. knows, with one final flourish across the rungs of the middle third and fourth, that two nil is a scoreline to look out for.

In his excitement he fails to register the first little tongue lapping up the droplets, then burrowing deeper, picking apart the threads. But when it is joined by another with an equal hunger, he finds himself hurdling the uninvited guests, then collapsing where he lands, the blood still redistributing, too soon for a full return to his legs. At eye level he sees whiskers poking out of snouts and the faintest glimpse of teeth, tiny turbines churning the carpet fibres over and over.

And then he shouts the place down.

9.

The new place is better. For starters, a house, with a garden. It is far enough from the rabbit hutches to feel like a fresh start, though in truth the tower blocks are only five minutes away. But it's a house, and there is a back yard and a fence and a neighbour.

And hopefully no rats.

The day they move in, the neighbour is clearing some weeds from just outside his front door. He goes inside as soon as he sees Mum and for all the steady traffic of boxes and cooking pots, there is no further sign of him, though raised voices can be heard coming through the partition. 'They could be talking about anything,' says Mum at one point, though no one really believes that. Still, it's just voices, so they focus on unpacking any foodstuffs first and then work their way methodically through the rest.

They eat off plastic plates, sitting cross legged on the floor, and it tastes fantastic. Chicken, rice, dhal. And then the plates are bagged up in a bin liner and put outside with all the other refuse sacks. But it's while the food is cooking, the flavours of *dupiaza* and *tarka dhal* gently wafting out of the back door and into the yard, that they hear some sharp words, then slamming doors, and a car engine roaring into life.

#

They get back from school some days, K. and his brother, and the neighbour is working on his car, front door open, music blaring from inside.

It makes no sense, '*Bee bop a lula*' but the singer at least sounds like he's having fun.

'Alright?' they say to the neighbour, but he doesn't look up or acknowledge them in any way.

Other times they come home to find his legs sticking out from under the car, and they ask him if he needs some help, though really they are trying to imagine what it would be like if he was actually dead and just lay there undisturbed for a couple of days, no one commenting because they thought he was fixing the motor.

He is big, and a little younger than Dad, but on days when the sun is up, and he is in a vest, K. never misses that gut spilling over the belt. Dad will only wear a vest when it's really hot, but when he does there's no gut, no surplus. 'Must be the dhal,' he often says, patting his belly, but it's just an act. Those days and nights on the benches, and now these days and nights first in the factory and then in the hospital, have cured him of all surplus.

#

There is a steady stream of visitors next door, often at weekends, and it can get rowdy. They turn up wearing strange clothes. Crepe soled shoes, velvet-trimmed, finger length drape jackets, leopard skin caps, and huge, showy rings on the fingers of both hands. K. later learns that the shoes are called 'brothel creepers', but the first time he encounters the phrase, in a random magazine he finds in the school library, he misreads it as 'brother creepers', and for the longest time after that he imagines that his neighbour is part of some weird sect, a branch of the undead in southeast London.

And when they get back from wherever it is they have been haunting, the music is cranked up again and those strange old/new sounds come crashing through the walls. *Lula, Baby, Wop bop*, at all hours, no matter that Dad is also not long back from a very different late shift.

They acclimatize to the ring pulls on cans and the clanking of bottles, but the one thing that still jars, past the alien sounds and the swollen laughter, is the lack of embarrassment.

The next day, without fail, there he is out in a deck-chair, pores soaking up the heat as if life is one big holiday. More tins and the Sunday papers to last from 'The Big Match' to the big sleep.

'*Odeh kono lajja nai*', says Mum, looking down from an upstairs window, K. and his brother trying not to giggle. And it *is* funny, the walrus occasionally stirring when a wasp or some other insect comes too close, but mainly just snoozing under angry headlines and a deceptively warm sun.

#

10.

It's Ladybird books and the Gingerbread man, but K. has already read these when he was really young, say five. He's seven now and this feels like a joke.

'Miss,' says the runt, hand shooting up almost as soon as the books are handed out.

'What is it now?' asks the teacher, who has barely sat back down at her desk.

'I've got to go,' says the boy, screwing up his face like that character off the telly. Then, looking round to check that everyone else is listening,

'I've got to do a whoopsie.'

The other children laugh and no one really settles down for the rest of the class, the teacher largely giving up when her voice, even as it is raised, becomes one of many. K. is bored by the whole thing. Just one big holiday.

#

'Fight! Fight! Fight!'

He'll hear that most days, shouts forming a circle, then a cluster, in one corner or another of the playground.

The teachers, like the uniforms, rarely on the scene in

time, and once they've waded through the ringside, their only job seemingly to put an arm around a sobbing child while another one, smirking, melts away into the crowd. As many girls as boys in the inner circle, faces lit up in a way they rarely are during class.

When it happens while he's in goal during three-and-in, the others are amongst the first to join the throng. By the time it's over and they've returned to the game, no one seems to remember that he was in goal, and the rest of the game feels sullen, the others resentful when he refuses to budge, and K. redoubling his efforts to save every attempt on goal and keep them out there as long as possible.

He avoids the huddles and throngs as much as possible, but at least he has an elsewhere—the game, the other players. Whenever he can, he also slips out through a side entrance, at first ten minutes here, then growing bolder half an hour there, to see if he's missed at all. He always makes sure that he is back for the afternoon head count but in any case no one ever notices.

Actually, that's not strictly true. There is someone who regularly spots him, who wishes she could do the same, just leave when it all gets too much, then pretend she'd never been away.

But that kind of courage, like the silent scream, is already gone, half vapour, half bark, and she's left instead with a stillborn ghoul, something shriveled and rotten in the back of her throat.

On his wanderings he makes sure not to stray too close to the big school. Groups of older boys often hang around nearby picking off the younger kids, lifting sweets, and dinner money and dignity, usually in that order. Sometimes he takes the long route back just to avoid the road where the main entrance of this school is. It takes him via the train station and up a steep bank where the danger signs are only there to be ignored and the rattle of the trains promises something, even if it is something short of distant glamour.

It is peaceful though, the only sounds other than the trains an occasional voice from the platform or the chirping of birds.

There is a moment between the first bite of an apple and the resumption of birdsong when he almost misses the third sound. But when he stops what he is doing and takes the precaution of holding his breath, there it is again, and this time he doesn't miss anything.

The rhythmic wheezing seems to be coming from a little further across the bank. Craning his ears, K. locates the sound just beyond a copse. As he draws closer, the wheezing seems to quicken. He tries to be as quiet as possible, but every sound is amplified by his nerves, and when he snaps a twig he fears he has already announced himself. A few more blundering steps and then almost without warning they're face to face, the wheezing cut short or perhaps it was finished anyway.

They look up but it's not the usual look he's seen on older boys when they want to make a point. As though they're not even looking at him.

He is surprised they don't say anything when they see him. The faces are blank, the eyes looking straight past him, through him, at nothing.

'Shit,' he says, but no one responds.

The eyes are gone, nothing. He's not really there, just a shadow draped over the tree stumps observing hollow saucers trapped in sallow faces.

'Shit, are you ok?' he asks. No reply.

The one with the bag slumps back, fingers loosening their grip. His friend already gone. Next to him, there in the weeds, a magazine.

Right there with its pages open at the centrefold, something he's never seen before. K. turns again and sees these boys, slightly older than him, almost certainly from the big school, lost to deep dreams of boredom and release.

Reaching down, he picks up the magazine and tucks it in his back pocket. He only feels bad for a moment and besides, judging by that funny clam right in the middle, they don't look like they're missing much.

#

Scrambling back up the bank, it is only when he reaches the top, and the gap in the chain link fence, that he remembers to look at his trousers.

The light corduroy, which can best be described as *halood* since they're not really orange, or yellow, is streaked with grass from the panicked ascent, and he hopes this can be explained away should the question arise without anyone needing to look into things more closely. *What's that on your trousers? Doesn't look like nothing to me. Wait, turn around a moment. What's that sticking out of your pocket? Where'd you get this from then?*

He's seen plenty of adults walking around with the papers, always the small ones with the big fat headlines, sticking out of their back pockets, T shirts often wedged in the slice of air between the paper and the top of the pocket. It's the same with the fags he sometimes spots tucked behind people's ears. As if to give an impression of being incredibly busy, so much so that they don't have the time or the luxury of holding both their fags and their papers, but yeah, nice to have a little stash just in case, and who's asking anyway? The last bit almost as important as the papers or the fags themselves. Who wants to know? Eyes flitting from the back pages to any perceived challenge, and then straight to some stunner just inside the front cover. Mum's right really. *Odeh kono lajja nai.*

K. is fairly sure though that this is not the kind of magazine to be showing off, and not just because it's in colour. He can't stop looking at that hairy clam either, and this forces him into several unscheduled stops on his way back to class.

11.

Luckily there is no one home when he gets back and he slips the magazine under his bed. They still share a room, him and his brother, but he's hoping the extra space in this house will solve that little problem.

When he comes back down to the kitchen, he is surprised to see Dad sitting there, wordlessly tucking into a plate of food. *Macher jhol* and the spine has been picked clean. Every now and then Dad fishes out a little bone from in between his teeth, and pretty soon the side of his plate resembles some kind of mackerel graveyard.

'How was school?' he asks, the last of the fish separated from the bones.

'Not bad,' K. lies.

'Anything good?'

'Not much really,' K. replies, then seeing that Dad is perhaps hoping for a little more substance, he adds the only things he can think of which don't involve wheezing or colour magazines.

'Joined up writing. The Gingerbread Man.'

They both laugh, though neither really knows why. And then drawing his son close, Dad kisses K. on the top of his head before heading off to the bathroom to wash his hands and splash some water on his face. He's still a little groggy from sleeping during the day, a habit he never fully masters, and fairly soon he will head out again for another stint under the neon strip lights and desperate, early hours abandon of the National Health Service. Trolleys and gurneys and foul, alcohol-fed abuse, but without even the buffer of needle and thread, or of one hand on the dispensary. And though no one says it, everything is graded, everyone carries the taint. Beasts of burden marked up as porters, *their* blue careful not to be mistaken for the blue of nurses, and a world away again from the officer class, the 'them' of medicine, higher learning and healing. Yet in Dad's case, there's a mind as finely sculpted as that face, and for all the sleep deprivation a hand more steady and an eye more detailed than the finest surgeon in this hospital.

Soon after, the shift patterns change again and Dad's home by early evening. By the time he gets back, the neighbour is usually out in the yard with some tins and a lot of noise for company.

Mum shaking her head as the sounds crash into the kitchen. To her, somehow it is just embarrassing for a grown man to be listening to this music, and *so loud*.

'*E murkho ke dekhecho?Ekta oshur moton shori diya baghan e boshe ache ar---*'

Dad cuts her off by putting the radio on, tuned in as ever to the World Service. The peep peep peep signaling

127

the hour also slices through the alien sounds coming from next door. A well-spoken voice mentions someone called George Davis and as if by magic the neighbourly racket suddenly abates.

So it becomes a ritual, the cut-glass accent on the hour every hour, the strange sense after a while that even the neighbour expects to hear the peeps.

Though if it is a tactic, it doesn't work when he has guests over. Mostly they turn up on weekends in an old fashioned, American looking light blue car that one of them drives.

Even without the sounds blaring out of the car's open windows, the roar then rumble of that engine announces their arrival long before they pull up outside. Mum is never impressed on these days but limits her disapproval to some accelerated chopping of vegetables and the odd comment about ogres.

K.'s brother tells him that the car has 'tail fins' and is a 'Cadillac'. It doesn't really mean anything but no other cars round here look like that and in a way both boys are impressed. Then again, when the occupants of the car step out both brothers can also agree that they look like *Showaddywaddy*, and that's not nearly as impressive.

If Dad is working on something in the backyard, he'll rarely look up, but the first time the car arrives and the strangely dressed men step out, he happens to be repainting the front door and can't help but be distracted by the noise of the engine. He sizes them up for a moment before resuming with the brush strokes. Watching from inside behind a twitching curtain, K. notices the men also briefly looking at Dad as they make their way up the front garden path next door. Even when they knock loudly on the neighbour's door and one of them sneaks another sidelong look at Dad, there are still no words exchanged.

It gets rowdy later on and all of them—Mum and Dad downstairs with their tea, and the boys in their bedroom pretending to sleep—can make out women's voices past the din coming through the fence.

The following day though, it's back to the peeps and the cut-glass announcer on the hour every hour from early morning, and late afternoon before anyone stirs next door. Again nothing is said but, as Dad chips away at the block of wood with a hammer and chisel and a look of determination which just seems to intensify with the heat, sweat rolling off a granite jaw, some kind of a point has been made.

12.

The neighbour now pretends not to see them when they get back from school.

'Alright?' K. always makes a point of asking him, not believing for a moment that he's actually fixing anything under the hood of his car.

He almost enjoys it now, this little afternoon charade, and is actually disappointed on those days when he comes back and there are no legs sticking out from under the car, mainly because those are the days that there is no car either.

'Where does he go?' K. asks his brother, as if he'd somehow know where the other creepers hung out.

'Dunno,' says his brother, 'but Ma reckons he's a *bhoot*.'

They both laugh, but it seems to tie in with what K. is already thinking. The undead, all that strange noise coming through the walls in the middle of the night, the way he never *directly* looks at any of them, especially Dad. How he only seems able to talk when he is around the fellow creepers. It all makes sense really. That weird smell too, grease and cheese and sweat, although to be fair some of his classmates also have that smell, as do one or two of the teachers. So maybe that bit's not about being a *bhoot* exactly. There's still all the other stuff though, no getting away from that.

Reaching under the bed, K.'s hands perform a confused sweep of the empty space. The mag is no longer there, and for a moment he panics. What if Mum has found it? He can't see her being too impressed by the clam, and can easily picture himself getting a *thapar*, making up some ropey excuse and then getting another for the lie. When he tries the bathroom door, it is locked and his brother calls out that he'll just be a minute. It makes him wonder as his brother never talks like that. Normally it would be 'What?' or more likely, if it is just the two of them at home, 'Fuck off!' in that lazy, don't-really-mean-it-but-wish-you'd-stop-bothering-me-anyway style that he's perfected from school.

Later, after they've had dinner, and Mum puts the kettle on for her evening brew, he checks again under the bed and isn't in the least bit surprised that the mag has miraculously reappeared.

#

13.

On his way to school in the mornings, K. starts to see those letters a lot more frequently. There they are, daubed on the wall just at the end of their road. And again, under the bridge, and yet again next to the shop on the estate. Even last year he doesn't remember there being so many NFs dotted around, but now they're everywhere, the F not always trailing off any more as though it had been done in a hurry.

Some of the more recent efforts, including the one outside the shop, have the added extra of 'Pakis Out', and plenty of this artistic quality has also infiltrated the playground.

The good days are when no one brings this up in front of him, when it's rush goalie and two-goal head starts depending on how shit the other boys think he is, until they find out the little Asian kid has got his shooting boots on and the first to five doesn't even eat into the first half of lunchtime. Class feels good on those days, the lack of attention from the teachers allowing K. to soak up some quizzical looks from the blonde boys, who even let him look at their books of Panini stickers.

Then there are the other kind, and he knows it is one

of *those* days from the moment he steps into the playground and sees older boys looking at him, saying nothing.

To start with it's quiet. The one big game of football that normally takes up an entire side of the playground has disappeared, as if gorged whole by the concrete itself. Then he'll hear the sounds, distant at first but gradually growing louder, closer. And as it draws nearer he can start to make out the words.

''Nal Front! Nashnal Front! National Front!'

He feels eyes burning into him from all sides. Looking around for what exactly, he's not sure. Support maybe. He can't find anyone familiar. The boys he normally plays football with have melted away, in their place a sea of indifference, marching along with its arms in the air.

'National Front! National Front! National Front!'

Oddly enough there are never any teachers around when this happens, the shouts booming around an otherwise empty playground. He wonders where they could all be, imagines there must be some other emergency they're attending to, then spots a couple of them having a smoke and a laugh near the dinner hall.

It's when the song changes that he starts to feel his pulse quicken, wishing that the teachers would hurry up and finish their conversation.

'Ding dong the lights are flashing, we're going Paki bashing.'

The chant sounds jolly the way they sing it, like a nursery rhyme. He can see the little conga line snaking its way towards him, those earlier scowls now giving way to smiles. K. recognizes a couple of the faces from the two-goal head start, but like his neighbour they're not really looking at him either.

No one's shouting any more though. No need. It's strangely calm. The arms aren't in the air either, or not in the same way. Some twenty feet away from where he's stood, wishing the concrete would also swallow him up like the football game, the conga line has come to a halt. The hands are clapping an insistent rhythm above their heads. K. has seen this on telly, when they show the football. Da da dada dah, dada da dah, England! The words have changed though.

'You're gonna get your fuckin' head kicked in. You're going home in a London ambulance.'

He looks at them, can see them staring back, but there's no real hate on the faces, just a little terrace smile and a confidence which makes him oddly jealous. He's stood there thinking there's not much he can do, and the little squadron facing him seems to know this too. It's why they can take their time, and all the twitchiness that's there in class seems to evaporate. There are no interruptions here, no 'stop that now' or 'where do you think you're going?' to break up the fun. No 'pack it in' either, though in a way he doesn't mind as it can often just sound like 'Paki in' to ears already primed. Life just one long party for these: no homework, no spelling tests, no nothing but this, the here and now of mischief. He knows he's cornered. They know it too. And there's that other thing too, the unspoken part which means the one thing worse for him than actually being here would be if he tried to leave. Running seen as 'bad form' even when the numbers are this skewed.

He's seen what they did to that younger boy, the unusually tall one in the year below with the funny hair and the freckles and the light skin. They enjoyed the chase, taunting him the whole way, golly this, sambo that, laughing at him as he grew tired, lurching away from one set of approaching hands and straight into the grasp of another. It didn't take much to bring him down—K. remembered he fell like a giraffe—and then they settled into their feast, punching, spitting, biting, and two of them held him down while a third removed his trousers, laughing the whole way. That was when the cry went up. 'Er, he's pissed himself! Dirty Black cunt,' and just as quickly as they'd gathered, all the fists and boots dispersed, shrieking 'He's pissed himself!' in a hundred different directions. No one had gone to help the boy, probably all thinking the same thing. No one wanted to stand out, offer themselves up as the next in line. K. had waited and watched from just outside the library, and it had felt like an age before the boy finally started to squirm back to life. Oddly enough he'd looked around to check if anyone was watching when he put his trousers back on, as if there was still some dignity left to protect, and when he got back up it was obvious he was struggling to walk. He headed towards where K. was standing, and as he drew nearer it became clear that his face was cut. The worst thing was the sniffling, even more so than the way his face was streaked with tears. K. had given him a look as if to say, 'sorry, mate' and then had gone into the library anyway, hoping he wouldn't be followed. He wasn't. So he told himself he was invisible, that the same thing which made the teachers ignore him also helped him pass by the mob unnoticed. And for a while he even believed it. But now this.

'You're gonna get your fuckin' head kicked in! You're going home in a London ambulance!'

14.

There's no let up from the *bhoot*. Night times are always the worst, that strange groaning coming through the walls, often blended with a woman's voice which seems to be offering encouragement.

'That's right. No, not there, *there*. That's better.'

The walls are paper-thin and K. and his brother lie there in bunk beds desperately trying not to laugh. Again they don't really know why it's funny, but it is. Some nights they hear a sound like a suitcase falling followed by just the woman's voice, and even through the wall and all that muffling, it is clear she is not happy. On one occasion they hear her repeating, 'Get up. No, not this. Not again. *Get up!*'

It all gets too much and they burst out laughing. When Mum goes to investigate, they both pretend to be asleep, but by then it's already gone quiet next door, and lying in the dark still wide awake, both brothers have more or less the same thought. Perhaps the walrus does have some shame after all?

All the same, the neighbour still won't make eye contact with them even when they say hello. The only time K. feels that he is properly acknowledged by him is that day when he comes home from school with his face all over the shop and buttons missing from his shirt. On this one occasion the neighbour actually looks up from under the hood and takes in the details: the half-open shirt, the cut lip, the bruising under the eye. There is no real surprise on his face which makes K. wonder whether he has some prior knowledge of the conga line. He still doesn't say anything but there's something in the look he gives K. which acts like a nod. Welcome to the neighbourhood.

K. is tempted to point out that he is from the neighbourhood, has lived here all his life and that they only moved here from two streets across, then remembers that nothing has actually been said. All the words are in his head, so he goes straight indoors and is sure that he can hear the man chuckling behind him as he does so.

When he gets in, the magazine is again missing from under his bed. He can't even wash his hands or check to see how bad his face is as he knows the bathroom door will be locked. So he puts his feet up on the wall and tries to think of nothing. Instead it's another surge, flecked red like his lip, driving down, down, pushing his head under the floor, into the ground with the ants and the worms. He tries to say something but the letters get stuck, pushing back up against a tide of red. And then they're washed away, trapped inside two huge tyres. Only when the current starts to slow can he see that they are in fact the two missing buttons. And then they're plucked from the crimson river, reattached to the shirt, and a little boy is back on his space hopper, looking down at his chest and a full complement of buttons. He frames the first of the buttons with a thumb and forefinger, and makes a victory salute with the other hand to let everyone know that both buttons are back. And although it hurts when he smiles, the corners of his mouth curl up for the first time since his lip was split. That scoreline again, 2-0, blood still rushing around in his head when he hears the sound of the bathroom door being unlocked.

Though it's early, the strange noises have already started up next door and neither brother can sleep. Creeping downstairs they see Mum and Dad on the settee laughing at something on the telly. When they're spotted they try to explain why they're not asleep, and for once they're allowed to stay up and watch telly for a bit. It feels great, a real treat; K. tucked in the middle, his brother next to Dad. K. laughs when everyone else does, though most of the time he doesn't know why. The important thing for him is to play along, prove to the rest of his family he belongs on this settee, laughing at Tom and Barbara Good well past his bedtime. Anyway, it's easy. He just follows the sound of all those other happy people enjoying the programme, making sure not to look at anyone else on the settee. Then Tom and Barbara's neighbour makes an entrance and K. gets the strangest feeling that he has seen this woman somewhere else recently. He spends the rest of the programme trying to remember where and it is only right at the end when Tom mentions something about 'local Conservatives' that it comes back to him. She *has*

been on the news a lot recently, ever since she became the leader of the party. The hair is the same but the voice seems a little different now. It's funny how television can play tricks on you, K. thinks, but he doesn't share this with anyone, doesn't want to spoil it for them, though he wonders whether anyone else has noticed. The Conservative leader, whatever that means, and she's actually quite funny.

Over the next few days he keeps seeing this woman on the telly, but she never seems to be having as much fun as she did that first time he'd seen her joking away with her neighbours. There are none of those funny expressions or the surprised looks, and he can't be the only one who's noticed as no one else ever seems to laugh around her. The really strange bit is when they introduce her husband and he's totally different from how K. remembers him, much older, and again, nowhere near as funny. Also, her voice is definitely not the same. Then again whose is? *He's* got one for home, and one for school, and come to think of it, another one for the bits in between. So it's not at all strange to him that this woman has one face for the news, and another for light entertainment. Actually the weird thing would be if she spoke the same way all the time around everyone she met. Aitch and haitch, really, though he sometimes forgets which is which, and that can cause a bit of bother. He had a look off Mum for saying 'wortah' one time, after she'd asked him what he'd had with his lunch. Funny enough what he was really thinking about when he'd said that was his upset stomach at lunchtime, and all that shepherd's pie, which he knew he wasn't supposed to be eating, pouring out of him like *jol*. Yet even that was preferable to spending the morning listening to his other classmates calling each other 'wankers' at every possible opportunity, but in that way they favoured, with the emphasis on the 'wan' and a near silent 'k'.

'It's got beef in it and it's good for you,' the dinner lady had said when he'd asked her what was in the shepherds pie.

Maybe it was the beans that had done it though. Either way there he was just glad he'd made it to the bogs before the runs had struck.

While he's in the cubicle, hoping no one else can hear the little air puffs before each fresh burst, he briefly tenses up when he hears other boys walking in. It confuses him as he listens to the sound of cutlery scraping plates, not a normal sound for in here, and it's only when he comes out of the cubicle some minutes later feeling a bit weak and embarrassed, that he sees a load of beans and two solid domes of mash floating in the urinal.

#

The peeps and the cut-glass announcer don't seem to have any opinion on the new Conservative leader, or on anything else for that matter. It's all very steady, a flow of facts and figures, the names of countries, the number of civilians, the day that such and such reached Phnom Penh, whatever or wherever that is.

Dad is out in the back yard a lot more, the weather staying warm and the shape of a chair beginning to emerge from a block of wood he has been working on. Sometimes when K. goes to investigate, Dad gets him to hold the block, or gently tap the chisel with a hammer, shadowing the action with his own big hands wrapped around both tools. K. loves it when this happens, feels very grown up half holding the hammer, and although he does nothing more than give the chisel the lightest of taps, Dad always gives an encouraging, '*That's* it,' as if it's the most important action of the day.

He also likes the way the announcer speaks. It's very different to his teachers, who generally say things he already knows but want him to act as if it's the first time he's ever heard them. Joined up writing, seven times table, Gingerbread man, blah, blah, blah. The peeps woman though, she's always saying surprising stuff, and pretty soon he learns about Cambodia and inflation and the Conservative leader, whose real name, he's surprised to learn, isn't Margo but Margaret. She speaks properly as well (the peeps woman), not like the dinner ladies at his school. Then again, those times when his feet are up on the wall and the blood is rushing to his head, spluttering out numbers and shapes and some light headed vision of the future, there is never any soundtrack. No background noise, no voices, no accents. And he has the strongest feeling that it won't do him any good to try and find one anywhere but in his bedroom. Better to say nothing than to say 'water', the mistake he made the day after Mum had given him that look. *La di dah* he'd been called that day, though in fairness that wasn't the worst of it. Which is how he knows to keep this stuff to himself. *Schtum*, the one thing he *has* learned in class, though not from any of his teachers.

15.

Usually, K. and his brother try to arrive as close to the taking of the morning register as possible, the less contact time with classmates the better to avoid starting the day on the wrong note. But no one could sleep last night, the sounds of the *bhoot* boosted by those of his fellow undead, who unusually for them showed up midweek, making a right old racket until the early hours. Dad had tried to have a word, then there were raised voices, some threats, all very non World Service. So it was an early start this morning, doors slamming and a lot of *shada lok* this and *shada lok* that.

Even so, when they get to school the caretaker is already busy, scrubbing away at one of the exterior walls with some kind of stiff brush.

'What are you doing?' K. asks the man, taking him by surprise given the hour.

'What does it bloody well look like I'm doing?' the caretaker replies, not even bothering to turn around.

Then his curiosity gets the better of him, and he looks to see who's asking. All of a sudden he seems embarrassed.

'Look, son, some people are just stupid is all.'

Drawing closer, K. sees the familiar 'F' tailing off into the brickwork. Unlike some of the others he's seen, this one has clearly been done in a hurry. And it's a lot closer to the ground than the one outside the shop on the estate or the one at the top of his street. The letters are also quite a bit smaller than usual, not that K. is complaining.

'You don't need to do that,' says the caretaker when he sees K.'s brother start scrubbing at the letters with another of the brushes lying next to the bucket and mop and fresh tin of white paint which the caretaker has also brought with him.

'Like I said, son, it's just silly talk. They don't know they're born.' His brother doesn't say anything, but carries on scrubbing, as though he knows they're up against the clock.

K. stands there for a moment, trying to think of the word, but it won't come to him. The brushes are making little impression on the letters, but in a few minutes the rest of the school will be here, pointing and laughing, and in that way he already knows, just those two letters are going to set the tone unless he can think of the word.

He thinks 'comfy', but that's not right. 'Hamfisted', not right either, though he likes the word. That furniture shop Dad's always threatening to take him to, but again, it's not the right letter. And then it suddenly appears in his head, the opposite of *schtum:* to trust someone with your secrets, to confide. He can even picture the page in the Chambers, 'confess', 'confetti', 'confide'.

'What the hell are you doing?' asks the caretaker as soon as he spots K. dipping the brush in the paint and completing the crescent of the 'c' in one bold movement the way Dad does. The 'o' is harder work and there's a bit of spillage, like the posters he sees advertising horror films outside the Odeon, where the film title is always in red with the colour seeping away from the letters like blood. It doesn't take long and then it's done, the wall encouraging strangers to 'confide', a place for everyone to go and confess.

He stands back, admiring his handiwork, and in the remaining moments before the other kids start to arrive, his brother and the caretaker apply another coat, gently caressing the letters and wiping off any excess. By the time anyone notices the fresh artwork, the sun has already dried it out, and it is somehow pleasing that for the rest of the day, particularly at lunchtime, it enjoys a steady stream of visitors who mainly pause for a moment and laugh, but not before putting their faces right up to the wall and having a little chat.

The runt seems unusually quiet in class today. K. can tell he's looking at him out of the corner of his eye, and he's also one of the few not to mention the wall, though he does go over to see for himself at breaktime. He looks puzzled and slightly suspicious after break but, though he keeps firing looks in K.'s direction, today is not a day when the fish will bite. Sadly, when it's time to go home, K. sees the headmaster directing the caretaker towards the wall with what looks like the same tin of paint as earlier. Waiting until the headmaster is satisfied he has shown leadership and turns back to his office, K. stops on his way to the main gates. The caretaker looks up and winks.

'Sorry, son. Been told to do it. Don't worry though, there'll be other times. Round here I'm sure of it.'

#

16.

London, 1975, '76, '77

'You've got to eat your greens, love, and this pie. Else you won't grow up to be big and strong,' the dinner lady keeps telling him any time K. asks what else there is apart from the pie. It's all very confusing. He's no smaller than anyone else in class, and one or two are smaller than him, though funnily enough most of the girls are bigger than him. Especially that Lisa, who wears those big wooden shoes and usually has something to say to Rachael. Something nasty.

'Er, you smell!'

Or that time, when Rachael was near the dolls house at the same time as the pincher, and Lisa had started to sing:

'*Stand by your man*,' like the song that was always playing on the radio.

Or really any time when she felt like giving out some advice, which was quite often:

'You know what you should do? You should play 'Piss chase'!' And all the other girls, and some of the boys, would be shrieking, while for Rachael, whatever words of defiance she might have had would just die in her throat again and she'd end up making some animal noise instead, a distressed grunt which only made the shrieking worse.

The dinner ladies don't even bother saying anything to Rachael, just slop the food on her plate and give each other looks, as though *she's* the problem, rather than those beans and the one-dish-fits-all choice of pie-and-muck or muck-and-pie. For some reason the trifle's good though, and whenever it crops up, K.'s there, sat alone after the main lunch rush has died down, spooning in mouthfuls of whipped cream but really just waiting for that first hit of processed fruit.

This is when he sees Rachael, still struggling to finish her main course, the dinner ladies cluck clucking at her to eat it all up. She will occasionally look up longingly across the assembly hall, but the toilets are far too distant a remedy, and in any case that escape route has now been cut off by one of the eagle eyed cluckers.

He's not to know she only goes to the lunch hall when he's there, those days she spots him sneaking back into school after his secret little forays outside. He can't know those words that keep dying in her throat are the same ones he tries so hard to stifle any time the teacher asks for a show of hands, or whether anyone knows the answer, or what else can they see in this picture? But if he just stopped for a moment, paid attention to something other than the fruit, he'd know. He'd see it, feel it, hear it beyond the cluck clucking, those letters staring up at him out of the parquet floor, repeating themselves on the formica tops, indented on the stainless steel vats with the dregs of the dregs, soggy, mushy, cold.

And he'd know, dried up in her throat, like all that wee burning shame through her clothes and into her flesh, a simple lament, spanning cruelties and time itself, this canteen, that lunch hour little more than an afterthought. Because those words also describe him.

'I'm here too.'

Why does no one ever listen? She forgets how many times a day she has this thought, but it usually starts in the morning as soon as she hears her mum calling her to get up, and sometimes doesn't leave her until she is pretending to be asleep again at night time.

'Rach, time to get up, love. You'll be late for school.'

Why won't mum listen? How many times has she tried to tell her she hates school? Just thinking about it makes her nervous. It makes her want to wee, and sometimes she wants to go in the middle of the class but when she tries to tell the teacher, no one ever listens then either. Sometimes mum practically pushes her out of the door when they are already late in the morning, but although she is holding her hand, her mum won't look at her the whole way to school. And the whole way to school she wants to tell mum, 'Can we go back?'

She hates the noise once they get there. Mum never sticks around or talks to any of the other parents, and the other children won't talk to her. But in class, while they are waiting for the teacher to arrive, they shout and yell and throw things and this makes her feel very nervous.

She has been hit with paper before, scrunched up into a ball and aimed at her head. When that horrible boy, Stephen Henbury, did this just the other day, the whole class laughed and it made her sad. She wanted to scream, but when she tried no sound would come. Why is it always like this, she thinks? She wants to scream at home too, at the ogre who is sometimes there, and at mum for letting him stay.

She wonders whether Stephen will grow up to be an ogre. He doesn't look like one yet because he's not big enough, but when he stares at her just before he throws something, or says something mean, his face looks different. It is strange to her. He looks scared then even though he is trying to scare her. She wonders if anyone else can see this but mostly they look scared too, even if on the surface they are smiling or shouting.

People think she's just a stupid little girl, but she's never been that. *She* knows that even if they don't. She knows for instance that the ogre can never take the place of her daddy, who she can't remember because he left mummy when she was still tiny, just out of mummy's tummy. She knows this because she hears them arguing sometimes when they think she is asleep upstairs. Just because she can't always say what she wants to, it doesn't mean there's anything wrong with her ears, she thinks, wondering why her mum puts up with it and hating her for it anyway.

'He was a lost cause, girl. Mark my words, if he hadn't walked out on you then, he would have done soon enough, once he realized the girl was handicapped.'

'Don't say that, Trevor. She's not handicapped, she's

just a little slow, is all. And don't you even mention her father in this house, not while you're under my roof!'

'Your roof! Don't make me laugh, girl. The only reason you've still got a roof over your head is because muggins here works all the hours in that bakery. Fucking coons and pakis, they don't mind the unsocial hours, but me, I'm used to something a little better than that. Maybe I wouldn't mind so much if I'd also grown up next to an open sewer, 'cos you know what it's like with that lot. They literally do shit where they eat. But girl, I'm from Bermondsey and that ain't what I'm used to.'

They argue like this a lot. Sometimes she hears her mum protest and when that happens, more often than not in the morning her mum will be sporting a black eye, or her face will seem puffy as if she has been crying. She knows this because even if her mum won't look at her on their way to school, she always makes a point of looking at her mum.

# #

Handicapped, though? She's not handicapped, whatever that means. She knows it's a bad word though, like 'Paki' or 'slag' or 'coon'. She's fairly sure of that. Anyway, she decides, whatever it means, it doesn't mean her. It's just that she sometimes struggles with words. They look funny on the page and they can get stuck in her throat like a bone or a cheese straw. In any case, just because the ogre said it, doesn't make it true. What does he know, she thinks? Nothing. He's stupid anyway. He thinks he's the only ogre.

He doesn't know about the other one, the one she has seen. It wasn't long ago, just after that big fight in the other school, when all the kids from her school beat up the kids from the other school and they had to call the police. Yes it was just after that, when they'd all been sent home early to avoid the same thing happening again. And she had just come out of the stairwell and onto their floor when she saw the different ogre, a different colour too, leaving their flat still buttoning up his overcoat. She remembered he was bigger than Trevor and that they were both, her and the ogre, staring at each other as he passed by. If anyone had asked her, she wouldn't have described him as a Paki, because she doesn't like that word. It feels wrong to her, mean, like one of those scrunched up paper balls that Stephen sometimes hurls. Then again, she thinks, no one ever asks because no one ever imagines just how much she sees, and hears, that they cannot. Or won't.

#

There is a boy in her class who she has heard some of the other girls, the horrible ones who hang around with Lisa, describe as a Paki. These girls, especially Lisa, also say things about her during lunchtimes, and sometimes in class too. She hears them but pretends not to, thinking that if that works with the ogre then why not here as well? It's so noisy in the classroom though. No one can sit still. Well, not quite no one, but the teachers always ignore her and K., the boy who sits next to her in class. He's the same boy Lisa and her friends call a Paki. But she doesn't feel that way about him. At least he doesn't pull a face when he sees her or sits next to her. Not like the others, starting with Stephen, who thinks he's really funny but isn't. It's not nice, she thinks, the way he says she smells and tells the rest of the class. She doesn't really but anyway, what can she do about it? It's not her fault if the thought of school, or the ogre (the first one) sometimes makes her nervous and then she tries to tell the teacher but the words won't come, or the teacher doesn't see her. It's not her fault if she is just left sitting there hot and wet and ashamed and hoping that no one will notice. But Stephen always does and is the first to pull a face and tell the rest of the class:

'Er, she's pissed herself! Smelly cow!'

It's not noisy then, she thinks. It's really quiet for a tiny bit and she can feel every eye on her. If only she were invisible then, she thinks, watching the teacher approach her, wondering why *he* looks so angry when it is her who's having to sit here in this mess.

'Now then, Rachael. What's the problem?'

He's not really bothered though. She can tell just by how he says it. He sounds bored and a little bit cross. It reminds her of the ogre when he asks how school is without looking up from the plate of food he is having in mum's kitchen. She wishes he wasn't there either. Anyway, that's when the rest of the class explodes, throwing paper and shouting, and she thinks it is odd because that must mean that the teacher is invisible too.

The boy who sits next to her, though, he doesn't say anything even though some of the mess nearly touches his feet. He is very quiet, like her, and also, like her, the other children don't really talk to him. She doesn't really know why although he is much darker than her, than any of them. When they use their pencils to colour in the little books they have been given, she notices that his skin is the same colour as one of the pencils. It is nice, she thinks. At least he has a pencil. He's got a funny name though, K. The class laughed when the teacher tried to say it, but she remembers he wasn't smiling. Then again, maybe it is something to do with also having a pencil? Having a name, that is. One that makes people laugh.

She hates her own name, Rachael Huntley. It doesn't sound right to her. Why can't she just change it? She doesn't feel like Rachael Huntley. She doesn't want to be that girl any more. Rachael Huntley is the girl who nobody sees, or hears, but everyone smells. She is the girl who gets laughed at or ignored, never listened to. Her mum won't look at her, even when she looks at her mummy, wondering why *she* is the one looking ashamed when it is the ogre who makes her feel that way. Rachael Huntley is the girl who doesn't like going to school but doesn't want to stay at home either. She hears bad words and raised voices, and she sees bruises and liquid spilling from her mummy's eyes, even when she pretends not to, holding her mummy's hand tight on their short walk from the flat to the school. And it's true, she thinks, even the sound of it makes her skin crawl. 'Rach'. 'Raitch.' 'Wretch'. She knows everyone thinks Rachael Huntley is a stupid girl. To the ogre's eyes, perhaps to others as well, 'handicapped'. But *she's* not the stupid one. So what if the words don't always come, if she sometimes struggles to say them? That doesn't mean she's stupid, just a little scared. Who wouldn't be in this place? But when they're not looking, or listening, the other children, the teachers, the ogre, even mummy, *that's* when she is. And that's most of the time, because really they don't see her or hear her unless she is upset. Anyway, the point is, she *can* read, she's not stupid and they mostly are.

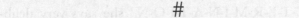

#

It is a struggle to start with. She can see the sounds and hear the letters, but until Mrs J., the librarian, comes over to help, her thoughts are as jumbled as the shapes on the page. But it is nice and quiet in here, and she feels calm, even if the shapes won't keep still long enough for her to follow them. It is curiosity that has brought her here in the first place. She wants to see where K. goes off to at lunchtime as he rarely seems to be in the playground. It turns out he comes here. Maybe they could also talk in the library? Even though he sits next to her in class, they never speak, but often when she looks up, she sees him gazing straight out of the window, and he just seems so bored. And then when the class is over and the buzzer sounds for lunchtime, he is always the first to leave but she hardly ever sees him in the playground, and rarely in the lunch hall. So she starts following him, making sure that he doesn't see her, and it turns out his hiding place is just a few short yards away. She keeps coming here even after she spots K. with that new girl, the one who has just joined their class. Michelle. At first she doesn't like it when she hears them giggling in one of the other aisles, but when she peeks around the corner and sees that they are not laughing at her but at some game they are playing with one another, she feels the hurt slide away to be replaced with something else which she doesn't yet know how to name.

#

'D-E-T-E-R-M-I-N-A-T-I-O-N,' she says very deliberately, thinking how much easier it is when she uses her finger to follow the individual letters on the page.

'Fantastic! You're doing ever so well,' says Mrs J., placing a reassuring hand on her shoulder. She feels so happy. This is the biggest, longest, most difficult word she has been able to recognize. Every spare moment she now has is being spent in the library. Mrs J. pulled a bit of a face the first time she came in but has been very nice since. That first day, when Mrs J. had caught her spying on K. and Michelle, she didn't really know what to say when Mrs J. had asked her what she was doing, so she'd just blurted out:

'Reading, Miss.'

'Mrs J., actually,' the librarian had said, pulling a bit of a face. But then her tone had changed. 'It doesn't really look like you're reading, if you don't mind me saying.'

No grown up had ever spoken to her like that before, and she wanted to tell her how lovely it was to be both seen and heard, but instead just started to cry when the words died halfway up her throat.

'There, there, love, there's no need for that,' Mrs J. had said, using her hands to wipe away the tears. 'There's no rush. You take your time, love, then when you're ready, you let me know and we'll find something for you to read. But in the meantime let's get you sat down over here and out of this sad face,' she said, placing a hand on Rachael's back and gently guiding her to a chair next to the desk where she herself had been sitting.

#

It is so much easier to learn, she thinks, without all that classroom noise. And Mrs J. is a far better teacher than any of her actual teachers. She doesn't get cross every time she, Rachael, makes a mistake. She wishes mummy could be like this, and sometimes she gets the feeling she could, if only the ogre would leave them alone. She knows he hits mummy and yesterday when mummy was upstairs, having a wash, he hit her as well. She had been trying to read the story book Mrs J. had given her, about the little chicken and the day the sky fell down, and hadn't heard him ask her about school. When he asked her again, but louder this time, she looked up to see him staring at her. He seemed quite cross.

'Think you can just sit there ignoring me?'

She didn't know what to say. It wasn't true anyway, she just hadn't heard him, she had been reading. She was still having to concentrate really hard to make out all the words. It was much more difficult on her own, without Mrs J. to guide her, but she had promised she would try her best to finish this story before the end of the week. And a promise, as Mrs J. would say, was a promise.

'I don't know why I bother,' the ogre tells her. 'Must be true what they say about fruit and trees.'

She has no idea what he is talking about, and so looks back down at her book.

'Don't you look away when I'm talking to you, little madam,' he says, a look of real anger spreading out across his face. 'I'm slaving away all the hours just so you and your mum can enjoy some of the nicer things,' he says, pointing across the kitchen. 'How many people round here do you think have got the latest appliances? Fridge freezer, cupboards fully stocked, every convenience. Never wanting for anything. And all I ask in return is for a little bit of respect. But no, little madam's too good for that now, isn't she? Look at her sitting there all prim and proper like little lady muck. . Well I've got news for you, girl. You ain't no lady and you'll bloody well show me some respect from now on. And if I ask you how school is, or what you're reading, or why. Or even if I just want to know why you look so bloody pleased with yourself with those stupid little glasses and that spastic look, then you'll bloody well jump to attention, Sir! Yes, Sir! And you'll bloody well put down whatever that nonsense is that you're pretending to read, and you'll tell me. Have you got that?'

And because chicken licken seemed so much nicer than the ogre, and in any case he was so cross and had said all those unkind things to her, she made the mistake of picking up her book and starting to read again from where she had left off.

#

No one can tell where he had smacked her, on the bum.

It doesn't sting like it did last night, but she doesn't much feel like reading today, or even pretending to. It makes her shiver just thinking about how he just kept smacking her harder and harder, and how the more she tried to scream the less the words would come. Mummy never came until it was too late, and she barely even remembers mummy sticking her head around the door and asking if she was ok. She *does* remember sobbing in her room, not caring anymore if her snot was getting mixed up with her tears on the bedspread. And she couldn't stop crying then, thinking if only there was some way that Rachael Huntley could become someone else, then that would make everything better.

But it's at school the next day, in the library, that the idea comes to her. She is glad Mrs J. hasn't said anything to her about it even though she can tell all is not well. It is clear she can. She's not like other grown ups. She looks, and listens. She knows all is not well with her star pupil. Rachael feels this when Mrs J. hands her a book to look at which is mostly photographs with just a little bit of writing, and without even mentioning the storybook about the little chicken. So she sits in her usual place, next to the librarian's desk, and examines the photographs. They are colourful, like the pencils they use in class, and many of them show the same person, each time wearing a different hat. She knows who this person is because she recognizes her from one of mummy's tea cups, which has a picture of this woman's face on one side. It is the queen and she must travel a lot, thinks Rachael, as every photograph seems to be taken in a different country. The little bits of writing underneath them are slightly different each time too.

'They're called captions, love,' says Mrs J.

She reads the captions, and sees that sometimes this woman is described as 'Her Majesty', while on other pages she is simply called 'The Queen'. And on still others, 'H.R.H.'.

'What does this mean?' she asks Mrs J.

'Oh that,' says Mrs J., seeing the letters the little girl is pointing to. 'Sometimes she likes to be a little mysterious, because, well, everyone knows her as the queen. So I like to think this is her way of saying, "but that's not all I am." She is a lady, after all, and we all need some privacy. H.R.H. means Her Royal Highness, love.'

This is great, she thinks. Three different ways of describing the same person. Perhaps one is never enough? Come to think of it, she's already been described as a spastic, as handicapped, as Rachael Huntley. And none of those make her feel happy. It wouldn't matter if she was the queen, but she's not. She has never even been outside this area, let alone abroad. Rachael Huntley, that is, the girl they all think is a spastic or handicapped. Just because the words don't always come but the liquid sometimes does. Which is when it comes to her. She needs some peace and quiet too, and Rachael Huntley isn't going to help her find it. Besides, that's not all she is. She looks, and listens, and learns, but the only person anyone else ever sees is Rachael Huntley, and that person does none of those things, and smells of wee. R.H. on the other hand, well that's another girl entirely.

#

17.

London 1975

The chair is almost finished, the only question remaining around what type of seat cover Mum will make on the old Singer sewing machine.

Dad looks pleased, and with the weather holding up he's finished it earlier than expected. K.'s brother is sitting down and getting up again to test the criss-crossed fibres where the cushion and seat cover will go.

'*Thik aache?*' asks Dad, though the way he is beaming suggests that he already knows the answer.

Then, spotting his other son, he asks him to find the World Service on the transistor, which for some reason is tuned into another BBC channel playing pop music. Turning the dial very slowly in case he misses the peeps, K. stops for a moment when unfamiliar sounds tumble out of the radio. He can't help himself, it just sounds so... strange, but not in that Bebop a Lula way that's popular across the fence. It is not often any pop music gets played here, and other than the occasional racket coming from next door, what he's used to are the peeps, or the dramatic sound of the TV news, or that jolly little intro to Tom and Barbara Good and their neighbour, the leader of the Conservative party. But this voice is like nothing he's ever heard, at times it sounds like whoever's singing is in pain or maybe they're pulling faces, as if they're both sad and funny at the same time. And then the voice asks a question, 'Ah do you remember your president Nixon?' and that's a name K. knows from all the cut-glass announcements. 'Yes! Yes! I do!' he wants to shout, the same way he wants to yell the answer to every question in class but ends up saying nothing, sitting on his hands while the teachers look right past him in an invisible beeline heading straight towards the snooty girls. 'Do you remember the bills you have to pay?' For once he doesn't know the answer, but even as he's thinking about it, the voice has moved on, telling him all night he wants a young American. Right at that moment a loud, 'Fuck off, Bowie, you poof!' comes through the fence, and it jolts him back to his search for the peeps.

#

Since that night when words were exchanged, the neighbour has largely stayed out of Dad's way.

All K. can gather from the snippets of Mum and Dad's conversation he has overheard since is that there were lots of men there, and something strange was going on inside. Dad couldn't say exactly what as he was only on the doorstep, but there was a funny smell, and some odd noises coming from inside, which is maybe why the neighbour seemed so agitated and in such a hurry to get rid of him.

The song also clearly aggravates the neighbour, and perhaps this explains why Dad tells K. to keep it on. Mum isn't too impressed by the song either, but quickly works out what's going on and leaves her lack of enthusiasm at '*Eta shunecho?*'.

For once there are no peeps on the hour, else they would have heard about George Davis and the Headingley pitch, the overnight 'outrage', the salting of England's wounds with oil; to add insult to injury the vandalism coming with England on the verge of a famous victory. The Ashes lost, spiralling inflation and the country going into recession, and all in all things about to get a whole lot worse.

#

18.

They're calling it 'the friendly final', a London derby between east and west. The build-up goes on all week in class but the only thing anyone says is what a bunch of wankers the team from the east are, though confusingly enough they're called West Ham.

'My dad says they're cunts,' says one of the blonde Panini sticker boys. 'Pikeys,' adds the other. 'And they're fucking shit.'

K. hasn't really given it much thought. Dad's never said anything about football, let alone called another team 'cunts'. Chances are he'll watch the game too, but only if they all are. Then again there's no knowing what kind of noises will be coming through the wall come the weekend.

In the event, Cup final Saturday passes without incident, and when the second goal goes in, K. feels pleased. Watching all those claret and blue flags and scarves at one end of the ground when Alan Taylor pokes in the rebound from close range, he can suddenly picture the boys in his class also watching these same images with their dads, except in those rabbit hutches the animals are all unhappy, and they are swearing.

After the presentation, he goes for a bounce on his

brother's space hopper in the backyard, trying to imagine what will happen when the question, as it surely will, comes up in class on Monday, 'So, did you see the game then?'

'Yeah, those pikeys weren't bad for a bunch of cunts,' he'll say and on this occasion the Panini boy will back down, too shamefaced by K.'s razor sharp wit, coming as it does on top of the earlier result, to do anything else.

By Monday morning though this no longer seems like such a good idea, and predictably enough when the question does arise, K. pretends to be busy with joined up writing, forced in the ensuing vacuum to listen instead to the Panini boys complaining about the referee, followed up by the almost inevitable, 'My dad says they're all thieves round that way.'

It still counts as a good day though. *They're* unhappy just as they would be unhappy later that summer when the pitch gets dug up and the Test match is abandoned. And really, he thinks, anything that makes these unhappy is just fine with him.

19.

The caretaker is right. They get several more chances to try out some public art, but the vandals are getting smarter too, and when they graduate from their favourite two letters to full blown words, the only cover up that will do is a fresh coat on the offending patch. *Pakis Out* is a bit predictable, but the caretaker seems especially annoyed by *Keep Britain White*. The letters are bigger too, higher up on the wall, and there's no question but that this is the work of older hands.

'These people. They don't know they're born, son. We fought a war against the likes of them, and now they're here telling us who's who and what's what. Pardon my French, son, but they're cunts. And they've got no class.'

K. doesn't mind too much on those days when he sees the caretaker with the familiar repair kit. At least it means there's someone else for him to talk to, an adult on the premises who is actually worth listening to. He likes the caretaker's stories about being evacuated in the war, and then missing London so much that he begged to be allowed back. The jokes people used to tell in the shelters, and how 'them' in government didn't like it one bit, the idea of a deep, underground solidarity amongst ordinary people away from the prying eyes of health officials or government inspectors. Whenever he says 'them' he gives K. a conspiratorial look, and nods in the direction of the headmaster's office, or at any teachers who happen to be nearby.

'They used to tell us we'd become defeatist down in those shelters, but that wasn't it at all. We just got used to not having *them* around, breathing down our necks every five minutes to check whether this was done or that was done, and then when it *was*, telling us it wasn't done right. No, it was just us looking out for each other, knowing the moment we poked our heads back above ground, more than likely 'they'd' finish off what the doodlebug had started. Do you hear what I'm saying, son?'

K. does indeed, and nods along, but in truth it sounds like another world, and when he looks up 'doodlebug' in the Chambers later on, his confusion just increases. Why would the larva of an ant-lion, which doesn't sound like a normal lion at all, be attacking the heads of ordinary Londoners during wartime? It is only when he looks more carefully that he sees the final entry under all that fluff about the ant lion explaining the word as wartime slang for a flying bomb.

Round the corner, on the grass verge, a group of boys from his class crowd around an older boy, crouched down with a magnifying glass.

'Er, d'you see that? That's disgusting!' 'Er, that's horrible!' 'Er, look at that!'

There's no point even going over there. K. already knows that something far less dangerous than an ant lion

has just encountered something every bit as deadly as a
doodlebug.

#

20.

It first appears on the bridge near the Odeon, then starts popping up on random walls and bus shelters. It's even shown on the news, painted on motorway flyovers, and really wherever there's more than two herberts and a spare bit of building. Instinctively K. knows it's a good thing, something about deflecting attention away from the nation's other favourite slogans.

G. Davis is innocent.

What? Who?

Then he hears some of the older boys talking about it at school, and before long even the Panini twins, who've not been the same since the cup final, are finding time in between sticker swaps for some commentary.

'My dad says he was fitted up by the old bill.'

'They're wankers.'

'Yeah, proper cunts.'

'Real wankers.'

'Yeah, total cunts.'

'Anyway, you got Gerry Francis? I'll trade you that cunt, Billy Bonds, for Gerry Francis.'

'Yeah he *is* a cunt'n'all.'

'Right wanker.'

But at least they're not talking about that other Davis on the telly, with his red face and his 'boys to entertain you'. Because then it's never too long before someone will start on the punkah wallah impression, and heads will be comically rolling, and the rest of the class will find it hysterical, and he'll just want that concrete to swallow him up all over again. In *that* sense he's very grateful to G. Davis, and whatever it is the man is supposed to have done, deep down K. feels he must be innocent.

#

He goes to see the caretaker whenever he can during break times, and more often than not the man is holed up in a room not much bigger than a broom cupboard which, he tells K., doubles up as his office. Every now and then he gets called away if something is broken or one of 'them' can't be bothered to sweep up some mess near their classroom, but after a while he doesn't mind leaving K. in charge of the office when he's gone. There's a little transistor in there, much like Dad's, and it's always playing pop music at a very low volume. Bit by bit the names start to become familiar. Slade, Suzi Quatro, Rod Stewart, and every now and then that singer who his neighbour had described as a 'fucking poof'.

One song in particular stands out. It gets played a lot too. It's nothing like the poof but it's still good. And a bit like the caretaker, the man sounds like he knows a thing or two. Something about spoiling the game, whatever you say, and then telling loads of lies. The voice isn't angry though, more like that word he'd learned just last night when he'd been looking up 'wanker': *wistful*. Make me smile, or run on wild.

He starts to write down the lyrics, and when a teacher passing by looks in but doesn't seem to register his presence even though he is sitting right there, K. takes this as a sure sign that he really can disappear as and when he chooses.

After that the days pass quicker and if it barely seems like yesterday when the graffiti first went up, then soon enough George, the 'G' of G. Davis, is indeed declared innocent and set free to a hero's welcome at the place K. only knows from the station announcers as 'London Waterloo'.

#

Maybe they were making room for him? It all happens very quickly, but that morning, just a couple of days after the George Davis release, when the house is surrounded and then the neighbour is led away, hands behind his back, gut spilling out of his vest, that's the thought that goes through K.'s head, watching the whole thing from behind the curtain. He's heard that phrase before, 'one in, one out', when they're made to run through the verruca tank before swimming. Maybe it's the same thing with prison, he thinks, and now that G. Davis is out, there's room for one more. Perhaps that's what it's really about, sorting out the timing, a bit like batting.

#

After he is taken away, other uniforms stand by the door while a procession of bags is brought out of the house. One of them breaks and K. sees what looks like a gas mask fall onto the pavement outside. There are also some weird looking sticks, all black, and several handcuffs not unlike the ones the neighbour was wearing when he was led away. Two of the uniforms are smirking, but the third, a woman, is struggling to see the funny side. And when another of her colleagues emerges from the house with a roll of film in one hand and a clutch of magazines in the other, he looks ashen faced.

'It's disgusting,' he says, though to K. he just sounds pretty much like any one of the boys from school when they're trying a bit too hard to make a point.

#

It takes the uniforms a while to bag everything up and make their enquiries. When Mum answers the door, they seem surprised to find a woman in a sari looking them in the eye and asking them what kind of a pervert has been living next door to her children.

'Er, it's not exactly clear that's what he was,' says one of them.

'I suppose you don't have any proof,' replies Mum, making no effort to disguise the sarcasm.

'Well that's why we're talking to all the neighbours, trying to get a better picture of who this person really is.'

'Is that why you ignored my husband when he told you months ago there's something wrong in that house? After that big, fat, dirty man and his friends threatened him?'

'Well, er, I don't know anything about that, madam, but I can assure you----'

'You've done that before. It didn't help,' says Mum.

K. joins Mum on the doorstep. This time he squeezes her hand, and she's immediately grateful for his presence, squeezing back, thinking this isn't exactly the life she had pictured for herself those sleepless nights alone on the ship, homesick before it had even left Bombay, the captain increasingly concerned when she failed to appear for dinner day after day, stomach knotted tight, clinging to some last vestige of home, the rotis filled with *shukhna aloo* prepared and handed over by hands wringing every last drop of love from that pier, the Arabian Sea already beckoning, a terrified young woman desperately preserving through willpower alone the final speck of *kalonji* before it would disappear forever in the beast's curdling waters. Yet it was from that same tumult that a foghorn would rise, its sound sending passengers scuttling onto the deck, and then, yes it's unmistakably him, waiting for her at the dock in high waisted trousers with a pleat, for some reason she can still see those as if it were yesterday, and is that a smile or is it relief? She can't tell, but in his other hand the train tickets to London already booked and a little shawl, which he wraps around her before something sharp, whistling in from a Northern sea, can pierce through the cotton. Back then it was nerves, all that unfamiliar that had first kept her awake then brought her to the threshold. Now, in the space of a few short years everything feels so familiar, more like a sickness, and though it doesn't begin or end with these uniforms she wishes they'd just go away.

#

Dhaka, undivided Bengal early 1900s-1947

Had it always been like this? She wasn't sure, but the pressure of K.'s fingers on her palm brought to mind another child, herself at roughly his age, or perhaps even younger. A little girl holding onto her dada's hand back in Dhaka. There had been monsters back then too, bigger ones than the *bhoot* next door or the one looking at her now in his unimpressive uniform. Back then all the beasts had been bigger. Wilder too. But somehow that was part of the excitement, a bigger world and its dangers coming into view for the first time. A little girl digging into her dada's arm as the beast drew near and her heart began to race.

#

Nishash prai bandho hai aasche. Ekta bishal shobdo. Gaatch shob uriegache. Eybar o aashlo. Chitka. Shomosto polapan jara shamnay boshe aache, chitka korche. Ta poray kanakaati.

Just a murmur to start with. As soon as the lights go out though a little ripple of unease, running from one end of the benches to the other. All day she had badgered her father to be allowed to go to the cinema, and in the end he'd relented, won over as much by her persistence as by the imploring note in her eyes. In a faltering voice she'd said her *dada* had already agreed to take her, and when that was met with an amused silence, had added that her older cousins, and an uncle would also be going. It wasn't far from the house, and if they were all going anyway, there was nothing to worry about.

Chinta koro na, Baba, aami odeh shonge thakbo. Orah neaashbe aar deaashbe.

She hadn't stamped her feet or made any kind of a scene, and her father, the professor, liked that. Yet another way in which she was so different to her older sisters. The eldest, also the most wilful, already married and with issue, and the next two most senior, though still at home, biding their time in that permanently alert condition broaching childhood and its remnants. Not yet women, but neither were they children any more. It was his duty to find them good marriages, in homes where they would be appreciated. Where they could grow to be women and raise families of their own. He knew from his own family, from several of his uncles, in one of whose households he'd largely been raised after his own parents had died while he was still very young, that not every match was a good one, and he had seen first hand the unhappiness this created. Wives and children largely abandoned to fates they'd never chosen. Hunger and longing and the bitter realisation that this life apportions cruelty to those least able to withstand it. He had heard the rumours of secret dalliances and a weakness for the flesh. Heirlooms squandered on liquor and nocturnal trysts. Brahminical virtue and castles of sand, piety slipping away with the other masks. He had also heard about the other families, the other children, the other wives occluded just the other side of the shame. But he had actually tasted the hunger, and he knew it was physical, as with those other hungers which had caused this despair. It was why he understood philosophy, its corporeality, long before he knew its name. To his mind, it came with a physical aspect. Tongues sharpened by hardship and bodies fed with resentment. Which is how he had always known, from a very young age, that impermanence was as much, if not more, a part of this life than any fineries. He had set that knowledge to studying, and learning, then teaching every spare moment that wasn't given over to fixing and mending whatever fetched up in the godown where he had secured some temporary work. The careless details of everyday neglect. Bicycles, cloth, the crumbling spines of ancient tomes. Some other world disappearing in the cross-stitch, in the threading and pasting and re-purposing. Each mended garment, or wheel, spinning calloused hands that little bit further from their torment. Every yellowed page caressed with love another possibility away from the jaundiced memory. Betrayal and its subsequent hardships absorbed in a dedication to the work itself. The restoration of spines an undeniably physical metaphor, mind and body once more realigned. By which point even the young man's detractors—and there were many, who decried both the shame of his high-born poverty and his willingness to work with his hands—started to recognise the value of that work, and of the mind which processed it. And where once the whiff of scandal and loss would have clung to him like an albatross, there was now a presence about this young man. An authority even, assigned to books, but assured by labour. Sons, and even one or two daughters, of the wealthier business people who still for the most part controlled local affairs, would be sent to the young man they had already begun to call *mastermoshai*. To help them prepare for their school finals, or in some cases just to imbibe through proximity some of that intellectual authority. And though he was young he understood his function within such arrangements. To provide an aesthetic flourish, an artistic sense by way of the mind, or to soften a machinery founded on commerce and calculation. *Just make an effort to listen to mastermoshai. He'll tell you how.* So these callow young people, who if fate had taken a different turn could just as easily have been his peers, would reluctantly sit in what appeared to the young teacher to be the palatial surroundings of their family homes, sometimes even with marble floors, while he attempted the often hopeless task of fine-tuning a largely non-existent artistic sensibility. But he knew he was accruing credit in the eyes of these families. That even on the marble an impression can be cast. So he persevered. And when the time eventually came, as everyone knew it would, for the young teacher to move to the big city and pursue his own studies there, it was with the support and financial blessing of one of these influential local families. The philanthropy, if it could be called that, came from a merchant whose daughter had married well, her in-laws impressed with her knowledge of the Greek philosophers as well as an in-depth appreciation of Bengali literature. Once there, in the big city, the young man, now a student again, rejoiced at its array of voices, its spines which had remained intact. And he drank from every literary pore, slaking the thirst only known by the once forsaken or the exceptionally hungry. That reputation for thoroughness, first forged in the twilit godowns of his youth, now took shape in a promising academic career. Knowledge, and its applicability, finding a home in Philosophy. The presentation of a life not yet fully formed. Ethics as much as aesthetics, hence *swadeshi* once the bodies had been fished out of the well at Jallianwala Bagh. The massacre of an unarmed crowd in broad daylight. The orders to shoot coming from English voices. Thus the fineries of English institutional dress put away in disgust. Though no one ever suspected the disgust of the young professor might have stretched further than a sartorial shift. Away from the Greeks and towards the angrier voices, the closer ones inhabiting this agora. To harbouring freedom fighters, whom the *Ingrezi* called by another name entirely. The professor married by now, and with a growing family of his own. Daughters as well as sons. And whilst a part of him dreaded the brokerage of their lives, in the approaches that would inevitably be made and the conversations that would unfold, he recognised that it was his duty to set the tone for those negotiations. To be present and, if need be, protective, but in a manner befitting his status. A professor of philosophy and a man who'd already earned the respect of his peers by taking a stand. Wisdom literally homespun since the massacre in Amritsar. *Swadeshi* but without any of the humourless severity that sometimes implied. He encountered plenty of that within his Department. Speeches, styles, a sectarian tint from mouths which he suspected were unused to hunger. And even then, as the youngest professor in the history of his Department, that didn't feel right, somehow. The examined life, the one worth leading, meant sacrifices, of course it did. But it called for generosity too, not this descent into reduced madness. For if his cloth was home-spun, his tastes were much broader. He loved Chaplin, and that walk. Beneath the hat and the jaunty shuffle, those hungers, too, were familiar. How they could nourish and restore, or just as easily consume their bearers with desire. He had known this all his life, that desire was never innocent, yet here were his esteemed colleagues, enraged by rhetoric in ways that were anything but considered. So he found other ways to make a statement. Through an informal network of concerned souls, of which, in that district, there were many, and under the guise of hiring temporary cooks or cleaners, he incorporated outlaws into his household and so fed hungers for something bigger than self. Subversion hidden in plain sight and the *Ingrezi* eventually gone. Chaplin was useful in other ways too, imparting humour as its own homeopathy. Which in his ever expanding household, its mosaic of girls and boys and curiosity, proved as useful as anything Vedic. Besides, what was the point of all those books, all those hours spent poring over dusty tomes, if he couldn't now find some words for his youngest daughter, gazing at him with those innocent eyes that he found so hard to refuse?

She had been incredibly excited even before they arrived. Though it wasn't far from where they lived, she had been quivering with delight from the moment that Baba had said 'Yes, alright then, you can go, but only if you promise to tell me all about it when you get back.' Her cousin, Shankar, had been to see a film the previous month, and it was all he could talk about. He had apparently also seen a tiger in the street a few days earlier. When he'd excitedly told her this, she'd felt glum. She never saw anything. Films or tigers or even monkeys, which everyone else saw all the time. '*Ekta Bandar aashlo, ar thik or paacha e upureh ekta thapar boshiedilo*'. She had laughed, along with everyone else, everyone, that is bar her *didi*, whose bottom was the one being slapped by the monkey. Her didi had earlier caught the monkey in the act of stealing some papaya and had sent it on its way with a firm slap on its bottom. And of course in this telling, the creature had bided its time, waited until nightfall to seize its chance. Her didi had ventured out to use the roofless outhouse—this was at their home in the countryside—and while she was cleaning herself afterwards, the monkey, which must have been watching her, had swooped down into the exposed outhouse and delivered the decisive slap. That was when Shankar had mentioned the tiger, but although he had been called *pagol* by the others, she didn't know why. In her head there were animals everywhere but for some reason they were always choosing to hide from her.

The cinema hall Mukul was on Nawabpur Road right before Victoria Park. As they arrived they saw its well-decorated marquee at the entrance and walls pasted with big posters announcing forthcoming features. Besides Mukul, there were some other cinema halls within walking distance but when she asked him her dada was unsure where these were. He seemed a little annoyed that he had to hold her hand as they went in, but once he saw that the foyer was full of little boys and girls who were also being chaperoned by older brothers, and cousins, and fathers, he appeared to relax.

As they were in a big group, and had arrived early, they had spent some time outside beforehand. Her dada had picked up some *jhal muri* from one of the roadside hawkers and though he seemed to be enjoying it, and had offered her some, she had refused when she caught its spicy aroma. To her, there was *ekto paad-e-gondo* about the packet. She told him and he laughed, though the *ferriwala* didn't look very pleased. To placate him, her dada bought another packet which he then gave to her cousins, who had also come along with them. She was briefly tempted by the pickled *amra* that another hawker was peddling, but it was already getting close to the time that they would have to go inside, so she decided against it.

They sat on the benches at the very front. She saw that apart from their group, made up of all the younger cousins and herself, as well as her dada and chotokaka, more or less the entire row was taken up by boys and girls her age. Looking around, and from the excitable voices making themselves heard over one another, it soon became clear to her that the cinema hall was full of groups of young children, with each batch being supervised by an adult. The noise was incredible, louder than anything she could ever remember hearing, and as usual the boys were keen to make the most noise, just like her cousin Shankar, who even now was telling people (strangers in the next row, not even their relatives) about the tiger. He didn't seem at all worried about any of it.

'*Ha, aami bagh dekhechi. Raasta e cholchilo. Aar aami ek fota bhoi payi ni!*'

'*Taale tumi kotthai thako? Tumi jongol e thako?*'

She saw her dada turn around to see who was making fun of her cousin, now that he'd finished the jhal muri and both his hands were free again, but just then the cinema hall was plunged into darkness. All of the shouting and noise of just a moment earlier magically evaporated, sucked away along with their courage by the pitch black. She found herself holding onto her dada, sat next to her.

Transfixed, she watched as the ship prepared to set sail for the South Seas. The city it was leaving from looked incredible, busier than any place she'd ever seen, even Dhaka. There were so many people all running around and shouting, and so much noise. And though she could understand why Ann, the actress, was getting onto the ship, it still made her feel uneasy, like one of Shankar's stories. It was an adventure, that was why she was going. And that made sense. She had wanted to see the tiger as well, of course she had, but Baba had told her they were so much bigger than either herself or Shankar. What if the tiger was angry? They would have to run away and she wasn't sure she would be fast enough. What if it just didn't like little girls? Would Shankar stay and help her, or would he leave her to deal with the tiger on her own? These were important questions. Baba had said that to her once, when she asked him what he was doing, every day sat there looking at his books. I'm looking at the important questions, he'd told her, and then he'd laughed. But what were these questions? He'd not said. If Baba didn't know, she somehow doubted Shankar would know what they were. Then again the *goree mem* on the boat didn't seem so sure either. Perhaps nobody knew, and that's why they were all running around this strange city shouting, or hiding?

She felt her breathing quicken when the island emerged out of the fog. She could understand why it was exciting, why the sailors wanted to explore the island, but she knew it was wrong. They should never have come this far. Something bad might happen to them. And the deeper they went into the island, the more she felt this in her stomach. She was glad her dada was next to her. Every so often she could tell out of the corner of her eye that he was looking at her, and this made her feel better. Perhaps she needed to do this more? Look out of the corner of her eye, pretend she was looking at, or doing something else. There was that one time when she had seen the new cook put something in a cloth bag and then hide the bag under the floorboard. She had pretended not to see anything, and in any case he hadn't seen her, but it was exciting to think he had a secret that only she knew about. At least that was better than thinking about his cooking, which was terrible. Ma had been getting fat again and so she couldn't make food every day, but his food was terrible. He couldn't make rice or dhal or anything really. But no one ever said anything about it, and when she got less fat again, Ma was able to show him how to make *baigun bhaja* and *mooshori dhal*. Then the police inspector had come and Baba had said something to him and the police inspector had left looking very unhappy. She remembered that. And not long after that the cook had also left but she didn't know if he had taken his bag with him. Even so, she still felt a little jealous. It was Shankar who had seen the tiger.

There was a huge noise. She was finding it hard to breathe. All the trees and the foliage were being uprooted. She heard thundering footfalls, which felt as though they were about to land on her head, and then suddenly, there he was. Ann, the actress, squirmed at the altar where the tribe had tied her a little earlier. She had known there was big trouble ahead for Ann the moment the chief struck the huge gong. And that was when the other noises had begun. As soon as the monster appeared she dug her fingers into her dada's arm. But at least she wasn't screaming, like all the other children sat in the front row. Once the giant gorilla disappeared into the jungle with Ann held in a huge hand, that was when it really started. Serpents, dinosaurs, explosions. She remembered a moment of shocked silence, and then one after the other, and in unison, and then apart again, the cinema hall was filled with the shrieks and cries of children. They wailed through the jungle, and the capture, and the ocean crossing back to that strange city where it all began. And then they carried on screaming through the escape, and the ascent, and the planes. So that by the time the beast was dead, shot down in a strange city, her dada's arm was marked deep by the pressure of little fingers and the cinema hall was full of that strange paad-e gondo that she'd earlier detected coming from the jhal muri.

#

In the years ahead she sometimes hears that gong, and sees the torchlit procession, on bad nights when fires have broken out in another *para*. When rumours abound and no one will sleep. The fires draw closer and there are terrible stories. This *bhadralok*, that *chokra*. Until that day it is not a story, but a blood-soaked little boy, unable to speak, who she finds herself washing, and dressing. A boy who had been with his family, trying to leave, when the marquee they'd been tricked into by a 'security' detail on the way to the airport was cut down from outside, and a mob wielding machetes had descended upon the stricken shapes just the other side of the tarpaulin. The boy had only survived by playing dead, lying for hours under his mother, her blood salt slowly drying out on his skin. Satisfied that there were no survivors, the mob had moved on by the time he emerged, and it was sheer good fortune that the first person who encountered him wandering bloodied and dazed was her dada, now working near the airport.

Arrangements are made, ironically by some of Baba's former students, who have acquired influence in this uncertain new country. Police commissioners and transport bosses, local fixers and chief ministers. So their passage at least is assured, and in tearful, fond goodbyes she sees the madness of what has unfolded. They no more wish him to leave than he to go. Yet that reluctance is cured by the memory of the boy, of the other bodies lying un-collected in once familiar streets. Of the fires which puri-fied nothing and the screams which went unheard. The Mukul no longer a dream palace, now just a space of horror. So they recoil from all they've ever known and leave behind the primal myth of place. The imperma-nence of one life, banished in an instant, while another hoves into view, downgraded, chastened and with one eye on destitution. And this time there is no need for Baba to say anything. She finally understands exactly what he once meant by 'the important questions'.

Calcutta, post-Partition

Shankar is still telling tales this side of the border. Fourteen of them in one room and he makes jokes about jhal muri. But she doesn't mind that. It's a reminder of happier times when the only monsters they saw were on a big screen. And if it's cramped here, she thinks, it is at least safe, and they are together. The years pass and little by little they start to establish themselves in this city. Her dada finds work, Shankar too. From one room they gradually expand to the next, and then to the upper portion of the house too, until they are finally able to call it home. But she has seen what those years of privation have done to her parents, especially Baba. Ma has continued to do what she has always done, to provide food and comfort and advice whatever the circumstances. And she is unconditionally loved for it. But Baba, who she never once remembers having so much as a cough back in Dhaka, is rarely able to speak above a whisper now, his health diminished these past few years. All the wisdoms of antiquity, but a living, breathing ethics shaved to the bone, the shock of departure something from which he never fully recovers. So she makes a promise that she will honour his name, wrestle with those bigger questions herself. She studies by candlelight and is eventually admitted to the city's prestigious University. And there she enrols to study Philosophy.

#

'*Aare, bhai, ekto jaiga koro. Didi ke namte din,*' said the young man with a stern look on his face which somehow remained simultaneously playful. This was clearly some sort of game for him, the pushmepullyou of the buses which jerkily crisscrossed the city. Still, she was grateful for his intervention. She had been delayed near the library today and her journey back to Paikpara was far later than usual. It was already dark and promising another downpour, the air pregnant with those early, fat monsoon droplets. By the time the bus lurched its way to the mouth of Tala Park the entire area was submerged, the deluge casting adrift any thoughts of a quick scamper home through the park. Despite the lateness of the hour the bus was still packed, and it took the young man's exhortation before space miraculously appeared and she was able to alight. Seeing her hesitate before taking a step into the waterlogged street, the young man, who she now recognised as one of the local toughs, scooped her up in a sinewy embrace and carried her the short distance to the first dry spot he could find, under an awning near the park entrance. She briefly thought about protesting, but was dissuaded by the purposeful manner in which the young man waded across the street bearing his cargo. Once he'd satisfied himself that she was indeed now on dry ground, he turned to leave, but before he did so, said to her in a very matter-of fact way, '*Oto deri te kanno baire, didi?*' She was stunned but before she could answer, he added, '*Professor moshai kamon aachen aajkal?*' If not exactly the dialectic, then there was still something in this encounter which brought to mind what she'd been studying earlier, until she had lost track of time and made her slightly panicked way home. The treatment meted out by Zeno to Socrates in Plato's dialogue, Parmenides. Her unsolicited chaperon was right though. It *was* late, no kind of hour for a young woman to be out on her own, with or without the Socratic method. What bothered her more was that this total stranger knew who she was, who her father was. Did he also know that they were refugees? She was still considering the young man's questions when another hand firmly grasped her arm. It was her dada, who must have been on the lookout for her, concerned about the lateness of the hour. This time there was no hesitation. She felt relieved, gently digging into his arm as she once had in a darkened cinema hall.

#

Those are some of the hardest times, in that one room,

barely space to remember all that they have lost. Yet that earlier life, the happier time is the one she keeps returning to whenever the sounds of breathing or wheezing which surround her, or sometimes just the sheer restless fact of their survival, wrench her from what in any case is rarely sleep itself but its vague promise. An improvised curtain rail and the flimsiest of cloth hanging from it their domestic *svarabhakti*. She congratulates herself for the thought, the candlelit hours of study each day nonetheless sharpening her perception. For all the privation, and there is plenty just in the daily struggle to eat and sleep, let alone to exhale artistry with the more functional thoughts, what she sees each night in that simple act of hanging the cloth is the physical remembrance that yes, they may have lost all but the one thing that truly matters. Dignity. The material is indeed a *svarabhakti*, the vowel separating the consonants. And either side of it, amidst the wheezing and the warmth of bodies, they have not forgotten themselves. Ma and Baba, herself, and a cousin sister who has joined them after her own family were lost to the madness. And just a few feet away, the other side of the cloth, her brothers, and a cousin brother, the occasional twitching of feet or muted snoring the only other signs of life in here during those twilight hours. Her eyes, by now accustomed to the darkness during all those nights she doesn't sleep, sometimes pick out the furtive shape of a gecko, eavesdropping on the semi-slumber from halfway up one of the walls. But it is when she hears the scuttling of cockroaches, back to whatever furtive lair they enjoy in the recesses, that she truly wants to scream. No matter how many times a day she cleans and dusts, the unwelcome guests never go away. She wonders whether she is the only one who can hear them, or if in fact her entire family is also awake in the shadows, nursing similar thoughts of anger and loss and shame. Outside there is the street and the strays, and she knows that she is luckier than some, nightly warming benches and dust. She sees lost souls every day when she takes the bus to and from the University. Sometimes in that same district they shuffle into view, only partially obscured by the vast mountains of books and decaying documents, bundled up and spilling over into the street. She sees that familiar look on their faces and feels hungry too, wishing they could all gorge on the sentences, right there in the street so that all of them could slip back into the shadows, or to whatever snippet they've preserved of the life they've left behind, but this time sated. She knows this in her heart, feels it like a physical pulse, that yes, all the lost souls, the strugglers, the refugees, retain hunger, for food, for knowledge, and for whatever larger memory that snippet belongs to. Who they were before, what they are now. The threads that bind as well as the ones that unravel.

Even after her brothers find work and they are able to rent more rooms in the same house, Baba's health continues to deteriorate. When she sees him bedridden, she fights hard to remember the tall, strong man of her childhood, telling her stories every evening which kept her wide eyed with amazement, no matter how tired he might have been after another long day at work. He doesn't say much now, the stroke robbing him of the storyteller's beautiful voice, these days little more than a harmattan whisper. She feels guilty whenever she has to leave him to go to her classes because she knows how much he will miss her. Not just the fact of her caring for him, taking care of the household to relieve some of the pressure from Ma, who she can tell is also growing more frail. It is more than that. Occasionally his eyes still light up when she tells him what she has been reading and how the words themselves are frequently not on the page. She describes the bundled manuscripts on College Street, their weight and texture. Her mind travels to the myriad stalls and booksellers these bundles seem to decry. She tells Baba they are like lonely travellers spilling their guts. And those guts smell of paper, of decay, but just underneath that of the glorious moment when pens first scratched paper and thoughts became something other than fleeting. When she says this to him she wants to believe that beyond the immobility, a thousand gestures, the smile and suspense of the storyteller's art are cascading down over the stroke-bound statuary. Once or twice she has seen him smile, or strain so hard to smile that every muscle seems to have gone into the effort. But of course it is the solitary tear she spots sneaking down his cheek which leaves the lasting impression.

With the money her brothers are earning they slowly furnish the house and establish themselves as a respectable presence in the neighbourhood. The professor's family. She knows this because she hears this, not only in the distant echo of that tough on the bus, but also over the years from the families of the pupils she now tutors in philosophy in their own homes.

Professor moshai kamon Aachen? Aapnara onek din shay para

te aachen.

And she thinks, yes, it's true, they have been living in the same house in that neighbourhood now for a long time. They have been there well over a decade, and though Baba hasn't worked for much of that time, everyone still calls him the professor. But she hears something else in this passing commentary, for it is not just her eyes which have grown expert at picking out geckos from darkness. In an apparently innocent enquiry linking her Baba's health with the amount of time his family has lived in that neighbourhood, she also hears the unspoken. The professor, an old man now, his health fading, and just one of his daughters still at home, still not married. She hears this even though it is never said because it is the one question books, and reading, can never answer. What will she do when he is no longer there? Mostly she can't bear to think of this eventuality, but sometimes the feeling is just overwhelming, that there is a bigger world out there than the reduced circuit of her studying, and teaching, and caring. And that world has spilled off the sentence and into the roiling entrails of some huge, uncontainable sensual beast. There is love and hate and ideas as yet undescribed, but all of it demands that she cast off the familiar cloak of these years, this neighbourhood, this family. It is unbearable and unnerving and she knows that if this is what is being said in passing, then behind the scenes eyes are being cast and other futures brokered. It is all a calculus and she knows this. Baba's failing health, her increasing age, and though she is from what others might call 'a good family', they are not wealthy. With each passing monsoon her prospects will only continue to diminish, along with Baba's health, and if one part of her would like nothing more than to stay, and stay here where she is needed, in dutiful attendance for the rest of time but loved and cared for too, she somehow yet knows that that will not be how her life will unfold. She knows that day will come when there is more than a solitary tear, when the torrent will flow through that door, into the narrow street where it will merge with the dissolved forms of the other lost souls, yet in her case with a destination—in-laws—and a designation—wife. When she thinks about such things they feel alarming, and appalling, and inevitable, so she tries to banish such thoughts from her mind. But that's the thing with inevitability. It can only be put off for so long. And she prays instead that when the day arrives that she will return home from one of her tutorials to find the rumour of strangers in her kitchen, of promises and commitments struck in her absence lingering in the air, that the man those promises lead to will appreciate just how much she has risked to be with him.

#

She is right. The local young tough's eyes aren't the only ones which are on her. Over the years she is spied by the acquaintance of another refugee family, and a report is made that there might be a suitable match with one of their boys, briefly visiting from Vilayet. The boy has expressed a wish to get married before he returns to London in a matter of weeks. His father has already passed and his mother is ailing, and in that broadly unspoken world of whisper and inference, this is taken as yet another sign of their 'compatibility'. Yet for all the thoughts she has banished, she never suspects until the day her Baba sits her down and says more to her in an hour than he has since all the trees were uprooted and the darkness crept beyond the Mukul. And though she is reluctant at first and cannot willingly comprehend the enormity of what is being proposed, she soon understands that this is not a dialectic. ...*At this time in her life... The last of his daughters... Will finally be able to rest knowing she is settled.* Once more, arrangements are made, yet the first time she sees him is on the day. She knows from her didis that he is handsome, but she knows very little else about him. And though they are sat within breath of one another, she hardly looks up all day. For all the clamour, and the pushmepullyou of the subsequent days, the respective clans lurching to-and-fro from despair to triumph, each one bargaining away another fraction of the past, she barely remembers looking up. The shroud there even when the material is removed. There for the three unhappy months spent in his family home, a garden compound in Berati where the only joy she feels is the sound of an occasional bandar scurrying up one of the coconut palms. And there, that terrible day, when she finally arrives at the portside in Bombay, gazing in awe at the gigantic hulk of the SS Himalaya and holding on to every last word which will delay her departure. Tasting the salt in everyone else's tears and feeling a sickness which never truly leaves her, even after the fog has cleared and her Skull Island has turned out to be a grim little place called England.

#

London, 1960s

'Ha kaare ki dakhos?'

She vaguely heard her husband's voice piercing the exhaust fumes. They were stood under the bridge by the busy road which led home from the market. He wanted to show her the best stalls with the cheapest food and the least unfriendly hawkers, but really all she was interested in was the young couple on the other side of the road who were openly kissing without a care in the world. She couldn't stop staring, for this was something new. People just didn't do this back home, or if they did, she'd never seen it. But this couple, who she guessed were no different in years to herself, seemed so uninhibited in their courtship display. It was embarrassing and wonderful all at once, and at some point her mouth must have fallen open while she stared. And actually that was something else that she'd already observed since arriving here just the previous week. No one looked at each other properly here, not the way she was used to. People looked, they stared all the time back home, on buses, in the street, in class, but it very rarely, if ever, meant anything bad, and more often than not the looks would be accompanied by a smile or a humorous comment about the bus, or the Chief Minister, or maybe just the outrageous hike in the price of fish at festival time. It was when they stopped looking that bad things occurred. When they would forget what another soul looked like and see instead shapes in tarpaulin marked for death. There had been so much forgetting around that time, and everyone knew someone who had forgotten, or been forgotten. The thought chilled her. She tried not to dwell on it. That had been so long ago and surely placing so many oceans between herself and the blood soaked memory of that little boy would help her forget? No matter, she felt it would always be there watching from the recesses like that gecko which had once slyly taken up residence with them. But time, and the physical distance, seemed to help and she was quickly able to return her thoughts to more recent events, to the looking rather than the forgetting. In fact, the only people who had really looked in the entire time since the S.S. Himalaya had left Bombay were the Customs Officials who had boarded the ship in the English Channel and the well dressed stranger who had been waiting to meet her at Tilbury. She'd felt him looking at her during the train journey to Victoria Station, which she guessed was named after the old Empress of India. And though this man wasn't entirely a stranger, in the sense that she had already spent an unhappy three months living with his extended family prior to making the journey, this was the first time that they had effectively been alone, away from that family. He had come back to London earlier than her for work and her last few weeks living with his family without his protective shroud had been a chastening experience. There were constant complaints about her food (too mild), her reading (too self-involved), even her language (too mannered) from brothers-in-law, cousins, even a *mashi*, such that by the time her passage to London had been booked and her documents had arrived, she was finally ready to strike out for that bigger life, however turbulent its waves or unspoken its alarm.

As she'd disembarked, she'd noted, with approval, his smart appearance and the hint of a smile as he gently chaperoned her onto what was called 'the boat train'. On that train itself, though it was late summer, she'd been struck by how much cooler the air in the carriages was compared to back home, though of course she'd first felt the cold at the port itself. That had been a shock, as far as she could tell nothing whatsoever to do with that word 'summer', but at least it had jolted her from the downcast torpor she had sunk into from more or less the moment the ship had left Bombay.

Now she felt a hand pulling her roughly by the arm and herding her away from the kissing couple.

'*E desh-e kokhono eta koro na*,' chided her husband, relaxing his grip on her arm as soon as she'd stopped staring. He didn't say anything else on their way home but she could tell he was embarrassed. She found it quite funny, trying hard not to laugh so as to spare his feelings. But her mind was full of questions. How could she possibly have known that you didn't stare in this country? And if that was the case, why hadn't her husband warned her about this beforehand? What must he be thinking now, she wondered, about this woman he'd also made a commitment to? The professor's daughter who'd turned out to be little more than a village idiot, albeit a well educated one.

This time she felt a little stab of indignation. What was she supposed to do? Pretend this kind of thing was normal? Though by the time they'd reached their front door she found herself nursing other questions. How long had it taken her husband to stop staring when *he'd* first arrived? Or was this sort of thing already normal for him? She realised there and then that she barely knew this man and was thankful he'd loosened his grip almost immediately. The other thing she couldn't quite shake from her mind was how unfriendly the hawkers were in the local market. When her husband had paid for the potatoes, the trader hadn't smiled or said thank you. And it was little better when they did speak. In any case she couldn't understand a word they were saying, the sounds so unlike any of the English she'd ever heard spoken before. It seemed to come from the back of the throat, an afterthought to a curse. Then again, what did she expect? This was all entirely new to her. Why would the language she encountered be any different?

#

So she did what she'd always previously done when faced with mounting questions, ones that required some investigation. She sought out the nearest library. How different could an English library realistically be from the ones she had frequented back home? Those places were at least somewhat familiar to her, and at that moment, familiarity felt like the most precious thing on earth.

This had the additional benefit, she felt, of getting her

away from her husband's cousins and one of his brothers, who they were sharing a tiny flat with. As far as she could tell, neither the brother nor at least one of the cousins was working as they just hung around the house all day. The flat was on the ground floor and whilst it had a little garden, she could only avoid them for so long out there. Already she knew from the bombast and the seeming lack of regard for anyone, or anything, considered an 'outsider' (to their family), that these two idlers would expect to be waited on hand and foot if she made the mistake of staying in. That was more or less what had happened back home during those unhappy weeks after her husband had returned to London for work and she had been left alone with the rest of his clan while awaiting her travel documents so that she could join him. Most nights she had cried herself to sleep, praying that the morning would bring the mercy of an envelope addressed to her. Just the memory of that brief time alone with his in laws made her shudder. So she made the decision to seek out the library, which would at least, she hoped, offer some respite from her in-laws. Her mind was made up after enduring several sessions of their boorishness around the nightly dinner table, when the greatness of her in-laws' family would be repeatedly invoked over *bhat, tarkari* and a sudden improvement in their dietary regime (her mild food again, though confusingly for her, this time evidently a good thing). It was a greatness that wasn't immediately apparent to her in her surroundings: in the cramped formica off which they ate, or the insatiable coin-slot meters which nonetheless seemed helpless to prevent the local variant of load shedding. Or in the thin white bread which substituted for *roti* but fooled no one. Or in the sounds of their upstairs neighbours, so close that they might as well have been sitting there too.

Hearing the nightly bombast of her husband's relatives, though not, mercifully, of her husband, her mind quickly wandered elsewhere. She thought about the last time she'd shared such a small space with so many people, and how different it was to this. Back then there had been laughter rather than boastfulness, and it was gentle, even when the bodies in that room were spent from their daily exertions, or wracked with such exhaustion, or anguish, that they could have been forgiven for bypassing a little gentility.

His relatives, though, were delusional. That much seemed clear to her, even in such a short space of time. All their big talk about the money they were going to make, the palaces they would build, and the honour that would bring, yet when she looked around what she saw was flaking plaster and some kind of a damp patch spreading outwards from one corner of the room.

The next day she ventured out on her own for the first time since she'd arrived. This time she walked up the road in the opposite direction to the market. Her heart was pounding even though there was hardly anyone on the street. It felt incredibly empty, and quiet, nothing at all like the streets back home, and this just made her feel even more exposed. The few people she saw barely looked at her, and when an older man said something to her as he passed, she remembered her husband's advice and made sure to look away. It was only when she'd carried on a little further and the man had already disappeared from sight that she realized he'd been wishing her a 'good morning'. And she felt briefly irritated by her husband all over again. She decided, for the next little while at least, and in his workbound absence, that he wasn't necessarily the best judge of what was good for her. She would ask the next person she saw for directions to the library. Or at least she would try to ask. She'd never really spoken English before. It was a language she had been made to study, and read, for her School Final Matriculation exams, and at one time she had memorized large portions of Shylock's lament and Portia's 'quality of mercy' speech for that very purpose. But to speak it, and to speak it with people who spoke such a strange sounding English, if the sullen hawkers were any sort of guide, was something else entirely. She felt her heart racing the nearer she got to the next pedestrian. It was hard to look her in the eye (against her husband's wishes) and form the words and smile all at once, and just for a moment she thought she might cry instead, the whole thing just too much to manage in one go. She felt the words slipping back down her throat, swallowed whole by some vaguely unspecified shame.

'Yes, my dear? Are you alright? You seem a little unsteady there.'

She felt bad for doubting her husband. This time the act of staring had almost cost her her balance, and she felt her cheeks burning with embarrassment. Perhaps she *was* that village idiot, all at sea in the big new city. No, that wouldn't do. She'd travelled alone thousands of miles just to be here. The least that journey deserved was a simple sentence. Gathering herself up with a supreme effort, she mentally rehearsed the phrases before blurting out:

'Liebri please. Good morning. You know where?'

The other woman considered what she'd just heard for a moment, then smiled.

'Mornin', my dear. Library? You're in luck, my dear. It's just there,' she said, pointing to a rather grand looking building a few yards away. When she looked to where the woman was pointing, it reminded her of the old colonial buildings in Dalhousie Square, and she was surprised when she was able to walk straight in without first being vetted at the door by some pompous official.

She'd smiled and nodded repeatedly to thank the woman for her help, and she somehow doubted her husband's relatives would have done the same in her position. Actually, she doubted they even knew about the library, although they'd been here far longer than her. Also, the woman was the first Black person she'd ever met and this, coupled with her own stuttering attempts to communicate in a foreign tongue, made it a morning of firsts. A double first, which pleased her no end.

#

When she took the book up to the counter, the woman sitting there asked her for her ticket, and she felt the embarrassment return. But the woman was patient, even if she wasn't as friendly as the lady she'd met earlier, and in fact seemed a little surprised when the form she had given her to fill out was quickly completed and handed back to her without any assistance. That wasn't nearly as hard as speaking, she thought, nonetheless pleased that the librarian was clearly impressed by her choice of novel and appeared as though she wanted to say something to her about it.

'Dickens?'

She nodded and smiled in lieu of the words that just wouldn't come.

'Have you read any of his other books?'

Again she nodded and smiled, but just couldn't bring herself to say, 'And Shakespeare, and Tagore, and Plato, and Socrates, and Bankimchandra, and the Upanishads. And I know what this must look like, a strange woman standing here in front of you smiling and nodding like a village idiot. But the truth is, she crossed oceans to get here, and long before that she swallowed libraries whole, ingesting formulae, and philosophy, and the careworn circles of history. And even before that she knew that sometimes guns were stored away along with knowledge, and that both could bring great empires to their knees. And she knew that if nodding and smiling wasn't necessarily the same thing as 'yes', then her answer would still be 'yes'. This strange woman understood all too well that opening line, because she'd already, in her short life, known both. The best of times, the worst of times.'

Afterwards she was grateful the words hadn't come, that their stored up frustrations still belonged exclusively to her mother tongue. It would have been unfair to say any of this to the librarian, she thought, especially as she seemed to approve of her reading choice. She nodded and smiled once more, leaving the library with the book in one hand and the newly acquired library card in another.

Mercifully there was no one in when she came back to the flat, and so by the time her husband returned from work she had already made some inroads into the book. Revolutionary Paris felt very far from here. Upstairs, the neighbours were arguing again. This seemed to happen at least once every day, but a mixture of that coarse London brogue she'd first heard in the market and the ceiling partition made the sounds utterly indecipherable. At any rate, she thought, in spite of the raised voices, there was no real menace here, and she felt grateful for that. As indeed she was for the small dictionary she found tucked away in one corner of their bedroom. It seemed to be the only other book anywhere in evidence in this flat, and its presence allowed her to look up those words which were unfamiliar and continue with her stop start progress through the story.

She remembered his question, how, in spite of his obvious tiredness when he'd come home, he had asked it with that same hint of a smile she'd spied when he'd met her at the docks.

'*Shara din eta kohcho?*'

She nodded again, placing her library card as a de facto bookmark and about to put the book away when she noticed her husband shaking his head, that same smile urging her to continue. She felt slightly guilty for underestimating him. Perhaps he'd also seen how bored she was, enveloped by the nightly bombast? At any rate she was happier now, carefully feeling her way across the bloody entrails of another time, another place, a foreign tongue. And in that simple gesture, encouraging her to continue, she saw perhaps that this man might not have to be such a stranger after all.

#

She could tell the librarian was surprised when she returned the book just four days later.

'That didn't take long,' she said, adjusting her glasses to make sure the person handing the book back was the same one as the rather confused young woman she recalled from earlier in the week who had taken it out.

'I liked it very much,' came the instant reply, the phrase repeatedly rehearsed on her way over. At one point she was saying it at precisely the moment that the same man she'd studiously ignored the other day happened to pass. This time he stopped, tipped his hat and said, 'Well I liked saying it to you very much, so I'll say it again—Good morning.'

It was a little confusing, she thought, as she hadn't been talking to the man, but she smiled and nodded anyway before resuming her protocol mantra.

She liked the smell of the books on the shelves, and in any case the library was warmer than the flat. Also, she had spotted a number of quite expansive looking dictionaries in one corner, and carrying them home would be difficult, particularly as she had no bag to put them in. But in all honesty she just didn't want to be home unless her husband was there, for she had no desire to endure more bombast or clean up after her slovenly in-laws, who seemed to regard her presence as the next best thing to a live-in maid. That was something else she'd learned the other night, after she'd closed the book and drawn her husband a little closer. Everything was a fresh language, even those bits which might have been familiar, so the pressure of thumbs pressing on a broad back, or the caress of tongues, just seemed to flow from her confidence starting to return for the first time since being in this place, and into some throwaway remark about 'kaajer lok' also being entitled to pleasure. Her husband had looked across at her then and told her, with a very serious expression on his face, that in this country no-one said 'servant' any more. The word was 'maid'. And she'd inwardly sighed, chiding herself for ever thinking that the journey from strangeness to intimacy, real intimacy at that, not just what they'd been doing, would be anything other than awkward, and painstaking. She also knew in that moment how much the success of such a transition, and thus her future happiness, depended upon her. Yes he seemed to be a good man, and he was certainly a man, but unless she could get him away from the pervasive influence of his family, she feared he would also remain ensnared in their delusions, forever a diminished version of the man he could have been. She thought about the last few months, the agony of leaving her own family and joining his; the torment of waiting for documents and daily having her confidence undermined by his relatives; the resumption of that sourness even after she'd made the long, lonely voyage here. And then she considered the all too rare pleasures during that time, each of which had accrued from being fully immersed in her surroundings. Staring at the kissing English couple, her own faltering attempts at dialogue, or brief exploration of the neighbourhood, and of course the absorption of a new language, its physical tangents and sensual properties. It dawned on her that the first major shift that needed to happen was a temporal one. The key to any future happiness lay in what she did now. How she lived, how she thought, and in that sense, if in no other, this called for a change of season, from past to present. Considering both the bombastwallahs and fonder memories of her own family, she resolved that how they lived then would have no bearing on what she did now. And even if it did, that she would still be present in her present.

#

The dictionaries help, though of course she resents her initially frequent recourse to them and the disruption this causes to her reading pleasure. Gradually though, over the course of the next few weeks, she finds that some of the more unfamiliar words—'gridiron', 'monopolized', 'comestible' - have started to resonate. She writes them down on a piece of paper which the librarian has very kindly given her, and they become familiar. She enjoys her days in the library, practising 'not so much' along with 'I liked this very much' in answer to the librarian's frequent enquiries about her latest choice of reading material. There are a couple of days when she doesn't feel so well and stays at home, after which the librarian seems genuinely happy to see her when she comes in on the third day holding the book of Maupassant short stories which she has devoured while laid up in bed.

'Well hello there, stranger,' she says. 'For one horrible moment I thought we'd lost you, my dear. So how did you get on with this one then?'

She smiles and nods, adding, 'I liked this very much, but some not so much,' thinking how nice it is to be missed, even for a moment.

It is still frustrating though, not to be able to converse properly, to say to the librarian that although she loves 'Boule de Suif' and many of the other stories, which convey an incredible sensitivity, she loathes the selfishness of the nobility, the way they first exploit the poor girl's kindness and then further degrade her for their own ends. 'Not so much' doesn't really feel adequate to this task.

#

The seasons do indeed begin to change, from summer to autumn and then into the frostbitten, smog-laden murk of winter. It is a brutal shift, one particular morning marked by fog so intense that visibility becomes a question of faith rather than formula. Sometimes she reads on the newspaper hoardings outside one of the nearby shops about people whose luck has run out in the gloom, faith misplaced along with their footing and lives abruptly curtailed in manholes or under traffic. Tragic lost souls, she thinks, knowing that even when the fog disperses the loss will continue. She recalls all too clearly the suffering of another time, unburdened by fog. The nights marked by fear and the days by scorching heat. That little boy in the tarpaulin, lost to the madness of strangers, and, still just a girl herself, her own desperate efforts to dry off his blood and offer some comfort. She knows that trauma brings its own seasons, of grief, despair and the fog that will not lift. And when she reads these headlines they conjure the acrid smell of fear congealed in scabs as much as the incomprehension of bodies lost to the elements. It upsets her every time and in another way makes her doubly determined to hold on to the slightly expanded circuit she has been building up these past few months.

She has her routine now, a little more sure-footed than before, taking in first the market and its often unfriendly traders, a back and forth down and then back up the busy road to leave the shopping in the kitchen for later. And then, once the groaning bags of fruit and vegetables have been dropped off, she heads back out and in the opposite direction to the library, where she is known, and where the seasons have indeed changed, from Dickens to Maupassant and now onto the Russians. It is lovely, she thinks, having somewhere quiet to read and learn. And cry, which she does more than once, tucked away unobtrusively in one corner, wracked by the beauty and the desolation of ultimately doomed love, its convulsions and torment hewn from the guts of families, societies, entire worlds aflame. She cries for the courtiers and for the peasants, for Tolstoy's Natasha and for Pierre, for poor, doomed Anna Karenina and for the system that condemns her. In the depths of winter she encounters Raskolnikov, her eyes welling up again, some distant echo in his nihilism of all those lost young souls from back home with the faraway look of madness in their eyes. She is certain of one thing though: the killing has always taken place, and as ever, it is largely pointless. More than once she thinks about telling the librarian this, but the words just don't come, even though she has been referring less and less to the assorted dictionaries.

#

By the time the factory gates hove into view, she feels she has greatly expanded her knowledge of the English language. Or at least of its great works of literature. She has been thinking about that on the bus this morning, her stomach knotted tight in the habitual fashion prior to any major journey. She has been in London several months and whilst she has known that this day would come, when she would have to go out to work, she perhaps wasn't expecting it to be like this. In her mind she had pictured an office of some kind, something more in keeping with her level of education, but when she had mentioned this to her husband he had just laughed, telling her that as far as the English were concerned, she knew nothing and should be grateful for whatever work was available. This stings her when he says it so nonchalantly, and she is still smarting from its implications of ignorance and servility as she gets off the bus with her husband.

It is a large electrical engineering plant near the dock-yards in Woolwich, where her husband has already been working for nearly six months. She doesn't know exactly what he does but recalls a little pride in his expression when he'd tried to explain to her that he was on 'piecework and differentials'.

She is struck by how busy it is. She hasn't seen this many people gathered in one place since she left India, people frantically lining up to use the lifts or placing cards in boxes. And everyone with one eye on the clock.

Her 'interview' as such consists of some awkward silence in a small upstairs office overlooking a vast shop floor while she tries to explain to the two men sitting opposite her that she doesn't really speak English but can read it very well. The men look at each other before one of them leans over to pull a book off the sparsely populated shelf on the far wall. He hands her the book, an engineering manual, and asks her to read.

'You want I read?' she checks, slightly embarrassed by the whole situation.

'Yes,' he says. 'Any page, wherever you like.'

And so she starts to read, still wondering if this is some kind of a joke that only they are privy to.

'Electrical and electronics engineering originally comprised electrical power, illumination, and both the telephone and the telegraph but has since moved into many other spheres of everyday____'

The second man stops her with a quick gesture of his hand. He is smiling, in fact both men are, and seeing this her spirits sink, thinking that yes, this is all one big joke to them, with her as the punchline.

'Well I think we've heard quite enough,' the man says.

'You know we have girls here from just up the road who can barely read the road signs, though they all seem to know their way to the canteen. And then here's you, all the way from the other side of the world, and you read perfectly.'

She wasn't sure what to think. It still wasn't clear whether she'd passed the interview or even what the job was. In fact she was only here now because her husband had arranged it.

'Anyway, you'll be working under my supervision, and if need be, I will cut short my own lunch hour to sit and talk with you so that your spoken English improves. Now how does that sound?'

She nods and smiles, as per habit, and is then slightly surprised when the man who has been speaking outstretches a hand for her to shake. She feels the other man's eyes on her as she leaves, wondering perhaps whether it is her sari he is looking at. It is not the first time she has had that feeling. Sometimes in the market she can sense the barrow boys staring at her once the goods are paid for and her back is turned. Initially she thought it must be the novelty for them of seeing such delicately embroidered cloth. But now she's not so sure. Besides, she already knows from her circuit that the people who wish to be friendly, or even the ones who are just curious, will try to talk to her. A smile, and a greeting, or a polite enquiry. The silent stares however seem to belong to another part of the local language, that bit stored in the back of a throat like a curse. The man whose hand she has shaken seems nice enough, but she's not sure about his colleague. Still, she thinks, it is good to be a little careful when finding one's feet, be that in dense fog or bustling factories.

#

Later, when she tells her husband about the interview, he laughs, and tells her in return that when he'd had his own interview, the two bosses in question hadn't been at all interested in his experience of using arc welders or angle grinders. Sizing him up they had simply wanted to know whether he played hockey (answer: 'yes') and whether he'd be available for training the following week in preparation for an upcoming company wide tournament (answer: again, 'yes'). He tells her that to English eyes, all Indians are either hockey players, or factory fodder, or troublemakers, depending on how big or small they are, and how much eye contact they maintain during the interview. And he smiles.

'So which one are you?' she asks.

'All three and maybe none of the above,' he answers, and this time they both laugh. They are sat in the canteen and two nearby English workers look over at them when they hear the laughter. This time she is left with the distinct sense that the English are the ones feeling excluded from the joke. The beauty of another tongue, she thinks, the present never purely lived in one register.

#

Rising and returning with the dark, struggling onto the

packed buses, the votive properties of punch cards, of clocking in, and out, of shop floors and lunchtime language classes, become her new routine. But though it is tiring and there are days when she just doesn't want to be up so early, she accedes to the discipline of it, just as she had once made herself study by candlelight, and mop brows, and clean blood, and travel another circuit, and cook and care in a city far hungrier than this one. This is the arithmetic of her life now and it sometimes makes her laugh when she is asked by the other girls in the canteen how she is finding it in London, as if this is the first great city she has ever lived in. But she knows their intentions are good, so she smiles and tells them, in her rapidly improving English:

'Not bad, but you know, some of these men on the bus in the morning, they don't smell so good.'

And they will all laugh, in a way that she has noted the English like to do, clutching their sides and giving one another sidelong glances.

They are nice girls, though. In fact, most of the people here are friendly, and she feels very few of those stares she has experienced down the market. Even the bosses like her, and they don't always seem so favourably disposed to everyone around here. She has seen other girls, boys, even some of the older men and women, shouted at for one reason or another, and whenever this happens, she feels relieved that she, at least, can mourn and lament her life's myriad sorrows in another tongue. She has seen the men wander off darkly muttering the curses of underlings the world over, and the women reduced to tears in the time honoured fashion. Yet with her, there is no such rancour.

She recalls one incident from quite early on, just a week or so after starting work at the factory. Her husband had bought her a second hand coat in anticipation of those cold, wintry mornings, but the lining was threadbare and a portion of it had, unbeknownst to her, been hanging down over her sari. This must have caught the eye of her immediate boss, who had pointed this out to her during their lunchtime language tutorial, and he had seemed genuinely concerned for her welfare. That same day she saw him berate another young girl for wearing torn stockings and yet another for clocking in a few minutes late.

Within a year her English has vastly improved, to the point that she is able to enjoy a joke with her boss about the condition of that old coat.

'We thought you were going to freeze to death,' he says.

'I didn't know how else to tell you, your country is cold,' she replies, smiling.

'Anyway,' he carries on. 'You dress so elegantly and that coat just didn't suit you.'

'I think it is the winter that doesn't suit me,' she says, still holding a handful of files which Mr. Cook, her boss, has given her to take to the Head of Engineering on the fourth floor. He has been impressed with how well her spoken English has been coming along, and has made it his personal mission to maximise her opportunities to speak what he strongly believes is the 'correct' form of English. To that end, and noting how well she had read when asked to do so during the interview and how unflustered she is by written materials, he has overseen her relocation from the shopfloor with its preponderance of what he considers to be the 'wrong' sort of English-speaker, and into his office, where she takes letters, ferries messages and files between the bosses on the various floors and continues to surprise him with her rapidly expanding turn of phrase. She finds this endlessly amusing, and wonders what Cook would think if he knew she had read Pygmalion in one sitting during an especially fruitful trip to the library not long before she'd started this job. She feels it best to keep this information to herself though, as she has already seen with her husband how touchy some people can get if they feel in some way outmanoeuvred by so much as a stray remark. Still, she thinks, making the short journey to the fourth floor, they have been getting along better than ever since that remark, the one she'd made about servants deserving pleasure too.

She wonders how Cook would react if he knew she was a philosophy graduate and that her father was a highly respected philosophy professor in his part of the world. She is no flower seller, she thinks, transporting the files. It is a fine line, a delicate balancing act between appearing educated, yet somehow incomplete since that education had not taken place here, and exuding the sort of pride or haughtiness which to the wrong eyes might seem a little 'naak ucha'. She knows that's a common complaint around here, has frequently heard arguments begin in the canteen or while waiting for the lift or the bus with the accusatory, 'You think you're better than me, don't you?'

Recently, though, while passing a table where some of her old shopfloor colleagues were sat in the canteen, she is sure that she has heard the accusation directed at her, for the first time.

'Think you're better than us now, do you?'

She pretended not to hear as she made her way over to where her husband was sat, waiting for her. But as she did, the follow up was undeniable.

'Yeah, look at her. Carrying on like Lady Muck. Wasn't so long ago she couldn't even look you in the eye or say hello. Not sure her fella would be too thrilled with the way Cook looks at her either. Randy old goat.'

She feels disgusted by the inference. She knows from their many lunchtime conversations that it is not like that, that Cook is married, with older children, and in any case that was never what it was about for Professor Higgins. But it's pointless trying to argue with people like this because whatever she says will just confirm whatever they have already chosen to believe. And just as she has never been Eliza Doolittle, she has equally never been a snob. That luxury, she knows, is reserved for the comfortably settled, not the recently uprooted, though of course her husband's family try their utmost to disprove her theory. In their case though, she has realized, somewhat begrudgingly, that the bombast derives from genuinely having lost everything. Some of them had been park bench refugees, and not all of his vast, sprawling extended family had made it across the border. Several of his relatives, including his older sister, had been lost to the madness and the butchery, and in the void this must have opened up for all of them, she could see how self delusion might have crept in with its own attractions. Their conversations bequeathed pomposity because the lives they had been left with were otherwise so bereft. It doesn't mean she approves of, or enjoys, any of it but she can see that there is at least a thread here unpicked from the stitch of a terrible wound, never fully healed.

The canteen snipers, on the other hand, seem to belong to another tribe altogether. Theirs is the long harboured complaint at the back of the throat, the sullen stare, the unsubstantiated rumour. She senses this clan too in the men who sometimes hawk phlegm not far from where she walks on the pavement. Smiles, even half-smiles, rarely play on their lips when they see her shopping for fruit and vegetables with her husband in the market. When they return home, both her and her husband are no longer surprised to find that the barrowboys have smuggled rotten produce in with their other purchases, yet if she tries to handle any of the fruits beforehand, a loud, guttural voice will reliably inform her:

'Don't touch the food! In this country we don't poke and prod everything.'

She wants to say, 'You don't wash your hands either,' but stops herself when she sees the other traders looking at her most unsympathetically.

Her husband sees and hears it too, and when this happens she can feel him bristling with rage. He is bigger than most of these traders, but he is alone and she senses that for now at least he would prefer to be seen as a hockey player to either of the alternatives they had previously joked about.

#

For all of that though, she remains popular in the factory. The snipers are in a minority, everyone else responding to her ready smile and unfailingly polite manner. She is known by the sobriquet 'sunshine', which she likes to think is a comment on her sunny disposition, though of course she has also overheard a less favourable explanation from one of the snipers.

'It's 'cos she thinks the sun shines out of her arse.'

She pays no mind, for just as she had found her feet once the winter's dense fog had lifted, she now stumbled far less over language, even its more careless or spiteful outbursts. The words don't describe *her* but rather a figment of someone else's unhappy imagination. Besides, it is Friday, the week is over, and her husband has promised to take her to the late showing at the Lewisham Odeon of the new James Bond film, 'Goldfinger'.

#

The same flat but a different set of neighbours upstairs. There are still occasionally raised voices but now they are accompanied, more often than not, by the sounds of loud music which do their best to wake her from her hard-won slumber. She considers it a minor miracle that the little boy she lies next to seems blissfully unaware. He is just a few months old and he is a quiet baby. Watching him sleep through the rumbling interruptions from upstairs, she knows it won't be long before they have to leave this flat. It was in any case too small even before the arrival of her first born, and whilst she has grown quite fond of this neighbourhood, some of its market traders aside, perhaps it will be nice, she thinks, to go somewhere new, with a little more space for her son to play in and for herself to breathe.

Leaving work wasn't easy, though. She recalls how sad she was when it came to her final day, her eyes welling up when she saw the amount of money and presents which had been collected for her, it turned out, from every floor in the building, including the one with the snipers. She really hadn't been expecting anything, and is even more taken aback when one of the girls who she recognizes as part of the sniper quartet, stops her by the lifts and tells her, one hand placed tenderly on her arm:

'We're really sorry to see you go. I wish you all the best, my love, and the little'un too.'

A strange lot, the English. Even the worst of the tribe sometimes not that at all. Then again, she thought, was it so different back home? Ordinary people often showed themselves to be far better than their so-called leaders. The girl's hand on her arm takes her back all those years to the memory of the tough and his reassuring presence on the bus. And then she's gone, though the steady stream of gifts continues throughout the day.

So many presents in fact that in the end Cook had to hire a car to transport the gifts, along with her and her husband, back to their flat. He'd warmly shaken her husband's hand and when it came time to say goodbye to her, she'd seen something in his face which oddly enough reminded her of her own father on her wedding day. Almost inconsolable grief nonetheless folded into the careworn creases of experience. Something else too. A father's immense pride in his daughter, in her courage and determination that this life will be lived no matter what. Not simply endured, but lived, really lived.

#

As to 'where' they will go, she's not entirely happy that that decision seems to have been taken out of their hands. According to her husband they are on some kind of 'waiting list' and will be notified as soon as a suitable property becomes available. She has read some of the stories in the local press about multiple occupancies in bomb damaged or neglected homes and of the dangers of homelessness, but she still struggles to connect these unsavoury details with her own circumstances. Besides, she thinks, 'homelessness' doesn't seem to mean quite the same thing here, and surely her husband, of all people, would understand that? She knows he has slept on park benches after Partition, as have at least two of his siblings. She knows this because he chose to share the information with her one evening after they had been to see another late showing in the local cinema and had encountered a man begging for coins under the same bridge where, some years back, not long after she'd first arrived in London, she had once been shocked by the sight of young lovers kissing. But if she was by now used to the frequently amorous displays on offer during the course of an average night out, then the sight of an Englishman begging still caught her by surprise.

'He must be homeless,' she told her husband, sad for the man but relieved he couldn't understand her.

'No, he's got a home, it's drink he lacks,' said her husband.

She felt he was being a little dismissive of the man's plight, and they walked the rest of the way home in silence. Yet once they were indoors, something in him must have relented and they communicated once again in that language which by now and in those moments was only theirs. She wondered whether every young couple felt this way? Or perhaps her husband was just then feeling particularly emboldened after watching the exploits of that suave British spy on the huge Odeon screen? Afterwards, lying next to her, his eyes gazing straight up at the ceiling, he told her in a very matter of fact way that he had once been homeless, after his entire family had been forced to flee from their ancestral home. He told her about the sister he had lost, and about others too, aunts, cousins, uncles. He told her how those members of his family she had been so unhappy staying with before her journey here, and those various family members who continued to live with them, on and off, now that they were here, well, they were the lucky ones. And he mentioned an older brother who had more or less herded them all to safety during those times of mob and madness. A brother who had come here with nothing, yet in a few short years had reunited several of the brothers and cousins in London. She remembered there had been no joy in his voice when he was telling her this, but under the deadpan, and in the darkness, she had sensed just a hint of pride. She remembered this brother now as being one of her chief tormentors during that unhappy period living with his family prior to coming here. He had never smiled at her or tried to make her feel welcome in any way. Instead she recalled his nightly complaints about her cooking and her introspection, at which point it suddenly dawned on her that the first time she'd heard the local barrowboys' complaint lodged in the back of the throat had been in another tongue entirely. The recollection made her shudder. This brooding, sullen, joyless man who yet somehow was the saviour of his entire clan. One other detail had stayed with her. When she had asked her husband where this brother was now, or what he did, the response was startlingly vague.

'*O aashe aar o jai, kintu bhagwan jaane o ki kare.*'

Her husband had fallen asleep not long after, yet she herself spent a fitful night, unnerved by what he had said.

He comes and he goes, but only god knows what he does.

#

On any given day, she can walk into her living room to find as many as six other people sprawled across it in various states of repose. Two of her husband's cousins, one of his brothers, though mercifully not *that* one, and now a couple of nephews, and a niece as well. They are friendlier than before, at least recognizing her presence now that she is the mother of a little boy. But already, even with her first born still just a toddler, she finds herself worrying that if he spends too long in this room around these people then he will grow up to be just like them, so casually dismissive of the outside world and, curiously she thinks, considering their all too recent transition from refugees to citizens, of the facts of their own existence. She doesn't want her son to ever be this inward looking, or for that matter so evidently terrified of the kitchen, for that is the one room she is guaranteed to be left alone in.

In another way though, this has been a blessing. Whenever she considers going back to work, she reminds herself of the look her son gives her on those rare occasions that she hands him over to the niece to hold while she uses the privy or prepares some food. It is not fear exactly, more confusion, and it is unbearable to her even for a moment. She has also recently met one of the upstairs' neighbours in the narrow hallway separating their flats. At the time she had been struggling to manoeuvre the pram through the constricted space between her door and the front door.

'Let me help you with that, my dear,' said the voice coming from just in front of her. Looking up, she sees a smartly dressed young woman, wearing a skirt cut just above the knee in a style she has been observing a fair amount of late. She nods, grateful for the assistance, noting the fullness of the woman's smile as she helps her readjust the position of the pram. It is a stroke of luck, she thinks, encountering this person just as she was also heading out.

'I'm Carol, from upstairs,' the woman tells her, extending the darkest hand with the most intricate nails that she has ever seen.

'Pleased to meet you,' she replies, unsure exactly how she should introduce herself or whether she should tell her her name. Nobody used first names back home, and aside from her *daknaam*, which was for close family only, the only other name she could think of right then was 'sunshine'.

#

Their meetings in the hallway become more frequent. She often times her outings to coincide with the start or the end of one of Carol's shifts, precisely so that she can talk, however briefly, with someone other than her husband's relatives.

It transpires that Carol, who is training to be a nurse, is originally from one of the smaller islands, and that her fiancé (which is a new word for her), who also lives upstairs, is from the big island. She nods and smiles, pretending to know the difference, but it is only after several more conversations that she is able to ascertain that Carol is from Grenada and her fiancé, Everton, is from Jamaica. She hears how softly Carol speaks, looking at her son, asleep in the pram, or on other occasions, when he is awake, quietly waiting for their daily outing, how lovingly Carol looks at him, calling him 'the little Buddha' and smiling that dazzling smile of hers.

In that instant it occurs to her that none of her husband's relatives have ever been so affectionate around her son. She can't recall a single gesture or sound from them to suggest warmth or love towards the little boy. A stark reminder too of why she has not gone back to work or tried to find another job since the birth. When she can't even count on relations (albeit her husband's) to help look after the boy, then why would she trust a stranger? Besides, where would the money for that come from? This has been troubling her for a while, that in spite of the fact that her husband is the only one who is regularly working and of how frugal she is with expenditures, there never seems to be any money left over at the end of each month. When she asks her husband where the money goes, he tells her:

'*E takar desh-e patiedichi. Aasholay odeh khub darkar.*'

But it makes her think, what about our needs here? She understands the impulse to send remittance payments to those less fortunate relatives who are still struggling back in the old country. She had done so herself when working, never forgetting the sacrifices her family had made to secure her passage over here in the first place. Yet she had also never lost sight of the other half of that equation, which demanded that this new life in Britain be a success so that all those sacrifices would be worthwhile. Her husband, she felt, tended to forget that he also has a family beyond his sprawling clan, and that that family has its own struggles to think about.

She has heard that tone of voice before, that night when her husband had first told her about his own struggles post-Partition. But if at the time she had detected a note of defiance, pride even, in his account of those dark days, she now realized that what she had actually been hearing was the sound of gratitude, and its lesser cousin, deference. It was clearer now. The remittances were part of some ongoing debt of gratitude her husband felt duty bound to honour, to his family, above all to the cussed facts of its survival. She knows then that he will never say anything to the idlers in her front room, or imagine that this life, here, could matter as much as some fabled here-after in a mythical place called 'home'. She picks up her son and holds him close, enjoying the gentle pressure of his breathing as his tiny back arches up and down against the palm of her hand. Now matters, she thinks. Every bit as much as then.

#

Carol comes back holding a tray with two cups of tea and a packet of Peek Freans' biscuits.

They are upstairs, in Carol's front room, sitting at either end of a sofa which still has a plastic covering draped over it. This is the first time she has ever been inside another flat to the one she has never quite got used to sharing with her husband's relatives. She had run into Carol, as was her wont, the previous day and been invited by her neighbour to 'drop by' the following day, which she was informed was Carol's day off.

'It'll be nice to talk without any of the men around to spoil things,' Carol had said with a conspiratorial smile. 'Besides, it's so cold in that corridor and that can't be good for the little Buddha, for his peace of mind.' She didn't really know what Carol had meant by that, but decided it would make a welcome change from her usual routine of avoiding the in-laws and agreed to knock on Carol's door once she had had breakfast the following morning. To her this flat seems bigger, more spacious, even though it has more furniture. Not just the sofa they are sat on but two other chairs with armrests and cushions as well as a small side table. Her eyes pick out a bouquet of artificial flowers resting in a porcelain vase in one corner, and just next to that a magnificently appointed wooden sideboard with a built in cabinet and some kind of contraption on the middle shelf. She must have still been staring at it when Carol set the tray down on the side table.

'Ah, so I see you were admiring the Blue Spot,' observed her neighbour, opening the packet of biscuits and helping herself to the first couple.

'It is beautiful,' she replies, still quite unsure of herself or of how she should respond to her neighbour's hospitality. She follows Carol's lead and takes two of the biscuits which are lightly dusted with sugar. Her son is sat on the carpet, tracing its swirling patterns with his index finger. He seems quietly absorbed in this task, occasionally turning himself around when the patterns dictate, but otherwise, true to form, a perfectly serene presence within crawling distance of the two women.

'That's more like it,' says Carol, watching a sugar coated half smile playing on her neighbour's lips.

'Have as many as you like,' she says, pushing the biscuits towards her.

'We have this back home too,' she tells Carol.

'The Blue Spot?'

'Yes, the biscuits. But back home we call them 'Peek Freans'.'

Carol laughs.

'Just for a moment I thought you meant the Blue Spot. And then I thought, 'she truly is a person of mystery', before I realized you were talking about the biscuits, my dear.'

'Yes, of course. What did you think I was talking about?'

'Ah well, never mind,' says Carol, dipping one of the biscuits into the still hot tea. 'So tea and biscuits, it's something you do back home too?'

'Oh yes, very much so,' she says, for some reason wondering why her old boss, Mr. Cook, had never encouraged her to moisten the biscuits like this during their many tea breaks and lunchtime language classes together. Feeling more comfortable, although she is still sitting on the edge of the sofa, she continues:

'We had Peek Freans biscuit factory near where we were living. They opened it in a place called Dum Dum where they used to have a factory that made special bullets.'

Carol places her cup back down on the table.

'So let me get this straight,' she says. 'You're telling me they used to make bullets in this place where they now make these biscuits?'

'First they try to give us a scare, then when they see that doesn't work, they give us sweets instead.'

'Lord of Mercy,' says Carol. A moment later, kissing her teeth: 'Raas.'

That's not a word she knows, but she has heard that sound before, the one her neighbour has just made, while on her daily circuit with the pram. She wonders whether her son has heard this too, the sound of teeth being sucked, often after some kind of argument has taken place, but sometimes, during overheard conversations liberally punctuated with such sounds, leaving her with the impression that this might just as easily be another way of saying, 'Really?'

They sit in silence for a short while, the only sound for the time being that of a little boy squirming first one way and then the other with a look which, his mother would have to admit, from a certain angle might resemble that of a young *bodhisattva*, though in this case enlightenment was taking place closer to Deptford than Dharamsala. Perhaps she is not alone in her thoughts because a moment later she hears Carol saying:

'He is so happy, the little Buddha.'

'Yes, he is a good boy,' she adds, suddenly overcome by the urge to gather him up in her arms and extol his virtues to the entire world, or at least to Carol. She resists the urge though and continues to dip the second of her biscuits into the now lukewarm tea.

Sensing the awkwardness, Carol changes the subject.

'So I saw you admiring the Blue Spot a little earlier.'

'The Blue Spot?'

'Yes, it's Everton's pride and joy,' says Carol, who was now standing by the contraption in the sideboard that she had indeed been intrigued by before. 'He'd be mortified if he saw me playing around with it, so it's a good job he's not here, and this is our little secret,' she adds, tapping her nose with a finger which her guest notes, with a little consternation, seems today to be missing its extravagant decoration. A moment later she hears a hissing noise which also makes her son look up from his reverie.

'No cause for alarm, my dear,' says Carol, adjusting one or other of the controls on the contraption. 'It's just the valves. They're a bit like us in this cold climate, and take a little while to warm up.'

The next voice she hears is somehow familiar, though she seems to be more startled by it than her son, who she now sees looking inquisitively over at her. This time though she does gather him up and stands there gently swaying with him in the middle of the room, hoping this will soothe away the shock to his reverie delivered by the contraption's unexpected conjuring trick.

'So mother and baby both like Millie,' says a delighted Carol, gyrating her hips and jutting out her elbows in a movement her guest has never seen before, or at least not in real life.

She knows this song, remembers hearing it on the radio and in the factory when it had been a popular hit a couple of years ago. Her husband had mentioned how much he liked this song too, and she could picture him humming along with its catchy melody as he carried out home repairs with the radio playing. Recalling this makes her feel less guilty about being up here, enjoying herself while her husband is out working, putting food on the table for his family. In fact, this is the first time she has thought about her husband all day, and that in itself is a minor cause for celebration. There is a life to be lived, she thinks, and that life carries on with or without her husband's approval.

At one point, as the record plays, she realizes she has in fact seen this dance before, the one Carol is performing, but only on the big Odeon screen late one Friday night, when her husband took her to see the first of the

James Bond films they would see there, the one where the suave British spy was undercover in Jamaica. She vaguely recalled a scene set in a bar where these inside out dances had featured. But this was better, in real life, the thrill of moving to a pop music record and pretending it was entirely for her son's benefit. When the last refrain of 'My Boy Lollipop' fades out, it is a mixture of euphoria and desolation that she feels but all the same she is still surprised to find her son fast asleep, evidently soothed by the stop start lullaby of a little girl from a small island with big dreams.

#

This time her son is sat in Carol's lap. They are sitting in her kitchen, in the downstairs flat. It is not long after that day they'd danced upstairs to 'My Boy Lollipop', perhaps three weeks at most. The night before there had been raised voices upstairs but without any other kind of soundtrack to temper their heat. Still, she hadn't paid any real attention, happy to be distracted by her husband in an unusually playful mood, given that it was midweek and that the following morning would see him rise in its brutal wintry dark. Now though, Carol is telling her, occasionally pausing to remove something from her eye, Everton has been offered a better job with a bigger joinery firm. This sounds like good news, so she wonders why Carol looks so sad.

'So you must be happy?' she asks her neighbour, placing two cups of tea on the small formica table.

She had been surprised by the knock on the door a few moments earlier, even more so to find Carol standing there when she opened it. There were never any visitors to this flat, at any rate none who weren't already related to the occupants. Luckily, today there were no signs as yet of the idlers, and at least the brother-in-law who had been staying with them had recently found work with a local engineering firm, courtesy of her husband. So it was relatively quiet and she was able to welcome her neighbour into her kitchen without having to run the gauntlet of some stray remark or disapproving gesture.

There are no biscuits, so she offers to make Carol some food but is waved away by her neighbour's protests.

'No, no, no, my dear, you mustn't. I just came down to tell you we won't be here for much longer.'

'Really?' she asks Carol, trying but failing to remember what that word was that Carol had used when she'd mentioned the move from bullets to biscuits in Dum Dum.

'The job, Everton's new job, is outside London and they want him to start right away.'

'But your nursing. You will carry on with that, na?'

'I want to, and Everton says I can do the training anywhere, but I'm not so sure.'

'Oh, why so?'

'I'm not so sure he wants me to finish my training.' Her voice begins to falter, and she takes a moment to steady herself, although she is already seated.

'You know what that man told me yesterday? He said to me, "Carol, my love, sometimes I wonder if you appreciate your good fortune." "Good fortune," I said to him.

"And just what do you mean by that?" And you know what he said? He told me I was lucky to have found a man like him, a gentleman, who knew how to conduct himself in public, and in private, which, by the way, was why he was doing so well and why job offers and money raises were coming to him like manna from the celestial above. And by the way, and since you ask, which I hadn't, did I ever stop to appreciate how he wasn't like so many of 'our boys' with their coxcombry and their fancy strides and those two-tone shoes, like the gangsters, and their pork pie hats? "Well let me tell you, Carol, I could have broken the colour bar too and spent so many nights, like those boys, constackling the English girls at the Rivoli, but I never have. And you know why? Because after meeting you I have cast temptation from my mind, but I do know this. That the girl who stays at home cannot be constackled, be that in a ballroom or in the workplace. So this is a blessing, Carol, this job and the money it will bring. And you know we don't even have to stay here any more. With the money I'll be making we can start a family and buy a home, with a garden, somewhere without constacklers, or coolie people and their curry stink, or everything bought on the never never.'"

Carol pauses. The effort it has taken to say this, and to a relative stranger, has left her on the verge of tears as if she herself were surprised at the depth of her sadness. Her neighbour looks at her sympathetically, though in truth she has struggled to follow all the details of what Carol has told her. She does, however, recognize the courage it takes to open up and share such personal grief, the more so with someone she barely knows. Sensing that there is more, she gently lifts her son off Carol's lap and sits down next to her neighbour, urging her to continue by placing a steadying hand on Carol's arm. Her instincts prove to be correct.

'So I look him clear in the eye, just so he knows that this is not play for me, and I tell him, "Everton, yuh tink seh mi born big?" And I tell him more because, well, you know, I'm not ashamed to admit it, by now he has properly got under my skin, and you might think this is jus' a lickle girl from a lickle island, but the truth, my dear, is bigger than that. And the truth goes so: that this nurse-to-be dreams of all of those things too. A house, an' a garden, an' pickney, but she's no longer so sure whether she wants a man like him in the picture. And yes, those were my exact words, 'like you'.

'And this man who I live with so long but it turns out I don't really know at all, this mean little man narrow his eyes and he say to me, "Well let's see, Carol, let's see how long you survive without me to support you." He already fix up to leave, a van is booked this weekend to tek him and his blasted Blue Spot and he was hoping me as well to the new place, which he say he already have secured by leaving deposit with the landlord. And he did this without ever telling me, as if I would jus' follow him, like a simpering girl. He say we all paid up here till the end of the month, and then it's up to me. I can either join him in his new place or see how long it takes for this city to crush me. He say to me it would be better all round if I didn't wait for that, what was the word he used? Ah yes, if I didn't wait for that eventuality. If I came with him now and dropped this headstrong foolishness about nursing that he's sure has only taken hold because of living in this city.'

Carol's eyes are streaming now. Not even the presence of the little Buddha can restore equilibrium and stem the flow of tears. Suddenly aware of her surroundings again, she feels a twinge of embarrassment, followed by a surge of relief. It has done her good to get this off her chest. She is comforted by the knowledge that a sympathetic ear exists just a flight of stairs from where she rests her head. Though it pains her to admit that Everton is right about one thing: it will be a struggle for her on her own in this city. The thought of this, coupled with the more reassuring sensation that she can always of course transfer her training programme from London to another hospital closer to where Everton will be working, helps curtail those earlier negative feelings. Perhaps a temporary detour might not be such a bad thing after all? Besides, how will she ever talk sense into that bull head of his if they are not even living under the same roof? If it was constackling she sought then there had already been many an occasion for this to take place. No, this is not what she wants, the smart talk from the boys in the high waisters. She knows she is a fine looking woman, Lord knows it has been commented on enough that even a blind man could see it. It is something more solid she seeks, a future. And this man, with his prickly manners and bullheaded sense of self-importance, oddly enough fits that bill. He knows how to build things, how to join them together, even if that's also foolishness and pride. But for all of that, she feels, deep down, he is a good man and he will take care of her. He is callow, like most men, and perhaps he just doesn't know how to say it. To her. Perhaps something got under his skin too? The coxcombry, the bravado of those other island boys he must have seen around. No, he's not one of those boys. He's a maker, not a taker, she thinks, and whatever it is that has been damaged here can surely also be fixed. Love? Perhaps that's the bit that needs the most work, that never quite fits right.

#

She thinks about her neighbour, even after she moves out, after they both do. Carol the first to go, a tearful goodbye not long after the day of her sad lament, Everton waiting impatiently outside, in the van with its engine still running. And within another couple of years, herself, now the mother of two young boys. A little brother, K., for the little Buddha, and of course their father. She had almost forgotten that her husband had long ago placed their names on a council waiting list. Then out of the blue a notification. The interminable waiting for that somewhere to become available is finally over, and one bright spring morning at the end of that decade they pack themselves and their worldly goods into a van to make the short journey to a neighbouring district and what they have been promised is a fresh start in a gleaming new flat. She thinks about Carol then, of the conflicting emotions she had seen on her neighbour's face at the very moment of her departure. She thinks to herself it is a look she knows, perhaps a look that women everywhere know. Optimism and hope, those

most precious of particles, smuggled in under the careworn default of resignation and duty.

\#

21.

London, 1976

By the time the last of the uniforms leave, a hundred versions of the story are doing the rounds. In one, the gas mask is a severed head, in another some kind of animal. There are sticks, and fingers, and dil-something or another, but K.'s not sure what this is. But most of them feature small girls and none of them leave out the magazines.

It is only then, with the rumour mill in full swing, that the council sends anyone over to clean the place. Next there's pest control, and finally decorators who spend three days solid in their overalls painting over every last inch of the house. When the van arrives some days later, they all watch from inside as a fresh round of pots, pans, furniture and bedding is unloaded with military precision inside an hour. The two men who have done most of the heavy lifting then drive off, leaving a third, who had largely been directing them as to where they should leave various boxes and items, sat on his haunches the way people do near the railway tracks in hotter climes. He is roughly the same age as Dad, maybe a bit younger, and there's a teenage boy with him, presumably his son. K.'s brother is the first to spot the earring that the teenager is wearing, but really they're all just enjoying the fact that this time it's not them carrying the boxes and trying to size up an unfamiliar neighbourhood.

22.

It's quiet next door, and for the first time in ages, perhaps since they moved here altogether, daily life doesn't involve a constant vigilance. For a while they half expect the rowdiness to start up again, the late night clamour of voices and loud music, cars pulling up, doors slamming. But when several days pass, and then a week, and the only sounds they hear are of pots and pans or the whistling of a kettle, a visible change takes place.

Dad is back out in the yard, a fresh block of wood just waiting, mute, for the surgeon's caress.

Macher jhol and even *cosha mangsho* from time to time are on the go in the kitchen, but the windows and doors are all open, and Mum doesn't appear overly concerned if the cooking aromas waft across the fence.

Dad still likes to keep the transistor outside while he works, but the volume has been turned down and as often as not it's not even on. When it is, the chances are that it's the Test match commentary spilling out rather than the cut-glass announcers they've grown accustomed to. K. sometimes gets the impression that the intermittent applause which can be heard is for Dad's handiwork, which, much like the events at Trent Bridge, is all late cuts, wristy flicks and raw power.

The temperature just keeps rising and the news has started to carry stories of people queuing for water at standpipes. With school starting early in the heat, and all over by lunchtime, many of K.'s classmates take to throwing stones at passing cars. It is not that he's not tempted, more that word will certainly get back to Mum, and that'll be worse than getting caught by any of the drivers. The other throwers have their regulation cropped blonde hair and T shirts—no buttons or collars to grab hold of. And there's that other thing too, which the drivers, or any witnesses, are unlikely to forget. A lot more detail in his case, which is just the kind of thing the uniforms enjoy.

So instead he's home every day before the teams re-emerge for the afternoon session, comparing the television and radio commentary during the drinks interval, noting that they seem to be having more fun on the radio.

If it starts slowly enough, under leaden skies and with a touch of breeze, pretty soon those are distant memories, the endless sun drying out the pitches, leaving a lightning fast outfield. That first pitch invasion, young England fans mobbing Greig as he takes the catch to get rid of Richards, seems a long time ago.

They're not as unruly as the boys at school, but there's a familiar desperation to all the histrionics, the jumping up and down, the swarming all over the pitch, which he's seen in a hundred playground skirmishes. England fans, English boys, always up to something though even they don't seem to know what. *Just what they do*.

The really strange bit, as far as he can tell, is that they

never know why. Viv Richards has massacred them for two days but Tony Greig taking the catch is the bit they hang on to. And even the adults seem to forget things all the time. When they complain about the Caribbean supporters 'encroaching on the pitch' they conveniently forget all those English boys who'd earlier set the tone. And the 'noise' of tin cans or drums which gets everyone so worked up, but only after yet another English batting collapse, doesn't seem so bad next to the shouts and jeers coming from the various Tavern ends. Late afternoon the apex (thanks Chambers, and he also recalls 'aperture', another good word), shirt sleeves roasting in the sun, giant plastic beakers of some yellowy liquid held aloft, a constant hum of throat and laughter of the kind he's only heard across the fence, though not since the old neighbour left.

This crowd is in good voice though, making its feelings known. The final hour of play on the Saturday at Old Trafford, and uproar at the Brian Statham end, or is that the Pavilion end? He can't be sure.

K. is right up by the television, the cherry fizzing through the tiniest fractions between survival and injury. Close looks much older than the West Indian bowlers, especially Holding, racing in to deliver another lethal jab. Close lets it bounce harmlessly off his body, but then winces, most of the crowd voicing its displeasure, the umpire stepping in, waving a gnarled digit at the sheepish bowler.

'Enough is enough, he says, and quite rightly so. Brian Close is going to be a mess of bruises when he eventually gets back to the haven of the pavilion.'

At least Close has the pavilion, K. thinks, but then he remembers the library, it's quiet solitude, the one place the playground never invades.

The barrage continues but Close and Edrich survive, and he reflects that sometimes in this life that's all anyone can do.

In a way it's good, the last rites can be administered on the Monday, when all the other boys in class will somehow forget there's a game going on. The same ones who were making so much noise on the Thursday just gone before Greenidge steadied the ship.

English boys with their short memories, and it's up to him to remind everyone there's a match about to finish. A day when he can look them in the eye and feel good about himself, the match its own compass, the evidence umpired and on television. No one wants to talk about this procession, tumbling wickets and castles of sand following the openers' brave resistance. Edrich and Close, two of the elder statesmen, show plenty of grit but the price of survival on Saturday is an early departure when play resumes on the Monday. Once they're gone, the collars up gum chewers who replace them prove no match for the West Indian pacemen. All mouth and menace when the Indians were here just two summers back. Roles reversed and they're strangely quiet now, little more than quarry for these pacemen. Parries first then jabs, and when they're done toying with the batsmen, the knock-out blow, stumps cartwheeling or a thin edge to the keeper, thicker ones feeding the slip cordon, Black hands throwing the ball up in celebration, the huddle an unmistakable show of strength. For all that these are the West Indies, and those hands waiting to pounce are definitely Black, K. is still pleased to see the ever dependable Murray behind the stumps. That goatee, the twinkling eyes, something brown, like him. Indian, kind of, but with added steel, and not at all like the mournful, slumped shouldered rabble who'd been such an embarrassment to him, to Mum at the schoolgates, maybe to countless others too, the last time India had toured. He'd hated them, knowing that to English eyes *their* weakness would become *his* weakness, cowering in the face of superior odds. And he's sure it's not just him, that those odds are making the wrong people bold well away from the ground too. A thousand petty insults, smiled or shrugged off even if inside it's burning, though everyone's assured *it's nothing serious, mate, it's just a game. And cheer up, pal, it might never happen, though wait, it just did and I missed it all 'cause I was in the kharzi. Speaking of number twos, they were a bit shit'n'all, don't you reckon?* So this feels especially sweet, payback of sorts though only Murray makes him feel he has any sort of claim here. There's no let up, Holding as ever saving his best for Greig. According to the old hands on the radio he has 'pulled something deadly out of the locker' for the England skipper, too fast, too straight, well under the radar of that exaggerated batlift. Something deadly alright and no amount of brash can defend against this. The fastest delivery, also the straightest, the one straining every sinew is *always* the one meant for Greig, who keeps getting bowled. Watching this ritual, K. gets the impression that this is about so much more than one man's wicket, or a few throwaway words earlier that summer. Spiting the seam, the obeah of lithe fingers, some ancient quarrel steeped in violence unanswered. He's as sure of this as he is of anything, a touch of Anansi in the spell being cast by Andy Roberts. And when it's finally over, Selvey the last to go, the catch by Greenidge comes as some act of mercy. It's a good day, this, one to share with the Panini boys and the snooty girls and every other face-less urchin he is forced to be around by the Inner London Education Authority, a rare moment to look the beast in the eye and feel... nothing.

#

On the Saturday, after the barrage, he goes out to see what Dad is doing, and when he's handed the *chakkudhar* K. feels very grown up, though he's glad Dad helps him keep it steady. The smell of barbecued meat floats across the fence, and this is the first time that any of them have heard the new neighbour since he moved in. K. can't be sure but thinks there are at least a couple of other people sitting outside with him, the familiar sound of the ringpull on cans alerting him to their presence. He can see Mum visibly tensing when the barbecue gets under way but these sounds, these voices, are somehow different to the ones she's grown accustomed to blocking out of late. She's not happy seeing her younger son holding such a big knife, but relaxes when her husband takes over from this strictly symbolic part of the ritual. Father to son then back again and the blade is readied once more. She doesn't really see the interloper, only hears the swearing, and the thud, and the scrambling away. But they all hear the raucous burst of laughter overlaying the sizzle from all that *kacha mangsho* across the way.

And then shortly after there's a knock at the door and when Dad goes to answer it, a stranger stood there introducing himself with two cans of beer.

Part Three

The Whole Point of No Return

1.

The Seven Seas, more or less, 1960s

The best bit of life is when a fresh port hoves into view, when one set of smells and noise and refinements gives way to another, close quarters discipline set aside for a manic curing of the flesh.

Many of the others spat out by the cargo vessels return spent from shore leave, the ink on their arms and backs its own seamy trail of conquest and consumption. Still playing on their lips the hint of liquor and something more carnal. But ask them what they've seen and J. is often struck by the mumbled responses or the puzzled looks. Beyond the skin tickled raw by needles, leathery flesh bearing the latest legend, he has the sense that the only other impression made by such places on these men is of a memento. One place much the same as the next: sex, fight, ink and if luck dries up the howl of pissing glass to go with the salt and brine of their occupation.

Something of the grubber has stayed with him though, that desire to go looking a little further afield, off the grid. In a fug until they reach Marseille, pondering over and over and hating himself for doing so, why no one was there to see him off. He couldn't know then, wouldn't find out until much later, that it was just too painful for his old man. Hadn't wanted to crumble in front of the boy, tell him how much he loved him, admired him for taking the step he'd never taken himself. How empty all that was familiar, those docks, the containers, the banter, would feel without his boy. And how sad, and insanely happy, that made him.

Then the wake up call in a narrow little alley near the port, other men's ink getting mixed up with Arabic and the glinting of metal.

He'd run and kept on running, until the laughter he thought he could hear faded into a southern air and his nostrils filled again with the smells of fish from the open market.

The first, and last time, he'd told himself, that he'd trust the judgement of the well-inked veterans around him.

For a moment in that alley, when a fresh cut appeared on the old lag's arm, all he could see was the disappointment in his old man's eyes, as if to say, 'Is that all the character you've got, son? Did I teach you so little?'

And then it's gone, and he can feel his lungs bursting, and all he knows is that he can't stop until the fear is just sweat and blood and fish and he is himself again.

The chants follow him from one ocean to another, only the accent shifts, curiosity always intact.

'Mister', 'Meester', 'English', and on one very funny occasion, 'Bobby Charlton' from a little boy in Alexandria whose old/young face smiled with some deadly intent. But unlike the Manchester man, J. has his hair, and a gift for laughter which travels well. And before long he's being led down souks and bazaars, the sweet sickly aroma of incense and hookahs, of tamarind and lamb kebabs, as normal to him as runny egg, bacon and tea once were.

He notices after a while that he is the only white man in many of these hidden alleys, 'Shukran' and 'Shukria', 'Khuda hafeez' and 'Namaste' just the passport to tea, and no little sympathy.

'Bobby Charlton, he very good player.'

To which he always replies, trying to imagine the smile on his old man's face,

'Bobby Moore, he's even better.'

His team, their team, from the right docks. Not the other lot, the scabs. But he scarcely even believes it himself, some image of the past floating in salt and brine, inviting him to comment, though he doesn't know why. The whole thing just serves as a reminder that no one was there that day to see him off, and his face will briefly cloud over, yet *that's* the moment when fingers are snapped and shortly after trays will emerge bearing sweet little infusions of chai, cardamom the first thing he picks up on. Or silver pots of mint tea, the handles so hot a cloth is supplied to avoid scalding.

Sensing an audience, he'll put on a bit of a show. It's the least he can do given the hospitality.

'Martin Peters too. It was West Ham you see who really won the World Cup, not England.'

And he'll bring a touch of a long forgotten East End into it, repeating for good effect:

'It weren't England wot won the World Cup. It was West 'Ammm!'

It never fails, the idiot Englishman routine, but he

thinks he can see genuine friendliness in these smiles. Can hear it in the laughter, can see it in the hands frantically beckoning more family members into the shop to listen to the funny Englishman. Then one day he comes back to the same place, seeking another respite from the tattooed veterans. It takes him an age, getting lost in the labyrinthine maze of alleys, taking care to avoid the little trickles occasionally running along one edge of the potholed concrete. Soon even the concrete is a fading memory, dust and dirt and alleys so tightly packed that the language rebounds even when words are directed into the dirt. Finally, just when he is about to give up, turn back, a familiar sight, this bicycle repair shop, that alley. Feeling his spirits soar he steps into the alley where he sees something of a crowd gathered outside the shop.

A dog briefly looks up at him before going back to its afternoon nap. And that's when he hears it, coming from the shop.

'Kaiser Franz. Twice the player Bobby Moore was. And Russian linesman very bad, otherwise everyone know Germany win.'

Before anyone notices he is there, J. heads back past the cycle repair shop, and once again finds himself running down ancient gullies, pursued by raucous Indian laughter and half remembered yet utterly alien sounds.

Gora pagol ke dekho!

The way back feels easier, dried fish some kind of relief as the stench of the alleys, all sweat and sinew, is left behind.

As he runs past the *bhel puri* stalls without stopping, and the green coconuts stacked up by the roadside barely break his stride, he knows he has to keep going. Back onto the ship and around those leathery smiles.

He realizes that for every throwaway impression he has spent so much time on, the only thing he was ever really perfecting was the art of self delusion. All that mimicry, that mockery, and the one possibility he never allowed for was that his old man had fought every last instinct of his to cling on to something already gone, and let him go.

He feels a deep shame burning from the inside. How could he not have known? His entire life, the old man working, grafting, rarely having anything more than a ceremonial pint at the end of the week, preferring it at home with a paintbrush or a trowel. No East End flash about the man, no need, but when the Blackshirts had tried to march through, him and his mates the first to mob up, instinctively aware that something a lot bigger than a handful of narrow Dickensian streets was at stake.

'Demeaning', about the worst thing he'd ever heard him say, looking on half amused but feigning disgust anyway while his son fished away for hidden treasure in riverside mud.

More lines around the jaw now, a residual grief tempered by the joy that *his* flesh and blood was the one who got out, saw another world beyond the hard faces and the shrunken possibilities, containerisation the new spectre stalking the docks.

'What happened to you, then? Touch of the Delhi belly, my old son?' one of the tattooed vets asks as J. rushes back aboard.

'Oh, fuck off, you silly old cunt,' J. replies, surprised at the words even as they come out.

'You what?!' says the lag, equally unused to hearing this kind of thing from the mild mannered cockney.

'You want me to spell it out for you?' asks J., a little cross now but still managing, just, to hold it down. Picking up on this, the lag thinks better of it for now and walks away looking a little pained.

The leathery skin, the tats, the bristling demeanour. All that peacock strutting, so sure of themselves no matter where they are.

It hits him then. These are the same boys, not all of them, just the cruel ones mind, he'd seen playing on the bomb sites when he was really small. It runs in their blood, the cruelty, picking on smaller boys or girls where others were just happy to play. He remembers the swagger moving from east to west, finding new targets for its spite. 'Recent arrivals'. West Indians past Bayswater, up the Harrow Road, in the Grove and off the Goldhawk Road. And maybe it was the easy smiles, or the sharper stitch on those suits, but something really got under the skin of these Teds. The trilbys worn at rakish angles, American sounds, but not *their* America. Who knows, perhaps they felt mocked by these newcomers, island origins in the shadow of the big place? All that languid, so defiantly bespoke, no matter what the insult. And there were plenty of those. Too often the eyes would follow the curse, and then they'd catch other eyes also looking, though this time with softness, excitement, longing. Perhaps they'd also see an echo of Black American GIs, and of every girl who'd ever spurned them for these exotic newcomers at the Locarno. And the curse would catch fire, mob handed ugly haring after lone prey, surrounding the hostel, filling the night air with its violence. But plenty of it got left behind in the shadow of the docks too, cursing and pointing and fooling no one with the Edwardian suits and the trumped up grievance. Then again they must have fooled plenty, else why did he leave? Or maybe they're not those boys at all but just random others, the accents straying far and wide from any Canning Town pure. There are Poles and Russians in the crews he's been a part of, the frozen spit of the Baltic in their lined toughness. Spanish and Italian too, and he's heard enough snippets of 'moro' or 'nero' when they're chatting among themselves to sense familiar allegiances. But for the longest time he has put up with it, believing his confusion is different to theirs, a less tainted red running through his veins.

He's disgusted at the thought of all those tats, dark little whores bobbing up and down on seafaring bodies, ink, blood, knuckles, spit smuggled in with the other fluids. But none of it really registering. Just whores. *They've all got their price* he's heard more than one of the inky vets say. And he's wanted to say, *Yes, and you've got yours but in your case it buys their performance* on so many occasions he's lost count.

Still, nothing ever *is* said, and the resentment just festers. *My old man probably battered yours down Cable Street once upon a time* just a thought to be nursed when the close quarters discipline starts to fray. 'Demeaning'. What his old man would have said.

So J. turns and walks away, as he doesn't want any of

these to see him cry.

He doesn't yet know the dread surrounding that word 'containerisation' in his old manor, East India Dock already in its death throes, something toxic spreading from the docks into the streets beyond. Even the noise of the disused becoming harsher, mouths opening less and less to spit out their sound and fury. Language itself falling into disuse, replaced by something meaner, sniping from the edges of memory. *They come here and they take our jobs.* Black shirts and black moods and Billingsgate porters, with no one saying it though everyone's thinking it.

This is the dread leaking from the gutters, and for now it's just a feeling, but one he knows well. All that distance, all those years he has placed between himself and a half-remembered past now feel more of a mirage than anything he has actually left behind. He knows then it is time to head back to the rubble of his childhood, to reacquaint himself with those ghosts still lurking in mud.

#

2.

East London, 1967

In a neat act of symmetry, no one is there to greet him as he steps off the sea and back into the low slung familiar of London. Although he has been back several times since he first left, this feels different. He vows to himself there will be no more running, or hiding. He's here now, here to stay and doesn't really mind who knows it this time.

Perhaps the resolve also brings surefootedness, as for once he's able to savour the familiar taste of dredgers and silt still lurking in the shadows of the power station.

'We built those floating harbours, son, the ones they used during D-Day. And this is how they pay us back, filling in the export dock and building that monstrosity.'

It's his dad and he's pointing to the Brunswick Power Station built on the site of the old dock. But he's not interested, not really. Still just a boy.

At the time he'd been bored, wishing the old man would hurry up with the guided tour so he could get back to the mudlarking. He'd had to leave in a hurry the previous day when he'd spotted a group of older boys who normally played on the rubble coming his way. Any other time he wouldn't have minded but today he'd spied a ring sticking out of the mud and knew the older boys would find it when they frisked him, so he buried it deeper instead. Now his thoughts turned to whether it would still be there when he went back. And the longer he had to listen to the old man banging on about the war and the endless sacrifices he'd made, the more he had the feeling that some other magpie would have lifted the stone.

'We were never consulted. No one ever asked us what we wanted.' This time it's not his dad, and there's nothing wistful about the voice.

Looking up from his reverie, J. sees a large man in a donkey jacket staring at him. There are echoes of his dad, though the old man would never have worn anything as crude as a donkey jacket. Then again the cap is familiar enough, as is the sentiment.

He quickly realizes the man views him as a kindred spirit, and it is not hard to see why. They are the only two figures left on the quayside, wandering aimlessly as if in a house stripped of all furniture. They cut strange shapes, a bitter January wind slicing through the empty shore. Though it is late there is a stillness in this place which feels wrong to both men. Where are the lighters, or the dockside sheds used to store the cargo? Where are the people?

'Containerisation,' says the big man, as though he knows what J. is thinking.

'Come again,' says J., still reeling from the emptiness of the place.

'Great big metal coffins, that's what they are. Like stuffing clothes in a suitcase.' Satisfied that he has got J.'s attention, the big man continues.

'It's all done beforehand, you see. All packed away

ready to go, so when the ship gets here there's no need for the likes of us any more. Just a couple of machine operators and then it's off to those depots away from here for unpacking. And they're all so bleeding happy about it, but no one ever asked us what we thought. They never do.'

It is a story he hears again and again in the coming weeks. *We weren't asked. They did this to us. Told us it would happen and then told us to be happy about it. But I tell you what, if there's one thing I'm not, it's happy.*

3.

Those first days, then weeks, he's happy to be back, rooming with his Nan just up from the Isle of Dogs.

She seems pleased enough that the prodigal sailor has returned, puts on a good show whenever he regales her with one of his far flung tales. But behind the smiles and the endless cuppas he can sense her disquiet.

Every now and then he catches himself looking at how tightly she grips her mug, the knuckles worn bare by these last years.

First his Grandad passed, after a lifetime of loading timber and handscuttling grain, waiting for ships to moor on the riverside quay in the endless scramble for work. And whether it was wool, or meat, or crate after crate of fruit to be unloaded into lighters or moved to the storage sheds, he'd always be home for his tea, riding his bike with a vigour his legs had no right to supply. He enjoyed his nickname, 'Balloon', as in 'don't let me down, lads,' and J. loved hearing his stories about the other men on the docks, the occasional filching of fruit and the general camaraderie of Grandad's little crew. Always with a smile on his face even when Nan would spend the evenings, more often than not, picking splinters of wood out of his hands.

He'd liked his ginger wine too but it was something else that got him in the end, his lungs filling up with little particles of dust which must have been building up over the years. Some invisible germ leaking from the wool sheds and the timber yards, from years of being forced to overload a sling. Handling the good stuff but being left with just the dregs, the weight of bananas and sugar and wheat, but never their taste. One time even a Russian cargo of furs brushing against the coarse wool of his shirt, sleeves rolled up, those germs, that chemistry of neglect, seeping into his pores. And day in day out bearing the weight of the quays with an easy smile and a ready quip. Because the only thing worse than the work was not having it. 'Dinting': the unspoken fear etched into all those faces gathered each morning at the stands in the 'Paddy's Market' for a job. The undignified scramble as queues would form outside the quays; work given out on an ad hoc basis depending on the number of ships and their cargo, the men instantly grateful for this small mercy though the joints ached and shivered, then bent or broke through the seasons. The small two-pronged hooks the dockers carried with them to help them carry sacks and cases; the bigger 'S' hook for the larger cases, the grain sacks or the bales of wool. And then that terrible moment each day after all the jobs had been allocated when the controllers would tell the remaining dockers to 'sling their hook'. The forsaken, the militants, the troublemakers, which Grandad assured him just meant anyone who refused to overload a sling, left on the stones carrying the terrible taint of the dint. In the end the hardship had got into his lungs and eaten him away from the inside. This big, proud man reduced to shadow and stubble just a spit from the quays which had been his life.

And within a couple of years his old man too, cut down by a sickness that should never have found him. Wheezing and spluttering and coughing up claret, telltale red stains on the handkerchief pointing him towards a box. Near the end losing all sense of taste, the crinkle cut chips with grated cheese mere shapes, baked apples or the apple sauce with pork chops just colours. Eventually his face not even his own any more, the mouth worn dry by the final rasping notes.

Poor Nan. It is a lot to bear, and there's not much left in reserve. She's holding on as best she can but J. can see this isn't how she pictured things. There's no one to hold her any more, comfort her, tell her it will be ok. All her life there has been and now they are both gone. She'd cried when the gate to the docks had been demolished during the Blackwall Tunnel expansion. Even before that when the export dock was damaged during the war and then filled in just after to make way for the power station. But they'd both made a joke out of it and the fear had soon passed. And she'd loved to watch them eat when they came back from a hard day loading the world's wares. Her boys. They carried the world on their backs and in their arms, but at home they'd tuck in to a homemade breaded fish and chip supper, or lamb with mint sauce or roast beef and Yorkshire pudding. And no matter how hard the day had been, or how many indignities they'd endured to find the work, there was always a smile and a compliment, and plates wiped clean.

He does his best, but knows they can never be replaced.

'Nan, do you remember that time Grandad's mate took all the oranges?'

'What's that, love?'

'The time his mate got caught coming off one of the boats with all those oranges and the coppers locked him up but forgot to take the oranges off him?'

'No, I don't remember that, love.'

'You remember, Nan. They forgot about him because something else happened on the docks that day, and by the time they remembered and came back to the cell, he'd eaten all the evidence. And they had to let him go.'

'Oh yes, I remember now, love,' his Nan says, loosening her grip on the mug for the first time since she sat down. There's a faint trace of a smile playing around the corners of her mouth and for a few moments she doesn't feel quite as lost as she has done recently.

#

4.

J. is sure it used to be louder round here. He remembers the main road at the top of the street being choked with all kinds of traffic carrying goods to and from the docks. Somewhere in that blur of movement were steam trains too, and the sound of foghorns on days when there was a real pea souper. A London particular, his old man was fond of saying.

Taking a left off the main road, he is surprised when he spots the old runny egg caff still there, tucked away behind the narrow terraces.

The blast of warm air carrying its own mixture of fat and steam and fags comes as a shock to him. He *has* been away a long time. Another of those 'particulars' but without the mystique.

'What can I get you, love?' asks the aproned lady behind the counter.

J. takes a moment to remind himself of the acceptable responses. It wouldn't do to ask for string hoppers or deviled chicken here, so he sticks to more familiar fare.

'Egg and chips, and a nice cup of tea will do me just fine.'

'Right you are, love. I'll bring it over,' she says.

That's when he hears it again. *We weren't asked. No one ever asked us what we wanted.*

Looking around he sees two men huddled over their breakfast, mopping up the last of their beans with a slice of white bread. The first to finish is the one who has been talking. Nursing his mug in a giant paw, he looks up at the man near the counter who has just turned around. J. also holds the talker's gaze for a moment, then looks away, sizing up a spare seat and a formica table in the corner.

'You see that's the problem with this place. Too many people, and it ain't as if there's enough work to go around for our own to start with.'

The other feaster has just cleaned his own plate and mumbles his agreement into the mug. This seems to encourage the talker further. Several men are eating at the other tables and though there's some loud slurping of tea, no one else seems to be saying anything.

'I mean why are they coming here? You have to ask yourself that. And where are they always hurrying off to? The other day I saw one of them shuffling along and you know what, he's got the nerve to pretend he hasn't seen me. So I says to him, "Oi, Gunga, where you off to then?" though maybe not those exact words, and he carries on ignoring me.'

'The neck on these people,' his mate cuts in, fully involved now that the scran has been mopped up.

'Anyway, I was about to have words with him when he disappears into this doorway, and that's the last I've seen of him. But I tell you what, that door might have been open just a crack but I reckon there were at least a dozen of them in there, all jibber jabbering away. And I'm telling you, squire, the smell. They're not like us, they're not used to being in clean places. I don't even blame them, they can't help it really. Different standards where they're from. No food hygiene, nothing like that,' he says, lighting up a cigarette. 'But what bothers me is who asked them to come over. No one ever asked us. *We* were never consulted.'

'That's right,' says his mate, wiping his hands down the front of his trousers. 'What about the people who've always lived here? What about us?'

J. thinks about saying something but decides not to. No one else seems particularly bothered by what is being said and he knows, according to local etiquette, he's only been back ten minutes. It wouldn't do for the newcomer to start venturing opinions. Not just yet. The more talkative of the duo starts picking at the back of his trousers with one hand, the other making short work of the cigarette.

The chips are nothing like the ones his Nan makes, crinkle cut with grated cheese, and J. finds himself regretting this little recce. He takes his plate back to the counter and this time when he pays for the food he makes a point of staring straight at the talker and holding eye contact. He takes in the details. Donkey jacket, jeans with a slight turn up, heavy boots. The man who'd spoken to him on the quayside the other night was dressed much the same. He'd also said something about 'not being asked', but at the time J. had taken that to mean something quite different.

'Food ok, love?' asks the aproned lady, wondering what else is going on in her caff.

'Yes, it was fine, thanks,' says J. recovering his

composure.

'You live round here then?' she asks. Then, pausing for a moment, 'It's just I haven't seen you before.'

'I've been away awhile,' he says.

This must be a line she has heard before as she nods her head without saying anything.

As he passes the talkers on his way out, J. mutters something under his breath.

'What's that again?' asks one of the men but without making a move to get out of his seat.

Right by the door, J. turns around, clears his throat and repeats, this time loud enough for the benefit of the whole caff,

'*Bhenchod*'.

Then he walks out without looking back and keeps going until the only sound which matters belongs to Nan hollowing out apples to be baked while he attends to the pork chops.

#

5.

He avoids the docks altogether after that. The air, of which he'd taken sentimental lungfuls when he'd first come back, is now just there, and he tastes it for what it is. Salt and sulphur and a whole lot of sad.

It is only on those occasions when Nan makes rock cakes or currant buns or one of her apple pies with cinnamon that he takes a moment to savour the rich, sweet aromas.

The rest of the time he moves through the old neighbourhood without fuss. It is easier without the blinkers, spit and snarl announcing themselves with a certain clarity.

He brings back the fruits from the market that Nan loves to boil down into conserves. Plums, gooseberries, blackcurrants, raspberries, and blackberries. He learns she's not such a fan of strawberries.

The transistor is often on, a habit he's brought back with him from the high seas.

'Your Grandad was the same,' she tells him. 'He loved to listen to the radio when he'd get in. He always said you had to pay attention, really listen if you wanted to know what was going on in the world. Sometimes they'd tell you things on the radio they'd never show you on the telly. And they'd only tell you because they thought you weren't listening.'

J. likes hearing the stories. They cut through the sulphur, sprinkled the salt and the ebb and the flow of lives which were never small, even if they were contained.

'A lot of stock would go missing from the orange cargoes,' Nan tells him. 'One time, love, Grandad's mate was stopped by the uniforms as he was driving off the dock. They must have had their suspicions, just never knew where he'd put the stash. So they made him get out of the car and open the boot, and never twigged even when he was doing that bow- legged walk. His missus wasn't too pleased when he got home though. Apparently she was picking bits of shredded orange out of his socks for weeks.'

And she laughs so hard and for so long that she can almost forget the ache and the shiver of that terrible loneliness. The nights when she feels herself crumple, all those moments, the hopes and thrills and fears which stitched them together and felt so ordinary then, nothing they couldn't face, the horrors of the doodlebugs and the limbs and the rubble strewn with red, the ordinary courage and the deep cut unity in those shelters, the 'them' of tallymen and spivs and their so called betters, and the 'us', always an us. Those nights, rising through all that empty a baleful whisper. *Where are they? They've gone. On your own now.* And she wants to cry and cry and cry until every last reserve is used up and she can go too.

#

6.

The first days are just numb. He is glad for the formalities, is just relieved to be busy with the arrangements. What type of wood, what sort of bouquet. Pallbearers? Which sermon, what about some snacks?

People he hasn't seen since the area was rubble, and others he doesn't know at all, offer kind words, some even placing a consoling hand on his shoulder, but inside he feels very little. *All gone now. You're on your own.*

He excuses himself at the point when one of the mourners comments on the large number of oranges neatly laid out on plates. The transistor in the back room is better company and trying to feel a way past his grief he learns that a young Londoner called Twiggy is taking the fashion world by storm.

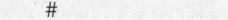

#

More people keep showing up. They say what they feel are the right things, throw in some detail about Nan and then gaze awkwardly into that space behind his head while the tea turns lukewarm and the words dry up. But no matter how stilted the conversation, some part of it will always serve to remind him that he wasn't there before, when he was most needed. It won't actually be said in so many words but he's already felt that disappointment in looks held fractionally longer than they need be. Or in the surprise that he should even know about her rock cakes or her special recipes for the apples. The years away have made him acutely sensitive to such details, the micro maps of possibility instantly laid out on first time faces. Ever since that moment in the alley in Marseille he has trusted his instincts, the part of his muscle memory which reads teeth and fear and flint long before eyebrows are arched or lines appear. That split second in which to catch doubt. Every pause flickering on the register of lung bursting flight, blood and Arabic and a swift hand movement with the shiv lost to the tiles and heat of those narrow, winding streets. Of course the memory was there all along, he knows that now. Ever since the sirens finally ceased and the shelters spilled them back out into rubble and wreck-ing balls and something altogether more unkind. Those figures playing near the bomb sites who turned out to be deadly serious, lacquered, with a comb and something else he'd never bargained for in the shelters. A sneer for the cameras, shot through with all the dirt and hollowed out flash of this new place. A cruelty he's not really seen before either, disdain for the young and the old alike, caps knocked off heads and a viciousness behind the brothel creepers and the Edwardiana.

#

The flow soon turns into a trickle, and before long it is just him and the fading brickwork, everyone else gone. Perhaps he should be less surprised than he is that the business of living is the one to which people devote their attention.

Best head off now. Things to sort out. Chin up, J., she'd have been proud.

But as he sits there, the tea barely warm, J. is surprised, taken aback even, by the indecent haste with which that business resumes again.

Work and money and kids, an endless parade of *he said, she said,* and *I kid you not, squire.* So by the time the brew has stilled, steam and the last vestiges of heat just vapour on the tip of his beak, the ebb and flow of antique lives have already been cast out to sea.

#

7.

East to West (London), late 1960s

He starts to walk more and more, the route taking him each time a little further from the docks.

He first does this when he follows the flight path of a blackbird which had briefly settled on the window sill. He watches it making regular stops on telegraph wires all the way up the street. But then it is gone before its beak or anything else has time to catch in the sulphur.

To start with it is the usual circuit past the terraces, the brisk sounds of the quayside still lingering.

He pauses by a half open doorway, oddly familiar sounds coming from within.

'Joodi paro ekto aloo peaaj neasho. Aar roshun. Sheta aajke dorkar.'

But this time, instead of circling back via the narrow streets off the main road, he keeps going past the electrical repair shop and the ringleted Jewish people, who he notices congregating away from the rubble of his childhood and closer to the turf accountant of this present. They briefly look up at him as he passes before getting back to whatever conversation they were having before.

It feels conspiratorial until he hears, 'Geoff Hurst destroyed 'em' in a thick, Cockney brogue.

Perhaps he has underestimated the area, he thinks. At school, the lure of the dust and the rubble too great to keep most of the lacquered boys in the classroom, he doesn't remember seeing too many ringlets. There were certainly boys with darker eyes, but little of them has stayed with him beyond a dim recollection of how quiet they were.

As Poplar gives way to Stepney and then on past the hospital, the streets get noticeably busier, but other than traffic he's not really looking out for anything. Occasionally he feels someone brush past, hears them make a last minute adjustment.

'Oi, watch where you're going, mate.' Bump.

'No, that's alright, mate, you're welcome.' Stumble.

'You silly little man!' Screech.

None of it really matters. The sulphur and its familiar tang now feel far away. In truth, everything does.

Some time after setting out he can no longer feel the elements. What breeze there is absorbs the sweat on his brow but there is no cold or hot any more. Just pavement and stones and tread.

A gentleman's barber advertises short back and sides for 4s 6d, but J. is not tempted. The old man was always very particular, never let the hair touch a collar. Grandad the same. He is different to them though, he knows that. They didn't exactly fight a war so he could grow his hair long but he doubts they'd have minded too much. At worst maybe a quip about some earrings and a skirt to go with, and then it would have been forgotten

Every now and then a strong scent of cumin wafts over, laughter coming from one of the doorways, but he rarely sees a face even though the street is right there.

He resists the temptation to pop into one of the caffs without a white face inside and ask for '*ek cup garam cha, bhai.*'

The hot, cardamom infusion beckons just the other side of the glass but he moves on, the cloves jogging another memory too.

Across the street muted laughter spills out of the pub, a thick pall of smoke hovering uninvitingly in the saloon bar.

'This way, darling,' jokes one of the drinkers when J. briefly sticks his head around the door. Again he is not sure what he is looking for and the words barely even register, clouded over in a fog of Marlboro.

On the next corner a familiar landmark. The old man used to bring him here whenever his boots needed fixing. The shop is still there, though it is more like a tiny box filled with laces and soles and the smell of old leather. Just enough room in the back for repairs and stitches from a bygone era. The owner, one of the old timers, whose memories stretch back to the Blackshirts and the street battles and the last time the old docks really made themselves heard. And though he was primarily about the business, he liked J.'s old man too. Always gave him a healthy discount once he knew which side of the barricades the old man had been on. As the money changed hands a conspiratorial smile and a nudge and a wink to their shared history.

He keeps going, past the fruit and veg and the leftovers near the crates being eyed up hungrily by random men slumped in doorways or others peeking furtively over bottles of hot fire. There are scavengers here too, he thinks, but no mud or mystery.

'Could you find it in yourself to help a poor soul in distress?'

He stops. The man who has addressed him is holding out a bottle, and J. can see that only the dregs of a dark liquid remain. He shakes his head, doesn't really know what to say.

'You can't help me then?' asks the man, trying then failing to raise himself up before roaring, 'Because I'm worth every penny!'

It confuses J. It makes no sense. The man is on the streets. He is not a performer. There is no show here. No telly. No cinema either.

What we have here is a failure to communicate.

The pavement remains narrow but the street is suddenly stretched by a lot more traffic. Everyone in a hurry too. Suits and three quarter length coats, umbrellas and briefcases carrying the important business of the day in a certain stride.

Purposeful. Straight lines connecting the crooked.

Their business the only one that matters, elbows sharpening behind a sombre façade.

No one really speaks here, though there is plenty of noise. And if there is a bump or a barge or a missed step, a loud sigh or tut tutting is the order of the day.

Some distance further, beyond the massive stone temples and the pinstripe threads, the pubs seem to recover something of their joviality, drink and smoke and the randomness of a dozen conversations floating in the mist. Largely just men too, tongues loosened by a kind of fever, the snippets of throwaway marinated in malt and grape.

Words and laughter rise in a crescendo, and J. can tell that there is a lot of effort going into this performance. Silence has been shepherded out along with any other doubts, smoke the only visible wall between the words and the nakedness of their ambition. He hangs back near the doorway and endures some more sighs as people try to push past.

'You coming in then, or should we all be worried?' he gets asked by one of the red faced drinkers standing just inside.

Again he doesn't know what to say, isn't really sure at all why he is even here. The drinker rapidly loses interest in J. once his friend returns from the bar with a couple of shot glasses. Business as usual, he thinks. I'm barely even here.

And in a Fleet Street minute the snapshots start to overlap, so that standing there J. can almost believe that these stories of oil spills and six day wars, trilby hatted inspectors and the skinny girl with a big reputation are somehow guided by the hidden pockets of conversation sucked in by the saloon bar maelstrom.

'That's not how I heard it. Yes, they had to bomb the tanker to burn the oil, but you know G., well it turns out his brother-in-law is a marine biologist and that's his stretch of coastline. And apparently they were still bringing in birds weeks later matted in the stuff. And there's more... '

Indeed there is. The longer he spends in that sodden

portal the more outlandish the drift. Tough Jews soaked in oil, matted for days under the black gold. Six days, bombings, everything turning toxic.

He is grateful for the light rain which is falling when he steps back outside, head spinning from an alphabet shrapnel. The sprinkle feels good against his skin, and eyes shut, face upturned, he accepts its caress. That first time he lets it guide him all the way back, the stories melding one into the other until debris is dirt and even the drinkers, the ones in the doorways with their crumpled dreams, have had their taste.

8.

The next day he retraces his steps, but this time without dwelling on the Fleet Street hacks. The day after that too. In fact every day for a fortnight he ventures a little further west, watching the streets widen and the shopfronts change.

As much as he can, J. studies the faces of the people he passes. There are fewer lines here, extravagant creases limited in the main to cloth. Mostly the men seem a little taller too, the impression conveyed by something in their gait and the quickness of stride. In these streets he also finds it harder to detect that unmistakable stoop, the invisible load the dockers would carry even when broad East End shoulders were held proud. In the photos on Nan's mantelpiece, Grandad and the old man always seem to be looking slightly up as though some hidden weight is still pressing down on them. The familiar trace of timber and bananas, grain and wool bearing down from the quays into the spine.

The smiles are gone too. He can't quite picture these men with the camaraderie of arms around shoulders for the photo album.

Then again that had been in short supply on the ships

as well, shore leave more of a cooling off period than anything else.

Even so he gets the sense that the briefcases and brollies are wielded like weapons on these streets, divining rods to keep the world at bay.

So he carries on, past the viaduct and its reassuring solidity. The billboards tell him that Bond will soon be back but the headlines are enveloped by the steam rising from chrome filtered machines in the Italian caffs. He presses on, through the unexpected gift of a park, leaves and shade a rare pleasure after so much bustle.

The currents converge on the baize, suits and stragglers and, to judge by their long hair and carefree manners, he's guessing students as well.

But he keeps moving, green giving way to grand buildings and facades which make him stop. Designed to make anyone stop, pause for a moment to take in their hugeness, all that stone, that money and sweat and sugar and weight and crooked and cruel, right here fronted by gargoyles in the beating heart of everything.

'Bow Street'. Grandad's mate, the one with the oranges, had fetched up here one time on a non-fruit related matter. J. can't remember how it turned out for the chap, but the street name has stayed with him.

From there on he tries to avoid the busier roads. If he sees a sidestreet which seems to lead somewhere, that is where he will go. After a while he forgets the ache in his legs, vast buildings occasionally broken up by cutaways to green, or a church courtyard. Then the madness again, steam and horns and everything criss-crossed up by Baker

Street and the waxworks, but a park to ease the pain and as much time as he needs.

More of those crumpled faces, the bench a prop for a show which he can tell is already over. But that's ok, for there are rules to this game and so long as the rules are observed and the good people with their prams and cameras and money are not inconvenienced, the men are left to their parklife.

The big houses and the cricket ground and then he's zigzagging his way across canals and past recent confusion, the council and the countess staring at one another with looks of mutual incomprehension.

'Try one?'

He stops, looks up to find a young woman holding out a lollipop towards him. She smiles and that's when he sees the beads in her hair, long strands passing by the edges of her mouth.

The officer class seems to have temporarily vanished from this area and he has no real idea how long he has been walking or where he is.

'Go on, try one, they're cosmic,' she says, never breaking from that smile.

He takes the lollipop, puts it in his mouth. The flavours swirl around for a moment, and he can taste something so light it floats in the roof of his mouth. He looks at this girl and her smile is the purest emotion he's ever seen. She takes his hands and they glide up the stairs and past a half open door of a stucco fronted house. That is when he sees all the other people, limbs entwined, smiling and weightless, adorned in faraway cloth, the sounds of some east framed by the high ceilings of their west. And he smiles too. It is beautiful and there are no lines or creases or frowns in this place. Just them and this moment resplendent in its cosmic purity.

'I told you it's good,' she says, looking into his eyes with no hint of malice. Then turning to the ink on his arm, she says, 'I really love that. Where did you get that done?'

He considers the ohm for perhaps the first time since he stepped back into his London particular. The needlework had been swift, deft hands carving the simplest of all the local insignia. It is the only memorable ink on his arm but in truth, as he recalls the hot, stabbing pains and that sense of release, he doesn't really know why it's there.

'You're different, you know. Where are you from?' she asks him.

For once he doesn't need to think about it. The answer is right there breaking through the death pall of silence which has bedevilled him of late.

'Mud,' J. tells her, the broadest of smiles on his face.

9.

At first it is days rather than nights that he spends away from the docks. He develops a taste for the 'royal' parks and the stucco fronts, the patchouli oil and the love beads. No one says anything to him here about the overgrown collars or the facial hair. They barely even notice the seasons, John and Paul telling them love is all they need, heads and freaks in a paisley swirl, circles of friendly love cemented by the communal smoke. He likes hearing them talk about fellow travellers, mystical awakenings near the banks of the holy river or in the mountains of Afghanistan. He especially enjoys their surprise that he knows these sites too, has seen a lot more besides, and the ohm spreads from the skin to the speculative. He avoids the lollipops though, and the tabs, after that first time. It is one thing to swap notes with flower children, quite another to lose all sense of self. Whenever the tabs appear he finds the docks reasserting themselves in spite of his desire. The faint whiff of 'demeaning' clouding the air as he politely declines.

Then he learns it is not John and Paul but Jerry and Janis who keep the napalm from the flowers. Happenings, be-ins, love-ins, the consciously dirty and the deliberately underfed. Calico skirts, boots, bare feet, antique military jackets. Yet even as it turns his head, the musings of bearded philosophers in flowing robes, some part of his brain, nourished on the quays on a diet of inventory and stock and loss, keeps returning to those crumpled figures in east end doorways, clutching at bottles and the vanishing dregs of their future.

And those days he finds himself heading back to the narrow streets, the acrid smoke, the sulphur and sugar sweat with no little regret.

#

It takes the old Jewish man a moment to place the long haired stranger when he hands in his boots for repair.

'Ah, yes, I remember now. Your father used to come by, did he not?'

'That's right. This was always his spot. He never went anywhere else for his shoes,' replies J., hoping in some indeterminate way to placate the old boy who has been looking disapprovingly at his appearance ever since he walked in.

It is warm and he has started wearing sandals, a detail which is not lost on the shop owner.

'You'll be needing something a bit more sturdy than those for when the sky turns again,' advises the old boy. Studying J.'s boots more closely, he adds, 'I'm not sure these can be salvaged though. I mean I'm good but I'm no miracle worker. What *have* you been doing with these, young man. Did they make you join the army? Is that what it is then, you've been on manoeuvres?'

'Something like that,' says J., and they both laugh. But if it is not quite a miracle, the patchwork repair still does the trick.

Although it is warm, he is suddenly pleased that his toes are no longer exposed when he passes the barber's a little further up.

Propped up inside on one of the hydraulic operated chairs, feet barely able to touch the ground, is a hard faced youth. Skilled Cypriot hands which would once have manipulated scissors and comb, and reveled in the dexterity, now reach reluctantly for the clippers. The buzz cut is over in the time it takes to repeat the same mechanical tracing several times on the willing skull. The barber goes through the motions, showing the youth the back of his head in the hand-held mirror. The youth steps down from the chair and scowls at J. when he sees him looking in. Then the next youth steps up and the barber places a fresh sheet round his neck. That is when J. notices the assembly line of identikit scowls waiting their turn with those little big man manners and that barely restrained fury he hasn't missed at all.

\#

10.

Once he realises he has places to stay in those wider streets, days, then weeks, pass more easily. The need or desire to head back to the scowls, but also the wit, grows ever fainter. There are some things he never quite gets used to though. Just for starters, the open belching or the friendship kisses. To a mind, and a body, reared on 5am starts and scrubbed doorsteps, it just looks, and feels, a bit sloppy. Dirty even. As for all that bodily exhibition, well of course there are perks, but the best he can manage is a faltering acceptance.

He still baulks a little any time he passes a long-johned hairy in the corridor. It is a constant reminder that he is just one of many in this place, passing through with the other seekers. Before long he gets used to the oatmeal-honey face masks favoured by the women, thinning the beets from recipes lifted from well thumbed paperbacks. But no matter how much they like to mention the natural ingredients and their mood enhancing properties, the obsession with appearance still seems a little odd. And oddly familiar.

For all their pilgrimages to India, or Morocco, it still feels strange to him how little of the local cuisine or anything else really they've brought back with them. He doesn't recall raisin bread and organic beauty masks on his own voyages to these outposts. But the sounds and the smells and the razor sharp army of eyes and mouths offering kindnesses and then nothing have never left him.

Yet he doesn't mention any of this, or the traces of mothballs which linger like an article of bad faith on the clothes of the weekend longhairs, whose ranks he supposes he has also now joined.

#

He sees the denizens of Haight-Ashbury, transplanted to London bedsits along with their corduroy and bearded affectations. The pouting, insolent lips of Roger Vadim girls, blowing cigarette curls only lightly laced with pot.

The seekers for whom this is just a stepping stone, the route to their Orient an acid fried antidote to the buzz cut thrill seekers of his east.

For some reason he finds this all quite funny, the utter solemnity with which the names of the high priests are evoked. Ginsberg, Burroughs, Leary, the streams of... something, or the dreams of growing golden corn from dung.

It never fails to amuse him how the easy smile which plays on his lips is misread time and again as a kind of worldly wisdom. And it seems to make him irresistible to a certain kind of seeker. Sometimes they take him along with them to West End clubs with strange names like Middle Earth and UFO.

He smiles in the dark where others take a trip, the back

of the stage morphing with oil slides stirring under the heat of the projectionist's lamp.

Other nights reconnoitring pubs with a rep for party intelligence and then the gatecrash of some unsuspecting host, girls and beads and tabs in the front to ensure admission. It is all quite funny, thirst for every possible intoxicant slaked on another's coin, hair flying and not a buzz cut in sight. But when he finally stops to look around at the headbands, the incense and the flowing dresses, though it is funny, it is just not fun.

11.

In spite of the late summer heat, he insists on wearing his boots nearly every day. He has found work in a hardware store, something of that wry smile translating to customer service and impressing the guv'nor. The ink on his arm and a strategic mention of the docks *that* side of the drink keep questions to a minimum from his employer. The assumption seems to be that provided he turns up on time and keeps his nose clean everything will be fine. It is the second time recently he's seen that look on a stranger's face on hearing the phrase, 'I've been away for a while.'

Much of the time is spent up a storeroom ladder, pulling screws and hammers and bolts from well hidden boxes and then bringing them back out front for the handymen or would-be fixers who make up most of the customers.

They like him too, a reassuring bulk behind the light brown overalls and very little idle chatter. None of the furtive glances or the adolescent smirking they have to put up with from the Saturday boys.

Lunchtimes he takes a walk around the surrounding streets, choosing a different one each day for the backdrop to his sarnies. Homemade of course, but increasingly with meat products smuggled inside when the other hairies aren't looking.

The work and the routine is just what he needs after those long, empty summer days. It means he can pay his own way too, though in truth he rarely sees anyone pay for anything where he stays. But the ham and the cold cuts taste good away from the seekers and he enjoys this time on his own much as he used to savour shore leave in another life.

Just a couple of streets away from the hairies and though it's still stucco, the paint here is peeling away, little flakes landing next to the weeds which are sprouting everywhere.

J. sits on a wall in front of one of these houses and ponders the decline, a tiny bubble of brown sauce squirting out of the sides of the bread.

He watches from the other side of the road as a big man enters the house opposite. Moments later there are shouts followed by the muted sounds of protest coming from inside.

'You can't do this to me! I've got nowhere else to go.'

A suitcase lands on the pavement, clothes flying out of it in mid air.

'What are you doing, man? Why are you doing this? I said I'm good for it. I will be by the end of the week. Just a couple more days, man, that's all I need.'

Records start flying out of the window, the big man removing the vinyl from its sleeves before hurling them, one after the other, like a demented knife thrower at the circus. Except that it is all so measured.

'Stop! Don't do that! Please stop!' says the distressed

tenant, but his words have no effect on the record breaker.

The little black discs keep smashing on the concrete, though one or two have their fall broken by the random clusters of weeds.

J. looks up in time to see the tenant lunging at the big man, hears a thud, and then several more before the big man reappears at the window from where he quickly scans the street. Even after he draws the curtains muffled sounds continue to leak outside from the room for some time. And then they stop.

When the big man strides back out he barely pauses to register the black splinters now strewn all over the pavement. He does however double check the other side of the street where he's sure there was a man sat there just moments before eating his lunch. Satisfying himself that the man is no longer there, he strides purposefully away, patting at an inside pocket in some involuntary reflex.

J. waits until his breathing has slowed a little, then nervously lifts his head above the wall. It was an instinctive dive into the bush in the first place the moment the big man had drawn the curtains. But his breathing is still laboured, relief and a kind of sickness taking over when the man had come over to the wall but not bothered to look in the front yard. He dusts down his overalls, though the sarnies can't be salvaged quite so easily.

By the time he has established there are no tears in the overalls, the tenant is back outside, foraging among the weeds for any unspoilt vinyl. For now at least he seems less concerned with the items of clothing or the suitcase, though it is clear that the records which have survived are the ones which have sought out a shirt, or some weeds, or in one lucky case, a thick, woollen coat for a softer landing.

It seems pointless to ask the man if he is ok but deep held habit makes him do that anyway.

The man looks up. One side of his face is already swollen, the ebony of his skin a dark blue mass of bruises, the left eye closing up, the lower lip cracked and cut.

He doesn't say anything but every movement he makes appears to leave him wincing with pain, one hand inter-mittently shooting to his ribs while the other continues with its hopeless task in the weeds.

12.

1s 9d at the pictures to see 'The Graduate'. He enjoys it, but there is an argument afterwards with one of the longhairs.

'They're all so plastic. I mean they were all so fake,' says the hairy.

'I'm not so sure about that,' says J. 'What about Mrs. Robinson?'

'Mrs. Robinson?!'

'That's right. Mrs. Robinson.'

'Don't play games, man,' says the longhair.

'I'm not. I mean it. She was no fake. The rest of them, maybe, but not her.'

'What are you saying, man?'

'Just what it sounds like. The rest of them, granted, they drop out for a bit, but at the end, did you see that look they give each other? They're not even sure they want all that freedom any more. At least that's what I saw.'

'Shit, man, that's not cool,' says the longhair, looking around for support. 'That's not cool at all. I don't dig what you say, man.'

The others are looking his way now, closing ranks around the offended party, offering him a shoulder and whispered consolations before turning back to J. with that wounded look so many of them seem to have perfected over the summer.

A young woman, recently back from Monterey with tales full of mystical sounds and vibes of pure love, then pipes up, pointing at J., 'I saw him going into that shop earlier on.'

'Which shop?' the others ask.

'The bad one,' she says, the California tan smarting under all that outrage. 'Where they sell dead things.'

There is a sharp intake of breath. He can see where this is headed. The way they ignore him even though he is right there a sure sign. As though he has already departed.

On your own now. Just you.

In the end it is something of a relief to him. It has been a while coming and really the only surprise is that it has taken *this* long. He has thought about this moment more than once recently, about what it would feel like. But now that it is actually here he is only struck by how little he feels.

One last bit of panto, more for their benefit than his , though he can tell there is still some fascination for all that unfamiliar in the eyes of these brittle creatures. He can feel it in their uncertainty, in those doubts about what will happen next.

How will the stranger who always wore boots react? Will he be angry? How will they defend themselves?

He sees the doubts flickering one to the next, the Nehru-collared huddle no kind of protection. And suddenly it is clear to him what needs to happen.

This is the moment to reaffirm his authority, its proof in calloused hands and the righteousness of labour. Ink and oceans and the careworn wisdoms of antiquity. Doodlebugs bouncing up the Mile End Road and a curious child unearthing mysteries encased in mud.

This is the time for old resentments and their machine tooled fury, for splinters lovingly extracted from hands and buzz cuts shaving bile to the raw.

And on any other day, a different kind of boy to have emerged from that rubble, with lacquer and a comb and a heart full of casual brutalities, might well have chosen this as his moment. But J. is not that boy, and it is questions, not cruelty, that fill his heart.

He is tempted though, especially when one of the longhairs places an organic paw on the California tan's shoulders and addresses J. with all the gravity he can muster.

'I think you should go now.'

He knows he should feel something, but in reality there is nothing. Not even when he lobs in the pantomime,

'I suppose a cup of tea's out of the question then? Herbal's fine.'

13.

He takes a room in one of the crumbling houses not far from where he saw that man take a beating. It is still close enough to his work and he knows from the time he has spent with the longhairs that for all their talk of peace and love they don't stray far from a very narrow circuit where all the faces are familiar, and very few are Black.

Often when he returns from work a Black family will be camped out on the stairs of one of these houses, suitcases in tow, waiting anxiously while curtains twitch. Then a young white man will appear with the keys to one of the flats inside and whatever bargain needs to be struck is done away from prying eyes.

Other times the suitcase will be travelling in the opposite direction, and the mournful protests, the shouting and the hitting which so shocked him before quickly loses its power to offend.

When removal vans appear he soon learns that the evacuees are invariably white, faces pinched tight, emotions pursed behind a parade of mattresses and tables, armchairs and the wireless. Occasionally a Hillman Super minx will pull away, creaking under the weight of some invisible regret, and with indecent haste a fresh cargo will arrive, Sunday best and on foot.

This street is a lot busier than the one he was on before. Many of the houses have been converted into flats and it is often noisy well into the night.

Still, he doesn't mind as much as some, the complaints starting off as description but quickly morphing into their true nature.

'It didn't use to be like this round here. I still remember how things used to be. A lot quieter before, people knew each other, knew each other's families, so you wouldn't get a racket until the early hours. And you could leave your doors open. Everyone knew everyone, do you know what I mean?'

'Not sure I do,' he lies, knowing exactly what the man across the road means.

'They weren't so bad back then either. But there's more of them now, and it's us that need to watch out.'

'And what is it again that we're supposed to watch out for?'

'You know, you don't need me to tell you that.'

'Well, I better stay alert then,' says J., the sarcasm washing clean over his neighbour.

His boss has no such concerns though. A lot more customers have been coming through his door since J. has been working there. 'Increased footfall' he calls it, using the jargon he has picked up from some manual he's always thumbing through. If it bothers him at all that most of these customers are Black, he never mentions it, his demeanour consistent, and consistently dour, no matter whose arrival the two tone doorbell announces.

The neighbour is right though, there *is* a lot more noise of late, newcomers sitting on porch steps and conversations heading way past the national anthem.

The youngsters on his street rarely say anything to J. when they are together, but they might sometimes nod his way if there are no peers to impress.

It is funny, the kids back home were the same. He finds himself thinking that more and more, even says it once or twice. *Back home*. So what does that make this?

#

One night, coming home late after the last show at the ABC, he decides to make a little detour via the old square with the longhairs. Perhaps it is the fresh memory of Bond and his suave Oriental exploits which make him bold, but when he passes another of the big stucco fronts a little further along and hears a loud, sweet vocal spilling out of the open windows he stops, and for once doesn't hesitate as he heads up the steps.

#

Inside there are people lining the stairs all the way up. It is an odd mixture, the usual longhairs of course, but there's more money here and a bit more flash, a whole house to play with and if the rug in the hallway is any kind of indication, some fancy interiors as well.

Black faces too, quarter length leather coats and champagne moving through the expected cloud of dope smoke. He doesn't recognize anyone from his street. Nor are any of his former comrades here.

Spying an open bottle of champagne on the table behind two of the Black men, J. goes to pour himself a drink.

'Wha' di rass do you think you're doing?' says one of the men, sporting a beret.

'Having a drink, squire,' says J.

'Is wha' kind of foolishness, this?' the other man cuts in.

'No foolishness, squire, just a drink, is all,' says J. making sure to measure the 'k' and maintain eye contact when he says 'drink'.

The first man shakes his head, throws a bored look at his friend, and they move to another part of the room, leaving J. to the bottle. Krug. A first for him.

Looking up, he spots his two inquisitors, happier now with glasses refilled as a couple of young women decked out in furs over long boots hold on to their every word.

He is holding the bottle, pouring himself a refill when he notices the wall mounted display cabinet full of Japanese plates.

'They're proper fancy, don't you think?'

Turning to his right he notices her boots first, then looks at her properly from the floor up. She is not as tall as the other women here and like him is clutching onto a full glass.

'Yes, they're nice,' he says.

'No wonder they're up on the wall then,' she adds, 'you wouldn't want your dog's dinner off them.'

They both laugh and then he stretches out a hand.

'I'm J.,' he says.

'Delighted, I'm sure,' she replies, offering a fake curtsey. Then, holding out her hand, she says, 'I'm L.'

#

There are Persian carpets and tapestries, antique silks and conch shells. As they take their own grand tour, they leave the perfumed smoke and the berets, the scowls and the furs, further and further behind.

On the wall they spy cracked canvases with faded nameplates and the higher they go the dustier the gloom. Until there is nowhere further and they race back down past the unsmiling wallflowers and the chemical enhancers, back past the Moroccan tiles and the solid English stone, and right back into the cavernous reception room where that popular record is playing, the one favoured by the porch owls on his street.

Them a loot, Them a shoot but this is no shanty.

And they're dancing together, hip to thigh, L. showing him how. They stay that way through the tommy guns and screeching tyres, paying no mind to the strange inside out dances happening around them.

'I love this one,' she tells him, spelling out the letters in time with the singer, 'C-A-P-O-N-E. Kerpown.'

As they're leaving they hear the sounds of an old piano as if held together by little more than dust. But he knows these keys from somewhere, is sure he has heard that lament before.

The curtain has fallen, now you're on your own.

They arrange to meet again and when J. goes to collect her one evening after work from an address nearby, he is surprised to find the door opened by a young boy, who can't be more than seven or eight, standing there with a quizzical look.

L. appears in the hallway behind him, straightening her coat.

'Well I see you've met each other then,' she says. 'J., this is my son, S. He'll be joining us. I hope you don't mind.'

#

After their first 'date', the three of them walking back from the ABC, Bayswater still laughing about Jim Dale's forward combed hair, he is surprised for the second time when L. slips her hand into his. More so when he thinks they must look like any other family round here going for a walk.

She has fun pointing out the Jean Shrimpton lookalikes on every corner, though Twiggy is her favourite, so elegant but with a mouth Barbara Windsor would be proud of. With the Shrimp, she reckons it is more pouty, a bit more affected, something for the press corps to latch onto.

There is an openness about her which is new to him. She doesn't carry on as though this is some indecipherable jungle, a ruined paradise full of junk and incense. Not like the longhairs in his previous place, clouding everything with swirls of smoke, a mystical fog descending from some cosmic portal. From which the only thing to ever emerge was more *dhoop*, though only he knows it as that. Or on a bad day those injured looks, some unspecified hurt at the wrong code, the wrong 'vibe', the wrong food being invoked by the uninitiated.

At one point, near Elgin Avenue, he finds himself putting a protective arm around the little boy's shoulder as a group of young men pass with a bow legged swagger he's rarely seen before this side of the drink. They have the same clippered scowl as the apprentice toughs he witnessed that time lining up for their buzz cuts.

Nothing is actually said, though the elbows are barely tucked in, and he is grateful for the presence of the little boy, an unwitting buffer through all that snarl. Even so, when he gets home J. makes sure to trim the beard, the sink in one corner of his dimly lit room rapidly filling up with the dead waste of these past months.

#

Things move quickly after that. Before winter properly arrives he has moved in with them, the decision made easier by the way S. allows him to place a protective hand on his shoulder, or guide him across the road in the busier streets around Bayswater.

He looks forward to their nights at the pictures, a treat after the dust and metal combination of the storeroom. Something of that packaging, the workaday fittings, settles on his clothes, and after a while he can even taste the metal on his tongue.

So those days spent wandering, a little boy sticking close to him and the contentment of the boy's mother, spill over into newfound joy, each time wiping away another fraction of the metallic taint. And they start to grow bolder, taking their chances with the repertory crowd in the fleapit on the Portobello Road.

It is a world away from the ABC and they make for a curious sight amongst the meths and the crazies and the ladies not dressed for winter; the young boy and his 'parents', no smell of fear coming off them, sidestepping the looks and the odd snippet of stray language.

They are untroubled by the noise, its randomness quickly familiar, the stares under occasional berets just a stylistic tic, a gauntlet for the uninitiated. But to them no kind of a marker at all, just nighttime ephemera.

And the stern faced men under the berets quickly lose interest, turning their attention to the more easily cowed, pre fab seekers with no ink and no lines under eyes that have already seen plenty.

So when the decision is made, it is hardly even that, more an extension of their weekday constitutionals.

In J.'s case there is no need for a van, or helpers, and he leaves one morning as unobtrusively as he'd arrived, a holdall in one hand and some vague street-specific nostalgia he feels he ought to cultivate.

#

14.

'Hammers.'

He looks up from the counter, where he has been reading about Jagger quoting Shelley down the park. If the pictures are anything to go by, the man is still a scruff and still enjoys being surrounded by other scruffs, though the ones on bikes with the studs and leathers and those Kaiser helmets look a bit of a worry. Not that anyone seems bothered. They're saying a hundred thousand went along. A hundred thousand!

'Sorry, what was that again?' he asks, making a note of the braces and the sideburns.

'Hammers, mate. You got any hammers?' the man asks again.

'Any particular type?'

'Claw ones, mate. The ones with the claw,' the man says, duplicating the upward motion of removing a nail with such a hammer.

Looking again at the man, J. realises it is not so much the sideburns or the braces as the ink on the man's burly arms which has caught his attention.

'Is that Celtic then?' J. asks, nodding towards the wrought iron pattern snaking all the way up the forearm.

'Eh?'

'Couldn't help noticing your ink. Just wondering if it's Celtic,' J. says.

'Nah, mate, it's English,' the man replies. 'Had it done here.'

'English?'

'That's what I said the first time,' the man repeats, his voice betraying a hint of irritation.

'So you know about tattooing then?' J. asks.

'Look mate, I just came in for some hammers,' the man says, 'So have you got ---

'The thing with western tattoos is they're generally a bit slipshod. The experts reckon it's because westerners haven't really come to terms yet with the three dimensional properties of the human body, not like the older cultures. You know how they used to do it in the South Pacific. They used to tie flint and bone together, tie 'em at a right angle to a stick, and then use another stick to drive the points into the skin. That's how they got so good, they had to be. Not like the artists here. Artists?! The neck on some people, eh?'

The man is staring at him, a silent rage behind the eyes, clearly unused to this type of carry on but also unsure as to how he should react.

'Oh and by the way, looks like we're right out of hammers too,' says J., balling then unclenching his fists beneath the counter.

#

15.

'Did it hurt getting that done?' S. asks him, pointing to the tattooed symbol on his arm.

'Not really, son. The man who did it was very skillful. He spoke very little English, but he told me to surf the pain as it comes in waves. And he gave me some good advice. Don't scratch it, don't swim, don't get it wet and don't sunbathe. Well it would have been good advice if I hadn't been in the tropics at the time.'

Did he really just call him 'son'? Ah well, stranger things had happened.

Of late he'd been seeing plenty of surly creatures, often on his way back in the evenings. The boots and braces, the cropped hair but without the scowls, out in the street having a kickabout with their neighbours, sounds spilling out of one or other of the open windows.

Every now and then he still catches a look but since the beard has been lost and the hair has followed it back above the collars he puts it down to unfamiliarity. In the unspoken protocol of locality, he's only been here ten minutes and they've walked this earth for all of an hour. Behind those manners he can see they're still just kids, copping a feel in the cheap seats while the real adults have places of their own.

Hard denim takes the brunt of the winter chill, the donkey jackets he's first seen on the docks making a re-appearance on these west London streets. He sees them coming out of John Collier's, armed with Fred Perry T-shirts and sta-prest trousers. And the donkey jacket gives way to a Crombie, Harringtons kept back for a rainy day. Before long it is a lot more than a kickabout that they share with their neighbours. The shift happens right there, right in front of him, the little urchins suddenly believing they're part of something bigger. And urchins no more, the tribe makes itself known. Peanuts. The half mast trousers and the shaved in razor partings some kind of shorthand, moonstomping their way through another noisy night, the neighbours there too, meanwhile the both of them unable to sleep, L. laying there knowing all the records but wishing they'd keep it down anyway.

Nights like those he is tempted to have a word, then wonders what might happen if he does, whether he might cop more than a look in return.

He doesn't pay too much attention to the headlines, but he has heard the stories of boots and bike chains and injuries.

He learns about the oxbloods and copies of 'Live Injection' clutched tightly to Harringtons. Sees it every other day, hears the streetside peanuts talking about 'bashing them' on their trips way out west to the Musicland outlet in Hounslow, the one with the good stuff, the Pioneers and their favourite, with the boss skinhead, Caleb.

Overhears them in a caff one time, full English on the

way, enjoying the discomfort their presence provokes, the other diners looking away or suddenly engrossed in the red tops. Looks up from his own mug of tea to see the proprietor taking their orders in one tongue and then finding another for the kitchen, sizzling and crackling and lament smuggled in with the Cypriot. Back on the shop floor a more localized complaint.

'I mean it's all that garlic, really. They smell.'

'You're right, it stinks up there. But they never say nothing unless it's that monkey speak. English, I tell 'em, speak fucking English over here and while you're at it, stop washing your hair in chip fat.'

They all laugh.

'So anyway, I'm up there pointing this out and one of them's had a go, some fucking Gandhi telling me to "please be getting away from my shop".' He puts on the accent, head wobbling for maximum effect.

'You're joking?'

'I know, the fucking neck on these. So anyway I did leave his shop, but not before turning the fucking place over. Give him a slap on the way out'n'all, cheeky Paki bastard.'

'Yeah, but did you get the vinyl?'

'Course I got the record, you dozy sod. What sort of a cunt do you take me for?'

#

The discovery comes one lunchtime when he is rooting around in the charity shop near his work. It is all the usual tat: crinoline and polyester, well thumbed Agatha Christie's. Leaning in to have a closer look at the James Hadley Chase, his foot encounters some resistance. There is a box of records on the floor, Tijuana Brass promising garish delights where Butch and Sundance fell short. Crouching down, he flicks past Tom Jones and Charley Pride and a couple of empty sleeves before his eye settles on the next image. At first he thinks they are Americans, they have that look of the vocal trios to emerge from there every so often. But when he looks again, the give-away is the foliage in the background and that yellow shirt. He might be wrong but something in their expressions just seems to scream 'island' to him. It is a country look he's seen before, but not here. 'Sufferer', the letters propping up their shoes, the island hunch borne out by the legend, 'The Kingstonians'.

Behind it, 'Club Ska '67' and a series of 'Tighten Up' records, volumes 1, 2 and 3. The rest of the box is made up of half familiar names on the smaller sevens. The Pioneers, The Conquerors, Derrick Morgan. He has heard L. talking about the Pioneers before and is sure Derrick Morgan's name has come up too. Some Caleb has been shedding his skin, J. thinks, as he takes the lot, has them bagged up and heads back to the shop with the loot under his arm.

That evening when he gets back, the peanuts are already in the street, eyeing up the locals with the usual mixture of boredom and mischief. One of the older ones spots the bag.

'What you got there?' he asks J.

'Nothing much,' says J., wondering why he's even bothered to reply. In all the months he's been here there has barely been any acknowledgement of his presence beyond a scowl here and a disinterested look there.

'Don't look like nothing much,' says the older youth, stubbing out his fag and clambering down from the wall.

The others have stopped their game, suddenly interested in this early evening tango. He is surrounded, a couple of the urchins with arms folded, the rest with hands still in pockets.

'Give us a look then,' says the older youth, looking J. straight in the eye.

'Afraid not,' says J., making sure to sound less agitated than he feels. The youth moves a step closer, the others in close attendance. J. can almost feel them smirking behind his back.

'Go on, mate, just a quick peek,' says the youth, feeling bolder with his family in tow.

'No.'

'What? I wasn't asking,' says the youth, his expression changing.

'Just as well I wasn't answering then,' replies J., composure returning after a brief wobble but still keeping as many of the urchins as possible in his peripheral vision.

'There you are. I was wondering where you'd got to.'

They turn around. It is L., in her apron still holding the duster she'd been using when she'd happened to glance out of the front window and seen a reception committee start to form around her fella. Suitably shamed, the urchins disperse, trailing some choice complaints about things not being how they used to while J. heads indoors with a levity he hasn't really felt since Nan passed.

#

16.

He is under the sink one morning, working the putty knife to remove all the old caulk from the joint.

L. had been going on at him to take a look at it ever since she noticed the stain spreading across the surrounding wall. Her suspicions proved justified when he'd gone to investigate, the telltale cracks in the caulking between the fixture and the wall the main cause of the damage. He'd scrubbed the joint with chlorine bleach, taking ages to dry it out with a clean rag wrapped over the blade of the knife. Though it is not warm the sweat pours off him as he works the knife, thinking this is the kind of thing he could manage in his sleep during those years when he was at sea. Now, not only is he struggling but he needs a helper as well. S. is right there, handing him the rag, then the knife, then the scissors with which J. cuts the nozzle of the caulk tube at an angle. In another way though it is good as he can tell the boy is enjoying the role of apprentice and he makes sure to provide him with a running commentary, stressing the usefulness of the boy's actions.

'If you can fetch me a rag. That's it, good lad. I'm cleaning it all out now with that bleach… And the rag's got to be wrapped over the blade. Now if you can get me that tube and some scissors. Good lad. It's like toothpaste really, just got to squeeze it out over the joint. And last but not least, got to let it dry out now. How long does it take? Good question. A few hours should do it, and then it'll be good as new.'

Ever since he'd given S. the pick of the records, the boy just wanted to sit and listen to him, whatever banalities he was spouting. That day after the near miss with the peanuts, L. had sorted through them and decided she only needed the Nicky Thomas single for herself, so he'd given the rest to the boy.

They quickly become his pride and joy, stacked up on the Dansette record player as he studies the sleeves, the artwork, the cast list of musicians and labels, Trojan and Grape and Duke tripping off his tongue the way other boys talk about James Bond or George Best. Things get easier with the peanuts too, the bass lines and organ breaks fending off the worst of their mischief. While at school he finally has something to talk about, the decimal point belatedly shifting, even if just by a fraction, in a routine unused to such interest. When the other kids talk about their families, the uncles, aunties, cousins, christenings, he still feels a little awkward—it is after all just the three of them—but at least the panic at what he might say should they ask him is no longer there. The three of them at home, just like the three of them on Sufferer, looking out, maybe seeing different things, but all sitting on the same block of stone.

Through Jimi, and Janis, and David, and Marc, past the spacemen in boots with lip liner and gloss, the hot pants and cold winters, the three of them on their block, seeing differently but looking, really looking, at one another. For the little tics, the details of a shift, hair and collars and method and mascara. And there it is in the candlelit greys of the powercut evenings, J.'s sideburns wobbling in the flame, L. more concerned with the metal stud newly appointed in her son's ear.

She looks at J., hoping he'll say something though she can't for the life of her imagine what. Somehow though, this feels worse than when S. had gone through that peanut phase, all elbows and bristle like the rest of them. But at least that had been familiar. The sounds, even the scowl, wholly unsurprising, though the look had never been quite right on him, and she'd been glad about that. Relieved at the lack of conviction when he ironed those collars, that small face belying a couth that the chewing and occasional cursing could never really hide.

This high up, in the tower blocks peering down at the old streets, the curses sometimes hang in the air, but it is not S. whose mouth curls at the sky.

#

When the opportunity had first come up, L. had been the one to get excited, a cloud capped view in the towers the fresh start she'd always wanted. And at first that's how she had felt, grateful each day for the miraculous panorama flooding through the windows. She loved that they were so far away from that other life on the ground, of metal and junk and peanuts, eyes and elbows sharpened on local stones. But soon there is damp and decline and what once felt new now drips in spite.

'Lift not working', the three words she most dreads, dragging her weary body up stairwells and past strangers, the bags of market value groaning under the weight of all that malfunction.

She thought S. would be happy to be away from the peanuts, but cloaked in sky he withdraws into himself again, studs and scars marking time behind a routinely closed door. And what can she honestly tell J. that he didn't know from the start? He was never keen, had only gone along with it because she was so adamant. She sees his relief in the mornings when he sets out for work, feels the slow burn of his resentment at the end of days which seem to just grow, the junk and smoke of the street savoured for every moment they delay his return.

She is alone up here in a way she has rarely known before, occasionally raised voices from the stairwell the only sounds she hears some days. Or the lift spilling out its cargo of petty resentments, wage slips and weariness fellow travellers in its mindless up down. Other times its doors open and she knows to not touch the sides, the up down provoking so many mindless acts in here.

One of the few times she laughs is when a couple of kids who've somehow fallen off the grid step in, clutching the sides marvelling at their own sense of adventure, to be here at all and with someone like her. From their accents she guesses they are not local, the strong smell of weed coming off them some indication as to why they are here. She notes the mildly amused look of incomprehension they give her as if to ask why she is standing in the middle? Oh, *that's* why. That's disgusting. You don't do that in your own lift.

Even then she hates herself for being that person who finds this kind of stuff funny. She never used to be this way, she thinks. She wonders what happened to that open hearted girl who danced and had fun and loved the vocal harmonies led by Jackie Bernard. That girl used to like people, and they liked her back, though not always in the right way. But she was nice, that girl, easier to forgive.

And some older habits creep into the lifts too, drink and fags and tally men a toxic ballast, everything perishable now, everyone a potential mark.

Her unhappiness the scent they follow up, knocking on doors, feeding off boredom and the hollow sound of lives which somehow, this high up, just stopped.

Backed up on the Dansette, the old records she can hardly bear to listen to any more. The day they come knocking, 'Singer Man' playing, Derrick Harriott at his best, there she is right by the turntable, the spirit of '67 frozen in time, noticeably out of place now. But she barely hears that broadest of bass lines any more. To her the long organ breaks now conjure up a funeral dirge, just making her more tearful and in the end almost grateful for the sharply wrapped knuckles on the door.

'It just needs freshening up,' they tell her, and how she longs to hear those words. 'No wonder you're feeling down, madam,' they say, looking around the flat with practised disdain, 'Didn't anyone tell you you're not a housewife anymore, you're a domestic manager. And like all good managers you've got to check the inventory, freshen up the stock once in a while.'

So the flat fills up with Prestige Pressure Cookers and Picnic Sets, Cornish kitchenware and Crystal Design carpets.

She lauds the 'simple geometric shapes' of Braun and tries to win J. over by including one of its stylish electric razors on the never never.

'No need for any more shaving creams or soap,' she tells him, though to his ears this just sounds like a lack of personal hygiene. 'It's got an oscillating motor and rechargeable batteries,' she says, remembering some of the tally man's schtick, though in fairness her mind has already drifted to the mixing properties of the Kenwood Chef.

So wrapped up with the stacking stools and the ant chairs, the ones made of ABS plastic and the ones with a metal frame, she has barely noticed the bigger design shifts taking place right in front of her. 'My week beats your year' in ransom lettering on her son's door. Inside, 'Queen Bitch' up on the wall, magazine clippings of a strange looking creature, a crooked smile and a streaked face. Vinyl stacked in a milk crate, English pastoral giving way to something more unhinged, a mortal coil crawling out of a carcass. Looking back and like everything else round here staring straight ahead because the only other place is down, into the bowels of failure, a splat on the concrete to be licked at by worms. And *this* English pastoral it seems is bookended by old style Jamaica, the peanuts staring across from one stone block to the sufferers on another.

She has somehow managed to miss the piercings and the cuttings, the trading of bristles for spikes, Bowie set aside for bedlam. All of this has passed her by.

Razor blades neatly laid out on a table, some coarse string through which they have been threaded. And next to them, peeping out of its sleeve, something suddenly, gorgeously familiar. The Slickers, 'Johnny Too Bad', and the briefest of flickers from a happier time, inside out dances and next to this, everything dizzyingly back to front.

She has missed all of this. When did that little boy with the sweet face become so angry? This creature of blades and blood, half-mast now full blown. When did this happen and how could she not have known?

#

She has grown used to knuckles wrapping on doors too, so when she hears that sound for the umpteenth time, L. barely gives it a second thought as she opens the door.

It is not the usual tally man or that familiar smile. The big man stood there with the baleful eyes invites himself in, those eyes appearing to make a quick inventory of the various rooms as he sweeps through the flat.

He stops near the Beogram 4000 turntable still housed in its protective packaging. Another sweetener for J., the Dansette destined for her son's room.

'State of the art,' the man says, repeating the words on the packaging.

L. stays silent, the shock still registering.

The man says something very quietly, as if to himself.

Then he looks over at L. who appears to be shaking.

'What do you think?' he asks her, snake eyes locking onto her trembling face.

'I'm sorry, I'm not sure I understand,' she says, trying hard not to cry.

'Maybe you didn't hear me before,' the man says. 'So I'll repeat, "the price of everything the value of nothing." And I asked you what you think of that.'

'I, I, don't know,' she stutters, snake eyes burning into her flesh.

'Well, I do,' the man says, raising himself off the arm of the sofa to his full height until he is towering over her.

'It's time to pay now.'

#

17.

West London, mid-1970s

J. gets the call at work from one of the neighbours. By the time he gets back there is an ambulance at the entrance to their block. Ticker Tape is already over the front door, a steady stream of unfamiliar faces passing in and out, largely ignoring him until one of them asks him who he is.

Luckily it takes longer for the news to filter through to S.'s school and J. is able to collect him before the uniform dispatch arrives.

And when all the questions have been asked and the formalities concluded, when they have been ruled out but no one, or nothing else seems to have been ruled in, *that's* when he is seized by a numbness, when he journeys into the metal in the storeroom, into its carbons, swallowed by dust and a longing to pierce his flesh with those old Tahitian flints, to cut and skewer and carve until all is liquid, a free flowing bloody stream just waiting for an ocean to have its say. But it is nails and screws and hammers he makes do with, as an old life is gradually dismantled, put away in boxes, sealed in bin liners.

With S., the razors are put away, and the scars allowed to heal. It is as though he wants to stop time, his flesh the portal to a distant age before any of this, the three of them walking and laughing, thick as thieves but with no need for loot. The Electric and the peanuts and an empire of signs in the junk.

#

So they walk, the journeys together the only consolation they know to offer one another. A tragic accident, they'd been told, she'd slipped, hit her head on the corner of the new worktop, but it doesn't sound right somehow, this girl who was always so steady, never missed a beat on the old inside out, and now she's supposed to have slipped, left them like this. What about the strange man the neighbour had seen walking away from the block shortly afterwards? Who was he? Where was he headed? Where had he come from?

They walk away from the questions, grow bored with the stock responses, the lack of progress, the 'calm down and reconsider'.

Before long even the tea and sympathy are in short supply, so they walk away from all that disinterest and keep walking, footfalls on the worn stones training the flesh, teasing, cajoling, telling them there's more, more of this grime, as much as you want, as much as you need, gents.

They listen to the awful details of strangers, flights to the afterlife delayed in A&E, a mugging in the park, don't go there, fellas, it's full of them - coons and pakis and pikeys and jakeys, and what a rhythm of despair that is, full throttle into the heart of the stink. In the doorways and stairwells and moth eaten coats, there's enough of this grime to last a lifetime.

So they plough on, the questions growing fainter, each step loosening that umbilical, the cloud capped and the stucco fronted now near-extinct traces of another life. Suits and braces and boots and skirts and hotpants and brylcreem and crepe soled spectres. They pass them all and then they leave the narrow streets behind, so that suddenly he is back with the pepper grinders and the spice merchants, though they're all long gone too. The boy looks on confused as they stop by a river basin, J. pointing to a sign up ahead.

Blackwall Tunnel Northern Approach.

'Why are we stopping here?' he asks J.

'Nowhere else to go,' says J.

'What do you mean by that?' asks the boy.

'Only one more road, son, and it goes south,' J. replies.

#

When the place becomes available they take it as a sign. Deep South perhaps the one spot in this city where their numbness will go unremarked too. As for this new place, no one else seemed to want it once they knew what happened inside. All that after dark of sex and perverts and masks and groans. Well, almost no one.

Meanwhile a death pallor has settled over their old flat, and perhaps it is that, or maybe it is the unanswered questions, the boredom of those whose job it is to take an interest, which helps them decide. Either way they take the plunge, and one unseasonably hot morning, of which there have already been a few in this early summer heat-wave, J. makes the arrangements and for the first time in his life waits with impatience for a van to arrive. Movers and cases and bags and boxes, and himself and S., all headed south for a fresh start off the grid.

Part Four

Some other South

1.

Calcutta, post-Partition

Back then it was all he could do to walk. Mornings the best, a quietness before the heat and noise of day, only the half eye of the *kutta* watching him rise up off the bench, stretch aching limbs and yawn. The other strays lined up in their dusty crescent, little bellies gently breathing. Human limbs splayed out too, his brothers snatching rest in these brief moments of respite, knowing the steel tipped lathis are never that far. For now just the three of them. Nila never made it through those days of chaos, of cutlass on bone, and worse. Their family, like their compound, until recently so formidable, scattered like strangers as if centuries of presence counted for nothing. Banished in an instant, the compound no match for the mob. The sounds from the jute mills warning enough. And perhaps they'd been lucky that way, though not Nila. Not their didi. No news from the others, farmed out before the havoc to relatives this side of the line. But as boys, and the strongest, the three of them slipping across under cover of darkness and tarpaulin, and now just biding their time hoping for a fresh start in a city which barely even sees them.

At first when the *kutta* follows him it stops at the mouth of the park. On the third or fourth day though, it decides to venture further.

In the narrow little gullies and lanes off Chitteranjan Avenue, all the way from the Bow Bazar crossing in the South to Sovabazar in the North, he senses the creature's tiny footfalls as it nimbly avoids the still largely obscured shapes beginning to stir on the pavement. It follows him past the cooking fires in their infancy and the lamps lit on chai stalls, and the rickshaw wallahs already on the lookout for the day's first fare, while others are still sitting or sleeping on their stationary rickshaws. The gentle tapping of bells against the shafts will grow louder as the city awakes, but for now it is little more than the nuzzling of early morning lovers.

The occasional looks he elicits from the rickshaw wallahs make it clear he is not part of this tryst, his value ordained in the days' old grime on that shirt, or in the giveaway particles of dust in the hair, the companionship of beasts a rare solace.

There are times he wants to join the cows nosing around in the gutters for vegetable waste, when the smell of overripe fruit mingled with the *dhoop* wafting over from the open fronted shrines makes him so hungry and sad that he wants to retch, right there in front of the crows who are also present. Within full view of the hawkers, then the *bhadralok*. Retch his guts up within earshot, interrupt the slap of laundry upon stone or the sound of metal cooking pots being scoured. Then he will look around and see the *kutta* sat on the pavement behind him, loyally awaiting the signal to move on. And something deeper than the gnarled flight path of his guts will reawaken other hungers, drive him on past the great iron beast of Howrah, that vast tide of humanity just beginning to form on its western bank.

Trailed by the smoke from open cooking fires and the promises of hot ghee, he passes a hutment made out of packing cases, brick, tin, bits of canvas and plastic sheeting, the whole structure held together with little more than defiance. Looking inside he can see a woman squatting down to light a cooking fire, a small child in attendance. As his eyes adjust to the gloom he is even able to make out a makeshift washing line being monitored by another young child carrying a baby held to her hip. They look at him and when they smile, he feels a deep well of shame rising from where only moments before he had felt sharp hunger pangs.

The *kutta* follows him all the way up to Dalhousie Square, where they ponder meals past in the Lal Dighi. From school he knows that this pond used to be the source of fish for the Governor's table, but the only marinade now is the diesel coming from the bus depot on the other side of the square. By the time they reach the General Post Office, the grandiosity of its Corinthian pillars feels like a sick joke mocking them, how thin they are, and somehow placing them amongst the ranks of the illiterate clustering nearby around the professional letter writers.

They see these men dotted around with the tools of their trade, sitting at fold up tables in the self important manner of court clerks. The ones without a table make do with upturned crates, pens, paper, envelopes and typewriters at the ready. Unlike the rickshaw wallahs they rarely look up, touting for business. There is no need.

The lifeblood of an ancient bureaucracy ensures a steady stream of clients who will seek them out. Indeed when he looks again he gets the strong sense that what he is really admiring is something else entirely, the letter writing just a handy prop. The memory jogged again from school, Sir with his glasses, handing down wisdom but always withholding just a little, making them wait for the full story. A portion here, a fraction there until even the most distracted of them is dying to know the rest of the tale. *So there was beef and pork in that resin and that was the spark that lit the touchpaper. And then what? So the Lumiere brothers had an idea. And then what? The English would play this game with a stick and a ball. And then what?* And eventually they learn to listen as a class, to crane their necks and close their eyes, and devour the promise of each word. And when the story threatens to evaporate, Sir feigning his own distraction in the passing of the allotted hour, they also learn how to spot when the rest of the story is imminent. A straightening in his chair, palms placed on the desk in front of him. *And then what?* An exaggerated yawn, strength sapped by so many words. *And then what?* By the end the other boys practically howling for deliverance, for the flames that engulfed the sepoys, for those first flickering images, for the stroking away of that hard red ball. And that's how he knows that what he's looking at today are the ancient signs, the ones he has been trained to see. Laid out on the crates, behind all the *bolluns* and the *aachas*, the patrician hauteur of the petty bureaucrat but in the guise of a storyteller. There it is again in the lowering of glasses, the holding of chins. He can practically taste it in the practised delay before acknowledgement once the initial approach has been made. A chin resting in a bony palm, kneading the raw materials of survival. Tall tales, tales of the here and now, perhaps even of the hereafter, but in their telling survival assured for both parties at least until the next time, the next episode crafted in the here of this concrete for the there of distant jute. Yet in his gut, perhaps in all their guts, the recognition that this need be no more than what it is. An encounter stretching back beyond the square and into the hinterlands of illiteracy, letters transcribed and remittances enclosed without a hint of bitterness anywhere in the transaction.

Watching this somehow keens his hunger all over. He is briefly ashamed of envying the illiterates who at least still have somewhere they came from, which they call home, and to where they can send those precious few *takar*.

This time the *kutta* is the first to leave the square, sensing his discomfort. They take refuge in the graveyard of the Armenian church which suddenly rises above the tightly packed buildings nearby.

Reaching into his pocket he pulls out a tiny piece of roti which his brother had distributed last night. He'd intended to make it last all day but the scene in the square has reminded him of some emptiness. About to place the roti in his mouth, something makes him stop, some tiny movement near one of the gravestones. And then the monkey is climbing, high tailing it back to some obscure vantage point. The *kutta* has not moved, sentinel sure on its tiny patch of ground. Without thinking, he tears off an even smaller strip of the roti and hands it to the grateful beast.

They walk for days, each morning a fresh route, man and beast trailing the city in their wake.

The rotis start to get thicker, his brother handing them out at night when only the *kutta* can see his dead eyes. The *how* never arises but the rotis keep coming, some now even fattened with a little filling of dried aloo. Nothing is ever said when the little packages are distributed, tongues as dry as the grass, questions congealing in the dark. And when he has the package in his hand, just out of sight by the bench, a little tail swishing its approval in the dust.

They linger by buildings with intricate ironwork balconies, past the nameplates which he loves with their promises of solidity, of function amid the chaos. 'Calcutta Cleaning and Shawl Repairing Works.'

Late morning and they are weaving in and out of the *boi para*, no one complaining when the *kutta* pauses to sniff at the documents, bound up like bales of hay and spilling out onto the pavements at regular intervals. The book stalls, some no bigger than a cubby hole or a tray sized table, never fail to delight him, the faces of their proprietors peeping out of the gloom, always ready with a wisecrack.

'*O aajkaal ki porcche?*' someone asks, spotting the *kutta* sniffing around some old exam papers, and they both laugh, the *kutta* largely unimpressed.

He looks longingly at the entrance to the Coffee House, stern faced young men manning a trestle table by the stone steps leading up. They seem amused by the *kutta*, offer him a *lal salaam* when he sidles up to the hammer and sickle painted on the wall.

He can hear the whirring of fans, and arguments, but there is no question of man and beast joining the people's revolution upstairs. So they head instead for College Square, offering their own salaams for the peace and the relative quiet of the quadrangle.

Looking around at the buildings, he is impressed by their size and scale. It is not country here. There are no rivers flowing through innocence, though it would surprise him if there are no jackals either. He points out to the *kutta* how solid these buildings look and they share some roti, admiring the grand designs of Presidency College.

After a while he starts to defer to the *kutta*'s wisdom, the University district left far behind, no more high minded sanctuaries from the heat, just the shade of on occasional awning, the *kutta* suggesting when a break is in order. The trot becoming more and more sluggish before the temporary respite, shade thrown over the crescent pose. But still watchful, as indeed is he, a city of strangers viewed from the haunches.

#

There are days they return to the park still carrying the reek of the tanneries, the leather merchants and shoe makers leaving their mark in a maze of antique lanes near Bow Bazar. Faced with his brother's inquisition he is too tired to even explain why they have sought out the stench, a hint of Canton in the place names. Sun-Yet-Sen Street, Hap Heng Grocery Store, and no work anywhere, though the narrow gullee buildings they pass are all about work. They see the ground floors of these buildings given over to every type of industry: washing, wire stripping, scavenging, recycling. But their hungry looks arouse something hostile in the street and they move on when the *kutta* catches the eye of one of the older traders.

And in a linguistic move which seems to further rile his dada, he has taken to using 'they' when describing his daily ventures.

#

The brothers are still able to set aside their differences waiting in line for the standpipe, triviality washed away with the first layer of grime and dirt. During these moments the *kutta* knows to stay out of sight, its appearance un-welcome amongst the desperate throng.

'*Aare, shalla, e kutta ke maro! O shob jol kheeye felbe!*'

And with a couple more fattened rotis to last them until the park beckons once more at night, they head out a little further each day.

They shadow the delivery women balancing huge baskets of kindling on their heads in a miracle of sinew and poise. The women of Harinbari Lane, touting other wares in dimly lit doorways, similarly ignore them, though he thinks he sees an occasional flicker of compassion on dark, careworn faces.

It is in the labyrinth of narrow alleys making up nearby Tiretta Bazar that he most feels his invisibility. It burns against him like a deep shame when the traders barely bother to look his way.

Another filthy refugee coming here to live off our charity.

In the fraying cotton of his shirt, the grime that the water rations can never really remove, he is less than a man, not even a customer. In their eyes, one dog being led by another.

The *kutta* knows too, its amble becoming a trot as they look to escape the pavement hawkers of Burra Bazar and the giant shadow cast by the green domed Nakhoda Masjid. Craning his neck to take in the space bound minarets, he feels the force of their presence. While he is admiring the way they tower over everything else in this *para*, a voice pipes up beside him.

'This is a magnificent example of the Islamic decorative arts. Did you know, sir, that its red sandstone edifice is modelled on the tomb of Emperor Akbar?'

He turns to see a short man with pale skin, the telltale red stain of paan when he opens his mouth. Something in his confusion seems to encourage the man to continue.

'Ten thousand of the faithful can pray inside. *Ten thousand!* And the gateway of the Masjid is built in the style of Buland Darwaza, sir. You might be knowing this, sir. Just like Fetephur Sikri, near Agra.'

He wants to say ten thousand things about the faithful, but in the event not so much as one will reveal itself. The *kutta* has already lost interest, ambling ahead amongst the hawkers and the trinkets, and the impromptu guide soon sees his confusion for what it is. Disinterest. What he doesn't see, what he cannot know before he moves on, is the strong sense of fear, the rising nausea pushing up against all that implacability.

They take refuge in the sweet sickly smells of the Mechua fruit market, trailing the dark looks and whispered insults of the faithful. *Heathen. Animal worshipper. Unclean.*

And still there is no work, no place in this great, heaving mass of humanity for him. Just a clue in the mountains of refuse, the dead skins of spoiled fruit. So when they return to the park that evening, he vows to look away from the city, from what has become the continual repulsion of its greedy bowels. And the next day, setting out as usual with a growing ration of stuffed rotis, man and beast for once turn their backs on the city and head north instead into its forlorn extremities.

2.

They still pass the occasional hawker, though the narrow lanes are quieter than the ones they have grown accustomed to. Every so often they see some unfortunate pushing an overloaded barrow. Here at least the bearer straining every sinew is not being assaulted by traffic from all directions. The ringing of bells on passing bikes a more likely local signature. Fewer taxis too. Clearly no need round here, meters switched off, drivers resting, the calculations for daily survival pointing south. To the places which have already spurned them.

A little further ahead the strangest sight. A young man rolling two large tyres, stride unbroken as he negotiates the potholes. He is evidently a familiar face, people calling out to him near the metal workshop, where he stops to have a chat. As they pass him, he seems unconcerned at any danger posed by his friends clustering around him with their *bidis* in hand. Indeed he is sat with his own, firing the tip as he takes a breather on the fat roll of rubber. No one seems to mind, a couple of hands already kneading the rolls as other calculations are made.

Though it is early, they are far from alone on the dusty pavement. Some way on from the workshop the *kutta* pauses, briefly concerned at the attentions of some young children. It is more playful than anything else, and the half-clad children are in any case called away by their mother, thrashing laundry against the kerbstones. Again he sees the brick, timber, tin, tarpaulin patchwork and feels a curious envy, but the *kutta* knows not to linger.

Five Point Crossing and Shyambazar barely register, the crude iron weights and hand held scales just another detail of this city's life which does not include them. The *kutta*'s paws briefly slide on the floor in the fish and meat section at the centre of the market. They quickly move on, the traders' shouts still ringing in their ears. And no sooner than the smell of death, the sharp, metallic tint of cleavers starts to recede, the *kutta* uncovers fresh torments hidden away. Marking the perimeter of this section, a recently used *boti*, the greasy red of its blade only just wiped down. The *kutta* pauses by the wooden rest on which the blade is folded down. In its fearful eyes some primal recognition, feet on rest, hands free, death grip, and for the first time since they set out anywhere in the city, it howls pitifully.

In his mind's eye other horrors, the blade slicing through human bone, neck held down by enraged, ecstatic hands. The screams from inside the mills, jute cutters working their frenzy, the slaughter soon just sacrifice, a ritual cleansing, the tethered lines of non-believers led like other beasts towards the blades. Before long the thrashing and hollering starting to abate, bowels evacuated, the stench of certainty mixing with fresh liquids.

Some distance from the mills, where they lived, his *didi*, Nila, secreting away a packet of jewels in the one place she knows that men with caustic souls will never think to look. When they have finished with their grisly assembly line they will surely come looking for another taste, of this much she is sure. So she uses her fingers to hollow out half a pumpkin and places the packet against its sweet falange. Then she replaces the interior, positioning the vegetable under the bed. The footfalls and profanities arrive before her brother, and by the time the army finally gets there, he is gently rocking back and forth, still cradling her lifeless head in his arms. And all around him are pumpkin seeds, scattered like spent cartridges. Locked into his rhythmic wake it is not time any more, or light, or noise which he senses, but a stillness he has almost forgotten in these days of mob and fire and machete and screams. Nothing moves, and there is no sound other than the numbed pushmepullyou. He doesn't know how long he stays that way, the tilt its own form of reckoning, the solitary pattern he can bear. His lips crack, hot, stale air pushing up from his insides. And still he continues to sway, a dead weight now no weight at all, so that when he looks down for the first time since he could bear to look again, he sees that his arms are cradling nothing but air. There is no head, no body, just one other figure beginning to stir under a bundle of rags in the corner.

'Just us now,' his brother tells him, pulling out a cleaver from the rags.

#

3.

The *kutta*'s howl seems to awaken other spirits near the Tala Tank and within moments the air is a cacophony of hooting and howling, shrieking and squawking.

Yet the sounds are somehow distant, an airbound complaint at all that filth and fury on the ground. Looking up he sees the shapes massing on the vast drum of the Tank, the whole reservoir standing on a platform at least thirty metres high. Like the minarets presiding over the godless streets, except that here there is the scuttle and scurry of creatures, the forsaken spirits of wings and paws and beaks born again within the spit of four million litres.

They idle near Teliapara Lane, the *kutta* finding some shade while he admires the cast iron street nameplate and the stone elephant heads of the corner building, their raised trunks pleasing supports for a first floor balcony.

This time they pass relatively unmolested through the nearby market at Sovabazar, but the *kutta* again makes haste when the displays of fruit and vegetables give way to the thicker tang of blades and poultry and fish.

It resumes a more leisurely amble when they chance upon Kumartuli, briefly fascinated by the earthenware and clay images of the Hindu deities, investigating one or two which have been left outside to dry in the sun before being painted. In spite of his hunger he finds sufficient discipline to talk to the craftsmen about the various Durgas and Kalis they are working on.

'*O conta beshi pachanda kare?*' one of them asks, seeing how the *kutta* is snouting around two particular earthenware Durgas propped up on the pavement.Again, they both laugh before man and beast continue their sojourn past the dusty godowns of Sovabazar Street.

Walking gets easier the further north they head, fewer of the small traders, the astrologers, the chai stalls or the ad hoc arrangement of sleepers and dogs, chickens and goats blocking their path. The blare of car horns becomes less insistent, though the ramshackle temporary shelters, their tarpaulin structures held up more in hope than expectation, continue long after pavement accedes to dirt track. So too the ever present piles of rubble sitting atop every pavement. Peering in beyond one of these dusty perches he sees that the excavation has been carried out to lay or repair the service pipes. He notices how in the failure to properly reinstate the pavement a little gully has appeared, bubbling over with the last rains of monsoon, the warm, heavy drops congealing into a meandering hump pockmarking the pavement like the scales of some giant lizard. The *kutta* rarely frolics near the rubble, its paws treading nimbly around the humps, some clue that this is not a place to dawdle.

The first time they linger around these mounds, something spooks the *kutta* and it refuses to go any further. He walks ahead but no matter how often he looks behind, the *kutta* is still sat at the mouth of the pavement incision, alert and unyielding. It remains a mystery until he hears the sound, the unhappy braying of goats up ahead. The unfortunate entourage is being 'encouraged' by a wiry man with a big stick, the prodding and the poking the source of their unhappiness. Looking over his shoulder he sees the *kutta* still sat waiting for him, as though it knew all along that this was the point at which he would have to turn back.

It is an instinctive decision, heading all the way back to the retching bowels, past the *thana* at Jorasanko, beyond the familiar crossing at Chitteranjan Avenue, until finally all they can taste is the condensed chaos of Mechua Fruit Market. And on this day they learn to savour the market streets carpeted in straw, fresh mounds to dispel the rumours of rubble and slaughter they have just fled. He revels in the mountains of bananas piled higher than many homes; in the pyramids of pineapples, melons, pomegranates, the sweet sickly excess of jackfruit and papaya. They weave skillfully amongst the coolies balancing unfeasibly large baskets on their heads, the *kutta* plotting a nimble path through the produce.

The noise for once does not disturb, drawing them instead to its epicentre just across the road from the market.

They watch silently as that dance as old as any of these streets gets under way, the auctioneers and potential customers haggling over prices and volume. At first his silence, if not his dress, marks him out as just another coolie awaiting the signal from fleshy, *banya* hands to deliver his load to the private transport of the successful bidder. But there is no load, no weight tethering him to this spot, just the curiosity of a newcomer, and fairly soon he is ignored entirely by the loitering Marwari businessmen, the razor sharp of their calculations cutting his pocket full of roti to the quick. Gorged on the noise, the smell of the skins putrefying in the heat, he leaves the market, the *kutta* following several paces behind with its snout still trained on the gutter.

The memory of the goats is further muffled in the pavement shanties of the rag pickers, stock strewn all over the street, the mounds this time made of cloth, the lizard shedding its harder scales. At some point the cloth runs out and the voices he hears are suddenly metallic, corrosive, the sounds refracted off a graveyard of empty cooking oil tins. They are passed by a steady stream of handcarts and bicycle carts loading up on their tin cargo, roped together in precarious piles, each change of direction threatening to send the whole lot spilling out into the road.

They pass the open fronted workshops and the open charcoal fires in which the tinsmiths heat their soldering irons. The *kutta* follows the arc of the soldering iron as it attaches the lid or base to the body of a fresh can.

'*O ekta kotte chai?*' enquires one of the men taking a break from his work.

Laughter again, but as the tinsmith looks up from the *kutta* to what he presumes to be its owner, he doesn't extend the offer to this man. Even though something in the way he studies the work suggests this man possesses a natural aptitude, some prior affinity between hand and flame. He gets back to work, squatting down next to the fire, hopeful that when he looks up again he won't still be assailed by two sets of hungry eyes.

Their presence barely raises a pulse by the metal bashing enterprises of Balak Dutta Lane, those cooking oil tins deemed beyond repair battered into submission for their resale value as scrap. The strong arms stay busy with the hammers, flattening, stretching, then bundling together the distressed sheets. He quickly sees there is no opening here, and for once even the *kutta*'s presence remains unregistered.

The banyan tree on Chor Bagan Lane offers the shade they seek and it is here, in its gnarled folds, that they pause for rotis. Later, gazing through the iron railings of the Marble Palace, he imagines the opulence of classical Rome, its fountains and statues, the nobility of its sculptures, the only thing gnawing at his guts some vague dream of flight from here.

'We have to go now,' he tells the *kutta*, not waiting for doubts to circulate, M.G. Road and Chittaranjan Avenue and Bow Bazar and Manicktala left to their bustle and trade, and this time when concrete morphs into dirt track, he keeps going, the *kutta* by his side.

#

Every now and then they are tempted by the gentle tapping of bells on the shafts of some rickshaw but it is only rotis he carries in his pocket so the trek continues on foot. At one point he nearly slips on the oil stained pavement where the stripped down engines and gearboxes of some auto graveyard have leaked their final protest. The whole area is awash with worn out motor spares, the innards of head-lamps, hastily patched up exhaust systems and worn tyres strewn in unloved, but still marketable, disorder. Perhaps this was where the young man with the tyres had been headed? He looks to see if he can pick him out from the serious faces gathered near one of the engines but when one of these men, sensing a bystander, finally turns around, a greasy rag tucked into his waistband, it is with the routine stare of a stranger.

#

They pass the nimble fingers of young children, rolling those few, precious strands of tobacco in a kindu leaf, then tying the bidis with cotton thread into bundles of five, ready for sale. It briefly makes him think of his own child-hood, carefree and country, leaping out of trees into the fast flowing current of the river. Then that one time he landed all wrong and his arm was smashed. Cradled in the strong arms of his dada, the one now dispensing rotis, at the time whispering encouragement through the blood. The memory of something sharp tearing his flesh snaps him back to the present, and soon the children too are left to their dextrous survival.

In his mind's eye he sees a penniless mendicant, wandering the extremities. Another sharp pain forces him to squat on his haunches, the sting bubbling up with the blister. So he drifts, tasting the air with the tongue of that beggar. Tasting its dirt and diesel until every last pore is blackened with soot and the only life yet to savour is liquid, the filth of these last days decomposing in the water. He sees then that the beggar is a sage, swimming from the shore to a rock island which will bear his name. And in the water the debris of that other life floating in the shallows, the lizard shedding its scales once more.

It is the *kutta* that wakes him, tugging at the sleeve of his shirt. He is not sure how long he has been sat there, eyes shut in his pavement meditation. When he stands the pain is briefly intense, and then it is gone, the blister just a detail, still there but not speaking.

Country again, near Berati, tails and fruit and simian-swift calculations, the *kutta* at once alert and sauntering, only the slightest of flinches when two figures appear from behind a tree, machetes drawn and a languid look in the eye.

In this garden of delights the kindness of strangers and a green coconut, the mouth sliced open with expert machete hands, its sweet, rich liquid greedily drained, the solid lining scraped bare with an improvised spoon made from the husk.

The strangers, fellow travellers from the jute mills, hidden under tarpaulin, swamp fevers left far behind. Wishing him luck they point him towards the airport, its great metallic beasts roaring through the torpor of the forsaken. And with the fuel of the impromptu meal still inside him, he sets out again, *kutta* in tow, towards the crazed howl of angle grinders and the unmistakable popping of electric arc welders.

#

It is a stroke of luck, the *chowkidar* on sentinel duty sufficiently bored that afternoon to ask him what he wants. He finds it easy enough to downplay the refugee angle, for that is not who he is. He just happens to be *here* now and there is the question of work. Somehow though, even before the chowkidar directs him to one of the workshops adjoining the main hangar, he knows his luck is about to change. In all his wanderings around this teeming city, this is the first time the question has been directly addressed to *him* and not the *kutta*.

#

4.

He grows accustomed to the acrid odours from the torches slicing through steel, his body instinctively arching back from the searing blue-white flashes. In his gratitude for the work he forgets to complain about the lack of any protective clothing, and the grime and the sweat and the occasional stray spark drip down off him and into his *chappals*. Still, for a minimal fee the chowkidar has agreed to keep an eye on the *kutta* while he is busy with the workshop inferno, though he shakes his head when he spots the new apprentice sharing some roti with the beast. A disbelieving 'aare' before he reminds himself that this young man is from the other side, country too, and this is just how they are.

That first night, when he returns to the park with good news, his brother says little, eyes locked on the tail frantically wagging in the dark. Only when the swishing stops does he look back up at his younger brother, telling him,

'I've got some news of my own,' before producing a set of keys from an inside pocket. He tells him how their other brother has found a place with some distant relatives, and that it is just them now.

It takes weeks for the ache and the raw of the bench to leave his back, but the room in Berati turns out to be a recently vacated dwelling in the garden he has already visited.

This time when he sees the brothers with the machetes, they smile their silent greeting, and he is surprised when it turns out that they know his *dada*.

The *kutta* stays with them, though only on the precondition that it remains outdoors. Each day when he returns from another round of oxy-acetylene torches, the *kutta* greets him like a long lost friend, its tail swishing a happy metronome in the dust. And every evening when his dada gets back from whatever routine he has found in this city, the *kutta* slinks away, the wildness of the garden compound its own sanctuary.

At first the other people in the compound are friendly to him, but as the months pass and his dada is out more and more, he sees something change in their expressions. For the first time since they arrived here, he sees fear in their eyes, gazes averted whenever his dada is around, and the easy smiles of winter replaced by a certain wariness even around him.

'Tomar,' says his dada, tossing him another set of keys, nodding towards the small house just the other side of the coconut palm.

He is initially confused, reluctant to enter what was until just now another family's home. How can this all of a sudden be his? It makes no sense, yet there are no traces of the family when he finally goes to investigate. Only when the *kutta* rests its head on the porch, untroubled by the black cloud of mosquitoes massing nearby, does he cross the threshold, allowing himself to dream the unreality of all that space again.

#

The morning he finds the note, it still bears the traces of wet, humid monsoon air. The *kutta* has slept inside out of the hot, heavy torrent, the musk of its fur heightened by the damp. He sees the note weighted down with a small stone in the middle of the floor. As he stoops to pick it up, the *kutta* looks over at him with a half interested eye.

'*You're on your own now. I've had to go. Will be in touch.*'

He reads it again just to make sure. It only briefly delays his journey to the airport, a strange feeling of emptiness followed by a kind of relief. But by the time the workshop hoves into view all thoughts have moved from the words to the blades, an apprenticeship in the balance and a *kutta* on the porch.

#

5.

Every so often he spies a couple of young men struggling to shift an enormous iron cooking pot into one or other of the temporary dwellings which seem to have sprung up almost overnight in the compound. Since his dada left without warning, people appear a little happier. The smiles have returned, caution gradually giving way to habit, the awkwardness of late slowly banished to an antique wild.

In the city itself though he sees other patterns which trouble him. The wrought iron grills, the steel shop shutters, and all around him the manufactured signs of withdrawal.

He sees the *ful jharu wallah* relieved of his sticks, which turn out to be nothing more than elongated dusters, by jumpy young men near the masjid. A similar fate befalls an unlucky *shaan wallah* in a different neighbourhood, another nervy tribe forcing him to set up in the street, the cycle wheel driving his grinding stone as he reluctantly sits showering sparks from the knives he is made to sharpen.

Even after the tools are laid down, sparks sometimes fly in the workshop too. One skittish set of thoughts meeting another, the return to the compound and the porch made sweeter by the anxiety these encounters always provoke in him.

When the apprenticeship turns into a job he knows he should feel happier than he does. He has work and a place to stay. Loyal companionship too, genuine affection in the nuzzling and devoted looks when he returns each day from the airport. No one has ever questioned his presence in the house either, though increasingly he sees the two brothers whom he met before this became his home talking at a distance and pointing his way, the eyes no longer so languid but the machetes still to hand.

There are days he seeks out an *Aakh wallah* just to remove the sourness from his jib. His spirits always lift when he spots one of these sugar cane presses, the wheeled handle feeding the lengths of raw cane through the contraption, its cogs and rollers extracting the cloudy, sweet juice with a tinkled warning. And for a while the bitterness will abate, allowing him to revel once more in the eccentricities of this city. Then the effect wears off and it is another pulse he senses, bubbling away, waiting to erupt from the city's exposed arteries.

One such day he is sat out on the porch, the *kutta* with its head lying flat, when the gentle bell of the postman's bicycle sounds on the dirt track running by the house.

In his eagerness to devour the contents, the flimsy blue of the aerogram tears where it has been gummed, the knife making an impatient incision. It is written in a familiar hand, only the place names are strange.

'*Tilbury*', '*Liverpool Street*', '*Trafalgar Square*'. One other phrase sticks out, his taste buds suddenly attuned to the ink, even the posture at which the pen might have been held in those far off places. After the bravado, a simple statement. *'There are opportunities here for people like us.'*

'Us'. Did he really use that word? It has been so long since he dared to dream about anything other than the machine tool rigour, sparks and routine and a deadening of the senses his only expectations. He realises how much his life has become absorbed by its mundane efficiencies, something as simple as a solitary word conjuring desire from the wild, scales once more slipping from the beast.

Us.

His heart starts pounding and he wants to share his excitement, but when he looks down, the *kutta* has already moved away, an unusually still tail just about slipping into the shadows.

Part Five

Red

1.

London 1976

The handkerchief Dad has pressed to his mouth helps absorb some of the shock and the worst of the stink.

    Shit Bucket Dettol Brick Glass Filth Decision

#

2.

His brother starts spending a lot more time next door, the sounds blasting through the wall. Since the last round of bricks and shit he seems to have found some refuge in the strange music that S. has introduced him to. K. feels it most at going home time, his brother's face full of sullen dread and barely a word spoken between them the whole way back. Of the two of them, it is K. who still pays attention when the caretaker occasionally greets them near the gates. His brother is already thinking about something else, so distracted he doesn't even notice the fresh letters on the wall or the smirking faces nearby. More than once, K. spots the runt among the smirkers and is tempted to have a word, but his brother seems largely disinterested so he leaves it, promising himself another time when the odds are more favourable.

#

3.

By the time the Test series reaches the Oval, the whole
country is parched, and even Peter West's face looks
unfeasibly dark. When he appears holding the mic at the
start of play there's a calmness about him which rarely
extends to events on the pitch. He likes to set the tone,
reassuring viewers that 'if they can just get through to
lunch without losing any more wickets then they're right
back in this contest', but in truth not even his smile can
disguise the reality. This ceased to be a contest the moment
Greenidge steadied the West Indian ship at Old Trafford.
When Close copped that hiding on the Saturday evening,
they were just the opening jabs. Ever since it's been
Black hands pummelling white bodies, the speed of the
pummelling accelerating with that of the bowling tracks,
stripped bare in the calypsonian heat. K. has loved every
minute of it, revelling in the chaos afflicting the bowlers
and fielders, then finally hurdling the boundary fencing
and straight into the crowd. The various Mound stands,
Tavern and Kirkstall Lane ends for once forced to put
their beakers down and to a man stand and applaud
the audacity of it all. He has loved the bell ringers in
their midst, the proud Caribbean folk giving their own

summary of the headlines after each contemptuous cut or pull or square drive or hook, Richards particularly savage on anything outside his off stump. Even Underwood, miserly, deadly Derek, made to look ordinary time and again, the ball smashed to the extra cover boundary on the up and nothing he or Greig or any of the others can do about it.

K. loves the noise as well, the way it changes over the summer. The sound of those early cloudcast Nottingham days already a distant memory. Ever since then a gentle infusion of cans and whistles, the air humming its approval for each brush stroke, stabs and swirls of colour in the stands, the English forced to look on admiringly. And the longer the summer heat has worn on, the more intense that infusion, rattling and shrill and somehow hanging in the air between overs. The older hands in the England team, Edrich and Close, look increasingly unhappy with the growing symphony, gesturing to the umpire, to each other, to no one in particular. At least that's what he sees. Their faces say 'this is not how it should be, not how I remember it.' But they are the brave ones, 'obdurate' someone says, and he looks it up in the Chambers. It seems about right, their resistance is stubborn but ultimately always in a losing cause. And he hates them with their unyielding faces, taking guard time and again as the cherry comes hurtling back, hoping for a quick outcome but loving their prolonged suffering anyway. He resents them their courage, putting themselves in the line of fire time after time, taking the hit on their body rather than giving away their wicket. Wincing and scowling and grumbling their way through another lethal new ball spell and, somehow, surviving it, dragging the last traces of 'how they remember it' through to another bone dry close of play.

It is hard for him to even see this as courage, these obdurate souls standing there in the face of a whirlwind.

No, what he sees are the angry eyes of disappointment. *How could they do this to us after everything we've done for them?*

Disbelief too, the air rich in smoke and teeth and tin. *Not how it's supposed to be. Just not cricket, old boy.*

He sees the uniforms and the smirks, the clipboards and the curses coiled into one cussed stance. As the Yorkshireman takes guard, a shift in the tectonic plates, all that murmur under the playground, behind the bricks, congealing in blood and bruises and shit and leather and stitching until his head is roaring in an orgy of happiness,

'Kill him! Kill him! Kill! Him!'

And then the circus rolls into town. A 'featherbed' they're describing it as at the Oval, all the experts agreed that this will indeed be a batsman's paradise. Nothing he sees in the first few days suggests otherwise, the match following the expected pattern. A huge West Indian innings, Richards again the architect, then the old hands putting up some resistance for England, the pitch devoid of all life. For once even the West Indian attack blunted by this most docile of surfaces, England batting time, confidence starting to return after this shakiest of summers. Only one man is still going full throttle, the silent footfalls of Michael Holding as he races in past the umpire, so quiet the man in the white coat doublechecks to see he's really there.

There alright, even on this featherbed the batsman clean bowled through a startled jump, the air thrumming with whistles again.

The fastest, and the best, as usual reserved for Greig, the boasts of early summer ringing in his ears like truth. All around the tic of something not right, too blond, too tall, too bold by half, rising up from one of those cracks in the Kennington earth, pushing up that trusted blade, the bat raised higher and higher anticipating the head shot. Instead another lethal yorker, the split second reaction time further reduced by the elongated arc the bat now has to travel.

He loves that sound, the irreversible cartwheel of broken stumps. And watching on TV, he can see that he's not alone, the square briefly overrun by young fans. These pitch invasions happen every time the England captain is dismissed, perhaps an opportunity to remind him at close quarters of the ill advised boast.

It looks like fun and he is envious of these young Black kids running across the turf, oblivious to the commentator's disdain. When the camera pans in, it is the determined look on some of those faces which stands out as much as the jolly. Lucky bastards.

What had India given him two summers back other than some kharzi jokes and a general feeling of embarrassment?

He hated them, nearly as much as the obdurates. They played as though they were scared to be here, the whole series one big apology for their presence. And as the humiliation went on, from one city to the next, transporting the shame to the regions, he began to hate the place they were from too. These players, slump shouldered, heads bowed, bullied, not once playing as if they understood. That here, in this place, this was normal for so many. Everyday life a series of insults to be endured, the butt, or was that the bud bud ding of everyone's jokes? They acted as though they didn't know, as though it was all new to them. *But you're not Pakis anyway.* And each time they were caught at gully or in the slips fending away a short one they just made themselves look a little more weak, their caution more like cowardice. He hated them for that too, held them in some way responsible for the boldness that started to appear on walls, through letter boxes, in playgrounds. For the chants and the lack of caution, face burning with shame at the bobbing heads, the comedy accents, the beetroot red of Windsor Davies, and for how everyone just started calling it 'the Paki shop'.

No wonder Mum and Dad had got out of there.

#

It is the last rites for England. In this most un-English of summers, rain will not be delaying anything.

Dad is out in the yard, the figure nearly complete. He keeps expecting Mum to tell him to have a look and ask Dad whether he needs a hand. But the call never comes, the only thing wafting through from the kitchen the rich, burnt scent of *baigun pora*.

Mum does actually linger for a moment just by the door, but when she sees K. sat there silently willing the bowlers on, it is as though she knows. He has been there since the start of play, the same manic intensity on his face now as when the first ball of the day was delivered several hours earlier. Her boy.

When England's last recognized batsman, the wicket-keeper Alan Knott, is clean bowled by a blind length break back, everyone senses the end is nigh. And this time when the camera pans out across the ground he can see the bell ringers, the white sparkle of their enamel, joy unconfined. But there's more, parasols held aloft in a Mardi Gras skip, whole sections of the stands weaving, thrumming away with the whistles. Before this summer, this series, it is not a sound he'd ever heard, the air heavy with a now familiar heat, bodies and bass and the surge of carnival just under the panicked survivalism. He's rarely seen the English look so skittish, and never in front of Black opponents.

And suddenly Greig is back out there, and it is the England captain who is on his hands and knees, grovelling in the dirt before the delighted West Indian supporters in the stands. It is all smiles under the late summer sky, the triumph celebrated with a confidence he can only dream of.

Something else too. These players don't act as though they don't know. He sees it in the way they thank 'their' crowd. Yet another five days when the normal rules don't apply. A full working week when life will get easier for these men and women thickening the sound. He envies them that, the kids too, so bold in front of the cameras. *Wha' di rass you looking at? We won!'* Behind the smiles, past the bubbly soaked shirt fronts, they leave no one in any doubt that they came here to do a job, and they know that this is just the start.

Peter West, for one, is fulsome in his praise, a gentleman to a fault, sounding the last generous notes of that summer.

4.

Dad is putting the finishing touches to the sculpture, rubbing along one edge of the wood which appears to be the left side of the head. When he goes out to investigate, K. can see that it is of a man deep in thought, hands pressed against his face in contemplation. Or is that despair, he can't really tell?

'Keep going with this,' Dad tells K., handing him the cloth, just relieved his son has finally stopped watching TV.

It is unusually quiet next door, none of the usual songs about sniffing glue or girls called Judy.

J. pops in, admiring the handiwork but looking a little troubled.

'Don't suppose you've seen S. today, have you?' he asks Dad, taking a moment to absorb the wooden miracle of the meditative figure.

Dad shakes his head, turns to K., thinking perhaps he might know. Rubbing the head, K. becomes aware of the two adults staring at him.

'What? What did I do now?' he says, genuinely not sure what he's supposed to have done.

'Have you seen S. today?' J. asks again.

He shakes his head, then stops as though he has

remembered something. Then shakes his head again as though it was nothing.

'What is it?' asks J., a little more urgency in his voice.

Putting down the cloth, he looks straight at the neighbour, enjoying this moment, feeling part of the big people's conversation.

'I heard him talking to my brother this morning. They said something about the Carnival. That's all I heard.'

J.'s face has clouded over, and K. now sees that he has Dad's full attention too.

#

5.

When they emerge from the tube at Bayswater, S. half expects nothing to have changed. Or maybe he doesn't really know what to expect any more. They make for odd viewing, a couple of spiky herberts and a little Indian kid in a carriage full of Black people. S. doesn't mind that they stand out here, the faintly amused looks they are attracting a welcome relief from the more familiar snarl of the Teds south of the river.

He enjoys the startled look on his neighbour's face, can tell he's never been around this many Black people before. Not so many sovvies round here, the style Jamaica proud. Hats, caps, teeth, tailoring, and a rumble even deeper than the bowels of this underground.

It is good to be back, he thinks, realising just how much he has missed this place. Though hemmed in tight, the sounds of corrugated iron melting under a Black Ark sun, he wants to breathe here, finesse his lungs with the smoky paste of jerk chicken, the low-fi rumble so deep it's felt before it's heard. Ribcage rattling like an abacus as the dreads string up, every available inch of wall, window ledge, street corner taken up by dark, unsmiling faces. Many more uniforms than he's bargained for, his neighbour for the first time looking a little worried.

'Coming down, coming down,' the chant of the crowd, barely audible at first over the tectonic thud of the pavement.

Then the cans raining down their Agincourt each time the uniforms move in, the roar of the Westway soaking up the crowd in the wire netting.

A tunnel of death for the Rover 2000s, running the gauntlet of rocks and stones and cans all the way up Ladbroke Road. He throws a token empty, vaguely hoping it won't connect, but not waiting to find out, and then they're running, past the Elgin, and down the alleyways he knows so well. As they turn into one of the narrow, stucco terraces, he sees something which suddenly reminds him of school, a scared looking white man being patted down by eager Black hands. And then just as quickly the group scatters, the screech of car tyres and uniforms spilling out of the black Maria. The only figure still not moving that of the unlucky white man, some deeper injury nursed under a frozen expression.

There's a sickness in the lungs, the taste not quite what it should be, but when they finally manage to get onto a train, gel expired and spikes lank, he is surprised when he looks over at the other two, slumped opposite and out of breath, the sweat still pouring off them. The other passengers look suitably disgusted at this shabby display of personal fitness but what really catches *his* eye is that of the three of them the one he knows least, the younger Indian kid from next door, is the only one actually smiling.

#

6.

London, Late 1976

When school starts again, K. has the strangest feeling that someone will mention the carnival and then someone else will mention the Front, and that's how it will start. But when that doesn't happen on the first day back, he is genuinely surprised at how little gratitude he feels for this small mercy.

The teacher asks them what they did over the summer, and when it comes to his turn all he says is, 'I watched England lose and it was funny.'

No one says anything but a tiny suppressed giggle comes from the table in the corner, where, just like last term, Rachael is sat on her own.

#

His brother is at the big school now so the new arrangement is that they meet after school just outside the shop and then walk back together from there. Neither of them is especially happy about this, but after what happened at the Carnival, it is the only way to avoid Mum embarrassing them both at going home time.

It still feels a little unfair to K., who doesn't see

why he should be punished for the sins of the brother.

Mind you it was funny when his brother got back late on the Bank Holiday evening and copped a right earful, suddenly reminded that the uniforms were the least of his worries. A reception committee for his brother and S., J. especially annoyed at S. for, as he put it, 'leading the younger boy astray'. Mum and Dad not much happier. *Why did we ever come here?* thrown in more than once before a shared look reminds them of exactly why.

So now this, his brother at the big school but K. the one who's expected to keep an eye on him, make sure he doesn't take any other unannounced detours after school. Walking back each day the writing is literally on the wall, the fence, the garage door, pretty much any surface really that hasn't yet been put behind locked gates. It is not even *their* wall, the insults as random as the canvas yet their venom anything but. *Enoch, NF, Pakis Out*, the paint dripping its intent. Other times it is all about *G.Davis* and for some reason, the one that never fails to make them laugh, presented in the favoured style of the day on someone's back wall, *G. Marshal is a Poof.*

'Gary up the gary,' his brother comments, smirking away as he does so.

K. doesn't really know why it's funny but smiles anyway, feels he ought to play along. Of late his brother hasn't been saying a whole lot to him, not since he blamed K. for blabbing about the carnival trip. So the words are a bit of an icebreaker.

'How's it going?' his brother asks, the first time he's done so since going to the big school.

The question takes K. by surprise, accustomed as he is by now to a quiet walk home, neither of them really wanting to let on to the other that they know about the mag under the bed or the triangle of hair on the centre page spread. No need to mention the locked bathroom door or the pages stuck together either. Come to think of it, why mention anything about his own lunchtime detours round the railway sidings and the sheer mind numbing boredom of it all, the only thing worse than scrambling away from the strange undead creatures clutching at polythene bags out of sight, the thought of spending one more second counting down the clock until the junkyard once more pushes away its beasts?

'It's going alright,' he lies, though for once it's almost believable. 'How about you?'

'Yeah, same,' replies his brother, the lies intact and the cosmic order for now at least relatively untroubled.

'What's it like though?' K. asks, curiosity getting the better of him.

'Different,' says his brother but not in a way that particularly makes him want to find out how.

7.

Lunchtimes get easier after he meets Michelle and the two of them start hanging out together. They take care to avoid the junkyard beasts. But in truth it is not difficult. No one else is ever in the library so they remain undisturbed, word games and finger paintings, hands held in the aisles, their own private domain. And that's a word they learn from the dictionary they find under a stack of old magazines in one corner. Pristine too, as if they are the first to ever consult its pages. They both like that one, the notion of being perfectly preserved. It only comes about because he's trying to prove to Michelle that 'privilege' has no 'd', and as he scans the entries, there it is, suddenly acting as if it was the real reason, the only reason to ever consult this page. He tells her she has a pristine neck, and she laughs, saying he is funny mirthful, and though that is not quite right, the error makes them want to stay, pawing at each other and at the pages, Mrs. J. occasionally looking up but never saying anything, able for once to sense children for whom some kind of obsession is just beginning.

#

8.

They think they are being careful, K. and Michelle, slipping away unnoticed when the other kids charge into the
playground. But they *are* being watched. A couple of times
recently, K. has had the feeling someone was behind them,
but when he has turned around all he has seen are the
standard kickabouts involving rush goalies and some stray
jerseys for goalposts. He never spots the little pair of snake
eyes following him from one of the games. Never imagines
the depth of the injury, at how 'hurt' those feelings were
in that first-day-back-after-summer silence. A throwaway
comment about which he'd thought nothing much. But
he should have known in that silence to listen for the unspoken. Then he would have heard the murmur which
would become a complaint, snake eyes and shark lips
narrowed into one cold, reptilian line. He should have
known better. His funny was never going to be their
mirthful.

#

9.

It starts up again when Greig and the collars up brigade head to India for the winter Test series.

Again, the opening skirmishes set the tone, and by the time the circus rolls into Madras for the third Test, India have all but thrown in the towel.

Following the occasional summary on the transistor, K. remembers what he should have been listening out for all along. Even when the England quick, John Lever, is caught out by the umpires, his sneaky vaseline strips making the ball talk, there is no comeback. No apology either and it ends in another crushing defeat for India. This time though he *does* hear it, that murmur again, the flightpath shifting in midair before the joys of late summer have even had a chance to settle.

From the little snippets on the news, the worst of it is that those collars are up once more, gum moving more confidently around the jaw than it has done for some time.

It is yet another embarrassment and he is just grateful for the lack of a live broadcast. The kharzi jokes start doing the rounds again, though this time, when India take all day to make just eighty three runs, the emphasis is on constipation rather than speed.

This is not how he wanted to see the New Year in, but it gets worse, and perhaps none of them are that surprised, though the shock takes longer to wear off.

#

No sooner has the painfully slow blockage of the Test been wrapped up, than a real burst of shit just after. And for the first time in months the bucket and mops reappear, disinfectant brought back out of the cupboards. Before long it is just like old times, glass being picked out of the carpet, and a standardized affectation of concern on the doorstep, everyone by now familiar with the drill.

So when he comes home from school a few weeks later and Mum and Dad are in the kitchen drinking tea but not talking, he senses that something is not quite right. That is when he hears the toilet flushing and then the sounds of heavy footfalls coming down the stairs.

Dad's face does its best to look happy, but it's not entirely convincing, especially as Mum can barely bring herself to look, let alone smile.

'*Aare dekho*. Look who's come to see you? It's your uncle.'

#

10.

London, 1977

The first few days not much is said. A whole lot of sidelong glances though, checking out the unshaven, unsmiling man having his breakfast, cornflakes like soaked cardboard spooned into an uncomplaining mouth with a huge paw.

Then he will head out and no one will see him again until the evening when he will once more sit with them at the table and silently devour whatever has been prepared.

He makes no attempt to engage them in conversation, and in some way this is good for K., avoiding the awkwardness of explaining an average school day, of having to say where he goes and with whom every lunchtime, and what they get up to.

Mach, mangsho, dhal, tarkari, and mountains of *bhat* all wolfed down without a thought for the effort that has gone into them. At first, K. puts it down to appetite. The man seems to be constantly hungry, so perhaps his mind is not yet attuned to these little courtesies. But when the pattern continues well into his second week, it begins to rankle. K. finds himself making a point of telling Mum how delicious each dish is. This is *khub bhalo* and that is *darun.* More than once he sees the man, his uncle, look up when he does this. Yet there is no smile on his face, nothing to suggest, 'Fair enough, I should have told you that myself.'

What there is hints at something else entirely, the deep set eyes locking onto the boy at the end of the table as though processing data for future reference. The noise coming from that end of the table is a highly unwelcome development as far as he is concerned. If he has to be here at all, he thinks, then at least let it be in silence. Let no one pretend any of this is about love or upset or any of those other weaknesses he'd long since been cured of. The cage had seen to that, its suffocating, cloying stink having never really left him, even all these years on. Lodged in his pores the dull contagion of duty, and not much else.

Family. Circling the wagons. A problem to attend to. As though they'd never really left those benches.

#

Only now does he properly look at the boy as if for the first time. This boy, K., his younger brother's eyes and an undeniable loyalty to his mum, or at least to her food. And he realizes that he is not really looking at his nephew, no, those mercies only reluctantly afforded to the silent, the mute, like K.'s idiot cousin, in double digits but still storing food in his beak as if he is a toddler, his fool mother rolling his food into little balls of mash, a crazy, perishable umbilical rotting away from the inside, the boy somehow hoping to slip under the radar but only succeeding in announcing his terrorised presence all the more loudly. Every time he stays with them he sees the repairs that haven't been made, the flaking plaster, the damp, the mould, that privy, and it disgusts him. He sees the one who doesn't know how to eat attempt to make himself invisible, head outside, shit in that box and stay sitting there for as long as possible, hoping no one's noticed. Not even daring to think about the x-ray eyes which have followed him all the way to his little shitpit of despond.

K.'s idiot cousin, so scared of life he is even afraid to chew, storing all that shit inside and for what? Some forlorn hope that it will all just crumble in his mouth so he can slip away to the other room where he still keeps his comfort blanket. He has seen that blanket, his *dombol combol*, and it's embarrassing, frankly. He makes a point of trampling all over it if ever he sees it lying around. A *dombol combol* for a growing boy! When he thinks of himself, of what he got up to at that age, it is worse than embarrassing. Disgusting! No spirit, no backbone, a healthy young boy still handed food parcels by his mum. This is why he's needed here. His brothers have clearly lost control, perspective warped by the comforts of this place. All day television, no load shedding, the constant stream of parasites banished to distant swamp clouds. It has made them all soft, he can see that. No blisters or lines or cuts or sawdust. Clean hands and full bellies. Yet for all of that one of them doesn't even know how to eat properly. A *mamaguy* built by and for this place. The boy sickens him and sometimes he just wants to hold his head under water so that all those balls of rot will come tumbling out, the shame there for all to see. But the boy does at least have the good sense to remain silent, and through the quiet he knows he is duty bound to observe protocol. *As long as he doesn't speak, he is not really here.*

The other one though, in this little bodged up box of a house, sat there trying to embarrass him in front of everyone. The cheek of it! When he looks up from his food he is barely able to recognize this nephew any more. Beyond the awkwardness punctured by the ongoing *khub bhalos* what he hears is not the voice of a little boy at all. No, in that constant interruption what he is able to infer rather is the sound of a challenge.

11.

The cold seems to scythe straight through his coat. He is barely out of the house and already he can feel it piercing through to his chest. In the playground predictably enough there they all are, T shirts and the occasional jumper but nothing else to even remotely suggest this is winter.

The girls at least are huddled in little groups, occasionally looking over at where the big game of football is going on, but very few of them are wearing coats either. One of the nasty girls from his class, Lisa, is pointing towards the library. She shares a joke with the rest of her group and they all laugh.

There, outside the building he knows so well, is Rachael, sucking her thumb and looking like the one person here other than himself who is actually shivering.

'Hallo.'

It is Michelle. She has crept up behind him, putting her hands over his eyes. Feigning ignorance, he goes, 'Denise?'

'No, silly. It's me!'

'Oh, is it? I thought it was Denise,' he pretends, hoping she hasn't picked up on the gratitude in his voice.

'You're silly,' she tells him, slipping her hand into his, the manoeuvre well disguised by the ample cloth of her duffel coat.

Perhaps it is because they are so wrapped up in each other's relief, that neither of them notices the little pair of snake eyes wandering from the big game to the perimeter fence, settling on a spot just beyond the cloth and whatever it is that they truly covet.

12.

They name the sculpture 'George Davis', but not in front of Mum and Dad.

'That's why his fingers are like that,' his brother says, pointing out the hands pressed against the skull. 'He's going, "Oh shit, I got caught",' and they both laugh.

They're talking to each other a lot more again, especially since their uncle turned up. He's rarely around when they get back after school, so they quickly learn to make the most of this time. When he does eventually make an appearance, it is often quite late. Eight, nine, more than once nearly eleven. But whatever the hour, a plate will appear and Mum will dutifully serve him whatever they've had for dinner earlier. Dad will sit with him no matter how rough his own day has been, though at least he's off the night shift now. And all they will hear from their perch halfway up the stairs is a series of grunts, the huge man beckoning with a rice stained paw for seconds.

As soon as he tramps back in the whole atmosphere changes.

Whatever they have been doing, watching telly, talking, a silent look from Mum tells them to take it upstairs, her own face suddenly tense in a way it hasn't been all evening.

'*Tomra upureh cholle jao,*' the instruction they most dread, not so much for themselves, but for what they're leaving behind.

'What do you think they're talking about down there?' K. asks his brother.

'I don't hear *them* talking,' his brother replies. 'It's only him.'

'Where does he go all day?' K. asks.

'I don't know. Not sure I want to either.'

They sit there for a while, contemplating the unopened box of Cluedo. Next to it is a little pile of Panini stickers he'd found recently on one of his unscheduled trips to the railway sidings. Another older boy, the eyes gone, clutching at the polythene bag. They must have fallen out of his pocket at some stage but the key thing was, as he'd read somewhere, that they 'weren't on his person'. The same zombie face as the other two, not even a flicker when K. had bent down to retrieve the cards.

'Does he talk to you though?' asks K. 'He doesn't talk to me.'

'What do you think?' says his brother sarcastically. 'No flies on your soup, eh?'

He's not heard that one before. Must be something they say in big school. It's annoying not knowing what things mean. Having to go along with stuff anyway, a weak smile and the vague hope that there's no follow up.

He needs to look that one up later, when his brother's not around. Maybe after he's looked up those other words. Abortion, that's a weird sounding one. Anarchy, again, no real idea. But that last one, submission, he's sure he's heard that before. For some reason it makes him think of the previous neighbour and those weird sounds that used to come through the wall. Something breathy, then a complaint, followed by the sharp crack of an open palm, or of something else.

13.

After the bombs go off in the West End, it's all anyone's talking about in class.

'It's those fucking paddies,' says one of the Panini twins. 'That's what my old man says.'

'Someone should have a word,' says the other half of the Panini equation. 'Dirty, fucking paddies!'

K. looks at them, the same age as him, still in single figures, but already talking and acting like he imagines much older boys do.

It's all over the news, but that can't be where they're getting this stuff from. He's only ever heard people talking like that around here, certain boys always very keen to bring their families into it. My dad, my uncles. That's what they say. The men on the news on the other hand remind him more of those people from the council who came round that one time with their clipboards after he'd made up all that stuff about having sisters.

The pincher looks around nervously, and K. knows straight away. The Irish connection. So *that's* where his surname comes from. But it's not an instinct which is particularly well honed in the rest of his class and the moment passes.

He has to admit though, it doesn't look good on the news, all those ambulances, people running around with cut faces, a lot of sirens. And right at the end some tiny report on 'the Indian fightback in Bangalore'. That was the bit he'd been waiting for, though for some reason it feels shorter today, only the briefest of footage before it's back to the West End. Finally, he thinks, some better news on the sporting front, though he's as surprised as anyone when it turns out the Indians *do* have a little bit of steel after all. It still doesn't excuse what's gone before, but it does make things that bit more bearable for now. He thinks how good it is to see those collars once more drenched in sweat, and how much he enjoys it when that confused look reappears under English sun hats. For a few magical moments looking at that sun bleached wicket and the panicked English faces it could almost be summer again.

Still, the fucking IRA with its priceless sense of timing, and now *that's* all anyone is talking about. Typical.

14.

Though it is winter, the more positive news from Bangalore encourages K. to dig out the small wooden bat which last saw daylight during those halcyon days when every drive was Viv, every cut Greenidge. It is the first time since the summer that he has felt confident enough to practise, the urge thickening when he hears the crackling transistor next door but one. It is the last day in Bombay and England are only just hanging on. The old lady whose transistor it is looks on approvingly as he throws the ball against the wall and leans into a classic forward defensive on the rebound.

She throws in an occasional, 'Elbow straight,' watching proceedings over a cup of tea at her half open window. Considering this is supposed to be the depths of winter, the weather could be a lot worse. She has known some bad ones too, the icy fog so thick that a shivery deposit has stayed on the tongue long after visibility has been restored. By comparison this is mild, the merest hint of something arctic settling on the teaspoon. Even so, she doesn't mind too much when a little draft sneaks in, taking some of the heat out of the feverishness building up on Test Match special. It is all noise and clamour in Bombay, everyone crowded round the bat and the fielders casting long shadows on that earlier English swagger. Seven down and not long to go, but in the end handshakes all round and honour salvaged. In all that excitement, she can't help wondering whatever happened to the sticks that used to be painted on nearly every wall round here. She doesn't see those games any more, all the boys wanting to be Compton or Hutton, and rough hewn technique honed through the smog. Nowadays the only things that appear on these walls don't seem so inviting. There is nothing playful or fun about those signs, and whenever they appear she feels embarrassed, slightly ashamed even. Mostly though it just saddens her how self discipline seems to have gone the way of so much else. The tea has cooled down and she thinks about breaking open a fresh packet of fig rolls. Once the formalities are concluded in Bombay, she closes her window, thinking what a shame it is to see this boy forced to make do on his own. His technique is not too bad either, though even at a glance it is clear to her that he needs to work a little on that elbow.

#

15.

Michelle's mum also does spelling with her in the evening. When she tells him outside the library he feels better about his own weekly tests, the joys of silent letters or unexpected vowels. She doesn't have a Chambers so he mentions the one that he's spotted in the library, and after that they begin to test each other, random pages and clusters starting to make familiar patterns. The day the page falls open at 'gum', he notices how captivated she seems, mouthing the words one after the other. Gunny, gunyah, gur. When she says 'gerr' it doesn't sound right to him, and sure enough it turns out, as he suspected, to be the sweet cane sugar Mum keeps stocked in the fridge.

Reading on, he sees that an unusually high number of these words originate in India. Gurdwara, gurkha, gurmukhi, guru. Somehow though he wishes the same were true of another prefix, 're', say, or 'st'. To his ear those sounds are more stable. Stable! Exactly. The word doesn't make him want to wobble his head and keep repeating it like some idiot. He is relieved that the English boys don't come here, that the chances of them ever encountering these words in this place are low. But he knows if they do, then the heads will automatically start to wobble and the gunny will make everyone laugh. The 'gu', 'gu', 'gunny' this week's bud bud ding. And from there the shortest of leaps to Gunga Din.

He turns the pages back to 'gale' and as they learn the difference between a galley, a gallery and a galleon, he becomes aware of how much easier it suddenly is to breathe.

#

Shortly after, there is one lunchtime when Michelle's mum comes to collect her. He watches as she bursts into tears and is then spirited away in a waiting car. That same lunch hour he is asked by one of the older boys to join the big game. The runt, who always seems to be part of these games, keeps taking his legs away, even when he doesn't have the ball, and K. is forced to sit out the last few minutes, rubbing his shins and wondering why he ever thought it would be any different.

Then in class the chewing gum has migrated from the door handle to his seat, though unlike Miss he spots it in time.

But at home when Mum asks him how school is, he just says, 'Fine,' hoping as usual there'll be no follow up.

Still, at least he has a football to practise with now. A gift from J., the crossed hammers insignia somewhere near the middle.

'Straight from the Academy,' J. tells him, though K. has no idea what he means by that. Even so, he's not unhappy that for the first time he can remember it's a proper ball that's balanced on his foot.

If he's going to survive any more of those big games, he knows he's going to have to toughen up, and some skills can't hurt either. But it takes a while before he is able to balance the ball more than once, flicking it up in the air three or four times as his foot gets used to the weight. Half the morning seems to be spent retrieving the ball after it has ricocheted off a shin or an ankle. Luckily no one seems to be around to witness the sheer lack of skill, though on a couple of occasions he swears he can hear an old lady's voice telling him to watch the ball all the way onto his foot. Watch it all the way.

#

The next day when Michelle tells him about her brother, her face again crumples. At least this time he is able to comfort her, putting an arm around her shoulder and letting her rest her head against his neck.

Though it is cold they are sat outside, on the mound, for once not bothered by the sounds of the playground.

'You watch. It'll be alright,' he says, remembering what Dad tells him whenever he gets that sad look on his face.

'How do you know?' she asks. 'They didn't even stop after they knocked him down.'

She starts tearing up again, telling him they don't even know if Junior will walk again. *Junior?* Weird name, he thinks, before reminding himself he's also got a *daknaam* only his family use. Still, Junior?

He is sad for her. It sounds horrible, the more he hears.

The only good thing as far as he can tell is that because it happened near the hospital the ambulance was right there so at least poor Junior wasn't left lying around for long.

'You'll see. It's going to be alright,' he tells her again, not sure if he believes a word of it himself.

When she cries afterwards and the loud wracking sobs keep coming, he tells her to 'let it all out', the way he imagines they would on television.

Again, the duffel coats insulate them from everything else that is happening around them. Else one or both of them might have spotted the runt peeling away from the big game, pointing up at the mound from a conspiratorial huddle.

16.

'Michelle Loves Pakis.'

Not strictly true, he thinks. They're still at the holding hands stage really. He's heard his brother telling S. about girls from the big school hanging around with older boys, but it's S. who says things like, 'She got herself into trouble.' He seems to enjoy telling them this stuff. Perhaps it's because he's older and he knows more? To be honest, he doesn't really know what S. means but, as with so much else, the key he has found, is to not let on.

The caretaker gives him a quizzical look when he appears with the bucket and mop. Looking at the latest newsflash, he wonders what this kid has been getting up to, though he has a fair idea. What the hell do any of these kids get up to? He sees them sometimes, sneaking back into classrooms, tampering with the light fittings, or with something. But even when they spot him, nothing seems to register. True enough what they say, he thinks. The lights are on but there's no one in.

Perhaps in his day they were no different at that age and it's just his memory playing tricks on him? He's found himself increasingly questioning his own mind. Tea and isolation and all those chemicals from the paint don't seem to be doing him any favours. Headaches and bad temper just festering away in that broom cupboard. Of late even the transistor has become a source of irritation, all that EMI stuff and then those bombs up west. It just doesn't seem right somehow. No one seems to care about anything anymore. Whatever happened to a bit of perspective?

'You alright, son?' he asks.

'Not bad,' says K.

'I'll give you a hand with that,' he adds, squeezing the mop.

'So there's no truth in the allegations then?' deadpans the caretaker.

'None whatsoever,' answers K., and they both laugh, making short work of the wallfront jibe.

#

17.

It's not hard to see why Junior looks happy, Michelle thinks.
They haven't even been here a week and he's already
found the main game of football, by the grass verge that
their maisonette backs onto. Even from this distance it is
obvious he's the best player out there, and, right as rain,
there he goes, showing off, balancing the ball on his head,
then on one shoulder, then flicking it up in the air before
balancing it on one foot and then flicking it back up onto
his head, where he lets the ball roll from one side to another
and then back onto the back of his neck, where the whole
routine had started off. It makes her smile, but then she
starts thinking about her dad, who taught Junior the ball
juggling trick in the first place, and her mood shifts again.

Dad was the whole reason they were here. At least
that's what mum says. She thinks it is all his fault. Says
he can't control his temper and can't let things go either.
All she knows is that someone said something to Mum, or
about Mum, and then dad lost his temper, and now he's
locked up because according to Mum, 'that's what they do
to men like your dad'. She doesn't know what happened
to the other man, the one who said whatever it was that
made her dad so angry, but she knows they had to move

out of their old place because that man knew lots of people there and they were all very unhappy about what her dad had done. Or what they were saying he had done. 'Two different things,' her mum kept saying, though less so in the last few days, since they moved here.

At least it was warm, she thought, heading out to take a closer look at how Junior was getting on.

'Watchya,' said the girl nearest the verge who had been watching Michelle walk over.

'Watchya,' she replied, as it turned out, to a sandy haired girl some years older than her who was wearing a pair of those short dungarees—'pedal pushers'—which had been really popular when she'd first started school a few years back. Michelle hadn't known any better then, but she was eight, nearly nine now, and seeing them on someone else they just looked a bit silly to her. Junior didn't have to worry about any of this stuff though. It felt a bit unfair, how boys could just pitch up in any old kit and it was fine, but girls spent ages thinking about what to wear. She didn't care much herself but she saw how long mum took to get ready any time they had a christening, or a family event to go to, round this cousin or that cousin's house. And the ones in north London all seemed to live in houses, never flats or maisonettes. And never on estates. It was embarrassing whenever anyone asked where they lived. She'd look over at Junior for support but he'd always either be stuffing his face with food or in the middle of chirpsing one of the more distant cousins. He'd told her once, 'As long as they're not first cousins, it's fine,' and then spent the rest of the time refilling his plate with chicken, rice, ackee, saltfish, dumplings and all the other goodies that seemed to have stopped, in *their* home anyway, since dad, as Mum put it, 'went away'.

Anyway, Mum always looked great on these occasions, whatever her mood inside. But the bit that Michelle would remember was the endless waiting for her mum to finally emerge from her bedroom with enough poise under her makeup to deflect any awkwardness which might arise later if her dad's name cropped up, as it was bound to during one of those impromptu Aunty conferences in the kitchen. No social gathering was complete without one of these breakaway councils. Always the same Aunty calling these meetings too, her mum's elder sister who made no secret of how much better her own kids were than Michelle or Junior, or how much better off her sister, Michelle's mum, would have been if she'd never moved south of the river, 'And with that man'.

Michelle hated it when her Aunty Constance, spoke about her dad like this. 'He's got a name,' she wants to yell at her Aunty. 'Just like you.' If she'd actually been brave enough to tell her any of this, she'd also have said, 'He's dad to us, and Patrick to you, and we don't like it when you say bad things to Mum about him.' But she can never quite work up the courage to do so, and the moment will pass with her sitting in the corner, or on the stairs, wondering why Junior is never around when she really needs him.

The last such gathering was only a couple of weeks ago, just before they'd moved here. Even Junior was very quiet that day as they'd traipsed across town to Aunty Constance's.

'Mum, do we have to go?' they'd both asked, even after they'd bought their tickets and were waiting for the predictably late train at the station.

At least the journey into town took them past the Peek Freans' factory in Bermondsey, where they made the biscuits. That was the one nice bit, Michelle thought, enjoying the sweet, tempting odour which briefly wafted into their carriage. The rest of the area didn't seem so nice though. Looking out of the window, she saw that it was one rectangular block of concrete after another, and kept thinking that the windows in these blocks looked so small, like the squares on mum's laddered tights.

After that, though, they'd more or less sat in silence all the way on the tube. The street where Aunty Constance lived was all houses. It had trees and neatly tended front gardens and all the cars were parked up properly. Not like where they lived, thought Michelle, with cars sometimes just stopping in the middle of the road and the drivers rolling down their windows to have a chat. This North London street was a lot quieter too, no one shouting out of windows, and if anyone was playing music it wasn't obvious.

It is a good spread inside though. She has to admit, her Aunty knows how to lay on a feast. All the usuals, rice, chicken, dumplings, but also a whole table full of the stuff *she* really likes: crisps and cheese straws and huge bottles of fizzy drink. The 'occasion' is cousin Mark's birthday. Constance's youngest, now seventeen, just a couple of years older than Junior. Michelle has never liked Mark. It might be because he looks just like his mum and he has that same way of looking at people, as if he's really doing them a favour just by being there. That's how he acts around her and Junior anyway, and she hates the fact that her brother either just plays along or honestly isn't as bothered as her by this. Or maybe he's just too busy feeding his face or making eyes at some girl his age to notice. Or care. That day, though, it was a little different. He definitely noticed. Everyone did.

'So, Junior, what's happening, man?'

They are in some kind of games room upstairs. All of them, the kids that is, the various cousins and their friends, have been packed off to this room which has got a pool table in the middle of it and a darts' board on one wall. The grown ups are downstairs, either splayed out in the living room digesting some of that spread, or in the kitchen, where Constance and the other Aunties are offering Michelle's mum support along with a few choice opinions about that man, that life, that side of the river. Upstairs isn't much better though. Mark has just asked her brother how he is, as if he cares or as if this is just like any other party gathering. He knows, Michelle thinks. They all do.

'Oh, you know, same as ever,' replies Junior, not making any eye contact. She thinks he looks nearly as embarrassed as she feels.

'Same as ever? You sure about that? That's not what I heard,' says Mark, clearly enjoying his cousin's discomfort. Junior doesn't say anything. Nor does anyone else, the room falling eerily quiet. In the silence, Michelle can make out the sounds of Aunty Constance's voice coming from downstairs, and then, a few seconds later, a whole chorus of female voices staging either their approval or disapproval, though even through the floorboards she has a fair idea which. Mark, though. What a wanker. And just as she's thinking this, her cousin starts up again, and she can see that he's nowhere near finished yet.

'Thing is, Junior, and don't take this the wrong way, but you can't turn up here acting all innocent when everyone knows what's been going on with your dad.'

She watches Junior stiffen and has the immense urge to walk over and slap Mark as hard as she can. Fucking stuck up wanker. But she knows that would cause even more problems for Mum. For all three of them, but especially for Mum, and she just doesn't want that. It was obvious on the way over that Mum didn't want to be here either, the way she kept pretending to read that paper just so she wouldn't have to talk to either of them, and see how unhappy they all were. She should slap him, Michelle thinks, and he definitely deserves a slap, but she knows how that would look. She knows what everyone else would say.

'Like father, like daughter. You can't blame her really, I mean she's from a broken home, no one to watch over her, give her some proper guidance. No one to keep her on the straight and narrow. That's what kids need, what they lack nowadays. Not like that in my day. *We* had rationing and national service and discipline, proper discipline if we stepped out of line. You couldn't get something back then, you didn't just half-inch it, you worked twice as hard until you *could* afford it. Didn't matter if it was butter or bread or a bloody fine pair of strides. We had community back then. Values. Not like this lot now. What a rabble, what an absolute shower.'

She's already heard some version of all of those complaints in the time it took for her dad to lose his temper, and then for other people to come and take him away. She's seen it in the way that kids she used to play with now just whisper and point. Or giggle, or say nothing. Like now.

'It's my birthday, man, and you can't even do me the courtesy of answering a straight question.'

She hates the way her cousin speaks. Who speaks like that? What an idiot. It is obvious the birthday boy is having fun, though. This just makes her hate him even more.

'Well, if you're not going to say anything, I might as well. This should interest you anyway, I know you like your football. So a couple of weeks back, you'll never guess what happened to me?'

Junior stays quiet, so Mark continues:

'So anyway, I got scouted playing five-a-side in Hackney. And then I get the shout. I've only been called up by Arsenal for a youth team trial. And that's when I thought, it's funny that, I get called up, but your dad's the one who was actually on trial. Except in my case it's a good thing, whereas your old man got sent down, didn't he, Junior? Call me old-fashioned, but that's not exactly my idea of 'same old', right?'

'Fuck off, Mark,' says Junior. 'Dad was right, what he used to say about you. Just like his mum, a constance pain in the raas!' That's when she sees him looking over at her, one of the few times he's ever needed to at one of these gatherings, and he gives Michelle a little wink at more or less the same time that Mark's balled up fist connects with the side of his face. Which is when *she* piles in too, sensing that something bigger than family honour is at stake here.

It is an awkward journey home, the three of them somehow managing to be even more sullen than on the visiting leg. Michelle can't understand why her mum looks so cross when it was all started by cousin Mark. He was the real culprit, not her or Junior. What was she supposed to do? Just stand there and watch while her brother got hit? And anyway, Mum, you didn't hear what Mark was saying about dad, so why are you acting like me and Junior are the bad ones here? The tube pulls into Euston and she is tempted to make a joke about how that sounds like Mum's name, Eustace, but when she sees the look on her mum's face, which she has been seeing a lot recently, she thinks better of it.

She can tell Mum's just waiting until they get home. She is going to get 'spoken to'. Mum's never hit them, not like some of the mums growing up round their old estate. She could hear it through the walls sometimes, the boys and girls she used to play with getting shouted at and then hit. A few times she'd also heard their mums, the ones doing the hitting, get shouted at and hit themselves, usually late at night when what Junior would call 'the man of the house' came back.

'Wait for it,' he'd say, nodding at the wall through which the sound of raised voices could be heard. 'Here's trouble. The man of the house is back.'

The hitting made a horrible sound, a dull thwack, but at least the shouting usually stopped round about then. Actually that was one difference she'd already noticed. When it was the mums hitting the kids, they often carried on screaming throughout the beating, but when it was the man of the house hitting the mums, all she would hear was that terrible thwack thwacking and then a whimpering sound.

She was glad her mum was nothing like that. Nor her dad, even though everyone else, from the nasty neighbours to Aunty Constance and sometimes even Mum herself, said that he 'had a temper which could get the better of him.' Well, she didn't know about that. He'd always been very gentle around her and Junior and even when he'd argued with Mum, it never really looked that bad to her. No shouting, and definitely no thwack thwacking. One time she'd walked in on them arguing in the kitchen and when her dad had spotted her standing quietly by the door, he had stopped mid-sentence, scooped her up in his big, strong arms and said to her in a very calm voice:

'Now listen to me, girl. Sometimes grown ups disagree and they're not happy with each other when they do. And sometimes things get said that maybe shouldn't be. That's why it's not good to stay heated for too long. But there's no need to put up with foolishness, and you know, your mother never puts up with my foolishness. Nor should she. But of course, being the man of the house, I have to puff up my chest anyhow and pretend there's still heat in my words when the truth is, your mother, Lord bless her, doused them in ice the moment she gave me that look. Yes, you know the one I'm talking about, because I see her give it to you too whenever you do some fool fool thing in your spelling book.'

She'd flung her arms around his neck and enjoyed just nuzzling up next to his bristly jaw. By the time she looked over her shoulder her mum had already arranged Michelle's spelling book and storybook on the table, so she kissed her dad on one stubbly cheek and without further ado made her way over to her mum.

Mum works for the Council now, but she used to be a teacher back home. Eustace used to be… Michelle finds something funny in the phrase but swiftly forgets this when her mum gives her another one of those looks. Dad's right, there's no need for language when it's all there in the eyes. Anger, sadness, and then that fancy word Mum had pointed out to her when they'd read the first paragraph of a local newspaper report together just recently: disappointment. It was a report about a football match in which Junior had been playing. Two of the local youth teams whose long standing rivalry, according to the report, *had spilled over into outright hostility. The disappointment felt by spectators was compounded by disgraceful scenes at the end of a bad tempered match when players from both teams confronted one another as well as startled match officials. Sadly, such scenes are becoming an all too familiar feature of our once beautiful game, now regularly marred by outbreaks of hooliganism seemingly every weekend. And this is not just a problem for the game at a grassroots level…* blah blah blah. It was so boring, she thought, quickly losing interest. Why were boys always fighting and girls having to hear about it afterwards? Junior had come home later that day with a cut lip, but Mum hadn't said anything to him about it. Just gave him a look instead, the one she, Michelle, was already used to. Dad had not long been 'sentenced', that was the word Mum used, and they were just about to move out of the area. And then they had, one of Mum's colleagues from the council helping them load the van which clearly said 'Local Education Authority' on one side, and then driving them the relatively short distance to this new place, with new people and a new school.

'Watchya.'

It's that girl again, the one who always seems to be out here whenever Junior's having a kickabout.

'You new round here, then?'

'Yeah,' says Michelle, knowing mum would hate it if she heard her talking like this. Not proper.

'He's really good,' says the other girl, looking over at Junior just as he feints a dummy around the goalkeeper and walks the ball into the net, which of course isn't a net but two jerseys placed on the grass a few feet apart.

'Yeah, he's not bad,' says Michelle, wondering why they are talking about her brother anyway. Looking up, she sees that he already seems to have made friends, or admirers, or whatever they're called. The game has apparently ended as Junior is now back to his juggling tricks, and is trying to show a younger boy how to balance the ball on his foot. It is all so annoyingly easy for Junior, she thinks. All he needs is a ball and a strip of ground and he's happy. But *her*, Dad never showed her how to juggle.

'You have to be clever, girl, like your mother. Play is play and that is all well and good, but in this day and age, a girl like you has to be smart in other ways. So I thank the Lord that your mother is around to guide you.'

What did he mean by that, 'a girl like you'? What if she *wanted* to know how to juggle, rather than just sit here with books, books, books and all this *blood claat* spelling? She's heard Dad say that when he's been cross about something or another but she doesn't know what it means other than that it is not a phrase she should repeat around any grown ups, least of all Mum or Dad.

Mum's not a bad teacher though, definitely better than the ones at school. Plus she just seems to know when boredom is setting in, because that's when she will place a hand on Michelle's arm and give her the other look, not the really scary one with all the anger, hurt and the fancy word she has recently learned, but look #2. It's calm and wise and bloody annoying, but she has to admit, it's bang on the money. Always makes her pay attention however far her mind has drifted.

'Look, Michelle,' Mum will start, which is how Michelle knows what's coming. The talk. It always starts off with that.

'I know this is hard for you, and you're probably think-ing, "Why do I have to stay in and study when Junior's out there enjoying himself?" But you know what you see as your brother just having fun isn't that at all. He's study-ing too, in his own way. All those games he plays and he's finally been noticed. Scouted, they call it. Anyway, that's beside the point. He's good with his feet and you, madam, are even better with *this*,' she says, gently tapping Michelle's forehead with one finger. 'The thing is, even though you were born here and brought up here, they will never really consider you an equal. So you have to be better than them, you have to study twice as hard, be twice as good, and even then you may only get half the opportunity. But it will come to you and you have to be ready for it when it does. So, let's read that paragraph one more time and then you can tell me all the new words you have learned.'

Her mum, whose name sounds like the big London station, knows just what to say to her, and when, but that's not been true of any of her teachers so far. In her old school they were very nice but she remembers feeling embarrassed whenever her mum came to collect her and would ask her class teacher why there was no homework. She got the feeling her teachers avoided her after that, and when all those things happened with her dad, and the other kids were pointing and whispering, she had the strongest sense that it was her teachers who now felt even more embarrassed than her.

God, she hoped Mum wouldn't carry on like that round here. It's not like she didn't already stand out, she thought, on her first day in the new school, unable to spot one other girl with braids.

The buildings were nice, though, more or less brand new. Very, what was the word she was searching for, the one she'd learned the other day with Mum? Ah yes, modern. Huge windows, lots of glass and a big playground. No sign of the teachers at breaktime either, and that was probably a good thing too, she thought. But the classroom, blimey, that was noisy. Shouting, screaming, throwing paper, and the only boy who looked like he could sit still and stay quiet also had this bored look on his face.

#

The teachers, Mrs. Allott and Mr. Lewis, are friendly. They ask about her last school and she's happy because, she thinks, this must mean they don't know about what happened with Dad, and maybe not even about Mum and the homework question.

'We like to think of ourselves as one big family here, and as part of that we all care about each other,' says Mr. Lewis, though in truth, she thinks, he doesn't look much like anyone in her family. Then again, considering Aunty Constance and her stuck up son, maybe that's no bad thing?

She catches the quiet boy in class looking at her some-times, or was she looking at him? She's not sure, but if he's anything like her, she thinks, he must be wondering when the buzzer will go for lunchtime, and when it does where he can go for some peace and quiet. Anywhere really just to get away from this cacophony. She likes that word, had read it in a match report on a First Division game on the back page of a newspaper someone had left lying around outside, close to where Junior had been playing football. She remembered the teams. Arsenal v West Ham with *a cacophony of noise coming from the North Bank*. Can't have been louder than here though, she thinks, watching where the quiet boy goes and following at a discreet distance.

The library smells ok, she thinks, much better than the classroom. Maybe that's because it's empty, or near enough. Apart from the librarian, there's only the two of them, herself and the quiet boy, though after a bit that other girl who doesn't say anything, who she has seen in class, also comes in but stays near the librarian. Still, that's the first thing she notices, how it smells empty in here rather than full, and it's a pleasing sensation. She smiles at the boy, who looks a bit surprised to see her there.

'Watchya,' she says, looking at the book he is holding in his hand. Reader's Digest. Odd sounding title.

'Watchya,' he says back after a short delay.

'We're in the same class,' she says, keeping her voice down so as not to bother the librarian.

'Yeah, I know,' he says. 'You're new.'

This time it is her turn to be surprised, but she's glad he noticed. Other than the girl who always seems to be around anytime Junior is outside playing football, hardly anyone in this place seems to pay her the blindest bit of attention. In one way, of course, that's good because she just wants to be left alone with her books and pencil case and whatever scribbled thoughts come to her. But it'd be nice sometimes to go out and play and shout and not have to think about anything. Like Junior.

'What's it like round here?'

'You really want to know?' replies the boy.

She nods, enjoying how the boy doesn't look away each time he says something.

'It's full of cunts,' he says, not raising his voice at all. They look at each other for a split second and then both burst out laughing. As soon as they hear the librarian getting up from her chair, the laughter is downgraded to giggling, which starts up again every time they find a strange word, usually a foreign one, in the Reader's Digest. Definitely more fun than learning with Mother, she thinks, especially once they start to regularly spend lunchtimes in the library.

#

But no doubt about it, that's a funny word, a little like what would happen if someone took 'aunt' and mixed it with 'can't', which is definitely how she feels about her Aunty Constance. *A constance pain in the raas.* The grown ups use it all the time, apart from the teachers, that is. She's always heard grown ups say this, even on the old estate. Some of the older kids used to say it as well, but here it's so common, even amongst the younger kids, that it shouldn't still sound as funny as it does. But it does. Everyone in her class swears, apart from her and her library companion,

413

K., and that other girl who sometimes comes in the library as well, the one who sits near the librarian. Actually that's not quite true, she thinks. Those posh girls, Emma and Rosie, who she can tell just from the way they sit, all upright and proper proper, think they're better than everyone else, all because they're posh and they don't swear. Stuck up, like her cousin, Mark. A right pair of cunts. Mostly though, what's funny about it is that she wouldn't dare say it around her mum or the teachers or the librarian or even any of the grown ups she *has* heard saying it themselves. But with her library companion she feels a little bolder. With him, that word's got nothing to do with her aunt, or *not* being able to say it. With him it almost feels secretive, even though it's as common as 'watchya' round here.

When it's going home time, they are the two most well behaved kids in their class. She can't believe what some of the other girls say to their mums when they come to collect them. Or what the mums say to their kids.

'Have you got everything?'

'What?'

'Have you got your bag?'

'What?'

'I haven't got time for this.'

'Piss off, Mum, you stupid cow.'

'Don't you talk to me like that! You wait till I get you home, you little cow.'

'Fuck off!'

Lisa on that occasion, but it could just as easily have been pretty much anyone in the class. At least she's not the only one who's shocked by this. She sees K. with his mouth still open until his mum arrives to collect him. *She* is wearing a funny looking dress, a bit like a really long skirt and it goes all the way down to her shoes. Some of the other mums stare at her but no one says anything. She's glad *her* mum doesn't wear funny clothes like that, but even if she did, she still wouldn't tell her to piss off and she definitely wouldn't call her a cow. Or that other word.

#

It's quite annoying sometimes when Mum gives her the 'twice as good' talk. *You have to be twice as good as them.* What for? What if I don't want to be twice as good, she wants to say? What if I want to be just like them? What if I want to eat their food, talk like them, act like them? What if I actually like cheese straws and crisps? I bet their mums aren't making them stay indoors all the time and read. Cold day, read. Hot day, read. Rainy day, read. Holiday, read. It's all I ever do. Makes me look stuck up. 'Sorry, Michelle can't come out to play. She's reading.' Not that anyone's asking, but if they were. And anyway, what's so bad about *them*? I reckon that's why I haven't got any friends, 'cos they all think I'm stuck up. But I'm not stuck up, I'm not like those girls in class, Rosie and Emma, or like Aunty Constance or cousin Mark. They're all stuck up and I don't want to be anything like *them*. Actually, they're just cunts. You know, Mum, I like saying that word. I say it a lot with this other boy in my class. We spend a lot of time together playing with words and it's much more fun than this. His mum dresses funny though. I'm glad you're not like that. And he's got a funny name. You know what he's called, Mum? K. I know, it's funny, isn't it? But he likes to read as well, and sometimes we draw words on each other's backs. I'll draw something first and he'll try and guess what it is, and then he draws something back. I like it when he draws. We just use our fingers. It's really nice until we have to be back in class. We can't really hide away there, and it's boring anyway. And loud. But I'm already twice as good, Mum. That's why I can do all the classwork in half the time.

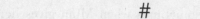

The other thing that's quite annoying is that Junior seems to be spending more and more time outside while she is stuck indoors. It doesn't seem fair even if Mum says he's not really 'playing' but 'practising his skills, the same way you are, just different skills.' She's not sure about that though. Didn't look like he was practising his skills when she spotted him disappearing into one of the neighbouring flats with 'watchya' on his arm. And she hasn't seen either of them anywhere near the grass verge for a while. Anyway, why would a talent scout, whatever that is, come here? It's just kids messing around with whatever they can get their hands on. Apart from footballs, stones, bricks, polythene bags, each other. And it's not exactly pretty, not like her Aunty's street, with houses and trees and nice cars. Their maisonette's not bad, but looking around, it's mostly just another kind of concrete. Why would anyone come here if they didn't have to?

#

Mum's job at the council is why they've got this maisonette. That's what Junior says.

'How else do you reckon we got this place so quick?'

'Dunno,' she says, dropping the 'I' like everyone does in class.

'It's not easy, coming by maisonettes,' he says. 'She must have got us bumped up the list because she knows people at the council. Point is, we're here now, so may as well make the most of it. Anyway, it's not that bad. Friendlier than the last place, that's for sure.'

'So you're making friends?' she asks him, thinking her brother and 'watchya' seemed pretty friendly to each other when she'd spotted them heading off together the other day.

'Yeah, aren't you?' he says, looking at her a touch warily.

'Yeah, sort of,' she says, wondering if K. properly counts as a 'friend', seeing as though when she first joined the class he was still sitting next to the girl who smelled of wee, the one who also goes to the library. It was obvious neither of them had made friends with anyone else and that was why they were sitting together. And maybe it was the same thing with her and K. Perhaps when she made some other friends she'd stop going to the library? All of which made K. a friend, but only 'sort of'.

Later, when she asks Mum exactly what a talent scout does, and Mum tells her, it still doesn't change her mind. Why would a talent scout come here? This, after all, is a place where no one seems to notice anything. Certainly not how Junior keeps disappearing with that girl, or how he rarely seems to have any football injuries any more, no sprains or cuts or bruises whenever he saunters back in from whatever he's actually been doing all day. Of course she's not to know that she's quite wrong about that. She's not the only one who notices. Visual notes are made, and words are spoken, but behind the scenes, much like her and K. sharing a private joke in the library. And she's yet to know that those eyes, the ones watching her or Junior, are narrowed, and that the words brought on by the visuals are inflamed. But perhaps she should, given what has already happened with her dad. Still, *her* eyes see more than most even if what they can't see is just around the corner.

She *is* surprised to see mum turn up at school in the middle of the day. At first she can't understand what mum is trying to tell her. Why is she crying? Why are they both crying? Why is this happening? Why *them*?

She cries again when they reach the hospital and she sees Junior, his face all bruised now and his legs! She can't even see his legs, just oblong shapes wrapped in bandages like one of those mummies in the Horniman Museum. One arm is in a sling and she is just waiting for him to get up out of bed and chase her around the ward like the caretaker on Scooby Doo, with all the bandages slowly coming away to reveal the villain's true identity. But he doesn't get up, doesn't even smile, and this is so unlike her big brother that she just bursts into tears all over again. He winked at her just before that fight with their cousin, Mark, and he was smiling and joking afterwards, though not of course while Mum was there, because that wouldn't have looked good for any of them. But that evening, after they'd got home and Mum had gone to the bathroom, he was laughing and joking about how Mark 'hit like a girl and probably kicks like one too, so he won't be needing an Arsenal kit any time soon.' He's nothing like that now. If anything, she thinks, *he's* the one who looks like he won't be kicking a ball any time soon. Then again, he hasn't been doing much of that anyway so what difference will a few more days here make?

When she is still visiting nearly a month later she feels quite angry with her mum, even though none of this is her fault. And it is the same thought which keeps passing through Michelle's head. What if Mum had also been paying attention? What if she'd stopped worrying about her daughter, who was nearly always indoors, and started to think for a moment what her son was actually doing when he was outdoors? It wasn't *her* who Mum needed to worry about. Mum should have been around a bit more and then maybe she'd also have seen Junior and watchya, and maybe she could have said something and then none of this would have happened. Ever since she first heard the news, Michelle has had an uncomfortable feeling that Junior's accident is somehow connected with his neglecting his football in favour of hanging out with that girl, watchya. That girl may be roughly Junior's age, but as far as Michelle can tell, *she's* not busy with anything. When they're together, it's only Junior who's neglecting something else. Though he's her older brother, she has been feeling especially protective of him these past weeks. At least she's been watching out for him, not like Mum. She would if she was around. But she's not there, she's always at work. The bloody council! She hated the bloody council and her mum's job there. She doesn't even know what her mum does but whatever it is, it stops her keeping an eye on Junior, though she never seems to miss any of *their* reading or spelling sessions. Then again it can't be that easy for Mum, now it's just her. If Dad was there, none of this would have happened. But he's not, and it has. And she feels mad at him too, for getting mad himself and then sent away. Why does it have to be like this? They are all careless, Mum, Dad, and Junior, and now it seems her older brother has even forgotten how to cross the road. The Green Cross Code. Look left, look right, look left again. Or was it right, then left, then right? She doesn't bloody know, but there is one bit of that she never forgets: Look!

'You might not think it, love, but your brother's been very lucky,' one of the nurses tells her, adjusting Junior's pillow so that he is propped up in bed, the better to see his various visitors. The steady stream from that first couple of weeks has reduced to more of a trickle now, but there is still a constant flow of gifts arriving on a daily basis, brought by friends, football coaches, even the occasional cunt like Aunty Constance, though thankfully not accompanied by her stuck up son. The nurses regularly collect the cards, chocolates and flowers when they start to pile up, and they're always ready with a kind word.

'Because of where it happened, right outside, there was no delay in getting him treated, so he should make a full recovery, though it might take a while. Yep, there's no doubt about it, love, he's one of the lucky ones.'

He doesn't look that lucky to her, but the nurse is probably right. It will take time but Junior will be back on his feet. And everything will be ok. It is only later that she hears from one of her brother's team mates, who's also visiting, that the car that knocked Junior down didn't stop afterwards and that the police had been trying to find out who was driving this car. Again, no one seemed to have seen anything, even though it was on a busy road right outside the hospital. And instead of feeling grateful, looking at all the cards and chocolates, some from the kids in her class who don't even know Junior, and from the teachers as well, what Michelle feels is a cold anger that no one ever seems to see anything. Except of course that they do, though she's not to know that... yet.

#

It's odd, she thinks. Since Junior's accident, everyone's much more friendly at school. The teachers, the other girls, even the dinnerladies. There's a boy in her class, Stephen, who K. calls 'the runt' because he's quite small and also because it rhymes with that other word, who has started talking to her at break times. He's not that bad, not at all like K. makes him out to be. Actually he's quite nice, asking after Junior and saying how everyone wants him to 'get well soon'. And he's not like K., all hidey hidey

421

in one corner of the library with just that old woman and the spastic girl from class for company. Anyway all that indoors stuff is getting boring. Who wants to stay hidden all the time? Where's the fun in that? Plus, it's much easier outside once you know people. And Stephen definitely knows people. He knows everyone, at school, in the playground, on the estate. He's quite funny too, always making jokes around the teachers and the other kids in class, especially that spastic one. This is new for her. She didn't used to think it was funny, and actually when she first joined the class she was a little bit worried that it would be *her* everyone was laughing at and throwing bits of paper at. Now she can see they're not interested in her, not that way, and it's a right laugh when the spastic girl has an accident in class, which happens more than once. Why should she feel sorry for her? She's a spastic, shouldn't even be at school, stinking up the classroom every day. And if it's so bad, why doesn't this girl say something? Can't be that bad then because she just sits there like one of the dolls in the dolls' house, except she smells worse than them.

Lisa and the other girls aren't so bad either. It's fun hanging out with them when Stephen's playing football or mucking about in the playground.

'We're going to the Paki shop, 'Chelle. You coming?'

'Yeah, alright.'

They get sweets there, Yorkies and Lion Bars, and hardly ever pay for them. That's a laugh too, she thinks, distracting the shopkeeper while Lisa or one of the other girls slips a handful of sweets into a pocket. Somehow though, she knows her mum would be really angry if she knew what her daughter was getting up to nowadays, so she never actually pockets any sweets herself, just lets her friends do that. Anyway, she's not actually doing anything wrong. It's a free country, she thinks, if she wants to ask the P-, Asian shopkeeper where he keeps the liquorice and then one of the other girls pinches something while his back is turned, that's not her fault. It's not a crime to ask for sweets, though round here it might be one to turn your back. Having the chocolate feels a bit naughty too. A right treat. Not like home, where Mum's always making her eat her greens and then do her spelling. Afterwards, Lisa will do her Paki impressions and sometimes one of the boys in the playground, usually Stephen but occasionally some other boy who's not even part of the group, will join in and they'll carry on bud bud dinging until the lunch break's over or they find someone else to take the piss out of. Best of all, there's never anyone around to stop them. No teachers, parents, other kids. No one ever says anything because no one sees anything. Except of course that they do.

#

Before Junior's accident, and then just after, they'd been spending a lot of time together, her and K., which must have been why they were holding hands and kissing and then touching each other when they thought no one else could see them. Sometimes in the library, then up on a little verge a short distance from the main playground, and then again in one of the darker corners of the estate, near a utility room. She's not to know eyes are on them, but perhaps she should. They both should. But it's warm and this is more fun than anything they are made to learn in class.

It's different with Stephen though. Sometimes she wonders if he even knows where the library is, but it turns out he's got his own hiding places on the estate. A broom cupboard she's never seen before, then access to an empty flat in one of the tower blocks. She doesn't really want to go in but he tells her it'll be fine, he's been here loads of times before and it's always been empty.

'I don't want to go in there,' she says, suddenly aware of how stale the entire corridor smells.

'What, are you scared?' he asks, not removing his eyes from her for one moment. He has been watching her ever since she arrived on this estate and joined their class. He has watched her sneak off with that Paki to the library, and he has seen her brother acting all lovey dovey with that slag from the next block. That's how he knows about this place. He followed them here the second or third time he saw them together, mainly because he was bored, but also out of curiosity. He'd watched them from the door, which was still open. He didn't really know what they were doing but they made a lot of noise and then the coon had looked up and their eyes had briefly locked before he'd run off. And if that was her brother, there was no point her pretending she was all nicey nicey. *Birds of a feather* and all that, something his old man says, though in truth, Stephen only has a vague sense of what that means. Point is, he thought, her brother wasn't nice, so what were the odds she was?

'No, let's go. We shouldn't be here,' she says, wondering

why on earth she had agreed to come along in the first place. 'It'll be a right laugh, they've got all sorts of stuff in there,' just didn't sound like such a good idea now.

He starts to flap imaginary wings and make a chicken noise.

'See you, I'm going,' she says, trying to push past him. He grabs her arm and shoves her roughly through the half open door.

'Be nice,' he says. 'Like you are with the Paki.'

She tries to push past him again, and he shoves her back again, this time more forcefully.

'Be nice, don't be a tease,' he says, never taking his eyes off her. She sees his lips moving and she hears the words forming, but it's a voice that's far older than either of them, than this room even, its damp, stale air dissolving into little particles of dust.

#

For a small boy, he's surprisingly strong, she thinks, slumping back onto the broken settee in the middle of the room. It is covered with a moth eaten blanket which smells strongly of damp and other mistakes. When she tries to get up, he hits her and then giggles. She can't see his face, just a blank oval pressed up too close. She feels his breaths scampering away across her cheek and his hands moving all over her. She wants to fight him, to squirm away, to hit him like she had with her cousin Mark, but when she tries she can't move her arms, her legs, her anything. He bites her ear and giggles, and his hands keep touching, pressing, probing. Her body is rigid, like one of those mummies, like Junior, but she knows this is not like any of the games she has played with K. in the stairwells, in the library, in the playground. She can feel his hands going lower and his fingers are rough, angry at what they don't know. He wants to hurt her, he's already hurting her and she just wants for all of this to stop. But when she tries to scream, the paralysis that has gripped her body slips down her throat and strangles the sound, leaving her choked and tearful.

The noise when it eventually comes is like nothing she has ever heard before. It arrives from so deep that it could have been summoned from the very guts of this room, its dust, its staleness. It begins with a barely audible moan, an acknowledgement of hurt, and then builds in pitch, an outraged quiver swelling its edges, absorbing fingers and rage and pressure and miscalculation. But this moan is soon a lament for all the classroom indignities, the strangled whispers, the frozen wastelands of so many childhoods. 'Let them play!' it says. 'But not like this.' And rising to a shriek, it's coated in shame, abandonment and a newfound boldness. Not courage, that was always there. But boldness. For it *is* bold, and audible, and the bloodcurdling sound which relays off the walls and the blanket and the two shocked bodies also carries them, as if on a carpet made of dust, back out into a bigger world. Another kind of concrete.

Stephen, startled, gets off her and quickly scrambles away from the settee. Michelle, finally able to move her limbs again, looks over in his direction. But she is not looking at him. She is staring at the doorway, where the spas-, Rachael, is stood, tears running down her cheeks but her arms folded in a pose of steely determination. It is *her* howl which has ended this, and for that, and for all the unkindness Michelle has seen this girl endure, for her own part in those humiliations, she wants to hug this girl and beg her forgiveness. It belongs to a moment just before this, when libraries and learning and fumbling with knowledge still felt like fun. One of the last words she remembered looking at with K., on a day when they'd been looking up 'atrium' in the dictionary. Atonement.

18.

They listen to the tape so softly, with the sound right down, that practically all they can hear is something which sounds like interference.

'This one's really good,' says his brother as the noise starts up again.

'How can you even tell what it is?' K. asks, genuinely impressed that to the trained ear one bit of noise can sound so different to the next.

'Just listen,' says his brother, 'you might learn something.'

He's got that same look on his face that S. has when he talks about girls. It seems to be a common thing round here, everyone wanting to look and sound a lot older than they are. But as ever when confronted with those little details of life he just doesn't understand, K. thinks it best not to let on.

Anyway, he's just glad they're talking again. The way his brother tells it, big school sounds like another world. Though from what he can gather, not entirely unfamiliar. Swots at the front, cunts at the back, everyone else hoping not to be mistaken for the former by the latter, or at least not to attract too much attention. He listens intently when his brother tells him there are some kids who turn up with streaks in their hair and others with ear studs. More Black kids too, not that they sound any friendlier. He learns that sometimes the older Black boys call the younger ones 'blubbamout' and 'picky head' but his brother doesn't say what they call him. It is odd hearing this stuff. It wouldn't cross his mind to be deliberately mean to some other kid, like that girl in his class, the one everyone else makes fun of. An image suddenly pops up in his head of those Black kids racing around the Oval turf in front of the cameras, the rules the last thing on their minds. He's never known that level of confidence himself, can only imagine what it feels like. As far as he can make out though, the one good thing about big school is that S. also goes there. And because he is in the final year at this school, he knows a lot of the older boys, which apparently comes in handy when it is a question of playground etiquette. Perhaps that's what J. had meant the time K. overheard him telling S. just before the new school year started, 'You make sure you look out for him, ok?'

K. just about manages to make out something to do with *'Black man'* and *'brick'*, then *'white people'* and *'thick'*.

The tape is mewling away, the sound of the heads going round and round the bit he really hears. There is a moment, just before the voice becomes even more mangled and the heads suddenly catch, when his brother hesitates. The split second delay proves crucial and he spends the next few minutes watching his brother gently respooling the tape with a biro wedged between the little plastic teeth on the heads. If forced to, K. would have described the whole operation as 'painstaking', another word he has Michelle to thank for. She'd only been looking up 'paisley' at the time because her brother had mentioned something about a 'paisley shirt' from his hospital bed.

'I've just about got away with that,' he says, sounding relieved. 'But you can't use this tape player until it's been cleaned. You got that?'

K. doesn't say anything, tries to look hurt, but in truth he stopped listening some time ago, even before 'eject' was pressed and the mangled, black wreckage *painstakingly* lifted out.

#

Then again, the reason they listen to tapes with the volume turned right down is because Dad is back on the night shift.

They convince one another that it is a skill, listening to things with the sound right down. That they can make out the tiniest recalibration of sound, ears trained like bats in some suburban cave.

Of course what actually happens is that they start hearing things no one else can. And certainly that no one else expects them to hear. In the shops, at school, on the bus.

'He just called you a cunt.'

'She said you smell.'

'They're about to nick something.'

'He's got no character.'

It also makes it harder to pretend they don't know what's going on, in that catch they sometimes hear in people's voices when they ask, 'And how are *you* getting along?' 'And how are *you* finding it?'.

They hear other stuff too. S. telling them about 'peanuts' when they are on the bus and they see kids with cropped hair waiting around near the station. On days like these it is a fine line between absorption and regret.

They want to look, to really stare, but daren't get caught out doing so. Yet they can't look away, everything about this tribe demanding their attention. Bristles, and boots, and three quarter length coats.

'There used to be more of them,' says S., 'but they're coming back.'

Then his brother says something surprising, which seems to catch S. a little off guard.

'Those cunts never went away. Some of us always knew that.'

S. looks at his neighbour, this little Indian kid, and his younger brother, who doesn't say a whole lot. But the one who goes to his school, the older one, there he is, sat there in his red jumper with the huge blue collars poking out of the top. This kid he spends a portion of every lunchtime looking out for because that's what he's been told to do. This kid he points out to Luke and Errol and the other Black boys in his class and when they ask him why, he tells them, 'He lives next door. He's alright, that little kid. He likes his sounds, you know?' And then when they ask him what sounds, this kid about whom he lies, telling them, Junior Murvin, Culture, all kinds of stuff he knows the kid has never even heard of but which he, S., has got tucked away at home along with the spikier stuff.

And now here they are on this bus with this kid telling him about peanuts as though *he's* the one that knows everything.

S. feels he should be more annoyed than he is, but really, when he thinks about it, the kid's right. These never went away.

19.

It is a quiet one today, no one around near the railway sidings. He has the place to himself for once, none of those half-closed eyes to scramble away from. Leaning back against one of the tree stumps, he removes a packet of crisps from his pocket. Salt and vinegar. Everything Mum hates. Still, he'd found it in the kitchen, just lying around. One of Dad's mates must have left it when they'd dropped Dad off after a recent night shift. The sharp tang of the first crisp surprises him. Only when the last flecks of salt have been retrieved from the corners of his mouth does he allow himself to take a proper look around.

The ground feels harder than when he was last here, a prolonged cold snap freeze framing all the dirty little activities which this place has been hosting. Not far from the stump he spots a couple of empty polythene bags and for some reason there is a small, individual running shoe right next to them. Just the one, no explanation.

He thinks about dropping the empty crisp packet in with the other foreign objects, but has a change of heart at the last minute, unclear as to exactly why that should make him a better person but fairly sure that it does anyway.

That is when he sees it. Half hidden amongst leaves

which have either been scattered in a poor attempt to disguise it or else which have fallen in some kind of a natural crown, the indigo lettering peeping out of a paper sleeve. Stooping down to take a closer look, K. spots a fine tear on one corner of the sleeve, but other than that it appears to be remarkably unblemished. He is really pleased about this. Always a good feeling when a situation seems tailor made for its own sentence. After all, he'd only been looking up 'unguent' that time he'd overheard the old lady next door but one. Overheard her lamenting to J. about kids nowadays with 'unguent' in their hair. Then he'd got lost in the prefix, one of those rare occasions when he'd thought it was all too much. A word maze, but seemingly endless. So there he was about to throw in the towel, for once defeated by the book. Perhaps he'd been looking in all the wrong places, he thought, casting his eye across the page one last time. Which was when it hit him. Right there, just below 'unbind', a shadow list of adjectives, mostly full of clunk, only one of which stood out, setting itself apart from the cluster. A triptych of balance, all poise beneath the line. And now this, an unblemished sleeve.

Inside, 'The Upsetters. A Live Injection.'

He wonders if his brother knows this one. It's not one of the names he's familiar with himself. Sounds a bit odd, frankly.

The disc doesn't look like much but he still wishes he had a bag to carry it in. Somehow the discarded polythene doesn't seem right. Anyway, even if he manages to smuggle it back ok, it's going to have to go under the bed. They haven't got a record player at home and if

Mum sees it, there'll only be more questions to answer and probably a bad outcome. Where, what, why? The last thing he needs, the second last being that centrefold with the weird triangle of hair, and what might happen if anyone ever fishes that out from under his bed. Discovery, he decides, is not an option.

20.

Junior, he hears, is making good progress. Michelle tells him several times during one lunch hour that the feeling has returned to his legs and now the doctors are saying it is a question of when rather than if he will be back on his feet.

Though they carry on holding hands, she doesn't rest her head on his shoulder quite as much. The tears have largely dried up too, though she still has her moments, especially when she describes how things are at home, how hard it is for her mum having to cope with everything on her own.

One time he only just manages to stop himself from blurting out, 'So where's your dad then?' but is glad he doesn't.

When he sees her talking to the runt not long after, he is tempted to ask her what she's doing, but just as he's about to go over he sees that she is smiling, enjoying whatever it is that the runt has said to her.

Somehow he doubts it's about the graffiti.

#

The teachers always make a point of asking her how she is, how her mum is, but most of all, 'And how's your brother getting along? A little bird whispered in my ear that he'll be back on his feet kicking a ball in no time.'

There are 'Get Well Soon' cards signed by the whole class, the runt's signature the boldest of the lot, and boxes of chocolates constantly arriving at the hospital.

Even the dinner ladies ask after her brother, those same, unsmiling harpies routinely performing crude autopsies on the lunchtime remainders, suddenly transformed into salt-of-the-earth wellwishers.

The worst of it is, she seems to love it.

He sees her lapping up the attention, everyone in on the act. Hears her tell anyone who cares to listen how wonderful everyone is at the hospital. All the doctors and nurses doing everything they can for Junior. Everyone's so friendly, and nice, and helpful. They all say it's a miracle how quickly Junior's getting better. Though he never hears her say a word about the porters.

Lisa and the other girls make a little space for her where they sit, and it's not long before they're sharing lunch hours together too. He even spots her laughing more than once when Lisa points towards the one girl never invited to join in the fun and games. Points at her with the usual intent and then shrieks with laughter, the others following suit, Michelle no different.

And when he rejoins the big game, and the runt, Stephen, comes scything in for another leg breaking challenge, he only just manages to skip out of harm's way and back to the familiar sanctuary of the library.

\#

It is quiet when he gets home. Dad back to normal hours, Mum with his brother at the dentist.

He's walked back with S. today, neither of them saying much. On the way, near the shop, they pass a couple of not-quite peanuts who can't be more than a year or so older than K. Their hair is short but not right up against the skull. He can tell they want to say something but the presence of the much older boy is a sufficient deterrent. Of late there definitely seem to be more junior skins popping up from the cracks. So far none on their street, but that day can't be too far off now. The runt's had a crop recently, as have one or two of the other boys in his class. They do seem to be on their way back. Or maybe his brother's right. These were never away in the first place.

\#

21.

It is quiet on his rounds, so he is sometimes home when the boy gets back from school. Habit is a harder thing to break though, and there is one time some weeks later when muscle memory kicks in during an interrupted nap. The tap tapping on the wall now a metronomic thud prodding him at the edges of sleep. Goading in its dull insistence. *You shall not sleep. You don't deserve to sleep. I won't let you sleep.* Shaking him from his torpor, leaden footed, groggy, the after hours pleading and the moaning and the bleating starting to seep into his tiredness. Every thud of the ball another reminder of unfinished business, overdue debts and, what's that? Oh yes, some snide dereliction of duty. 'Please, Mr.__ , just a couple more days. I'll get it to you, I promise, the full amount. That's all I need, just another day or two.' It is what they say, always a version of the same thing, but he knows behind the words, hands are rubbing together, faces frozen in that split second before the smirk. And they are mocking him, he knows it, he can feel it, he can practically taste it in the bloody red drip drip seeping into his thoughts, each thud another nail in the coffin of respectability. Of protocol, courtesy, just basic bloody manners. It is business, nothing more, but that's not how they treat it. How they treat him, with their lies and their indiscipline and yes, their greed, always trying to hang on to what's not theirs, to hold on till the last possible moment before, oh look, what's this? What do we have here? Were you trying to keep this from me? Put yourselves in my shoes. How would *you* feel? What would *you* do? I can't just let this go, you know I can't do that. You've only yourself to blame. They force him, oh yes, they force him to respond, the thud thudding every frozen rictus that has ever plagued him. Through the dirt and the dust and the cage and the cold, every hand offered in fear, every word spoken in a whisper, tap tapping, thud thudding against the side of his head. Something seeping from the sides, a haunted replica of that night watchman all those years back, propped up but already gone. The eyes looking straight ahead, into that beyond of everything, nothing, some hint in the fireflies, footprints in the dust. Or this money dry fuckry of cheese, gut and drink. The indiscipline of it all. That woman in the tower, crying and then falling, and yet it could all have been avoided. He considers one of his large paws, but really indiscipline and greed were her downfall. To think they once had an empire. And worse, that we let them. It sickens him. He sickens himself. But the mocking persists, metronomic in its certainty. Sleep is all he desires, and it is the one thing which is withheld. All those whispers congealing into a murmur, red seeping down into the vaults. The roar barely suppressed, red pouring in through the sides, staining everything. Filling up, liquid and unwilling and suddenly it's hard to breathe and it's all he can do to lift himself up and let the painted scales slip away, the roar once more confined to its box. The pretence just gets harder. That's all. But it is mid afternoon and that means a matinée. It is only when he emerges moments later, barely stifling a yawn, that he sees the boy gripping the bat handle with both hands. His nephew again looks surprised, but it is not really fear that he senses in the boy's eyes this time.

#

22.

He makes a point of going to pick the boy up from school. Unannounced of course, as experience has taught him that the element of surprise should never be underestimated.

There is no one at the gates to ask him his business, so he just walks in.

The school though. All those low buildings and the glass canteen and the unmanned gates. He's not entirely sure what it was that he'd been expecting, but it's not this. Everything so bright and modern and new, though it is clear the inmates have been doing their best to change that, some half cut foolishness scrawled on a perimeter wall. A little further in, nearer the classrooms, a cluster moves away from a gangling half caste boy when they see him approaching. The boy's face, he's seen that look before. Just doesn't really expect to find it here, in a school.

And those little rats, with their pinched faces, scurrying back to their ratholes. Clusters of them everywhere, some milling around for a while near the gates, but mostly just dispersing, especially when their baby snake eyes meet his. And that's a look he's certainly seen before, the plastic defiance just a tap away from powder. *Give them a tap and watch them crumble.* Looking up at the towers, at their little peep holes, the slits carved out of their sides, he sees nothing so much as familial weakness encased in concrete. Rats in a barrel, really. They'll do his job for him. Rip each other apart before he even gets there. Yes, that level of weakness is bound to eventually fetch up on his radar. The little rats, bad stock being raised by worse. One generation after another growing up with excuses, sleeves rolled up but no hint of work in those arms. Soft around the gills too but evidently, if what his brother says is true, sharp with the curses and accurate with the bricks. Dirty as well, hence all that shit to go with the shards. Cheese, ham, beef, chips, beer, whine. As though the stink can just be ignored. And if they even go near his nephew, well…

After his initial surprise, the boy has been fairly quiet. It is not clear what he's thinking. He's already seen him hoodwink the rest of his family, so he's not about to second guess the boy now. Still, his nephew looks as though he could use a laugh, so he wheels out the panto sketch he already had prepared about interrogatives and *pranams*, which lightens the mood and satisfies his curiosity. Partially, at least.

#

23.

Just a few weeks ago he and Michelle were barely talking. Every time he'd see her, she would be with Lisa and that horrible group of girls, or sharing a joke with the runt. Yet now it's just like it was before, every lunchtime the two of them secluded in the library, or on the mound, words and patterns tracing their addictive swirl in his head, on his back, across his lips. These days she doesn't mention Junior so much either, now that he's back on his feet. No one does, and in a way, K. is relieved, the nasty girls and the dinner ladies back to doing what they do best. Pointing and bullying and sneering and none the wiser for their brief foray into compassion. Things feel more or less back to normal again, as though the natural balance has been restored. The junkyard once more relinquished to the beasts.

'I love that word,' she says.

'Yeah, but what would *you* relinquish?' he asks, not entirely sure what he's trying to say.

She pauses, gives him a little sidelong glance.

'You'll see,' she replies, with only the vaguest idea of what she even really means.

#

24.

It starts up again in May. This time though, as soon as he hears the first wave of chanting, he doesn't hang around. They're straight into the library, himself and Michelle, where Mrs. J. looks as though she's been expecting them, in spite of the warm weather.

It doesn't last long, perhaps because the usual targets aren't around. The chant quickly peters out, 'National Front' stripped of its usual menace until only one voice can still be heard over the static. Even from inside they are able to make out the unmistakable sound of the runt, a lone ember still trying to stoke the fire.

'I hate that boy,' says Michelle, breaking the first rule of the library.

Pretty much ever since she has been back in school and away from the hospital, things have returned to how they were before Junior's accident. But he is still surprised to hear her say this. And in the library. For all the pages they've thumbed through here, all the lists and cross references, the finger tracings and whispered confidences, that's the one word that's never come up. Hate.

'I really hate that boy,' she repeats, just in case it wasn't clear before.

Mrs. J., who feels she ought to say something, instead leaves her desk and comes over to where Michelle is sitting. K. looks on as she puts an arm around her, but the real surprise comes when he sees Michelle's shoulders start to go up and down in the telltale manner and then the water-works as she buries her face in Mrs J.'s shoulder, the librar-ian gently reassuring her,

'Don't worry, love. Whoever he is, he's not coming in here.'

It is when K. turns around to make sure no one else *does* come into the library that he becomes aware of someone else in the room besides the three of them.

Peering round the bookcase he sees a pair of plimsolls poking out from the end of the next row of shelving. It is the half caste, a weak smile on his boat, but in his eyes something more. A look of infinite gratitude. And in that moment, framed by old Readers' Digests and a sobbing girl in the other corner, it is utterly, spellbindingly clear.

It is so simple, he can't believe he never saw it before.

They have all chosen to be here. In the whole time that this school has been his anxious little world, he doesn't ever remember being in the same room as other people who have chosen to be there. And chosen knowing full well that he will be one of them. Somewhere in those lists, under the magnifying glass, in the warped-perspective-lifting-dome of the letters, at some point within all of that, a little portal must have opened up. And in their hunger they needed no encouragement to dive in, thrashing around frantically at first in that alphabet soup, so much to learn and hardly any idea where to start. But gradually, lunch hour by lunch hour, the frenzy started to soften, and one by one the exiled letters began to form themselves back into words. Simple ones at first, or simple enough for them given their home spelling head start. Cupboard, separate, friendly. Yesterday's frenzy barely a splash now, and the shapes and the sounds become more complex. Preternatural, relinquish, smorgasbord. This is their world, their room, their language which they have chosen, and because they have chosen it, they become fiercely protective, rushing back to safeguard its treasures every breaktime. They love that they have found this place, and perhaps even more that this place has allowed them to find one another. Mostly though, it is just the giddying, dizzying excitement of knowing that they are no longer forsaken. That some sanctuary exists in which to cast off the old skin, *relinquish* those traces of the past. A place of their own in which to whisper, and giggle, and learn, and laugh. And as it goes, somewhere to hide out too.

#

Later, he puts an arm around Michelle, and she starts to cry again.

'What's the matter?' he asks.

'Nothing,' she says. 'It's nothing you've done.'

'What is it then?'

'It's nothing. Honest.'

'So why are you crying then? And you were crying before and all,' he says, thinking about her earlier outburst and what she'd said. 'Is it Stephen?' he asks, and when she doesn't answer, he repeats, 'It's Stephen, isn't it? What's he done?'

That's when it finally comes out, her eyes tearing up all over, and this time he lets her carry on until every last bit of snot and remorse has been spent and the only thing left intact is the little monstrosity her words have painted.

Touched me there. Said no. Touched me again. Got angry when I said no. Don't want to. Told me I was a tease. Got really angry then. Told me he was glad Junior got knocked down. Told me he knew who did it. Told me they didn't even care.

He knows he should be more shocked by what he has just heard. But when she's finished, he doesn't say anything, watching as she dabs away at her eyes, then tries to absorb some of the snot on his T shirt with a tissue. Even when he tries to summon up the outrage, it is not exactly shock he feels.

What was she thinking? Again, he barely stops himself from saying this aloud, but this time the thought doesn't go away so easily.

He should probably tell her that it will be fine, just you watch, but today the words don't come. Instead, what tumbles out is this.

'Have you told anyone else?'

In the pause that follows, he knows he has caught her off guard.

'What do you mean?'

'Exactly that. Have you told anyone else?'

She looks vaguely hurt at the question, but he can't see why. It seems a perfectly reasonable thing to ask.

'Why are you asking me that? Didn't you hear what I

was saying about-?'

'Oh, I heard,' he interrupts. 'That's why I'm asking.'

'You think it's my fault, don't you?'

'No, of course not. That's why I'm asking, have you told anyone else?'

Her face looks as though it's about to crumple again, and he wonders if he's being a bit hard on her. Then again, as far as he can tell, no one got hit, no one actually got hurt, and she's had more sympathy in these last few weeks than he can remember in a lifetime.

Strictly speaking, that's not actually true, he thinks, reconsidering the 'accident'. Junior, of course, did get hurt, although he's getting better now. And don't they just know it? Everyone and their dog, everyone's favourite dinner lady, classroom fiend, playground bully, all in on the act, right up until the point that Junior gets back on the crutches and takes his first few steps away from the bed. Then all that sympathy, the cards, the chocolates, the reassuring hands placed over hers in the lunch queue, all of that just melts away and it's back to the main feature. The peeps announcing that the Front got more than a hundred thousand votes in the recent elections, and the chants starting up again in the playground. And here she is, spending all day in floods of tears, even though no one got hurt and no one got hit. And acting for all the world like she doesn't know any of this other stuff. As if it's the first time she's ever heard of, let alone met, his old friends, the Front and their highly familiar local cheerleaders. As if any of this is somehow surprising.

'You're the only person who knows,' she says

eventually, the accusatory tone no longer there.

'Well, let's keep it that way then,' he says, drawing her close to him and feeling only slightly guilty about how much he is enjoying the shift that just seems to have taken place between them.

#

25.

The first day back from India, a volley of stones and other missiles comes hurtling towards his head. Instinct makes him reach for the dustbin lid, and the metal is dented by how hard some of the stones are thrown.

The assailants pedal away fast on their choppers, back into the concrete labyrinth, though he suspects they might be back later.

It is still the summer holidays, but he knows his brother is thinking the same thing, anxiety keened by the latest soundtrack, the thrash metal symphony of rocks bouncing off improvised shields.

Actually, even while they were out there, they'd spoken about it then. The scalping still fresh, big, fuck off ants pouring out of the fruit sack, eyes barely recovered from the naked flames which had licked at them for hour after hour, and the one thing they were genuinely worried about, how their bald heads would be received by the other little scamps filing out of the hutches.

'What do you think it's going to be like when we go back?'

'I dunno.'

'I hope it's going to be alright.'

'Yeah, course it will.'

Neither of them really believe it, but with nothing much else to hold on to, the equation is simplified.

In the couple of months that they are gone, the area seems to have undergone not so much a transformation as a consolidation. The Chambers has been really helpful to him in tracking the changes on his head, from scalped, to bristly, to cropped, each transformation marking a shift in mood. Startled refugee, seething immigrant, seasoned skin. He can't even believe he's thinking it, but it's true, it does feel different when the bristles finally form a well trimmed pad and the cutthroat slices the memory of the ants back into tiny atoms of gunny sack. And when it's done, he is equally surprised that he wants that cutthroat again to pare back the only collars he has. Maybe for some other stuff too.

As for the area, it hasn't so much changed as intensified. It's true. Definite signs of consolidation here.

Bunting barely back in the cupboards but the flags are everywhere, and they're *praahd*. The cabbie couldn't stop talking about it on the way back from the airport. Street parties and dancing, and apparently everyone joined in, though K. has a hard time believing his uncle danced a merry jig with the neighbours. The cabbie kept looking in the rearview where he could see them sat either side of Mum in her sari. Kept looking and kept using that word. Proud.

For Queen, and country. That's what he says at one point, Mum knowing straight away and giving both of them a warning look in the awkward silence that follows.

It is the one they know from a hundred bus journeys, whatever the insult, absorbed in the eyes, their focus retrained as self discipline. The gist always the same. Not now. It can wait. Don't give them the satisfaction. So no one says anything, but somehow it feels as though the cabbie's been given the last word.

Our Queen. *Our* country.

Dad pays him, but as the Granada pulls away from the kerb, leaving them to struggle up the footpath with suitcases packed tight, they all feel a little bit smaller.

Once the bulk of the unpacking has been done though, they decide, K. and his brother, to test their close-cropped souvenirs against the prevailing current of neighbourhood opinion. Though obviously that's not what they tell Mum. The version they wheel out for her benefit is all about fresh air and needing to stretch their legs after being stuck on that plane for so long. In the end, as much from weariness as anything else, she relents at the mention of the Russians and that mickey mouse aircraft.

'Alright then, but don't be too long.'

'We won't. We're only going round here,' they say, gesturing to nowhere in particular.

There's been a right old knees-up while they've been away, evidence of the long hangover strewn all around. One of the first things they notice are the bins still overflowing with empties, the remnants of fig roll packets, Angel Delight, and someone's been busy with the Vesta. The walls are a lot busier too, hardly any without some kind of writing on them, and something else they spot right away, there are very few trailing legs on the individual letters now. They get the impression that these artists were not in a hurry, the second bone dry summer on the bounce ensuring no seepage. It doesn't look as though the uniforms have interrupted anyone for a while now. There's none of that slap-it-on-and-scarper they're used to seeing. Whatever's up there seems quite measured, almost as though an older, steadier hand has been involved. And they have to admit, looking at the neatly clipped phrases, that a certain clarity of purpose and thinking has gone into this. Not only is all the signage neat but it appears to have grown in confidence too. They see that Enoch's back, Pakis are out, and the Front never went away. But now, for example on the wall next to the shop, just under the NF someone has calmly added 'Rights for Whites'. Again, no seepage, not even a hint of circumstantial objection. (K. feels a guilty thrill at the thought of this. He still can't quite believe he got away with spending an entire day with the Chambers out in Calcutta when he was supposed to be learning his *gayatri mantra*. 'Circumstantial' had come out of that session. It was a great word. He'd loved it then and it was just as impressive now. Ah yes, the minute details of everyday life. And this, the perfect opportunity to apply his newfound learning, the one he'd been waiting for ever since those fluid syllables had reached out to him from that humid late afternoon sitting. The only thing sweeter than the words on the page, a chance like this to lob them into his world. So that for once it's him who's ruffling the brick-work, the words spoken and the smallest of detonations left hanging in the air. He recognizes this for what it is. That rarest of moments where the interior demands its audience and the exterior is forced to listen. It almost never happens and he'll be damned if he's going to miss this chance to show how all those hours buried in the arcane are really about this. Bricks and paint and flesh and blood, all of which actually *live* on the page for him, so that he can taste them, touch them, intoxicate himself with their fumes, all the while giving the impression of innocence. The very opposite of here and now and almost everyone else he knows. The one boy round here who stays quiet not because of what he doesn't know but precisely because of how much he *does*. Show it and he knows it really is going home time in a London ambulance. Keep schtum and he's seen how everyone thinks he's much smarter than he is. Not because he's sitting on wisdom but rather because it's the lie which needs guarding. So for once he says it, a guilty little thrill as the words move from the page to the place.)

'There's been no circumstantial objection here. Look how unflustered the brush strokes are. This lot had all day to paint these. Some cunt probably give 'em a medal an' all at the end of it.'

His brother gives him a sidelong glance, wondering if that's just the jetlag talking, the last bit definitely sounding like it's for the benefit of anyone else who's listening. But though there are a couple of older boys also within earshot, neither comments on K.'s analysis. For now at least they seem more interested in the iron grill shutters pulled down over the face of the shop. The ones which are also sporting an NF logo, though this time spray painted as though it *has* been done in a hurry. In an unusual touch, someone has drawn a prick next to the logo. Or maybe that's a carrot, K. thinks, the irony somehow lost on the thickly veined grills?

Both of them have also noticed how the one thing which seems to have gone unremarked on this opening recce is their haircuts, yet strangely, mixed in with the understandable relief at this fact is a less easily explained sense of disappointment.

That aside though, if the local artwork is anything to go by, there's been some kind of renaissance while they've been gone.

On their way back they pop next door eager to see what reaction they'll get. Instead, when an ashen faced J. opens the door, he seems to barely notice them. Inside they find S. holed up in bed with the curtains drawn, his cheeks still puffy.

'Shit. What happened to you?' they ask, reeling from the shock.

S. struggles to sit up, wincing as he does so. He squints at them for a moment through a half closed eye.

'I could say the same thing about you,' he says, clutching at his ribs when he tries to force a laugh. 'You look like a pair of bloody peanuts.'

'Yeah well, so does half of this area now, so at least we won't stick out,' says his brother, instantly aware of how optimistic that sounds.

'Oh, I still think you'll manage somehow,' says S., clutching at his sides again, the other two just looking on thinking it's not that funny. But they don't say anything as the poor sod's clearly in no position to defend himself.

'So what happened then?' his brother asks again.

'Teds. Fucking Teds. 1977 and muggins here is still getting jumped by Teds. Would you believe it?'

'How did it happen?'

'My own fault really. I should have known. All this Jubilee stuff and I really should have known that lot were always going to come out for it. They love all that royalty shit. There's some place they all go up the Elephant. Well, I know that *now*. Anyway, it was bad timing mostly. They were spilling out just as I was walking past, and let's just say they didn't take too kindly to what I was wearing.'

'Which was what?'

'Oh you know, the ripped drape, that shirt with the safety pins. They *really* didn't like that. You know what they said when they were giving us a kicking?'

'No, what?'

'The big one. There's always a big cunt, isn't there? Well, he was going, "You fucking punks, you're always taking the piss, wearing that shit and then putting that stuff in your hair. It's disgusting. Well, have some red in there as well, you cunt! Have some of that!" And that's about it. Don't remember much else. J.'s not happy though. Well you've already seen his boat, you don't need me to tell you that. Anyway, he's been telling me I was better off as a peanut.'

'Don't be daft. We're the peanuts now,' says K., and then they all really do laugh, S. cursing him as he can literally feel the stitches in his side about to pop.

When they come back out, that's when the stones start raining down on them, though luckily, with moving targets to pitch at, the windows for once are left alone.

When it is over and they are able to finally put the lids down, K. hears the sound of manic pedaling, a faint trail of laughter heading back to the rabbit hutches. The pain of delayed recognition, he thinks. Nothing goes unremarked around here. Or if it does, it never stays that way for long. But that first day back, yeah, it's still a shock to the system.

26.

That morning, Dad's just come off the nightshift. It is a Saturday and for once even he can't disguise the system-weary slump in those broad shoulders. Coming off the back of the worst night of the week it is all he can do to take off his shoes and slump down into the armchair his *dada* seems to have procured from somewhere.

K. makes a particular effort to be up before Dad gets back from those nights of strip-lit crazy. Somehow Fridays are the worst, the one shift no one wants. This one clearly no exception, the knots in Dad's shoulders entirely predictable.

Dad closes his eyes, moaning his approval as the little hands knead the bunched up pockets of flesh. He stays in that position, head tilted back ever so slightly, the hands mostly making no difference but supplying a crucial impression of care. Later when they bring him a cup of tea, he manages a smile. It is sleep he really craves, but these small mercies are the first real reminders that he is home.

#

Not long after Dad turns in, Mum's voice only just audible, the door opening and closing, and then she's in the kitchen, Dad's snoring already starting up.

'Don't make any noise, your dad's trying to sleep,' she says, as she always does on these mornings after.

He asks whether he can go to his cousin's a bit later. She says no, he's not old enough to be travelling on his own. He doesn't tell her that's what he does all the time anyway, pretends to look upset. She asks whether he wants to do some spelling, he says no, maintaining the hangdog look. She feels bad that he is in a sulk but he has to learn it's not safe these days walking around on your own. That poor boy with the turban, look what happened to him. He says he doesn't need a turban, just look at this, pointing sarcastically at his head.

Then his uncle appears, says *he'll* take the boy to his cousin's. He's got to head out soon anyway, and it's on his way. So really, it's no trouble.

Mum, still reluctant, and slightly wrongfooted by the offer, asks K. what he wants. Then immediately regrets it when he says he wants to go to his cousin's anyway.

#

27.

London, Two Sevens Clash, August, 1977

Though he's seen his uncle once or twice since they got back, it still comes as a surprise when he sees his changed appearance that morning.

A thick beard now covers more than half his face, some grey mingled in with the recently acquired woolly coating.

He realises how neglectful he's become these past few weeks. How little attention he has been paying to the details. Whole swathes of life just passing him by, a fog circling above that streamlined skull he's become obsessed by. So wrapped up in his own loss of hair that he's somehow missed the rug that's sprouted in the next room along.

When did he become this neglectful?

When did this happen? Whatever else he can be described as, he has never been guilty of being *that* person, the one who says nothing because he sees nothing. He's always hated those people, the boys and girls around him who act so innocent, their eyes narrowing with the pin point accuracy of snakes in the moments just after. The teacher walking away, wondering why he bothers, it's just kids having fun. No harm done, he thinks, heading back to his fags and the crossword, and directly behind him, in the one place which is always a blind spot, the looks of wide eyed innocence morphing right back into a nest of vipers. Venom leaching into the ground, eating into the concrete, and after a while the hissing and the writhing *becomes* their innocence, scales and flesh, owl eyes and those of a snake absolutely interchangeable. But if anyone ever asks, they're just kids again. Rough and tumble, that's all it is. At least that's what the teachers say. And it's always backed up by the parents. No, not my Stephen, not my Lisa, they'd never do *that*. They're just kids. You need to lighten up. And a word to the wise, son, of course it's nothing personal.

Except it is. And now he's in danger of being just like them. Becoming one of them. Seeing only what he wants to see, then snucking behind childhood's readymade alibi at the first hint of trouble. Shit. When did this happen?

28.

They walk the short distance down the hill to the high street, and then up past the bridge to his cousin's. At least G.Davis is still being celebrated round here, he thinks, the allegation proudly refuted on the bridge. And there are precious few signs of leftover bunting adorning these houses. Actually what *does* catch his eye on the way up past the Odeon are a lot of black Marias parked up in the side-streets, their snouts sniffing each other's tail pipes.

Though it is still early it is unusually quiet on Lewisham Way. It seems a little odd given that it's a Saturday and no one's working. Then again the drizzle and that breeze had made them think twice before setting out. Still, he doesn't mind too much. It is less of a slalom than usual, and in any case he's working hard to keep up with his uncle so he's grateful for the largely empty streets.

#

'Wha' di rass you stop me for? Natty no work for you.'

'Shut up, Rastus. Where were you going?'

'Wha' it haffi do wid you?'

'Don't get lippy with me, Rastus, we can make life very

difficult for you. Now, where were you going?'

The uniforms turn around, surprised they didn't hear the footsteps coming up behind them.

At the mouth of his cousin's road, K. and his uncle hear the exchange taking place a little further up, behind where another convoy of black Marias is parked.

Several uniforms are on the street, two of whom are questioning a tall Black man in a Fred Perry polo.

They stop when they see the boy and his uncle stood behind them, the bearded man with his arms folded.

'Move along now,' says one of the spare uniforms not involved in the questioning.

K.'s uncle stands there, not saying anything, the faint crackle of the police radio audible from one of the vans. The uniform who has spoken thinks about approaching, but something about the absolute stillness, the near total lack of movement in the man standing opposite seems to unnerve him. In that split second delay a further crackle, then a message suddenly relayed from the van.

'Sarge, we've got to go. They're here.'

After the last of the convoy moves off, the Black man looks over at his uncle.

'You heard that, man. The Front, they're here. We haffi put dem under heavy manners, now. I'm telling you, star, we haffi do that.'

Still no movement from his uncle but then a barely perceptible nod, no other words exchanged, the two men heading in opposite directions, *Wat a liivanbambaie* tipping out of an open window.

'Yes, dread!' someone calls out, though it's just him

and his uncle walking past.

#

By the time they leave his cousin's several hours later, that's when the difficulty occurs. The crowd is all heat and noise, the earlier chill largely forgotten. Streets which had been so empty before now filled with the friction of loud-hailers, placards, bodies on the march. 'The police are the real muggers' held up for the benefit of the police helicopter circling overhead. No one objects as they join this procession at the mouth of the road. Hardly anyone even seems to notice the man with the beard and the young boy with him who slip quietly into their midst. Their eyes are elsewhere, rumours beginning to circulate. *Thousands on their way from Brixton. Asians being attacked on the Isle of Dogs. Someone has been killed by the police.* Passing through the crowd like an electric current, voices occasionally rising above the fray. *They're coming! Let's have 'em!* He follows their eyes but they're already gone, no longer afraid. Looking around him, the improvisation is familiar. Chair legs, bottles, half bricks, and dustbin lids as shields again. Then the air is choked. Brickdust, confusion, and suddenly everyone's running, small groups peeling away down side streets, and he sees chunks of wood being ripped from fences, the crowd pushing him sideways, the last thing he hears a heavily accented man telling people to look out, 'they're gonna use Belfast dildoes'. Someone helps him back on his feet, but it is not his uncle. 'Don't worry, son, stick with us, you'll be ok,' someone else says, but he's not listening. In the distance, close to where the police coaches are beginning to disgorge uniforms, the sarnies and flasks swapped for riot shields and batons, something else has caught his eye. A bus, lurching red out of that mist, and somehow he knows that's where he needs to be.

It is a frantic scene by the time he finally makes it home. Technically still late afternoon but Mum, Dad, his brother, J., even S. are all huddled around the television, stern faced reports coming in from just up the road. The odd thing being how different it all looks on the telly. In the kitchen the radio is on, and the trouble is being blamed on 'diehards from outside the area'. They all look up when he walks in, relief initially outweighing anger. In fact it takes a while before anyone realises his uncle is not with him.

29.

Though it is a Monday, the school holidays are still in force, and it is with mercifully downgraded expectations that the caretaker goes in to work that morning. In an unusual move, the headmaster had called him at home over the weekend to remind him that today was a big day for the school. Of all the local schools, *this* one had been chosen as the venue for the special educational conference, and he shouldn't need reminding that there would be some very important people there, including the local Mayor and someone from the Department of Education. Press too, you know what they're like if they get a whiff of something ministerial, so anyway, that's why I'm calling. The school really needs to look its best. Let everyone see why it's a flagship. I know you know, and you do a marvellous job, but I wouldn't be doing mine if I didn't mention this to you.

Still, the caretaker is not overly concerned. The kids haven't been around for the past few weeks and the school has only had a skeleton staff presence. All of which has meant far less for him to worry about. None of that horrible, scratchy bog roll stuffed down the loo, or clogging up the cisterns. No canteen gruel to fish out of the urinals, hardly any electrical emergencies either. The peace and quiet has been highly welcome, classrooms for once places of contemplation, all the chairs and tables neatly arranged, nothing for him to wipe off the blackboard, only dust to sweep up off the floor. It won't take long to pull the wool over the delegates' eyes, have them purring away about the 'award winning design' and 'open plan learning environment'. He'll give it a little spit and polish first thing, be on hand with a ready smile for any of those official types who fancy themselves a bit of a humanitarian. The occasional sort who like to make a show of talking with the lower social orders, parading their concern as a virtue in front of the other suits. Before it's back to the important business, none of which involves fraternising with the ancillary pay grades. Overthinking it, as usual, but even as he chides himself for this, he makes the decision to not go in early that morning.

#

When he does get there, the first delegates have already started to arrive. The initial signs that something is not quite right in the shaking of heads and arms on shoulders, the little cluster refusing or unable to move away from the plate glass windows circling the assembly hall. Then he sees the headmaster striding towards him with a look of fury, only turning back when a flashbulb glare goes off.

It takes almost an hour for the fire crew to arrive, check the building, and then finally gain access past the uniforms securing every entrance.

In that time the flashbulb goes off more than once, an officer immediately remonstrating with the cameraman but perhaps too many witnesses present, local dignitaries among them, for him to do much more. Many of the delegates are now visibly distressed or being comforted by others, more than one ambulance having arrived on site.

For that entire hour the award winning design ensures that anyone who wants to know can.

There in the assembly hall, strung up from a ceiling beam, the body of a man in an army surplus jacket. Although he is several feet from the windows, a slit is clearly visible running across his neck just below the jawline, where the chin meets the neck. And the man's tongue is hanging down through the wound, almost as though it has been pulled through.

Of course it is another picture which appears in the papers as more details start to emerge over the coming days. *South London School Horror* even makes it to the red tops, though their interest seems to wane when it is pointed out that the victim whose son, Stephen, attends the very school where the gruesome discovery was made, and whose last known movements involved straight arm salutes at the recent National Front march, had at the time been enjoying, like the other marchers, the not inconsiderable advantages of a police protective cordon. At which point it becomes easier to look elsewhere, the eyes of the world suddenly trained on Memphis and the choking-back-the-tears static

coming through on every airwave that the king is indeed
dead.

#

30.

They travel to the airport to see his uncle off. He seems in unusual good humour en route, at one point suddenly producing a cricket ball from his bag, as the cab sails over the Westway. 'Take it, you need practice,' he tells K., making sure to heavily accent the words.

Though it is late summer, his uncle is wearing a three piece suit. He is clean shaven too, the shock of his face back in session almost as jarring as the threads. If they didn't know better they'd actually say he looked happy that morning when he finally emerged from his room.

K. doesn't remember him saying too much else. Just one other detail sticks in his mind. A hint of disgust on his uncle's face at the tearful immigrant goodbyes taking place all around him in the terminal building, and a measure of relief that the genuine antipathy he seems to inspire in K.'s brother, and his own sister-in-law, will at least spare him these agonies. And then he's gone, beard and breakfast already in the past, the memories he's heading back to not so easily shaken off though.

#

31.

Bengal, 1947

Striding across the dirt track, he soon reaches the building with the thick plume of smoke rising from it. As he draws closer he senses in his nostrils, even before he is able to see, that the flames licking at the cloyed atmosphere have merged with the smoky residue of charcoal and dung cooking fires. On the pavement outside, impassive, heavily made up faces look up at him with no fear, the light dimly reflecting off lipstick and bangles. Only when he looks down does he see that they are not made up, the pavement spotted with something other than paint.

The stench hits him then, ragged, numb, oozing the chop of metal on bone. But if there is noise, he can't hear it, the sound already muted, lips moving, words forming then stillborn in the throat. Moving into the building, not even the sounds of his own footfalls audible through the roar of nothing. Something, blood, adrenaline, a novocaine tremble, rising up from that vault, pumping, surging through thickly veined, system built arms. Lifting the words on its current, sweeping them up past all the other words that have died in there. *Family. Together. Us.* Pushing them up through the stink of rotting flesh, the acrid, charcoal burn in his nose, all stumps and saucers and

reaching out to *dada*. Spreading out through every parti-
cle of his beard, each hair crawling with intent. Into the
serried ranks of *nayi, na, no* pounding above his eyes. And
back out into the smell of death, arms windmilling under
the mask, confusion in those other eyes, the shock of 'why'
unable to see beyond the mask, past the beard, stopping
short of realisation until the knuckles connect. By which
time of course it is too late. The lips and words and paint
making no impression on skin supplied by system rigour.
An extra layer to process the shock, one for the silent
scream, the other man's eyes still on his beard on their
way down. The briefest of flickers as the system struggles to respond to the gratitude in the woman's eyes. A
look tells her to go, run, and she does, the system left to
its mechanics, how he likes it, on his own. Picking up the
cleaver that the woman's assailant has dropped, he walks
toward some shapes his eyes have drawn through the hazy
smog. A group of men, more women, a child. Nobody has
seen, their eyes inflamed, the taste of meat and meaning
too strong to resist. They don't see him, the mask slipping,
scales fully shed. Until he is right by them, chop, gash,
delay, tendons severed to stop the rats from crawling away.
A break to tell the women, the child, go, run, now. But the
words die, trapped by the smoke, by something, and they
run anyway, from the men, perhaps even from something
worse. A dead eyed beast the last thing they will remember
about this place. The rats try to scuttle but the tendons
are gone and they can only slither. Lips forming 'o's and
eyes wide, then flickering, desperate, one last appeal to
the shadow holding the cleaver. Or to something. But he

hears no sound, some part of him immune long before this, and all he sees are shapes and numbers and weak. In the heat, the trails already gloop, salt and dust toasting in the shadows. And then the rats are being caught by their tails, the chop and quench easing their futile slither. Tired now, the smoke in his lungs, system slowing up. Chop, slice, bone, then stagger, splutter, a pause, the rhythm cut short as the smoke pours in, then one last burst, slash, chop, quench. Tails and wings, the rest purified by flame. No noise, more a feeling, a pattern, some work. A system. His. Until finally it is just him crawling from the stink, some of which clings to him long after the slice of another blade removes the hirsute mask, apparently leaving no traces.

#

32.

London, 1977

At Heathrow no one is saying much, the plane arcing its way upwards through something hazy. They watch it all the way into the clouds, Mum the first to turn away once the plane has disappeared from view. It's Dad who eventually breaks the silence though, clapping his hands together with an ever optimistic, 'Carry on regardless.'

And then they're gone, the rare indulgence of cabs both ways not lost on the passengers. The driver on the return leg is an older Sikh, only mildly curious as to where their luggage is, the Guru Nanak pendant on his dashboard flapping gently in the late summer breeze.

It feels better than the last time they made this journey. This time round there's no bunting or barbed comments, just a steady *kara* on the steering column.

#

The whole way home there is concrete. Buildings, flyovers, slabs, jutting out at strange angles, disfigured by something, by what? It's hard to say but no one really cares, least of all K. and his brother. Strangely enough it is only now, sitting on the back seat of a minicab heading home, watching the city they live in go past, that they realise how little they know this place. They see this central London grey as if for the first time, its towers and noise so different to that familiar hymn of muted violence, the one which has been stained right into the fabric of their childhood. The people here just walking about, at least that's how they seem from the backseat, conjuring a word K. had always coveted but never dared indulge: *carefree*. If there are peanuts around they are staying out of sight, so too the anxiety they bring, the balled fists, the pinched faces, everything, the mood, the mentality heading south once that machine-tooled sneer hoves into view. Only now, at the end of this long hot summer, weaving fresh lines in the city of their birth, the sole peanuts who appear to be in central London right at that moment simultaneously press their globes against opposite back windows. Press them and, yes, exhale, as though finally they're on holiday. Perhaps it's the heat melting away those stark grey edges. Maybe it's nothing of the sort, just some other shift in the tectonic plates. Either way the mood feels lighter, jocular even.

'Look at the state of that,' K.'s brother says, pointing out a genuine fashion casualty near the Embankment. 'He looks like he's offed a baboon and nicked his face.'

They both laugh, hoping Mum's none the wiser, the tragic, polyester-clad creature shuffling past, none of the adults bothering to comment, but Mum wondering when exactly her boys became so mean.

The cabbie looks in the rearview, equally unimpressed. *Ingrezi*. English boys. An entire summer of this crap. But he can tell the rain's not far off and before long the days will shorten, and when that happens, he thinks, with a bit of luck all this petty, this adopted English joy in another's misfortune will also be swallowed up by the gloom.

#

The man's not really there at the Embankment. Or perhaps he's been there all along, lurking in the silt. The cab barely even registers as it passes, just brown faces, teeth, pointing. Near the mud of that ancient riverbank, his suit, a threaded patchwork of dirt. But he senses these kids are laughing at him, whiteman in disgrace, maybe they can even see the piss stains spreading outwards? Another night of sleeping where he fell, the decline matted in his barnet.

He reaches up to touch his hair, the gesture briefly hinting at defiance, dignity even, but the kids have already lost interest, their world at least on the move, heading somewhere, his, whoever he is, more or less fading from view.

#

'And does anyone know what that commemorates?'

Stifled laughter. That's a lot of syllables for this classroom.

'Anyone?' the teacher persists, surprised that the bored and fidgety looking right back at her hasn't already morphed into loud and unruly. Then again, Stephen ('the runt'), so often in the past the catalyst for the shift, hasn't been seen since the terrible events of late summer. What that poor lad must be going through, she thinks, to know that happened to your own father, and in broad-----

'The tomb of the unknown soldier,' a voice intones.

It's that brown kid, the one whose name she can never quite remember, but whose face definitely doesn't belong. He rarely says anything in her class, so it comes as something of a surprise. More so when her eyes eventually manage to pick him out from the assorted rabble. It's the same kid alright but there's something a little different about him, she thinks, not quite able to put her finger on what. In any case there he is suddenly very sure of himself, cropped hair, a tight little grin and leaning back ever so slightly on one of the chairs nearest the windows.

'Yes that's right, very good,' she says, but before she can carry on he's already interrupted her. 'It's where they put people with no name, as if a baboon had killed them and stolen their faces.'

Laughter again, but this time there's a slightly nervous quality to it.

#

It's there alright, in the mud, laughter and all the rest of it, swirling around in the only way it knows how. Where else did any of it come from but mud? There submerged in its artful pools our hungers and cruelties, and the fun we had with both. And it is to mud, even if it is only of the most sculpted variety, that we must eventually return, bedded down with our instincts, hollering, yowling and yet somehow managing to do so in absolute silence. Utterly portentous and-----

'Oh, do put a sock in it, son,' a much needed voice of reason pierces through the tumult, the one which has been steadily building up in his head ever since the teacher had asked his class the question.

There are always other voices, of course there are. But that's the thing with masks, he thinks, not that they slip to reveal the truth, but that as one falls away another is already in place. *The truth*, don't make me laugh! From mud to fishes to chlorine, the beast has always been there, shedding its scales, regrouping, such that now, here, in the midst of all this award winning design, no one would even suspect.

Notes

A quick primer for the uninitiated or even the just mildly interested.

George Davis, who crops up throughout the story, often in the form of defiant graffiti, was a quasi-mythical figure for assorted dissidents during the 1970s in Britain. He became a sort of folk hero for some, yet another example of an innocent man stitched up by the system. His case, which saw him convicted for his alleged role as a getaway driver in an armed robbery, was viewed by many as a blatant miscarriage of justice... except not long after his release, following a judicial review, he did commit a very similar offence. A bit like the Harmony hairspray ad at the time, 'Did he or didn't he?' Answer: he did, but not that time. Anyway, during that period leading up to his original release, one of the more high profile stunts carried out by his supporters, involved sabotaging the Test match pitch at Headingley, in Leeds, with the vital match between England and Australia finely poised. The pitch was dug up and the surface rendered unplayable by liberally spraying it with oil. More pertinently, perhaps, kids all over Britain discovered that the mere mention of George Davis, man, myth, graffiti, seemed to rile a certain type of grown up: authority figures, teachers, virtually the entire middle class. So of course they did the only decent thing and shoehorned him into every other conversation from about 1975 onwards. And spraypainted his legend on walls and bridges all over London.

Margo Leadbetter, played by the actress Penelope Keith, rose to prominence in 1975 as the snooty but likeable Tory neighbour of Tom and Barbara Good in the popular BBC comedy, *The Good Life*. The first episode was screened in the same month that Margaret Thatcher became the actual leader of the Conservative Party, and in some way the fortunes of these two characters were forever after intertwined. The key difference of course was that Margo, whilst a snob, was basically a decent sort, while Margaret turned out to be the Cruella de Ville of British politics. Sadly, the decent sort was the fictional character while the nightmare we call Thatcherism was all too real.

Test match cricket, a magisterial sport, takes place over five consecutive days (though back then, in the 1970s they had a rest day in between, usually on a Sunday). So-called because over such an extended period of time a Test match allows for a true test of character, stamina, skill and courage to unravel. The Indian political theorist, and cricket fanatic, Ashis Nandy, has memorably described cricket as 'an Indian game accidentally discovered by the English'. Suffice to say, throughout the 1970s, India were embarrassingly bad at the game, and the timid exploits of the national team would regularly transfer feelings of shame, humiliation and barely suppressed rage upon already beleaguered diaspora populations in the

UK. Caribbean diaspora populations, though experiencing many of the same pains and prejudices as their South Asian neighbours, did at least have the salve of a truly magnificent, world beating cricket team during this same period. As the neighbourhood wisdom went, it was really the only time a group of Black guys could gather, throw a hard ball at a white man's head for a period of up to five days, and emerge triumphant, or at least not in custody, even though the whole thing had been televised. But yes, keep telling yourself it's only a game.

Colonialism had some chutzpah though. The British Raj. Basically the half-inching of anything that wasn't nailed down—i.e everything—and the building of extensive railway networks the quicker to transport half-inched materials to the nearest port and then back to dear old Blighty. And then if anyone complained, a quick round of hangings, or man-made famines (Bengal, 1943) or just plain ol' shoot 'em ups (Jallianwala Bagh, Punjab, 1919) to restore order. But look, at least 'the natives' got Christian missionaries and cricket out of it. And it turned out they quite liked cricket. And then of course, when all the raw mats had already been scalped, having an exit strategy that involved partitioning the land and leaving entire communities to the mercy of the man made borders. Oh yes, not forgetting the fostering of communal resentments or the bit about legging it before the proverbial shit hit the fan. Considerably north of a million dead and ten million instantly displaced when the newly drawn up borders came into effect in August 1947. The provinces of Punjab and

Bengal were both sundered to create West and East Pakistan respectively, though bizarrely enough, both portions were separated by a vast chunk of land in between, aka India. So that was always going to work out well. Partition, truly putting the psycho back into geography.

Acknowledgements

Some time ago, each of the proto-junglist London MCs aka 'The Ragga Twins' made it clear on their far-sighted debut LP, that 'Reggae owes me money'. Yet that journey into an expressive art form's past actually turned out to be a wild, itinerant ride into its junglist, postindustrial future. For as Toni Morrison, herself channelling something of William Faulkner, reminds us, 'the past is never past'. So it has been with the writing of this novel. What began as a settling of scores with a cantankerous inner voice, turned into something else entirely. It was 2013, and the voice had started up again, just after I'd made the difficult journey, in accordance with my late father's wishes, to transport his ashes back to the old country. He was a playful, open-hearted soul who had had every reason not to be, and it seemed to me, for that fact alone, that I owed him something more than a return trip to the Ganges. A story, perhaps, with all the trimmings.

Along the way, there are a number of folk who deserve special mention for helping see this cantankerous beast across the line. Firstly, everyone at Jacaranda, but especially Valerie and Cherise, for their support and suggestions, and for helping to bring the story to this stage. Abdi Sanati, Stephanie Young, David Fairhall, Ben Mango and Dianna Frid for taking the time to wrestle with earlier drafts. William Mazzarella for his detailed comments on both initial and subsequent drafts. Friends all, and fiercely present, in the unspoken conversations that always occur below the line. A sibling roar to my brother, Partha, who uncomplainingly made the time from a punishing work schedule to cast a forensic eye over proceedings. Heidi Mossman, for the tea, sympathy and the ongoing literary conversation. Mick Mahoney, for being a true gent, a serious scribe and a London particular. John King, for the words of encouragement and for inviting me in to the dissident corners of 'Verbal'. My old south London spar, Nick Bendall, for titular inspiration. Juliet Amissah, for always being there. Aase Hopstock, and Kamillah, for that gorgeous cover design. My nephew, Raoul, for his sharp aesthetic counsel. Paula Myers for keeping the faith from afar. Reshmi Meyer for the words of wisdom, and for recognising that 'old skool' doesn't always mean 'old fool'. London itself. After all, as one of its wisest chroniclers, Robert Elms points out, 'London Made Us'. And finally, Nadia and the two boys for making home, well, home.

About the Author

Koushik Banerjea was born in London, where he still lives. Telling stories—a love of books, words and the escapist properties of alphabet soup—seemed natural enough to a child growing up around an unreliable television set, no social media and frequent power cuts. An absence, then, which it transpired was anything but. In a former life, he survived the Hatfield train crash, deejayed as one half of 'The Shirley Crabtree Experience', and peddled his academic wares as a postcolonial theorist at the London School of Economics. Also from that earlier life, an unexpectedly long stint as a youth worker. His short fiction has featured in 'The Good Journal' and in 'Shots in the Dark', a Cultureword collection of crime stories. He has also been published in the 2018 Writers Resist Anthology (Running Wild Press), and in the online literary journal, 'Minor Literatures', as well as in 'Verbal' (London Books), to which he has been a regular contributor since 2016. *Another Kind of Concrete* is his debut novel.

VIRAGO

MODERN CLASSICS

499

Daphne du Maurier

DAPHNE DU MAURIER (1907–89) was born in London, the daughter of the famous actor-manager Sir Gerald du Maurier and granddaughter of George du Maurier, the author and artist. A voracious reader, she was from an early age fascinated by imaginary worlds and even created a male alter ego for herself. Educated at home with her sisters and later in Paris, she began writing short stories and articles in 1928, and in 1931 her first novel, *The Loving Spirit*, was published. A biography of her father and three other novels followed, but it was the novel *Rebecca* that launched her into the literary stratosphere and made her one of the most popular authors of her day. In 1932, du Maurier married Major Frederick Browning, with whom she had three children.

Besides novels, du Maurier published short stories, plays and biographies. Many of her bestselling novels became award-winning films, and in 1969 du Maurier was herself awarded a DBE. She lived most of her life in Cornwall, the setting for many of her books, and when she died in 1989, Margaret Forster wrote in tribute: 'No other popular writer has so triumphantly defied classification . . . She satisfied all the questionable criteria of popular fiction, and yet satisfied too the exacting requirements of "real literature", something very few novelists ever do'.